7 GENERATIONS

7
GENERATIONS
A PLAINS CREE SAGA

BY DAVID A. ROBERTSON

ILLUSTRATED BY SCOTT B. HENDERSON

HIGHWATER
PRESS

HighWater Press gratefully acknowledges the financial support of the Province of Manitoba through the Department of Sport, Culture and Heritage and the Manitoba Book Publishing Tax Credit, and the Government of Canada through the Canada Book Fund (CBF) for our Publishing activities.

HighWater Press is an imprint of Portage & Main Press.
Printed and bound in Canada by Friesens
Cover, interior design and colourization by Relish New Brand Experience

Library and Archives Canada Cataloguing in Publication

Robertson, David, 1977-
      Seven generations : a Plains Cree saga / David Alexander Robertson ; illustrated by Scott B. Henderson.

Contents: Compilation of four previously published graphic
      novels: Stone, Scars, Ends/Begins, The pact.
Also issued in electronic format.
ISBN 978-1-55379-355-7

      1. Cree Indians--Comic books, strips, etc. 2. Cree Indians--
Juvenile fiction. 3. Graphic novels. I. Henderson, Scott B II.
Robertson, David, 1977- . Stone. III. Robertson, David, 1977- .
Scars. IV. Robertson, David, 1977- . Ends/begins. V. Robertson,
David, 1977- . Pact. VI. Title.

PN6734.S49R62 2012   j741.5'971   C2012-905122-5

22 21 20 19   6 7 8 9 10

HIGHWATER PRESS

www.highwaterpress.com
Winnipeg, Manitoba
Treaty 1 Territory and homeland of the Métis Nation

FSC
www.fsc.org
MIX
Paper from
responsible sources
FSC™ C016245

To Jill and our four children: Emily, Cole, Anna, and Lauren — the future generation

— D.A.R.

To Angela for all of her support and sacrifice

— S. B. H.

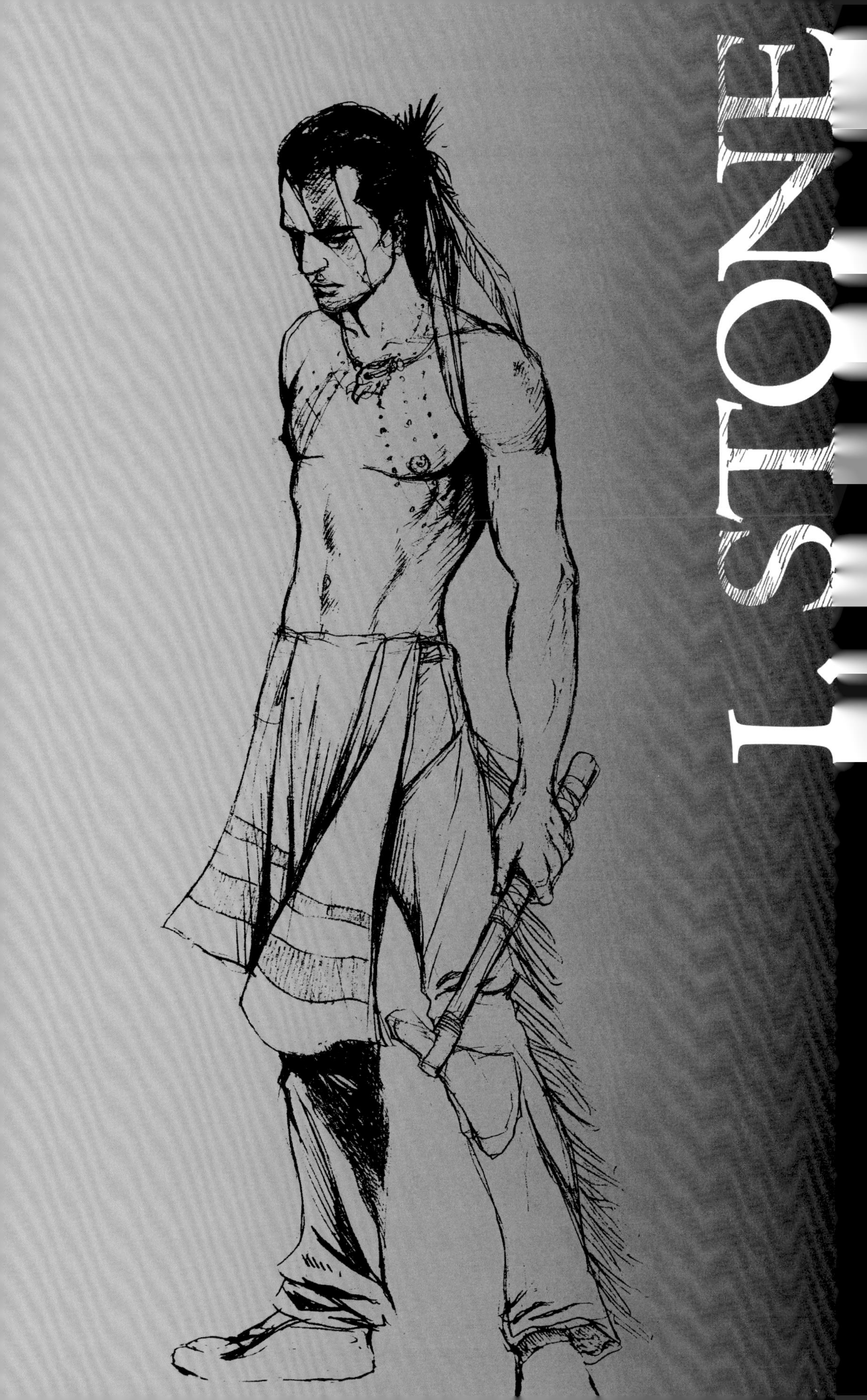
STONE

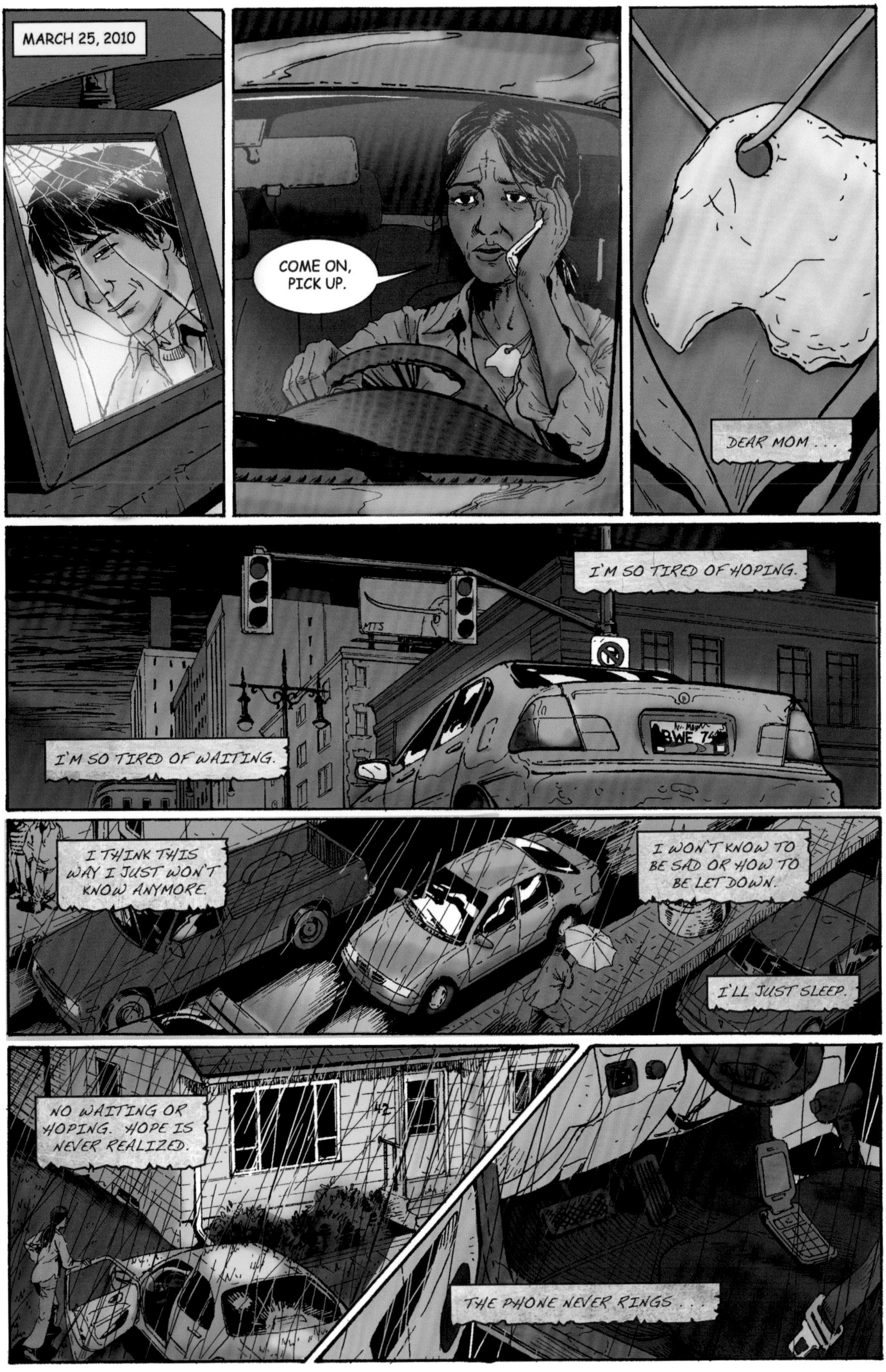
MARCH 25, 2010
COME ON, PICK UP.
DEAR MOM . . .
I'M SO TIRED OF HOPING.
I'M SO TIRED OF WAITING.
I THINK THIS WAY I JUST WON'T KNOW ANYMORE.
I WON'T KNOW TO BE SAD OR HOW TO BE LET DOWN.
I'LL JUST SLEEP.
NO WAITING OR HOPING. HOPE IS NEVER REALIZED.
THE PHONE NEVER RINGS . . .

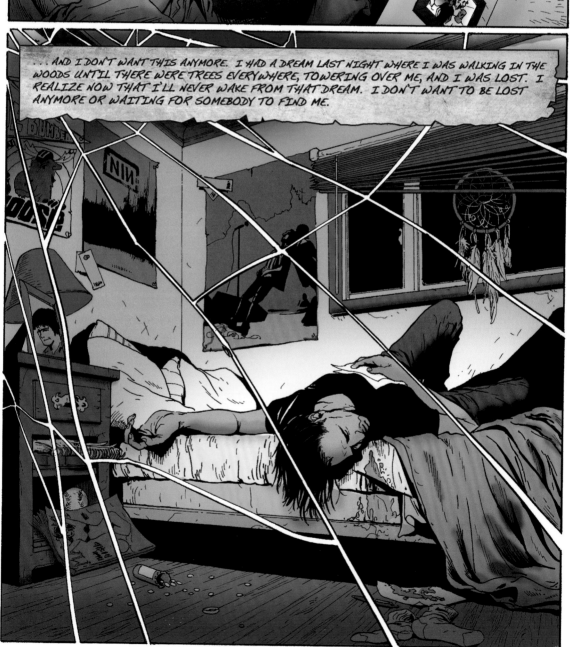

...AND I DON'T WANT THIS ANYMORE. I HAD A DREAM LAST NIGHT WHERE I WAS WALKING IN THE WOODS UNTIL THERE WERE TREES EVERYWHERE, TOWERING OVER ME, AND I WAS LOST. I REALIZE NOW THAT I'LL NEVER WAKE FROM THAT DREAM. I DON'T WANT TO BE LOST ANYMORE OR WAITING FOR SOMEBODY TO FIND ME.

PLEASE FORGIVE ME.

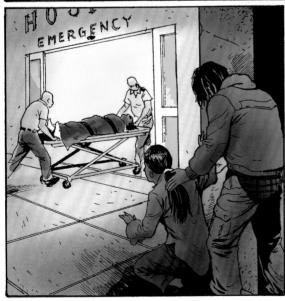

LOVE, EDWIN

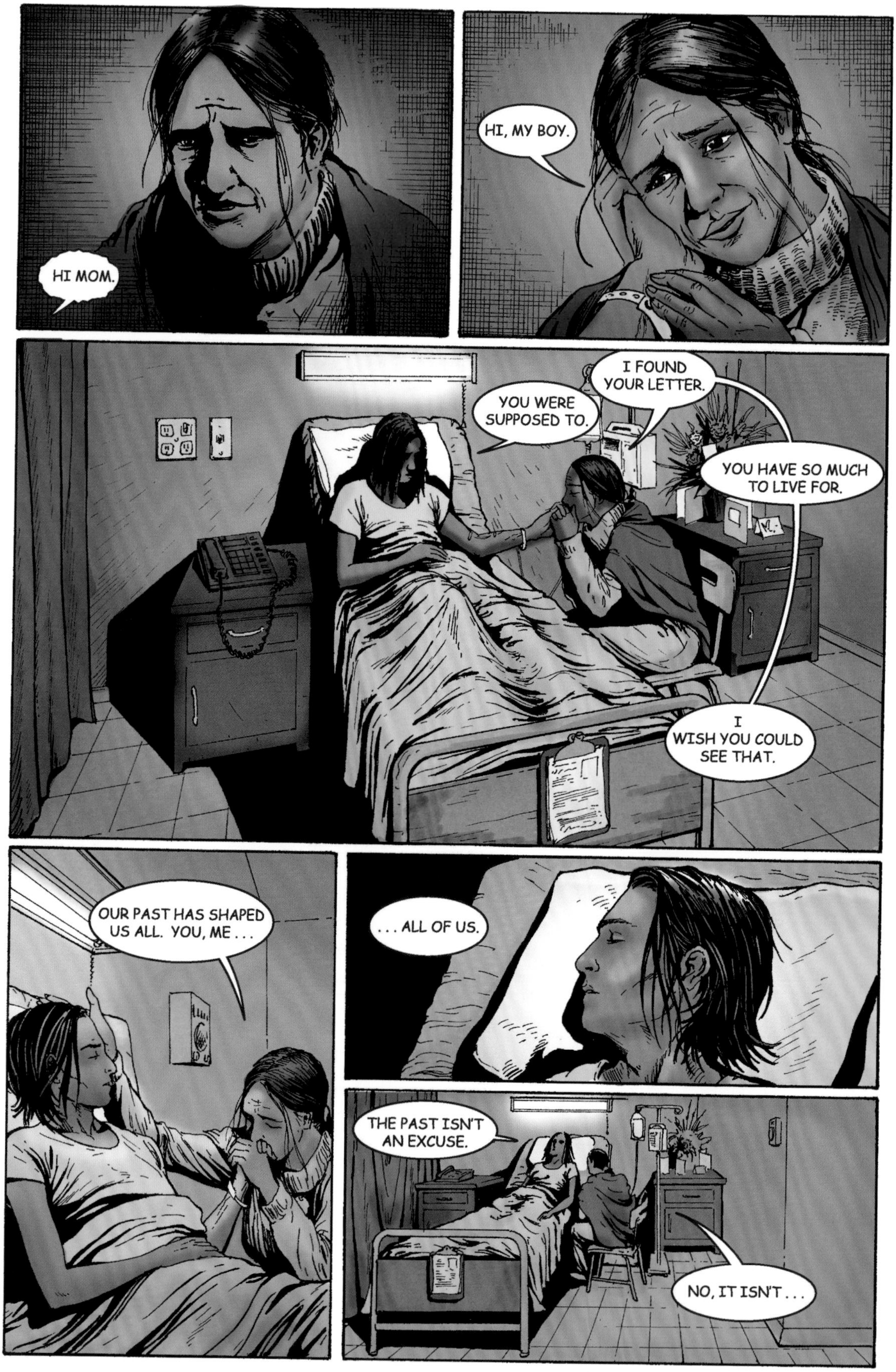
HI MOM.
HI, MY BOY.
YOU WERE SUPPOSED TO.
I FOUND YOUR LETTER.
YOU HAVE SO MUCH TO LIVE FOR.
I WISH YOU COULD SEE THAT.
OUR PAST HAS SHAPED US ALL. YOU, ME . . .
. . . ALL OF US.
THE PAST ISN'T AN EXCUSE.
NO, IT ISN'T . . .

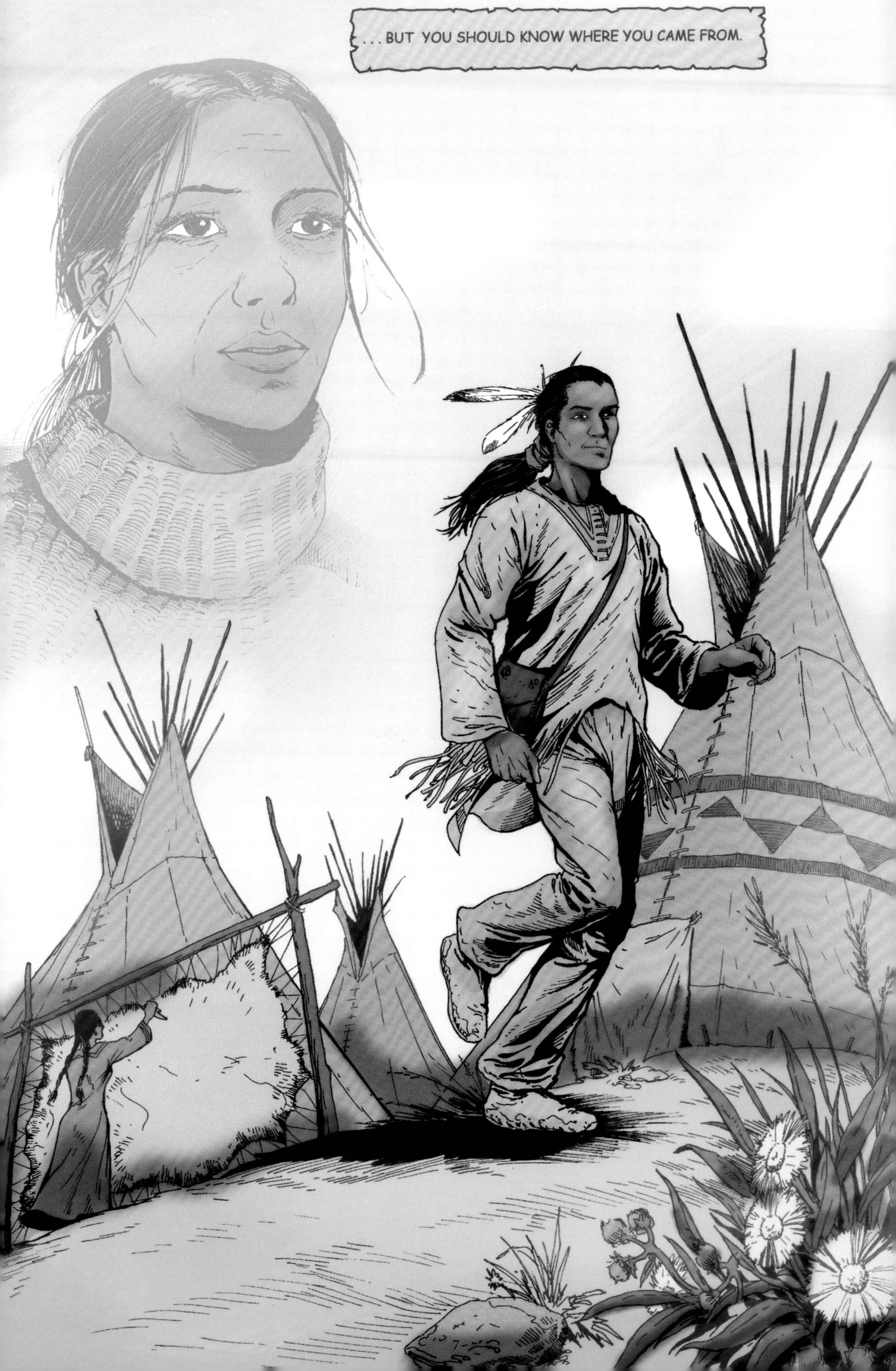
. . . BUT YOU SHOULD KNOW WHERE YOU CAME FROM.

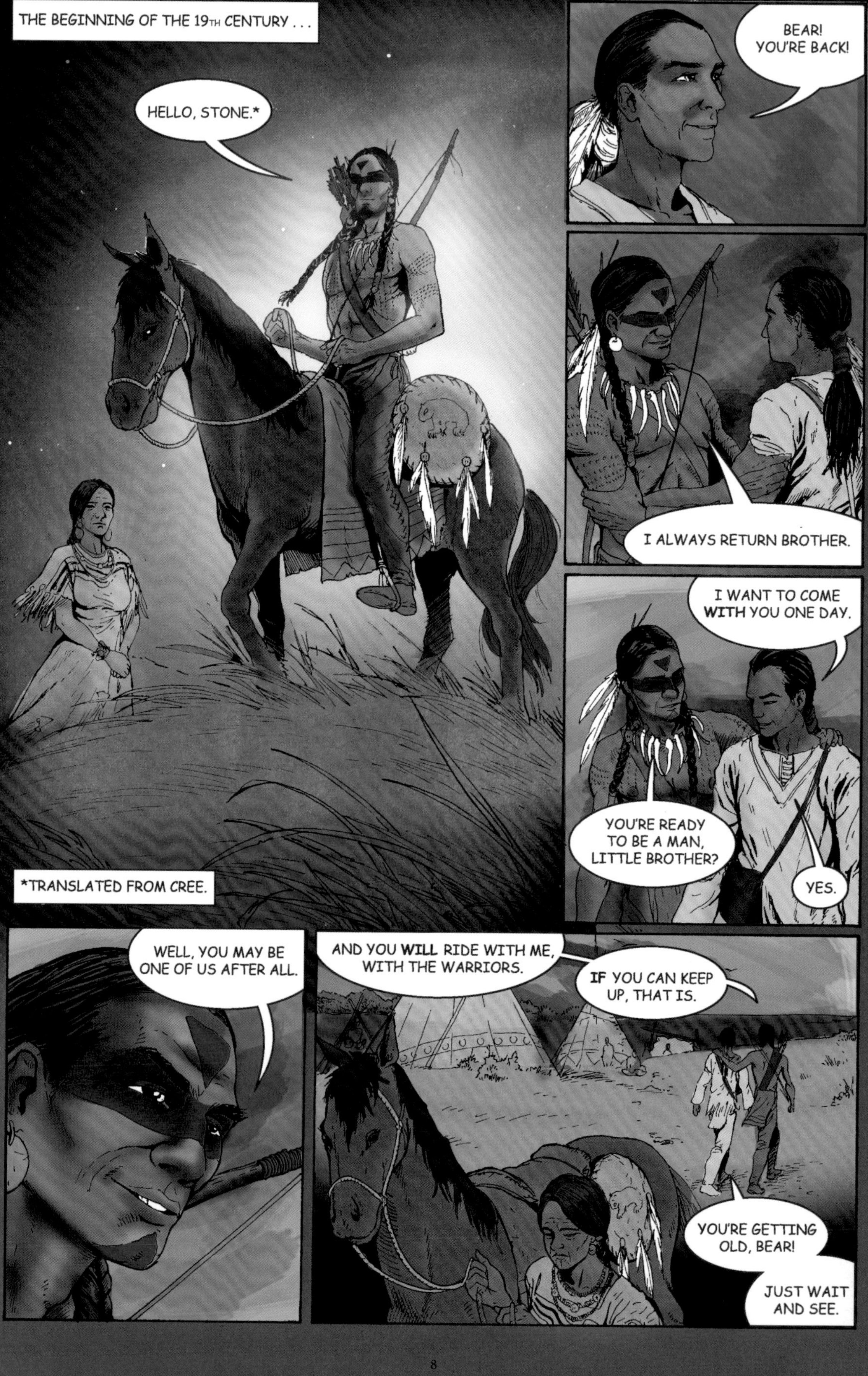
THE BEGINNING OF THE 19TH CENTURY . . .
HELLO, STONE.*
*TRANSLATED FROM CREE.
BEAR! YOU'RE BACK!
I ALWAYS RETURN BROTHER.
I WANT TO COME WITH YOU ONE DAY.
YOU'RE READY TO BE A MAN, LITTLE BROTHER?
YES.
WELL, YOU MAY BE ONE OF US AFTER ALL.
AND YOU WILL RIDE WITH ME, WITH THE WARRIORS.
IF YOU CAN KEEP UP, THAT IS.
YOU'RE GETTING OLD, BEAR!
JUST WAIT AND SEE.

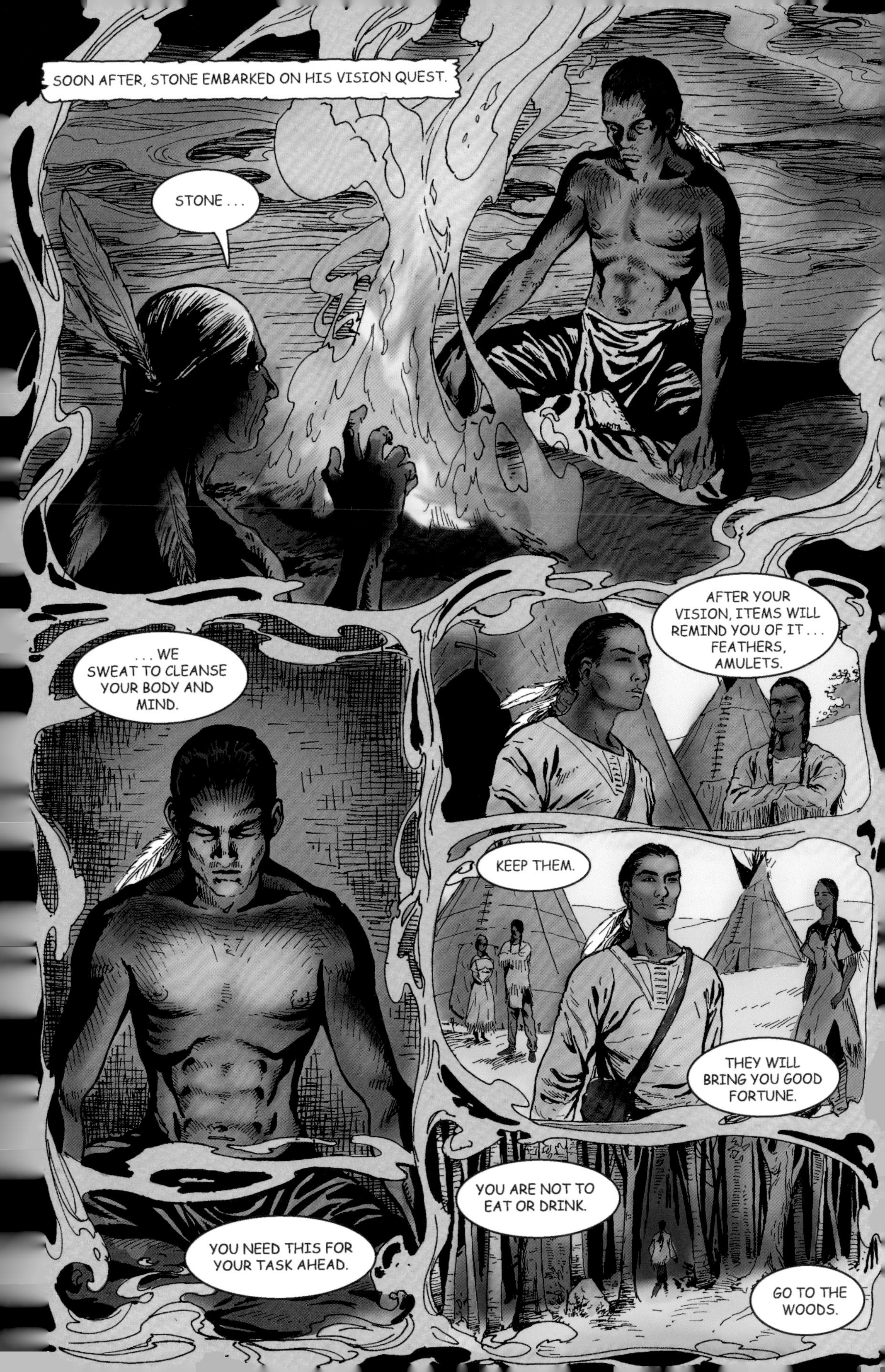

SOON AFTER, STONE EMBARKED ON HIS VISION QUEST.
STONE . . .
. . . WE SWEAT TO CLEANSE YOUR BODY AND MIND.
YOU NEED THIS FOR YOUR TASK AHEAD.
AFTER YOUR VISION, ITEMS WILL REMIND YOU OF IT . . . FEATHERS, AMULETS.
KEEP THEM.
THEY WILL BRING YOU GOOD FORTUNE.
YOU ARE NOT TO EAT OR DRINK.
GO TO THE WOODS.

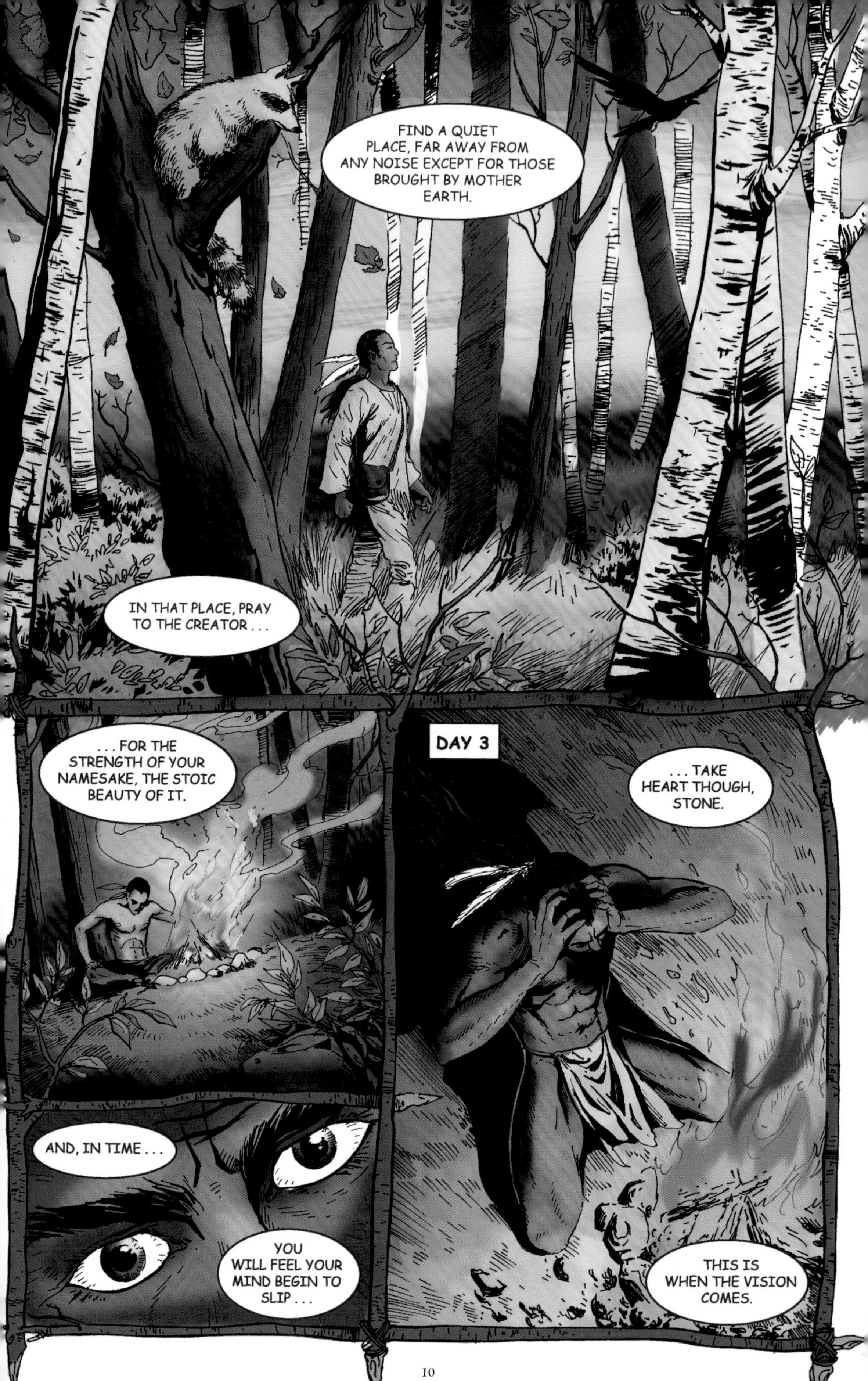
FIND A QUIET PLACE, FAR AWAY FROM ANY NOISE EXCEPT FOR THOSE BROUGHT BY MOTHER EARTH.
IN THAT PLACE, PRAY TO THE CREATOR . . .
. . . FOR THE STRENGTH OF YOUR NAMESAKE, THE STOIC BEAUTY OF IT.
AND, IN TIME . . .
YOU WILL FEEL YOUR MIND BEGIN TO SLIP . . .
DAY 3
. . . TAKE HEART THOUGH, STONE.
THIS IS WHEN THE VISION COMES.

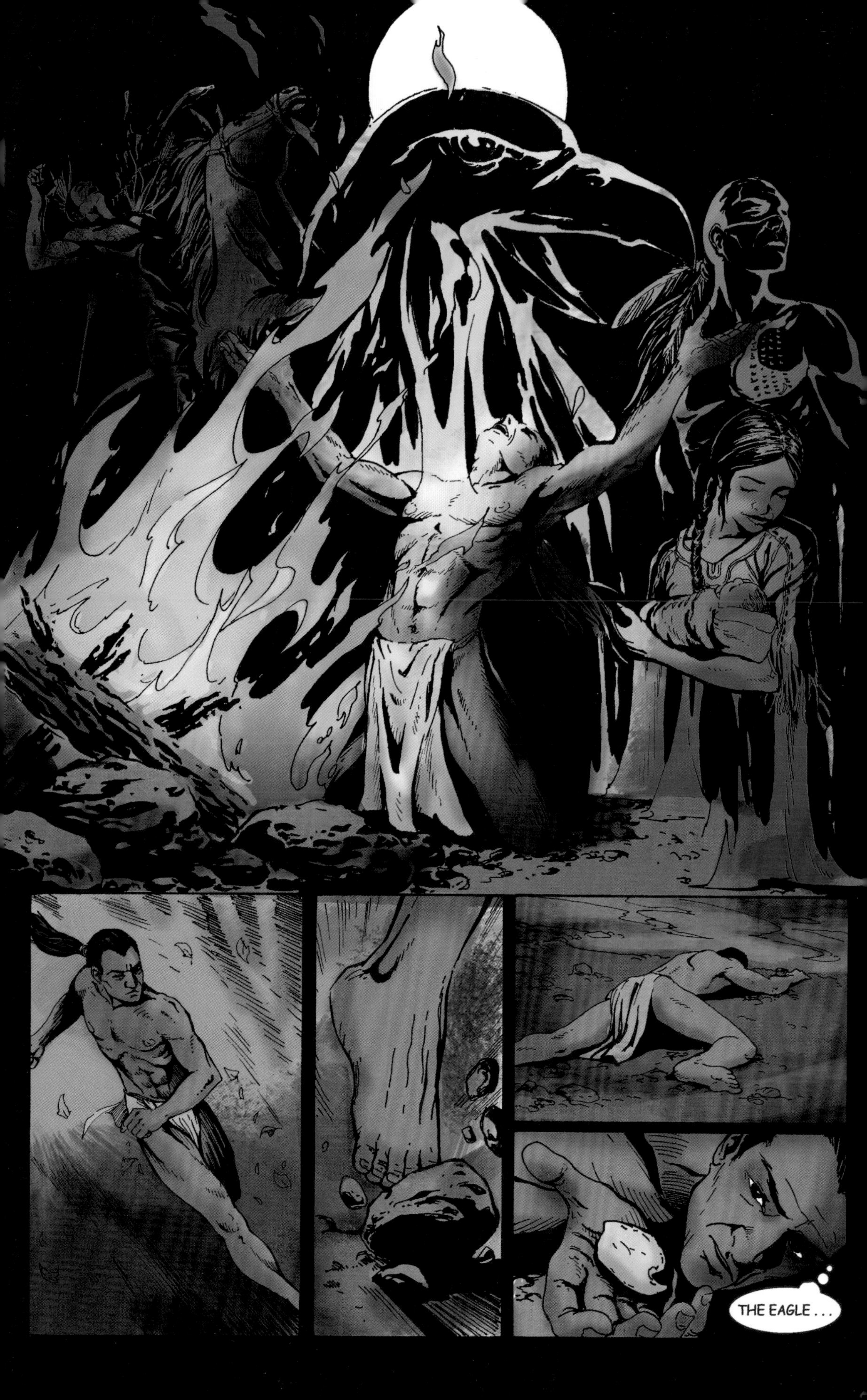
THE EAGLE . . .

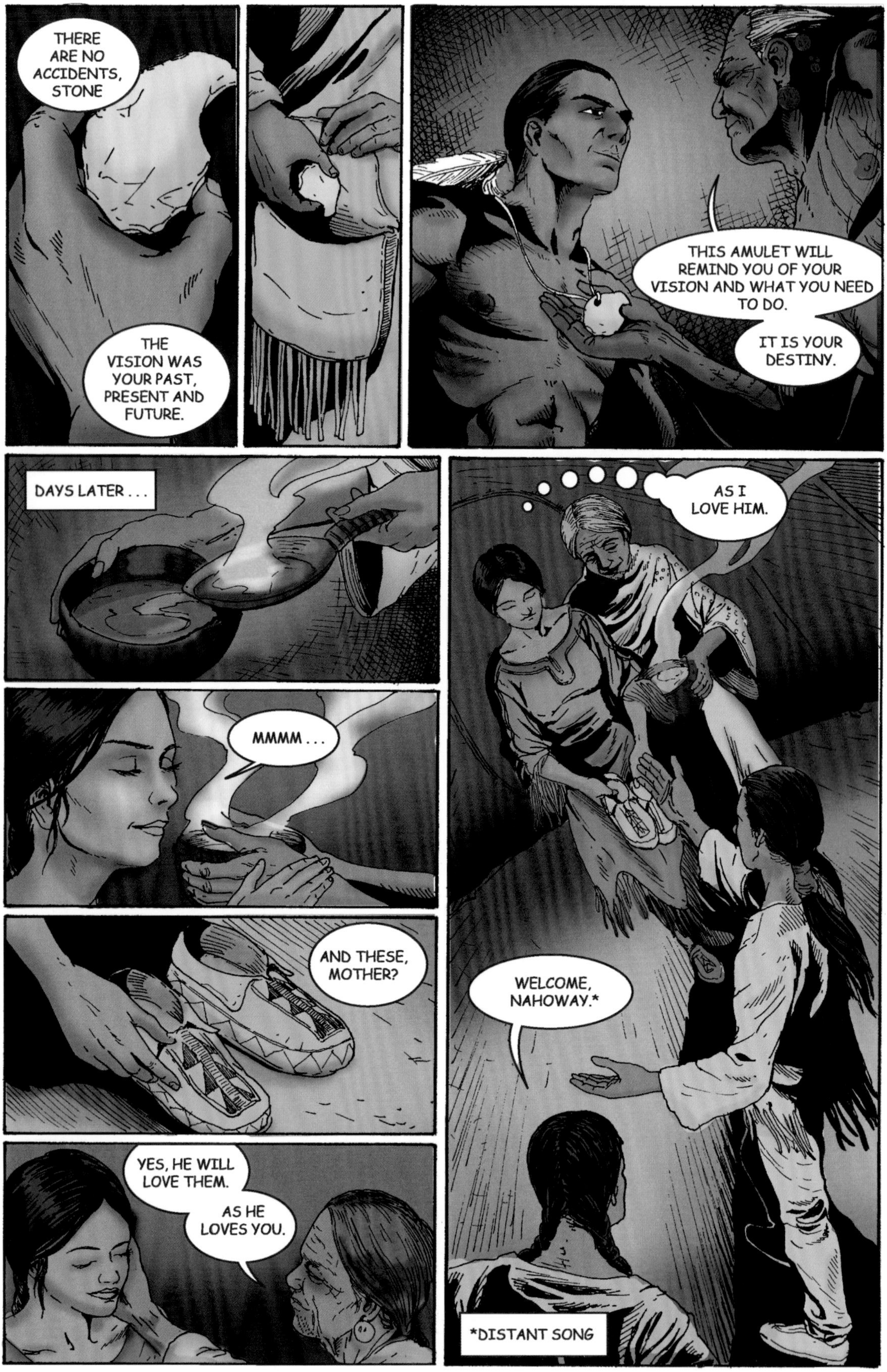
THERE ARE NO ACCIDENTS, STONE
THE VISION WAS YOUR PAST, PRESENT AND FUTURE.
THIS AMULET WILL REMIND YOU OF YOUR VISION AND WHAT YOU NEED TO DO.
IT IS YOUR DESTINY.
DAYS LATER . . .
MMMM . . .
AND THESE, MOTHER?
YES, HE WILL LOVE THEM.
AS HE LOVES YOU.
AS I LOVE HIM.
WELCOME, NAHOWAY.*
*DISTANT SONG

THEY WOULD MARRY.

CHILDHOOD FRIENDS . . .

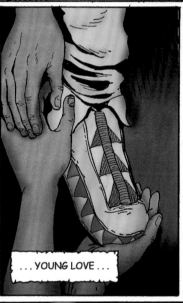

. . . YOUNG LOVE . . .

THANK YOU.

. . . THEIR FAMILIES STRENGTHENED THIS BOND.

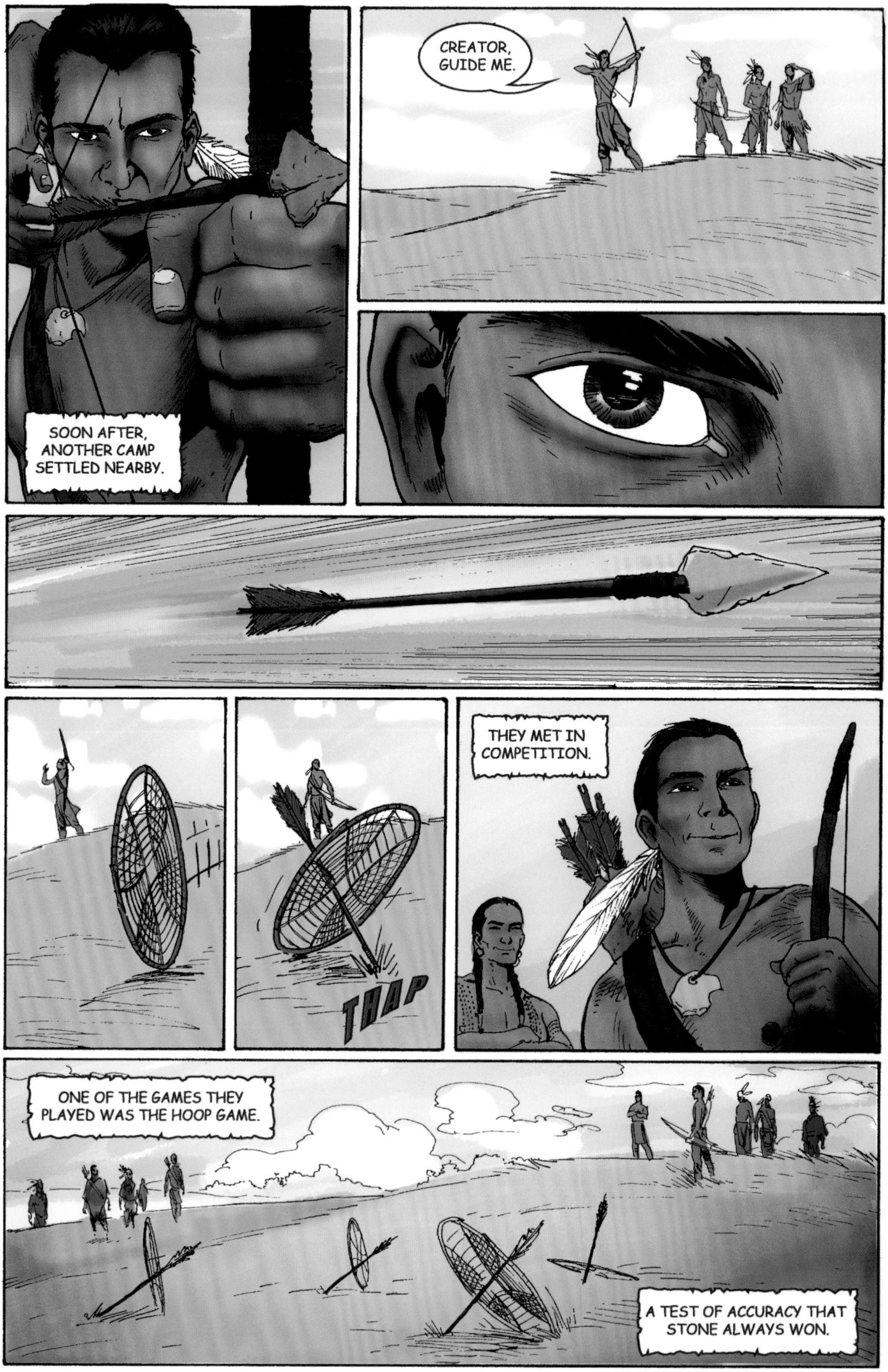
SOON AFTER, ANOTHER CAMP SETTLED NEARBY.
CREATOR, GUIDE ME.
THAP
THEY MET IN COMPETITION.
ONE OF THE GAMES THEY PLAYED WAS THE HOOP GAME.
A TEST OF ACCURACY THAT STONE ALWAYS WON.

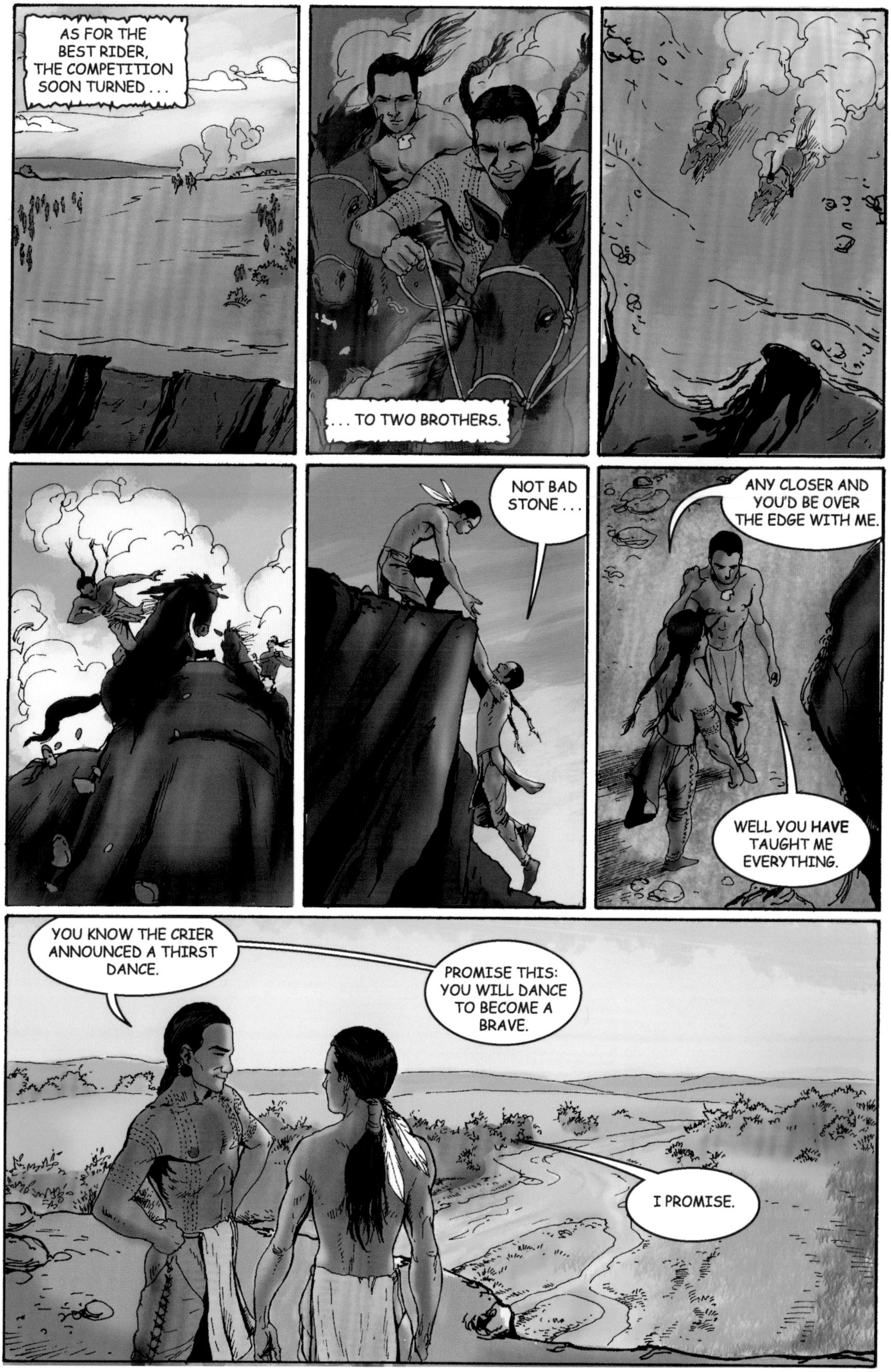
AS FOR THE BEST RIDER, THE COMPETITION SOON TURNED . . .
. . . TO TWO BROTHERS.
NOT BAD STONE . . .
ANY CLOSER AND YOU'D BE OVER THE EDGE WITH ME.
WELL YOU **HAVE** TAUGHT ME EVERYTHING.
YOU KNOW THE CRIER ANNOUNCED A THIRST DANCE.
PROMISE THIS: YOU WILL DANCE TO BECOME A BRAVE.
I PROMISE.

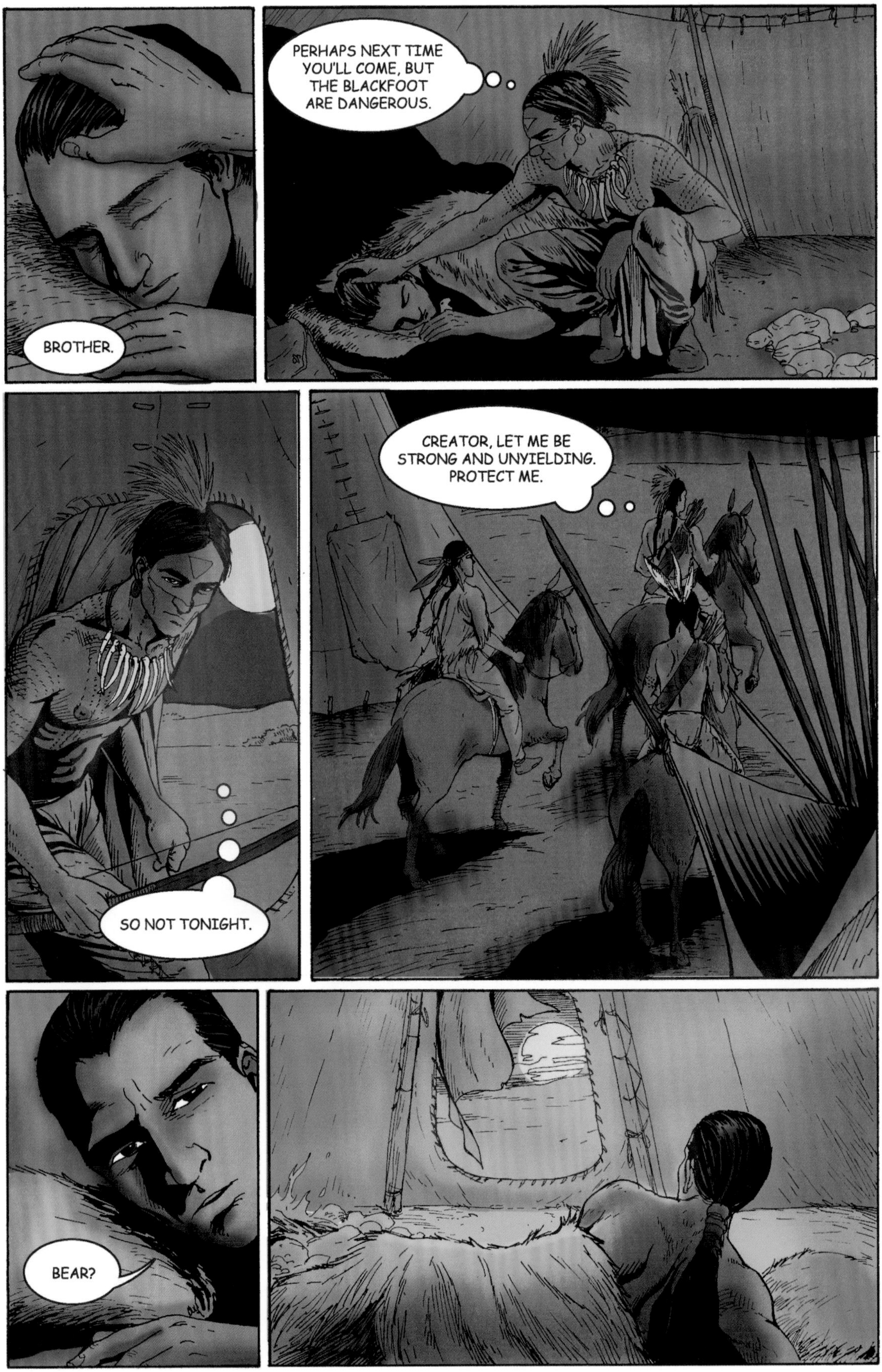
BROTHER.
PERHAPS NEXT TIME YOU'LL COME, BUT THE BLACKFOOT ARE DANGEROUS.
SO NOT TONIGHT.
CREATOR, LET ME BE STRONG AND UNYIELDING. PROTECT ME.
BEAR?

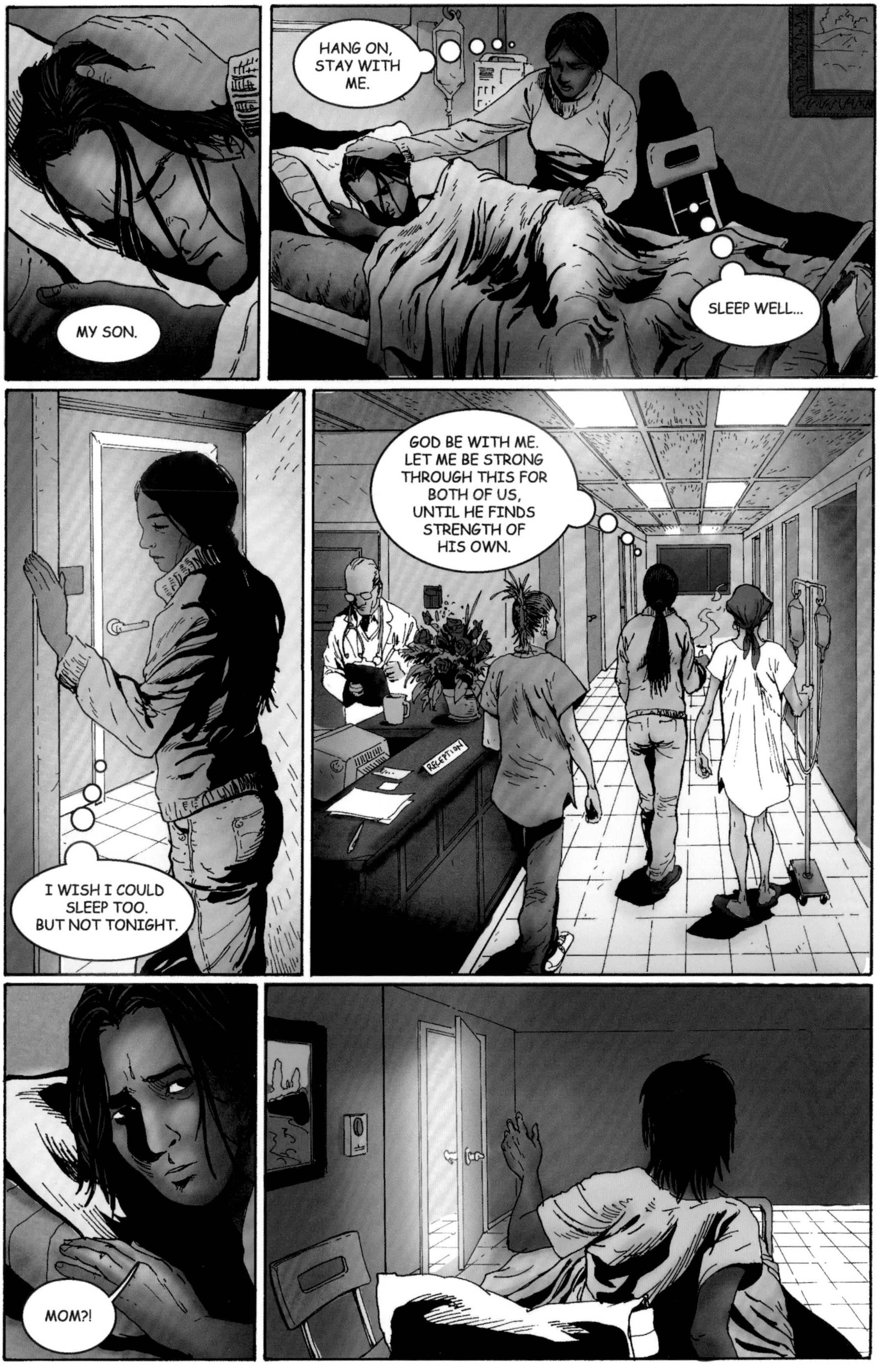
MY SON.
HANG ON, STAY WITH ME.
SLEEP WELL...
I WISH I COULD SLEEP TOO. BUT NOT TONIGHT.
GOD BE WITH ME. LET ME BE STRONG THROUGH THIS FOR BOTH OF US, UNTIL HE FINDS STRENGTH OF HIS OWN.
RECEPTION
MOM?!

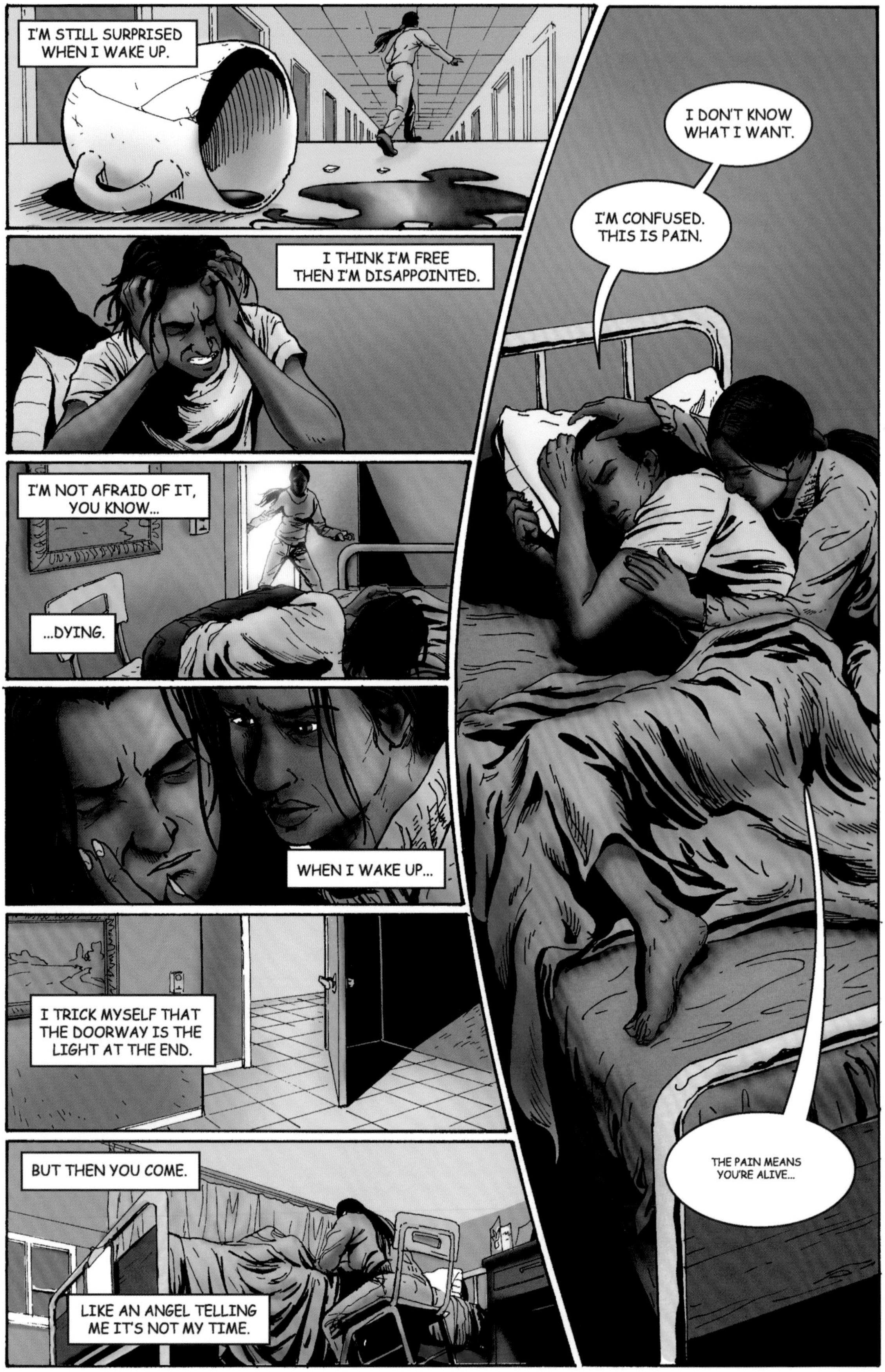
I'M STILL SURPRISED WHEN I WAKE UP.
I THINK I'M FREE THEN I'M DISAPPOINTED.
I'M NOT AFRAID OF IT, YOU KNOW...
...DYING.
WHEN I WAKE UP...
I TRICK MYSELF THAT THE DOORWAY IS THE LIGHT AT THE END.
BUT THEN YOU COME.
LIKE AN ANGEL TELLING ME IT'S NOT MY TIME.
I DON'T KNOW WHAT I WANT.
I'M CONFUSED. THIS IS PAIN.
THE PAIN MEANS YOU'RE ALIVE...

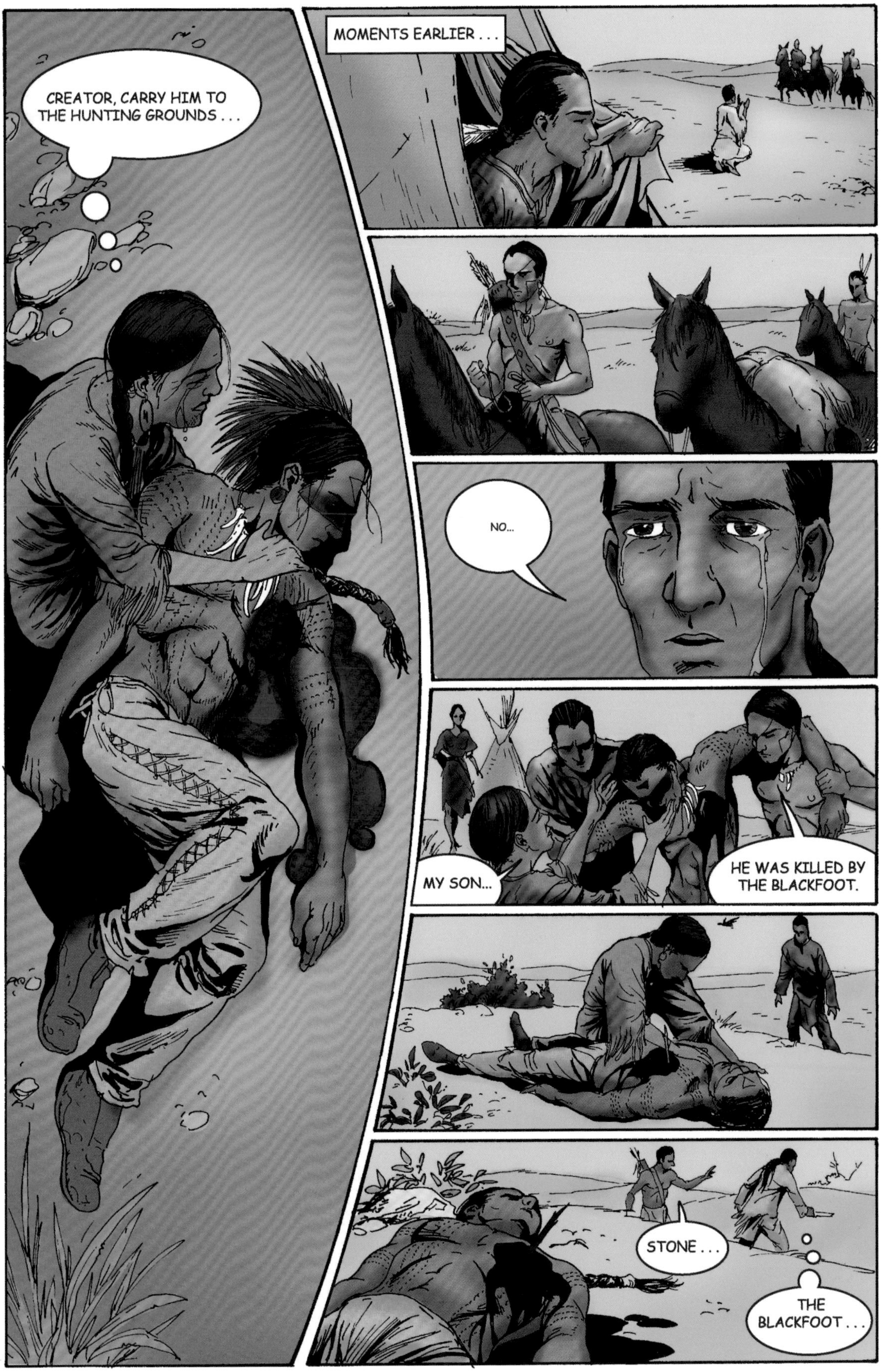
CREATOR, CARRY HIM TO THE HUNTING GROUNDS . . .
MOMENTS EARLIER . . .
NO...
MY SON...
HE WAS KILLED BY THE BLACKFOOT.
STONE . . .
THE BLACKFOOT . . .

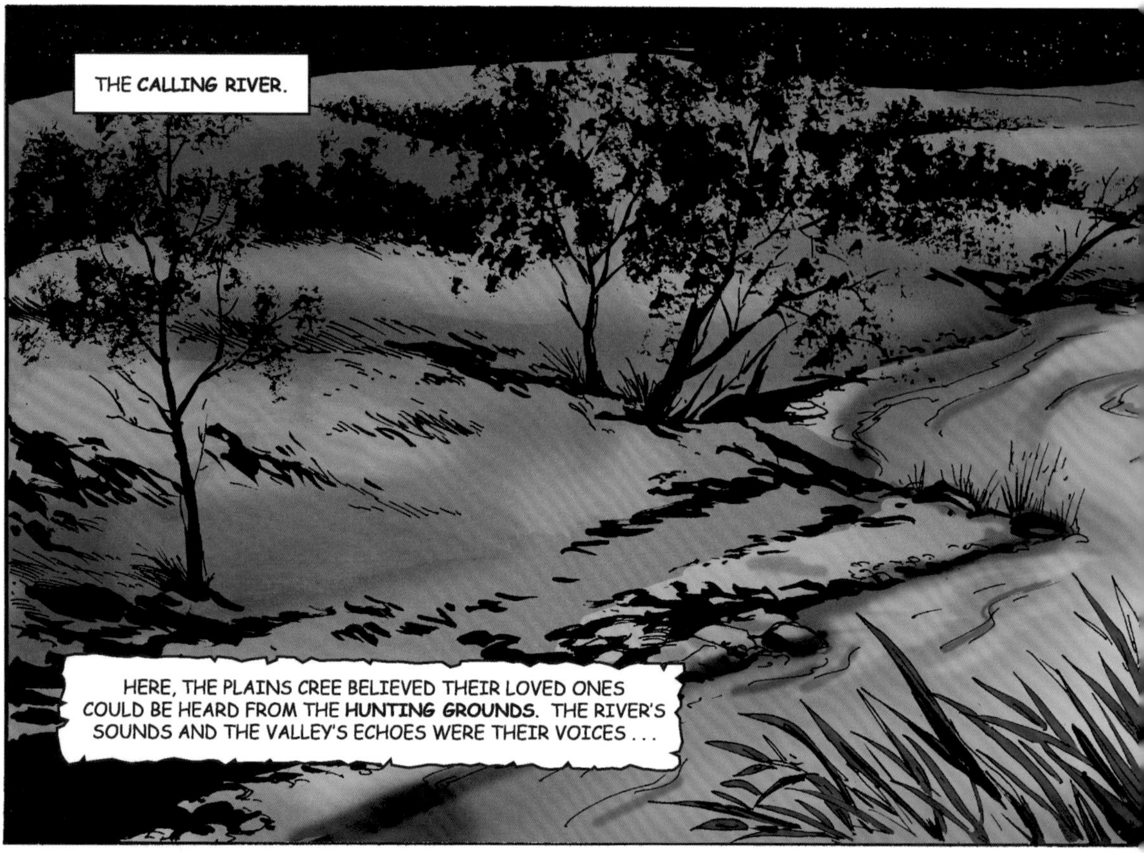
THE CALLING RIVER.
HERE, THE PLAINS CREE BELIEVED THEIR LOVED ONES COULD BE HEARD FROM THE HUNTING GROUNDS. THE RIVER'S SOUNDS AND THE VALLEY'S ECHOES WERE THEIR VOICES . . .

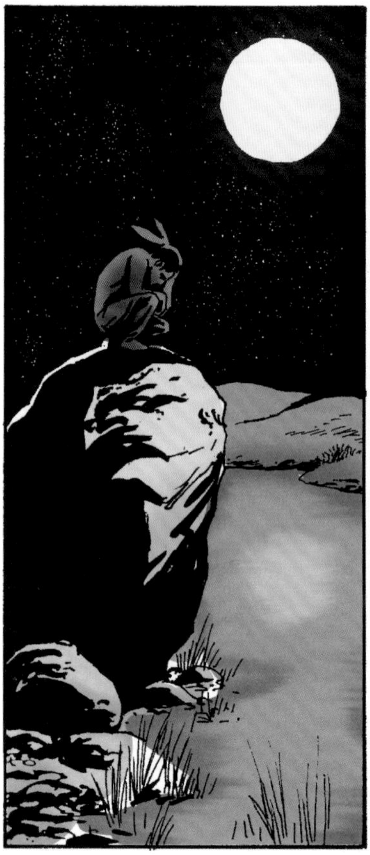

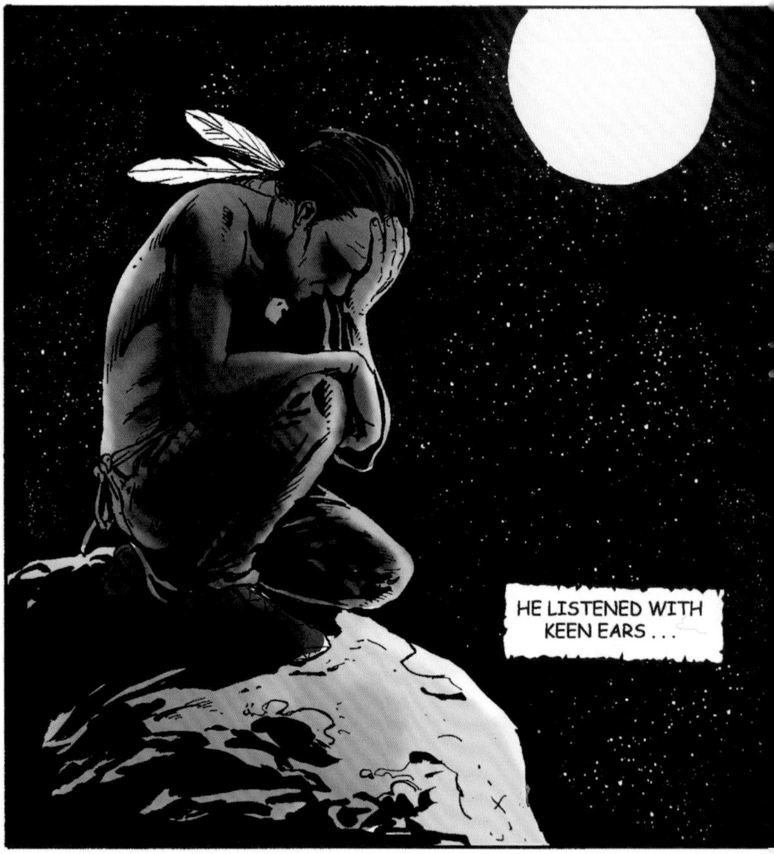
HE LISTENED WITH KEEN EARS . . .

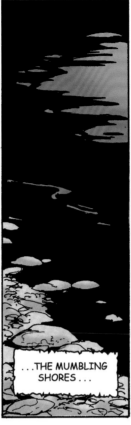

...THE MUMBLING SHORES...

...THE WIND THROUGH LEAVES LIKE FAINT WHISPERS.

...PRAYED THAT HIS BROTHER MADE THE JOURNEY.

STONE...

BEAR?

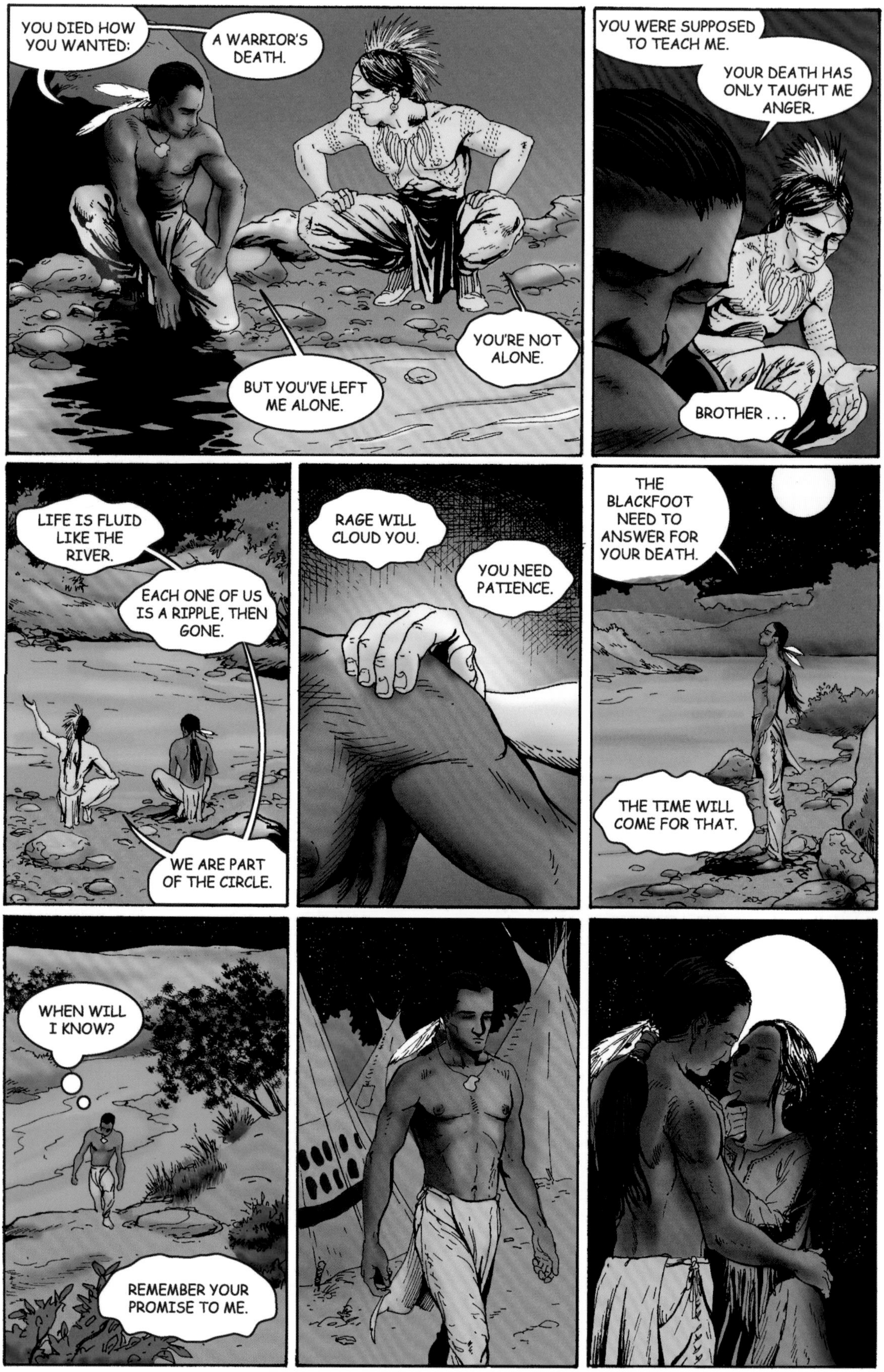
YOU DIED HOW YOU WANTED:
A WARRIOR'S DEATH.
BUT YOU'VE LEFT ME ALONE.
YOU'RE NOT ALONE.
YOU WERE SUPPOSED TO TEACH ME.
YOUR DEATH HAS ONLY TAUGHT ME ANGER.
BROTHER . . .
LIFE IS FLUID LIKE THE RIVER.
EACH ONE OF US IS A RIPPLE, THEN GONE.
WE ARE PART OF THE CIRCLE.
RAGE WILL CLOUD YOU.
YOU NEED PATIENCE.
THE BLACKFOOT NEED TO ANSWER FOR YOUR DEATH.
THE TIME WILL COME FOR THAT.
WHEN WILL I KNOW?
REMEMBER YOUR PROMISE TO ME.

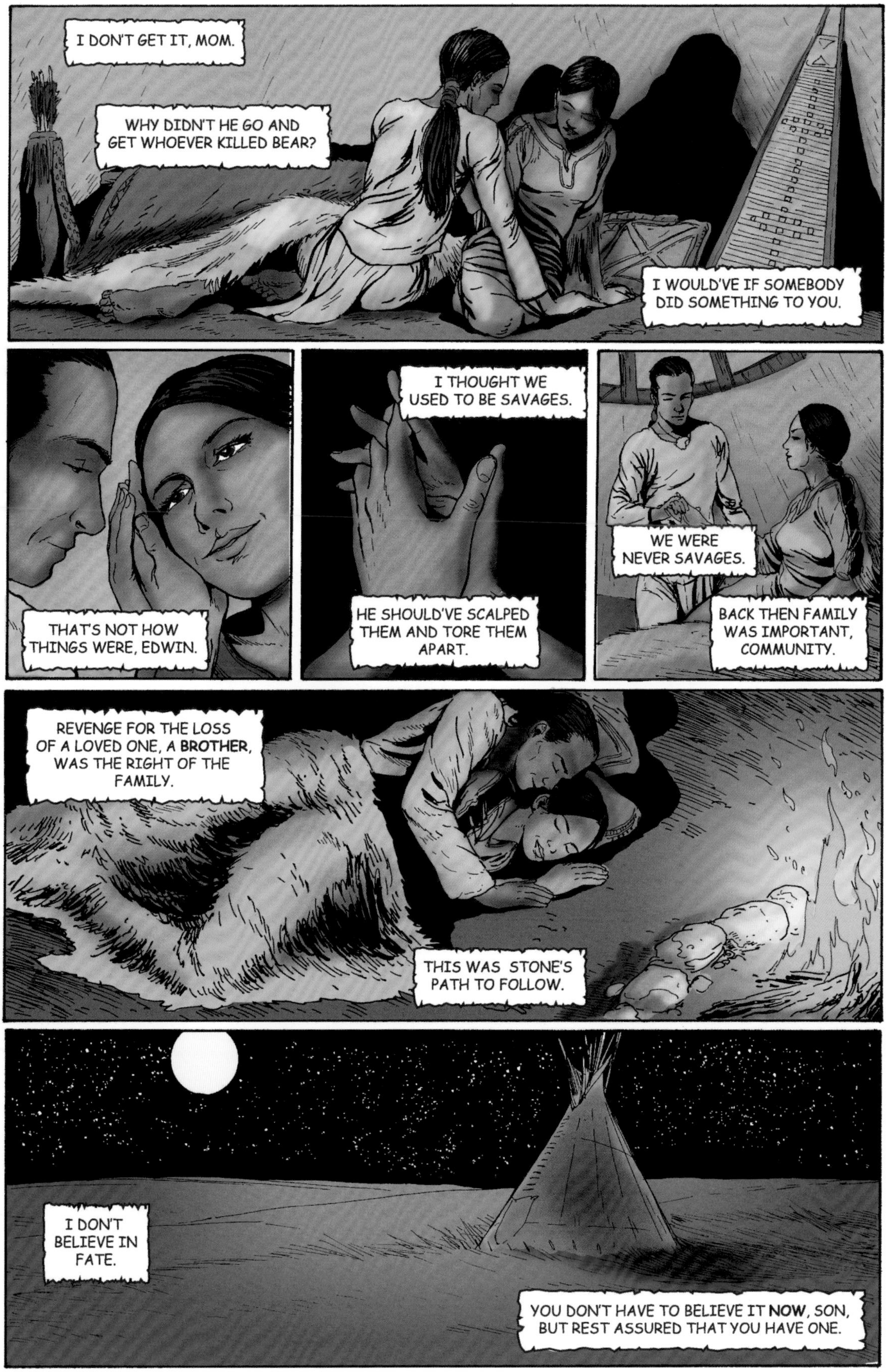
I DON'T GET IT, MOM.
WHY DIDN'T HE GO AND GET WHOEVER KILLED BEAR?
I WOULD'VE IF SOMEBODY DID SOMETHING TO YOU.
THAT'S NOT HOW THINGS WERE, EDWIN.
I THOUGHT WE USED TO BE SAVAGES.
HE SHOULD'VE SCALPED THEM AND TORE THEM APART.
WE WERE NEVER SAVAGES.
BACK THEN FAMILY WAS IMPORTANT, COMMUNITY.
REVENGE FOR THE LOSS OF A LOVED ONE, A **BROTHER**, WAS THE RIGHT OF THE FAMILY.
THIS WAS STONE'S PATH TO FOLLOW.
I DON'T BELIEVE IN FATE.
YOU DON'T HAVE TO BELIEVE IT **NOW**, SON, BUT REST ASSURED THAT YOU HAVE ONE.

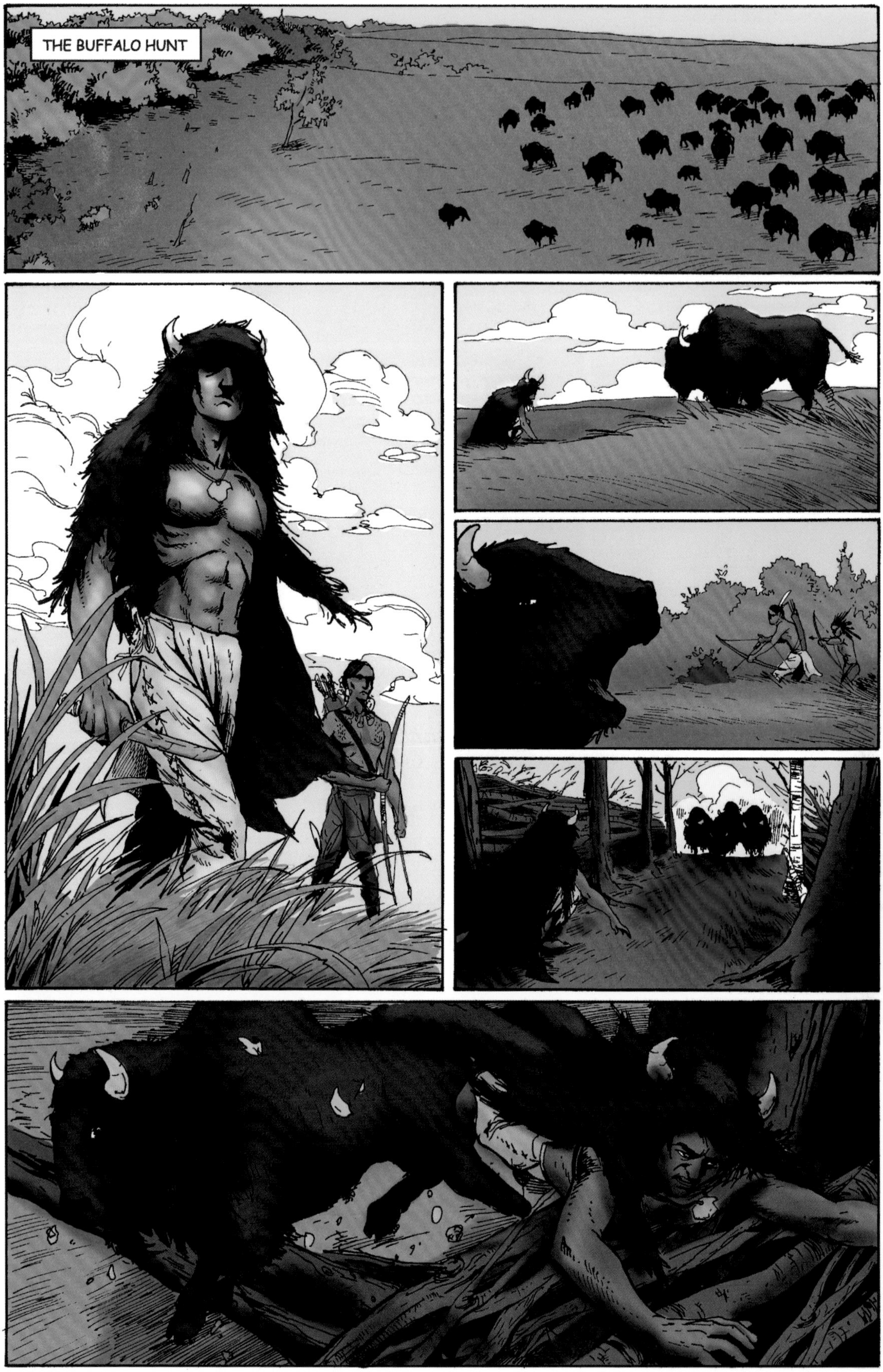
THE BUFFALO HUNT

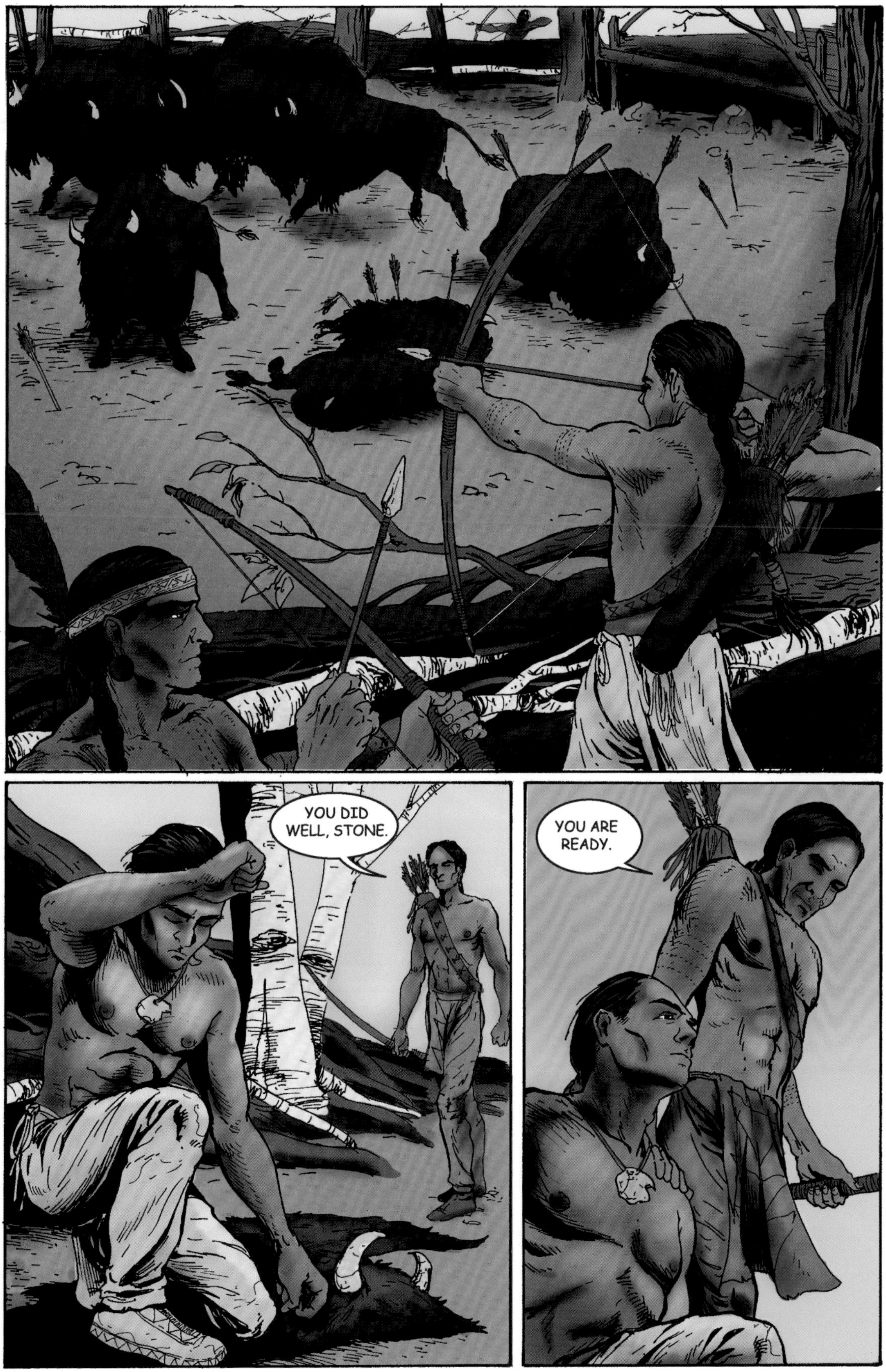
YOU DID WELL, STONE.
YOU ARE READY.

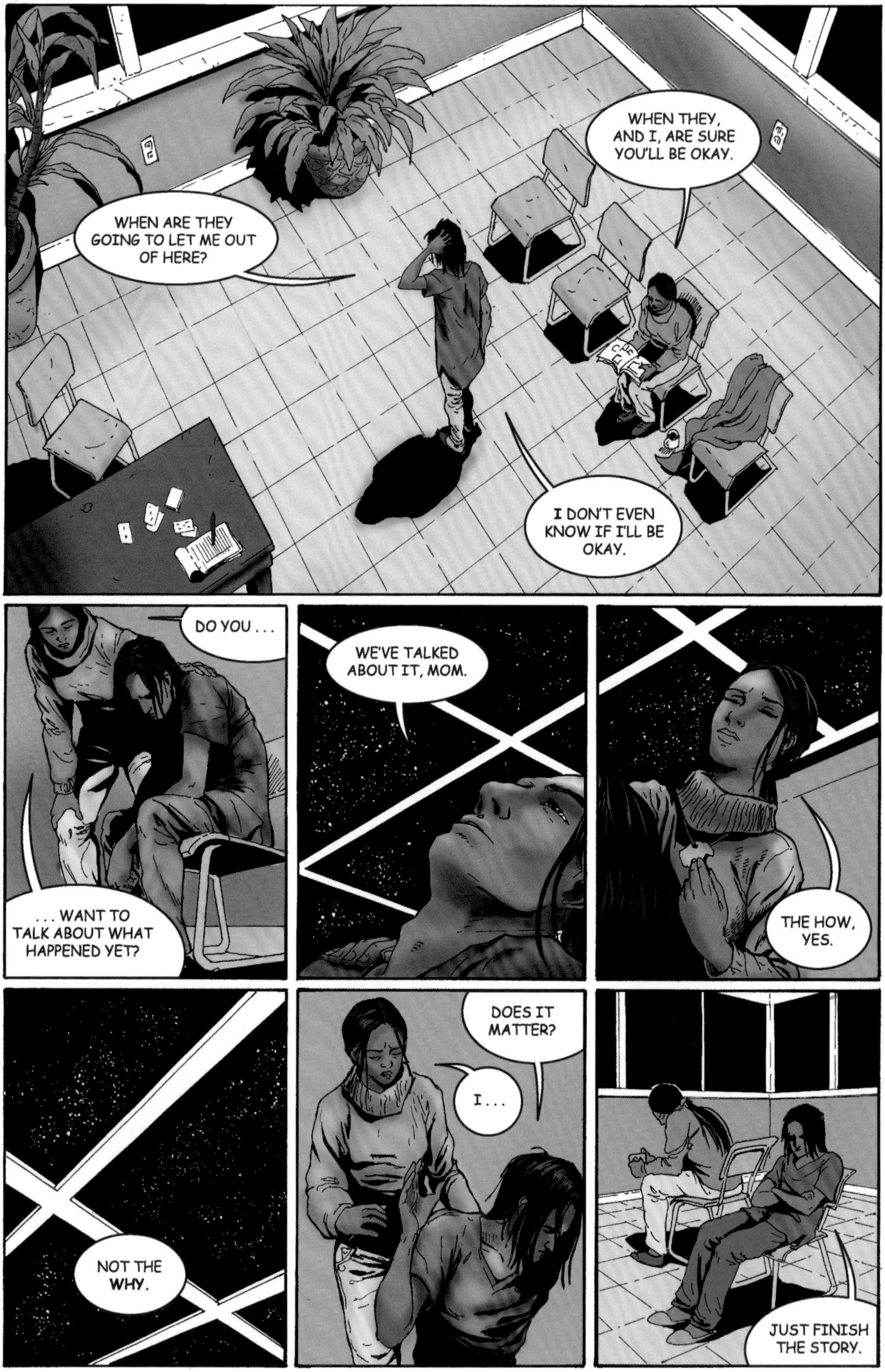
WHEN ARE THEY GOING TO LET ME OUT OF HERE?
WHEN THEY, AND I, ARE SURE YOU'LL BE OKAY.
I DON'T EVEN KNOW IF I'LL BE OKAY.
DO YOU . . .
. . . WANT TO TALK ABOUT WHAT HAPPENED YET?
WE'VE TALKED ABOUT IT, MOM.
THE HOW, YES.
NOT THE WHY.
DOES IT MATTER?
I . . .
JUST FINISH THE STORY.

TWO MONTHS LATER . . .

THE **THIRST DANCE** WAS AN ANCIENT CEREMONY PRACTICED BY OUR PEOPLE.

THE DANCERS DANCED FOR DAYS WITHOUT WATER OR FOOD.

TO HONOUR THE GREAT SPIRIT.

DURING THE THIRST DANCE A SELECT FEW PARTICIPATED IN ANOTHER, MORE PAINFUL DANCE.

IT WAS CALLED THE **MAKING OF A BRAVE.**

THESE YOUNG MEN FULFILLED VOWS TO UNDERGO TRIALS AS AN OFFERING TO THE GREAT SPIRIT AND TO PROVE THEIR BRAVERY.

IT WAS STONE'S LAST TRIAL TO JOIN THE WARRIOR SOCIETY.

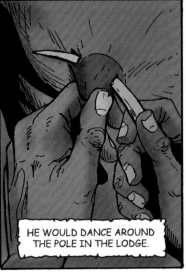

HE WOULD DANCE AROUND THE POLE IN THE LODGE.

WHEN THE TIME CAME HE WOULD DANCE BACKWARDS AND RIP THE SKEWERS FROM HIS SKIN.

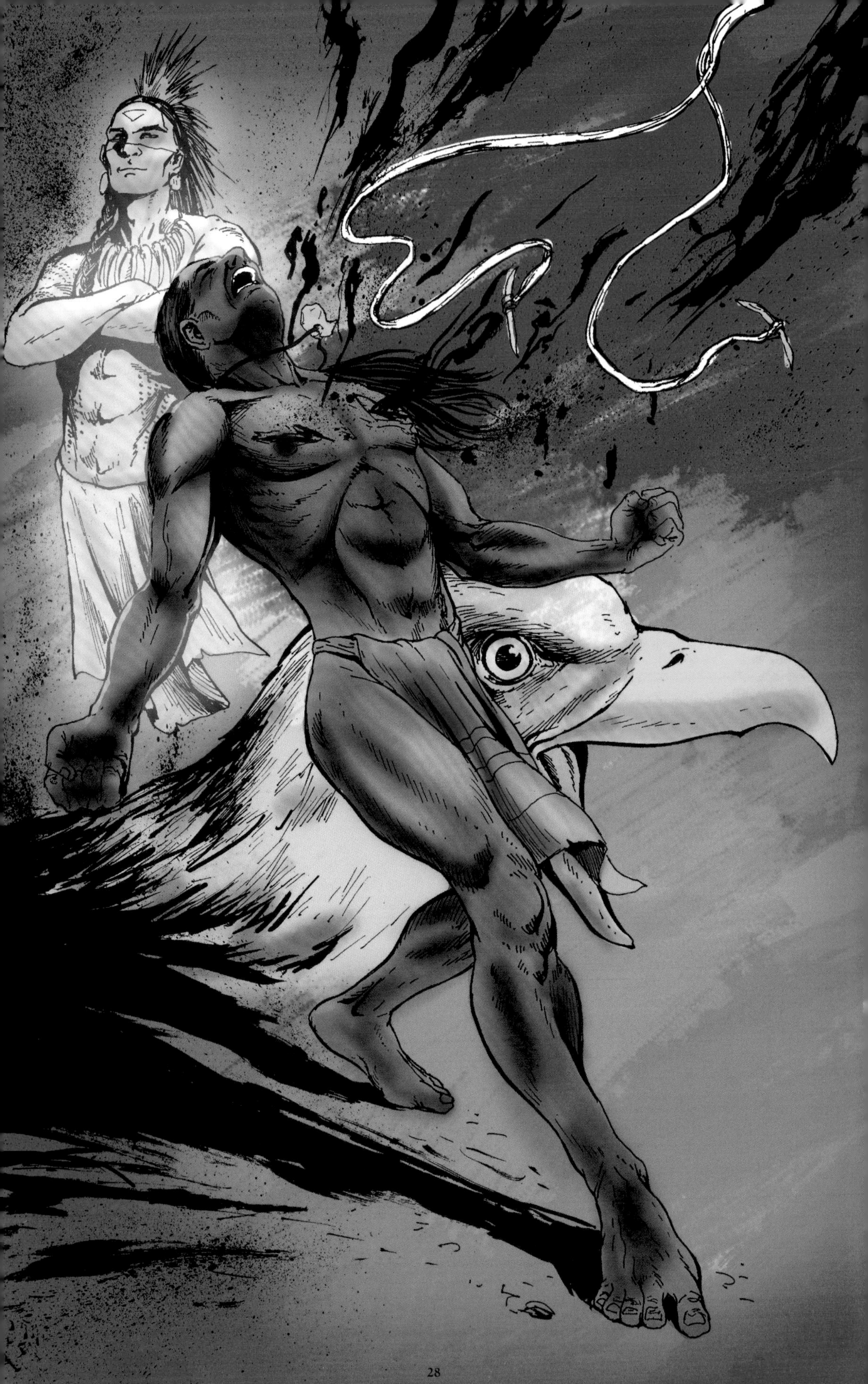

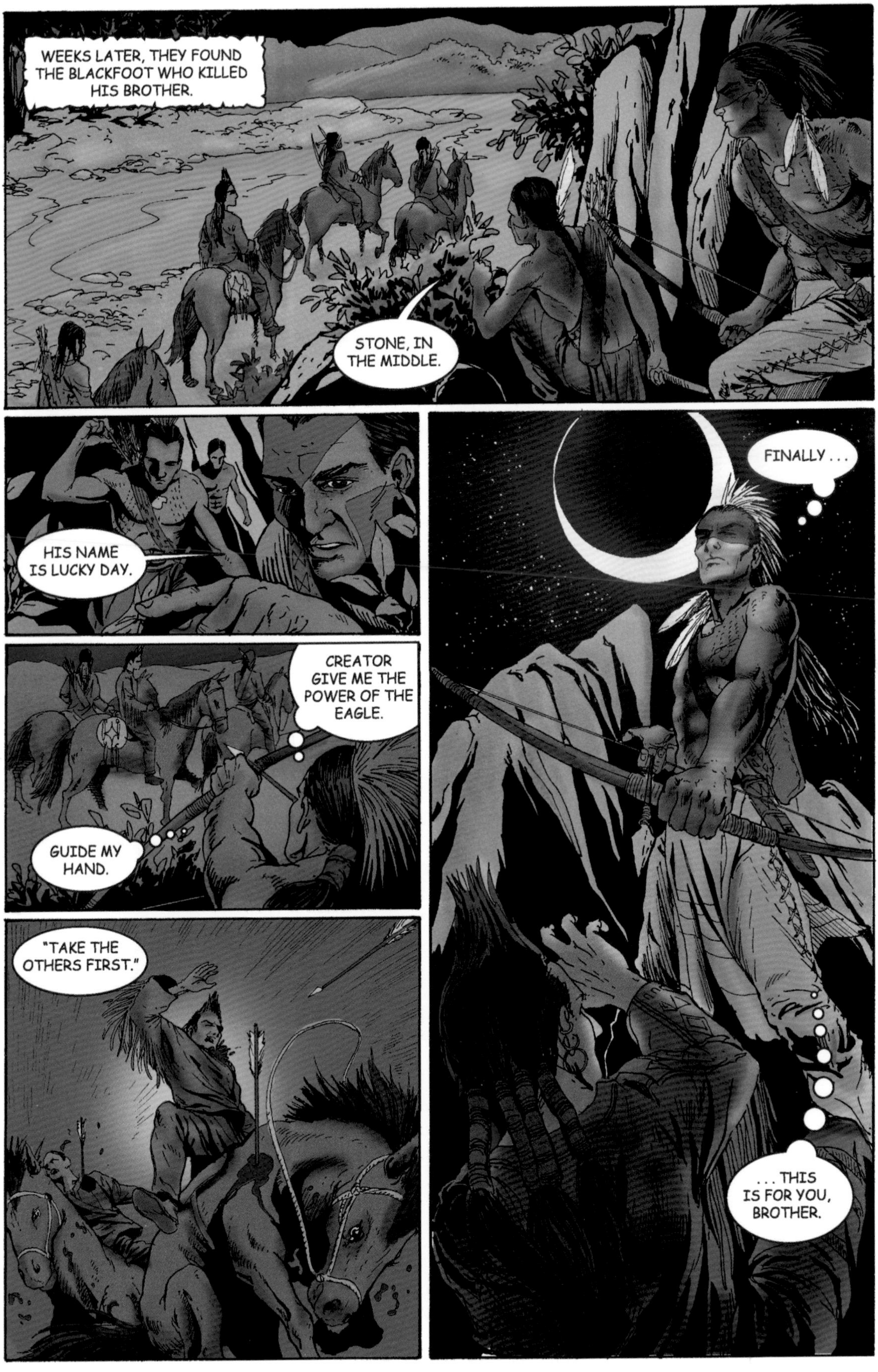
WEEKS LATER, THEY FOUND THE BLACKFOOT WHO KILLED HIS BROTHER.
STONE, IN THE MIDDLE.
HIS NAME IS LUCKY DAY.
CREATOR GIVE ME THE POWER OF THE EAGLE.
GUIDE MY HAND.
"TAKE THE OTHERS FIRST."
FINALLY . . .
. . . THIS IS FOR YOU, BROTHER.

THUMP!

AND IT WAS FINISHED.

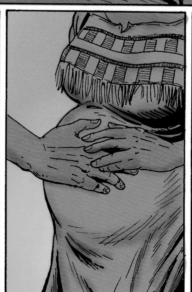

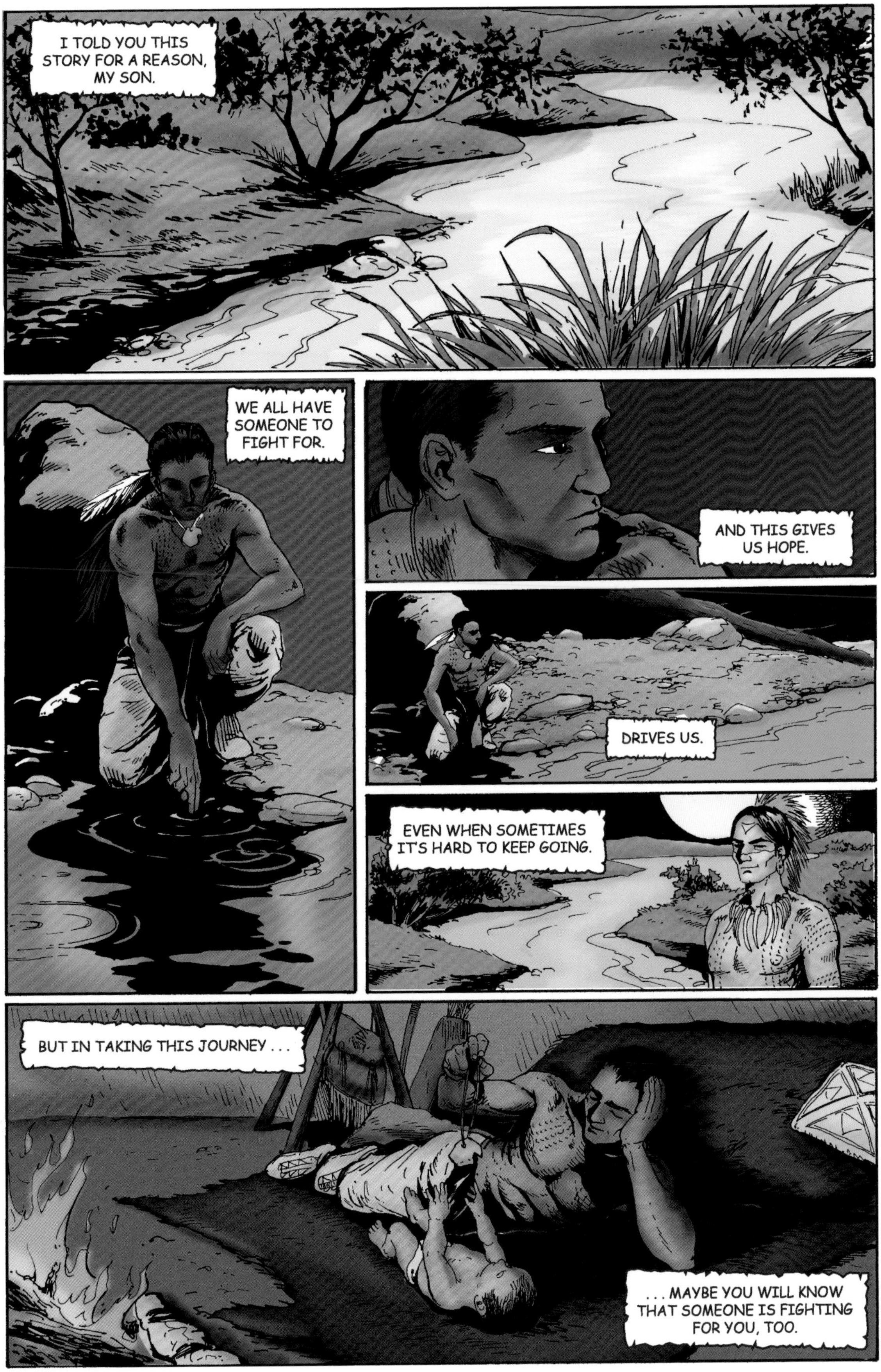
I TOLD YOU THIS STORY FOR A REASON, MY SON.
WE ALL HAVE SOMEONE TO FIGHT FOR.
AND THIS GIVES US HOPE.
DRIVES US.
EVEN WHEN SOMETIMES IT'S HARD TO KEEP GOING.
BUT IN TAKING THIS JOURNEY . . .
. . . MAYBE YOU WILL KNOW THAT SOMEONE IS FIGHTING FOR YOU, TOO.

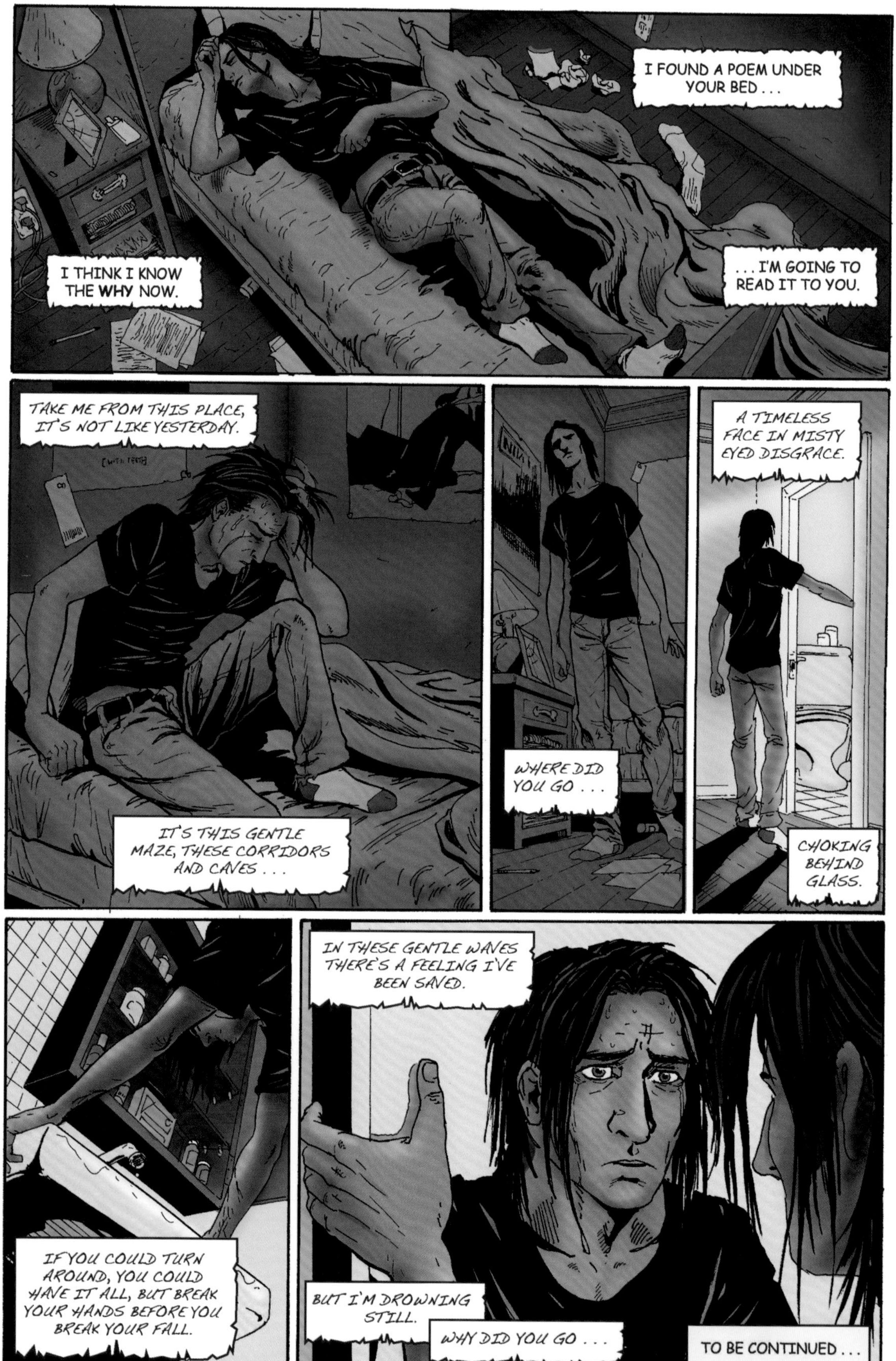
I FOUND A POEM UNDER YOUR BED . . .
I THINK I KNOW THE **WHY** NOW.
. . . I'M GOING TO READ IT TO YOU.
TAKE ME FROM THIS PLACE, IT'S NOT LIKE YESTERDAY.
IT'S THIS GENTLE MAZE, THESE CORRIDORS AND CAVES . . .
WHERE DID YOU GO . . .
A TIMELESS FACE IN MISTY EYED DISGRACE.
CHOKING BEHIND GLASS.
IF YOU COULD TURN AROUND, YOU COULD HAVE IT ALL, BUT BREAK YOUR HANDS BEFORE YOU BREAK YOUR FALL.
IN THESE GENTLE WAVES THERE'S A FEELING I'VE BEEN SAVED.
BUT I'M DROWNING STILL.
WHY DID YOU GO . . .
TO BE CONTINUED . . .

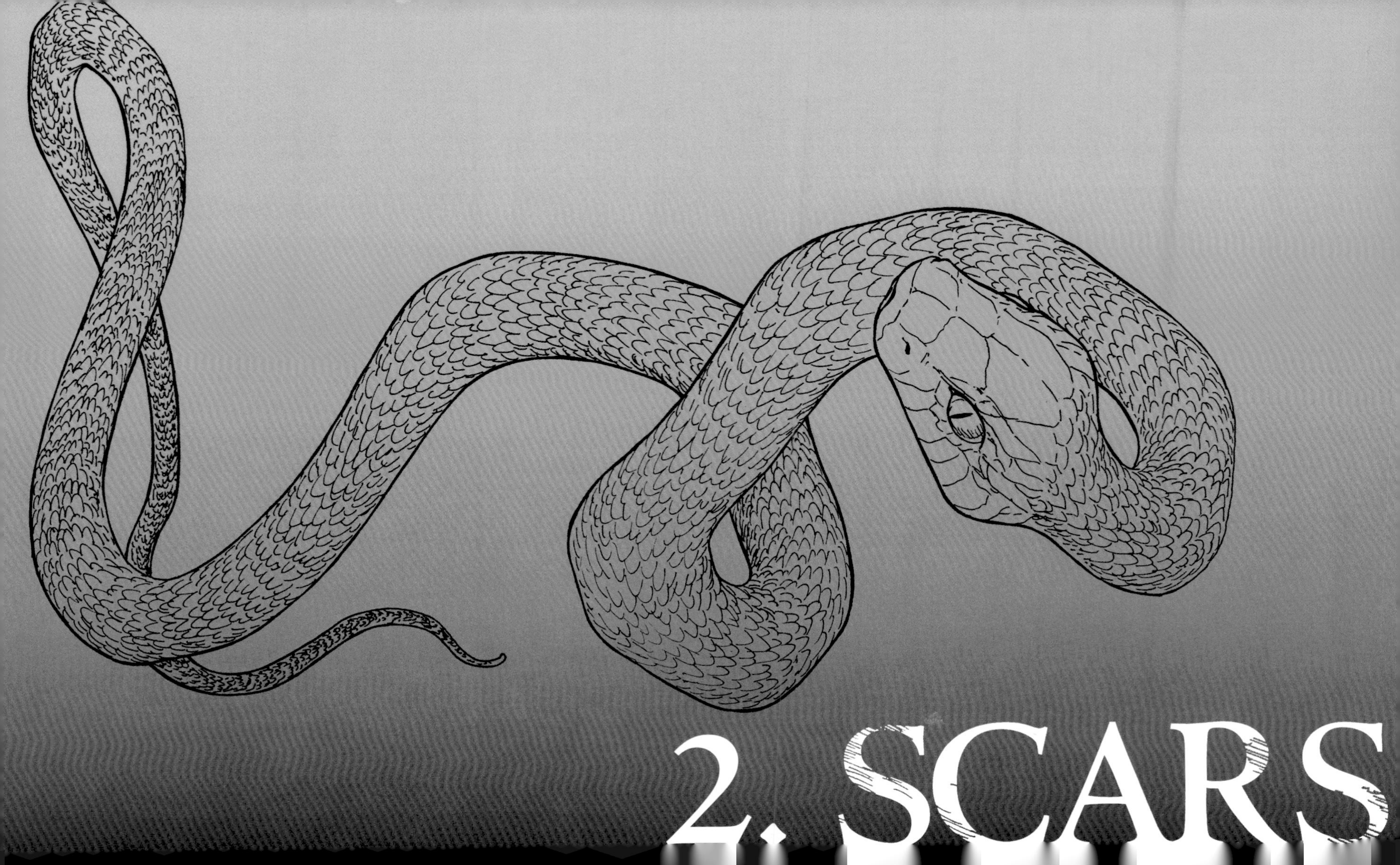

2. SCARS

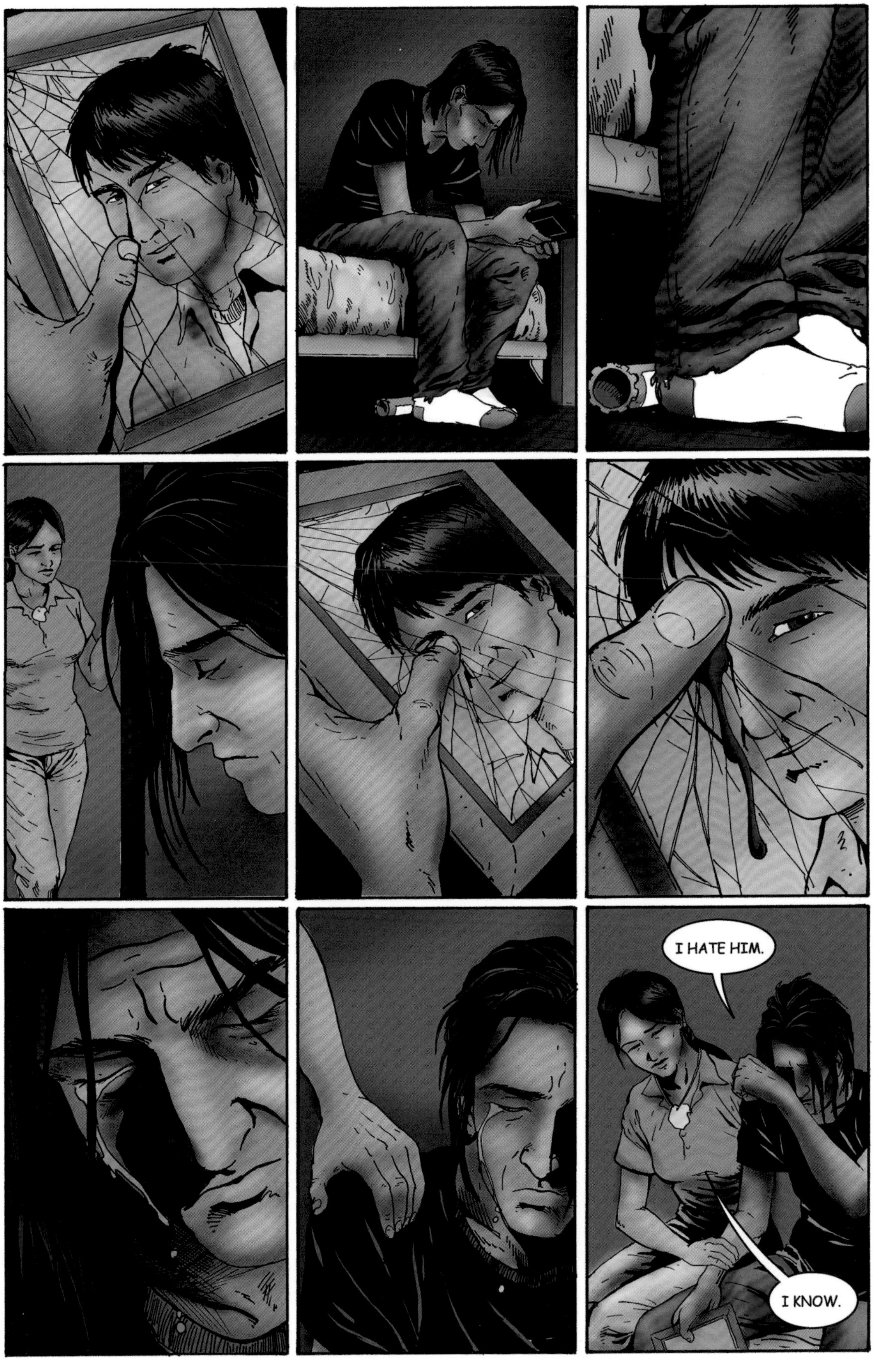
I HATE HIM.
I KNOW.

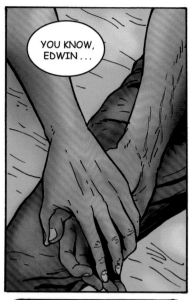

YOU KNOW, EDWIN . . .

. . . SOMETIMES . . .

. . . WE LOVE SOMETHING SO MUCH . . .

. . . WE HAVE TO LET IT GO . . .

. . . NO MATTER HOW MUCH IT HURTS.

MOM, I DON'T UNDERSTAND.

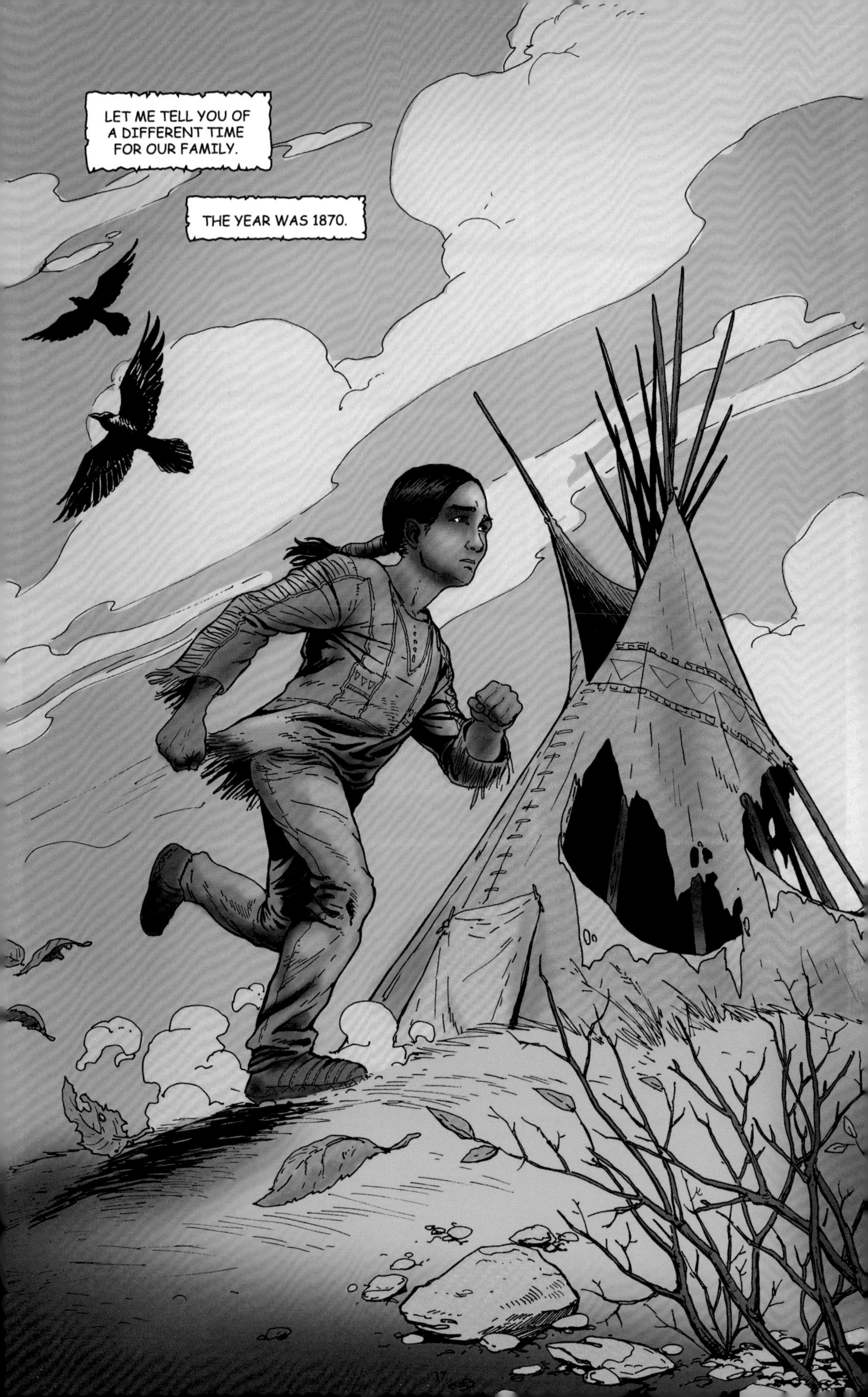

LET ME TELL YOU OF A DIFFERENT TIME FOR OUR FAMILY.
THE YEAR WAS 1870.

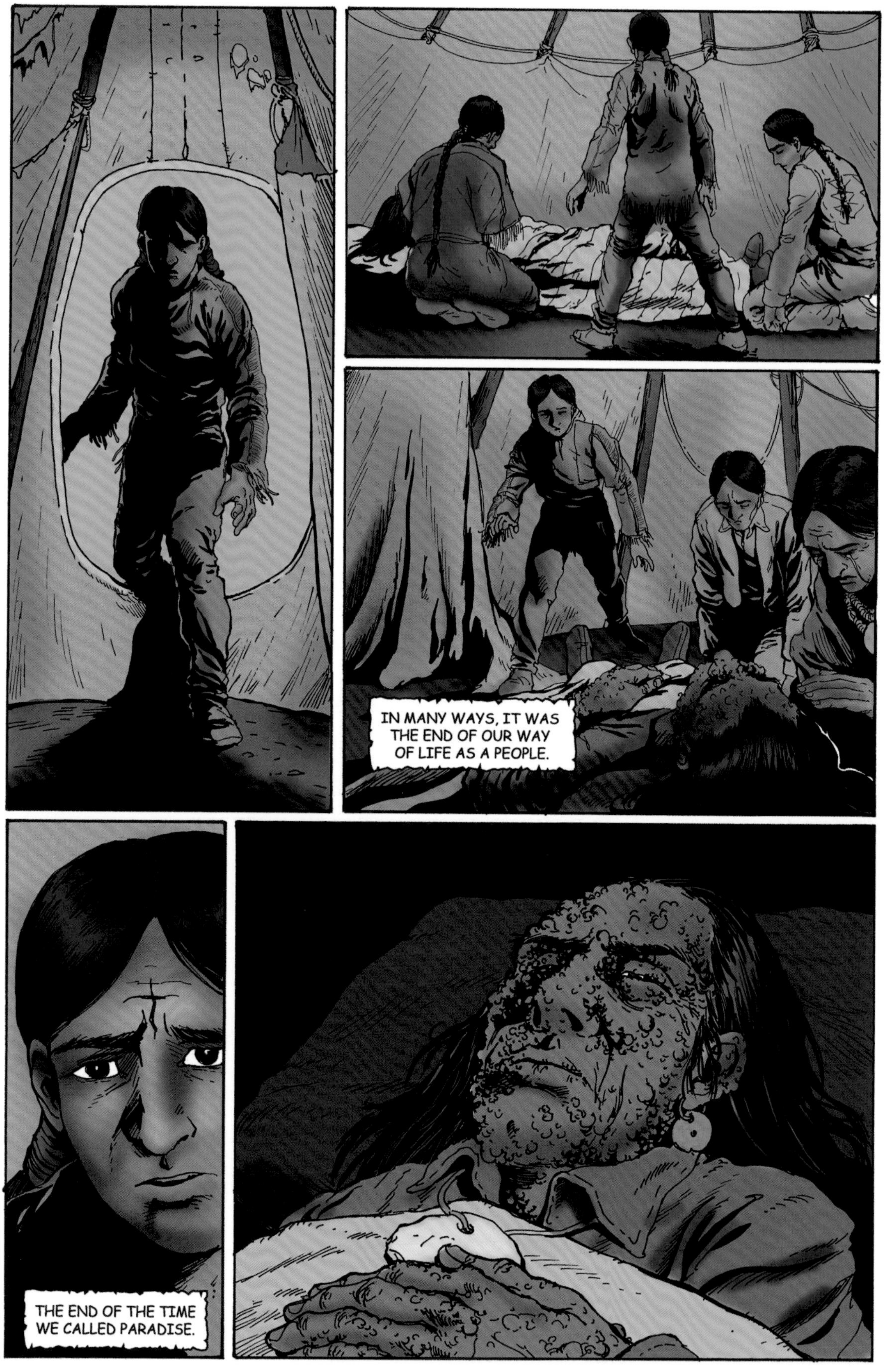
IN MANY WAYS, IT WAS THE END OF OUR WAY OF LIFE AS A PEOPLE.
THE END OF THE TIME WE CALLED PARADISE.

WHITE CLOUD . . .

YES, FATHER?

YOU NEED TO LEAVE HERE . . .

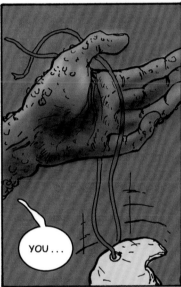

YOU . . .

FATHER!

LEAVE HIM, SON. HE'S GONE.

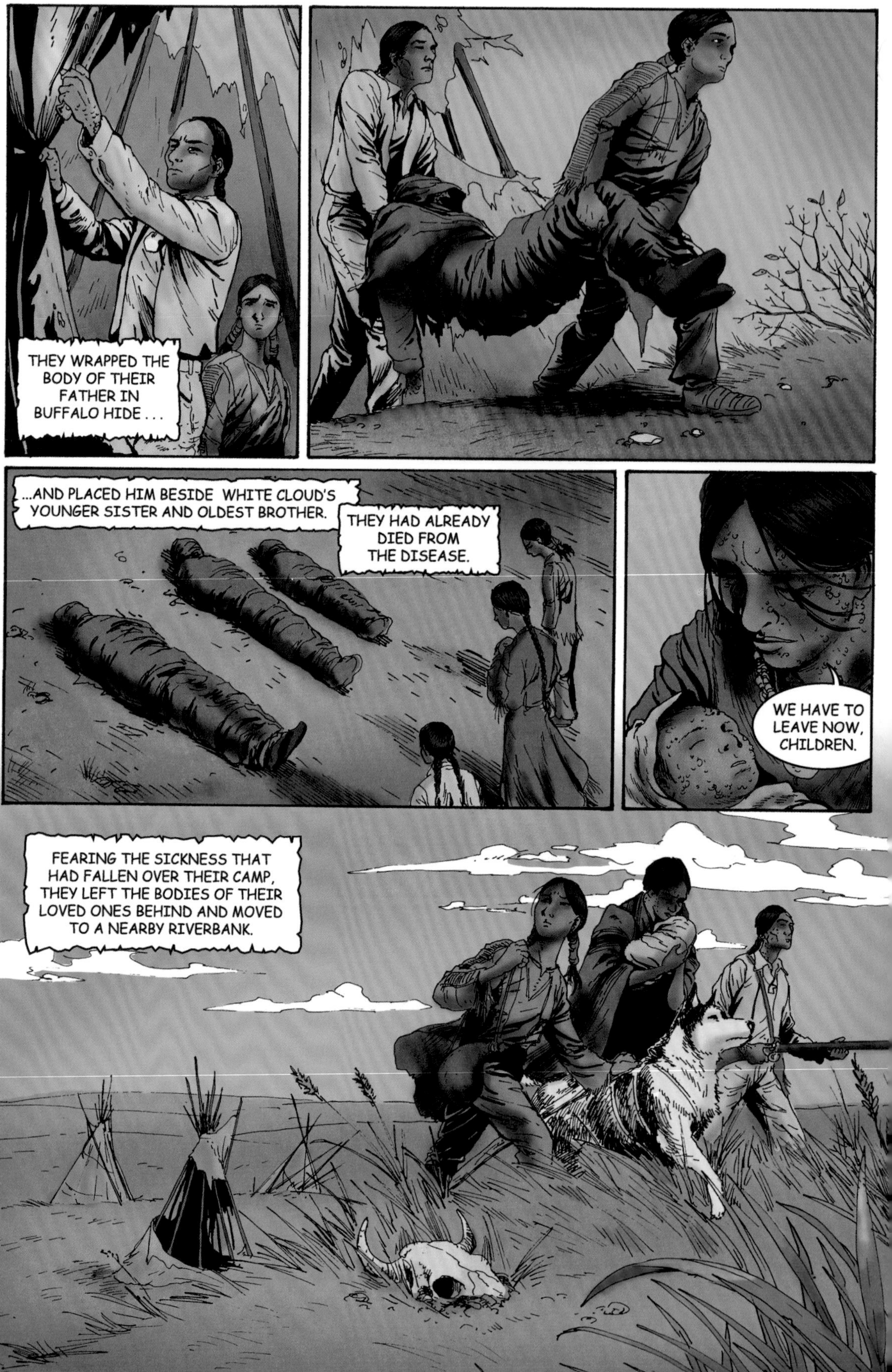
THEY WRAPPED THE BODY OF THEIR FATHER IN BUFFALO HIDE . . .
...AND PLACED HIM BESIDE WHITE CLOUD'S YOUNGER SISTER AND OLDEST BROTHER.
THEY HAD ALREADY DIED FROM THE DISEASE.
WE HAVE TO LEAVE NOW, CHILDREN.
FEARING THE SICKNESS THAT HAD FALLEN OVER THEIR CAMP, THEY LEFT THE BODIES OF THEIR LOVED ONES BEHIND AND MOVED TO A NEARBY RIVERBANK.

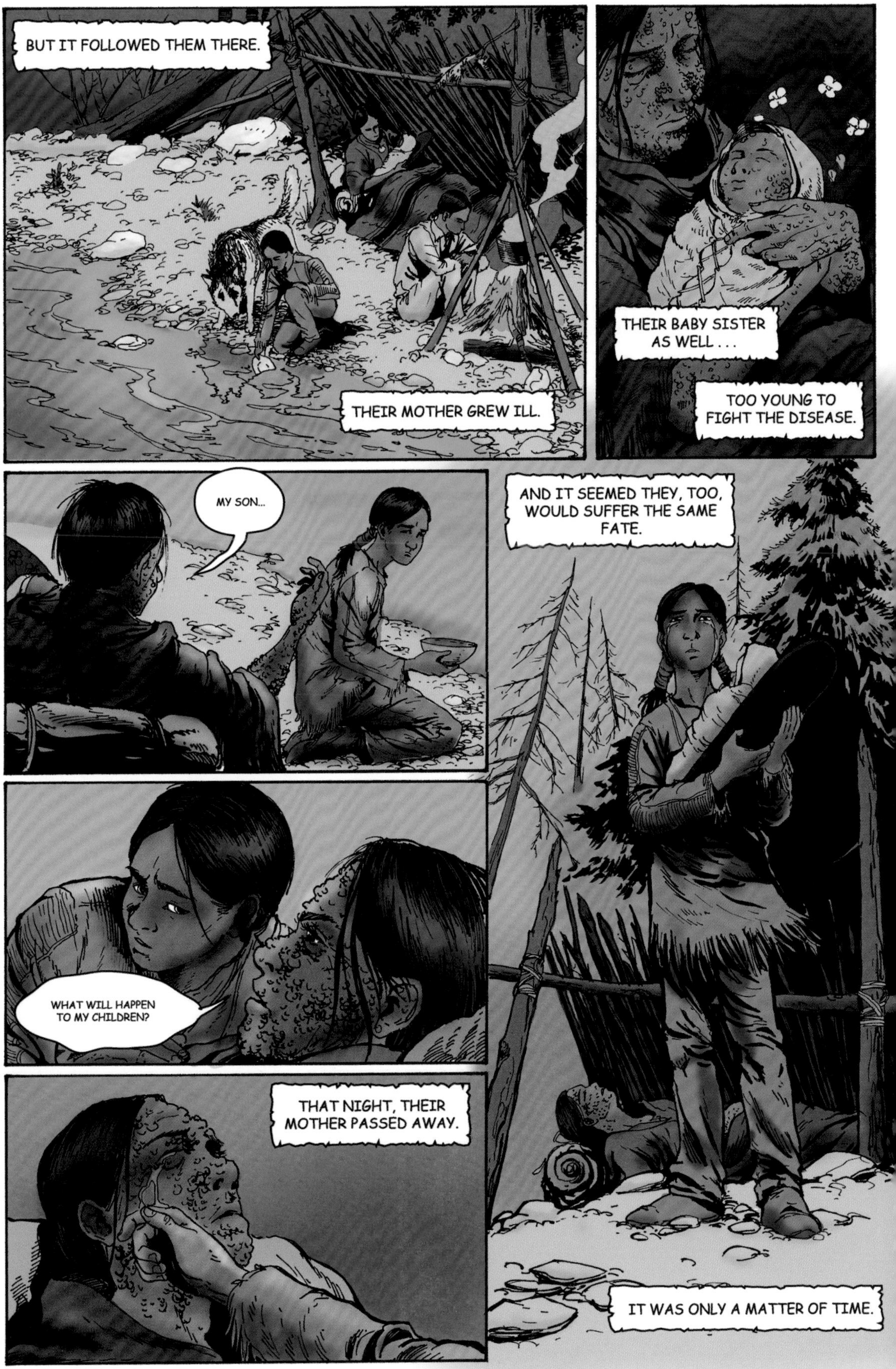
BUT IT FOLLOWED THEM THERE.
THEIR MOTHER GREW ILL.
THEIR BABY SISTER AS WELL . . .
TOO YOUNG TO FIGHT THE DISEASE.
MY SON...
WHAT WILL HAPPEN TO MY CHILDREN?
THAT NIGHT, THEIR MOTHER PASSED AWAY.
AND IT SEEMED THEY, TOO, WOULD SUFFER THE SAME FATE.
IT WAS ONLY A MATTER OF TIME.

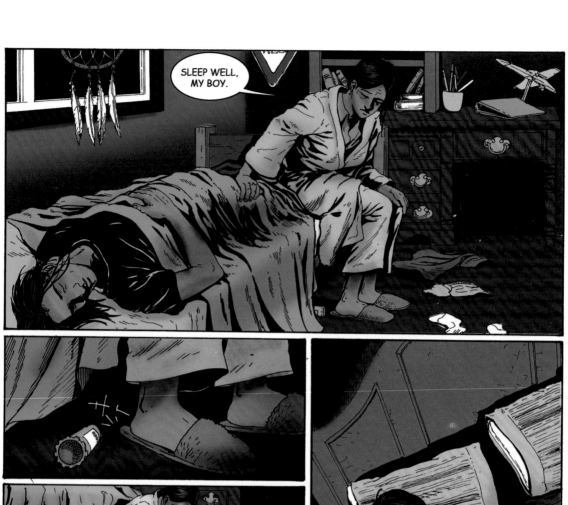

SLEEP WELL, MY BOY.

WHAT WILL HAPPEN TO MY CHILD?

IS IT ONLY A MATTER OF TIME?

DO YOU WANT TO HEAR MORE?

SURE.

THE NEXT MORNING, WHITE CLOUD SUDDENLY HAD HIS BABY SISTER AND OLDER BROTHER TO CARE FOR.

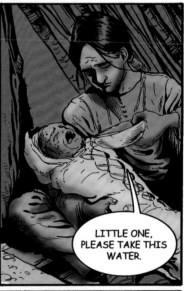

LITTLE ONE, PLEASE TAKE THIS WATER.

WE NEED FOOD, BROTHER.

I'M NOT HUNGRY.

YOU AND SISTER NEED TO EAT.

I'M GOING TO FIND SOMETHING.

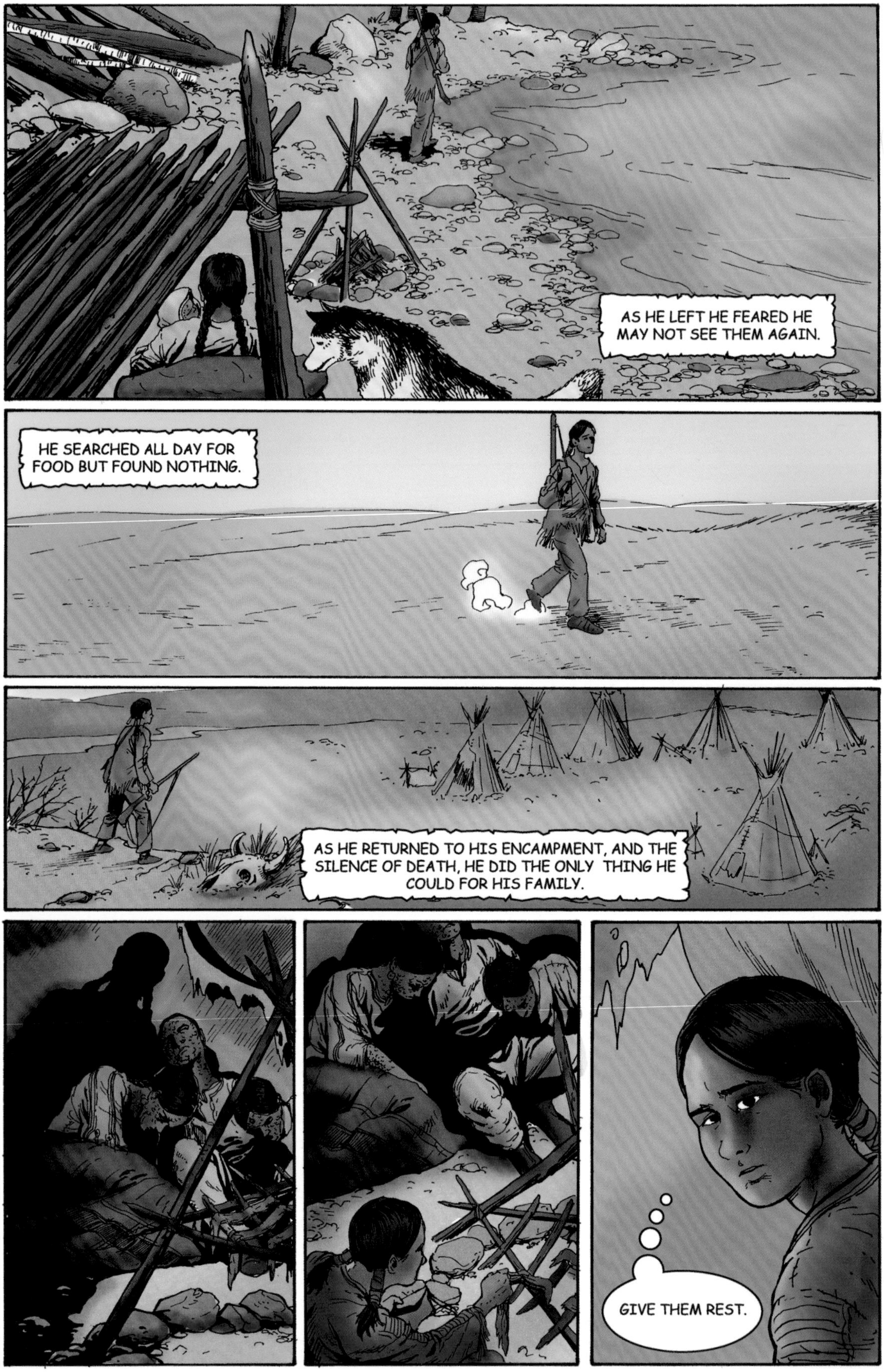
AS HE LEFT HE FEARED HE MAY NOT SEE THEM AGAIN.
HE SEARCHED ALL DAY FOR FOOD BUT FOUND NOTHING.
AS HE RETURNED TO HIS ENCAMPMENT, AND THE SILENCE OF DEATH, HE DID THE ONLY THING HE COULD FOR HIS FAMILY.
GIVE THEM REST.

EVERYONE'S DEAD BACK HOME, BROTHER. THERE'S NOTHING HERE TO STAY FOR.

SHE'S DEAD.

CREATOR, CRADLE OUR BABY SISTER IN YOUR ARMS.

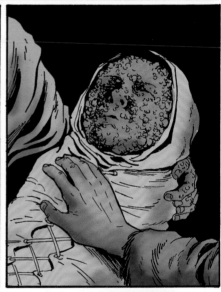

I WILL STAY. **YOU** WILL GO. I'VE NO HOPE LEFT BUT TO DIE HERE WITH OUR BABY SISTER. I WON'T LEAVE HER AND MY TIME IS COMING.

MAKE SURE OUR FAMILY LIVES ON. LEAVE ME, PLEASE.

YOU CAN SURVIVE

I . . .

I DON'T KNOW WHERE TO GO.

YOU WILL FIND YOUR WAY

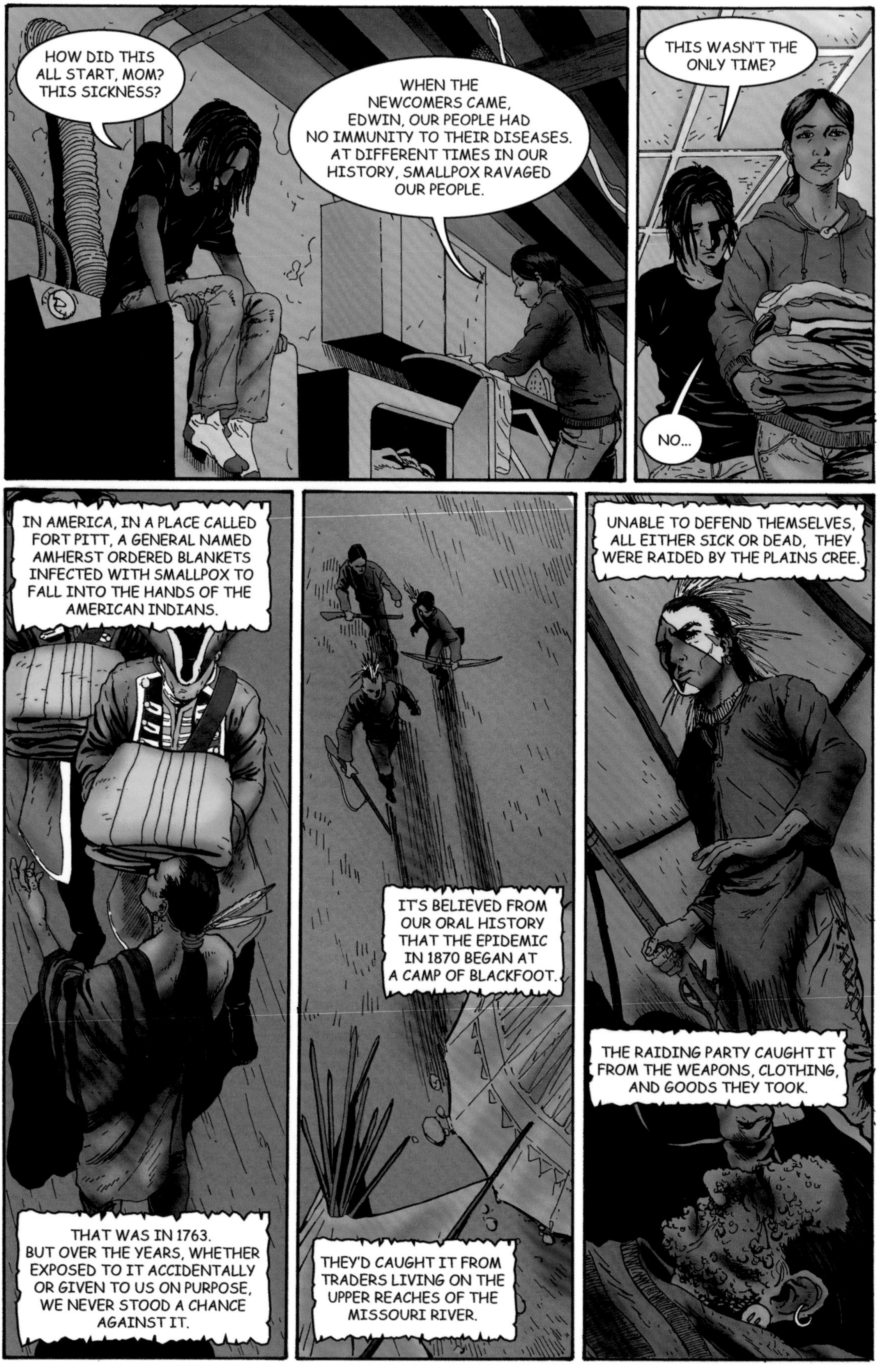
HOW DID THIS ALL START, MOM? THIS SICKNESS?
WHEN THE NEWCOMERS CAME, EDWIN, OUR PEOPLE HAD NO IMMUNITY TO THEIR DISEASES. AT DIFFERENT TIMES IN OUR HISTORY, SMALLPOX RAVAGED OUR PEOPLE.
THIS WASN'T THE ONLY TIME?
NO...
IN AMERICA, IN A PLACE CALLED FORT PITT, A GENERAL NAMED AMHERST ORDERED BLANKETS INFECTED WITH SMALLPOX TO FALL INTO THE HANDS OF THE AMERICAN INDIANS.
THAT WAS IN 1763. BUT OVER THE YEARS, WHETHER EXPOSED TO IT ACCIDENTALLY OR GIVEN TO US ON PURPOSE, WE NEVER STOOD A CHANCE AGAINST IT.
IT'S BELIEVED FROM OUR ORAL HISTORY THAT THE EPIDEMIC IN 1870 BEGAN AT A CAMP OF BLACKFOOT.
THEY'D CAUGHT IT FROM TRADERS LIVING ON THE UPPER REACHES OF THE MISSOURI RIVER.
UNABLE TO DEFEND THEMSELVES, ALL EITHER SICK OR DEAD, THEY WERE RAIDED BY THE PLAINS CREE.
THE RAIDING PARTY CAUGHT IT FROM THE WEAPONS, CLOTHING, AND GOODS THEY TOOK.

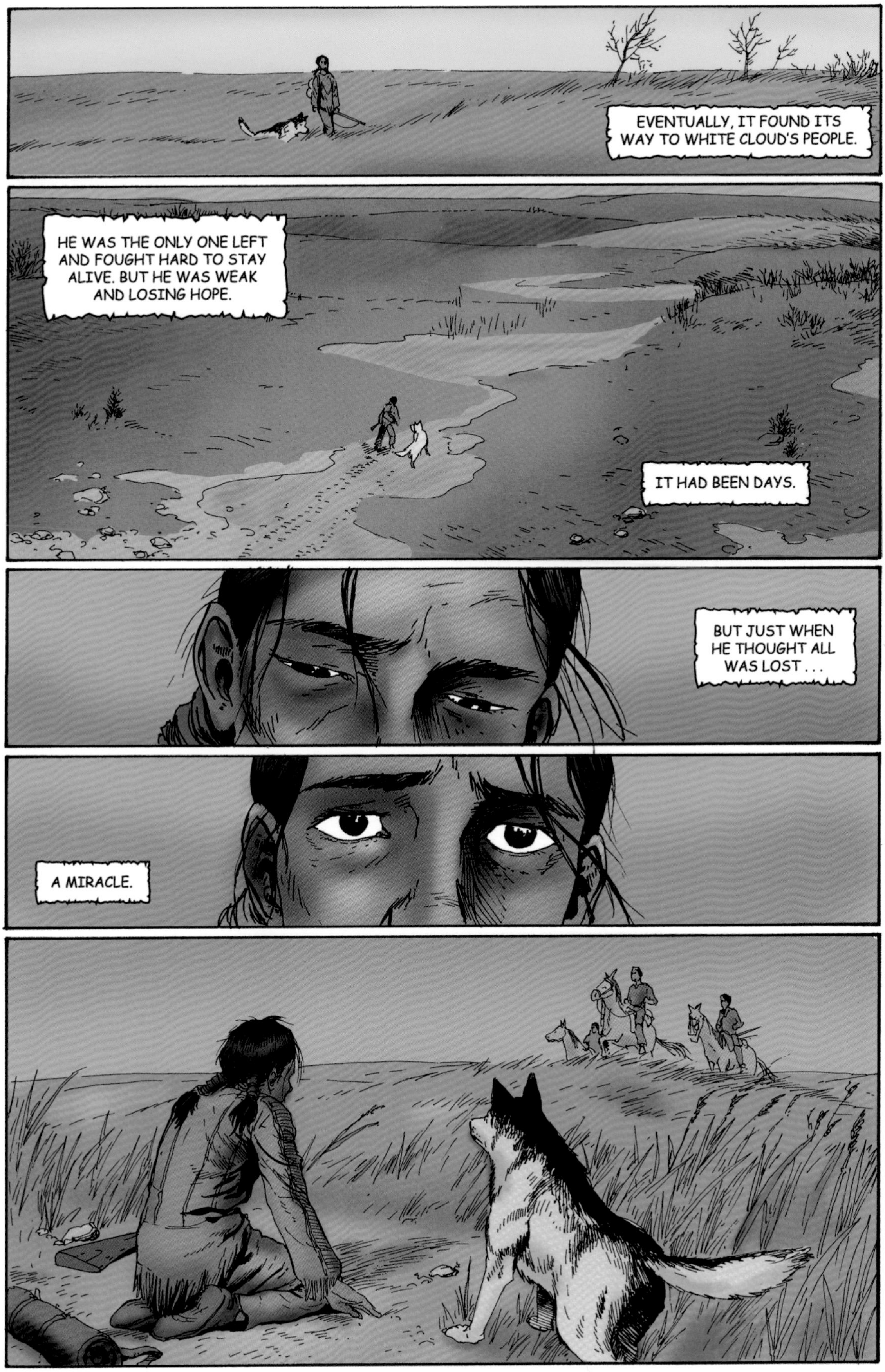
EVENTUALLY, IT FOUND ITS WAY TO WHITE CLOUD'S PEOPLE.
HE WAS THE ONLY ONE LEFT AND FOUGHT HARD TO STAY ALIVE. BUT HE WAS WEAK AND LOSING HOPE.
IT HAD BEEN DAYS.
BUT JUST WHEN HE THOUGHT ALL WAS LOST . . .
A MIRACLE.

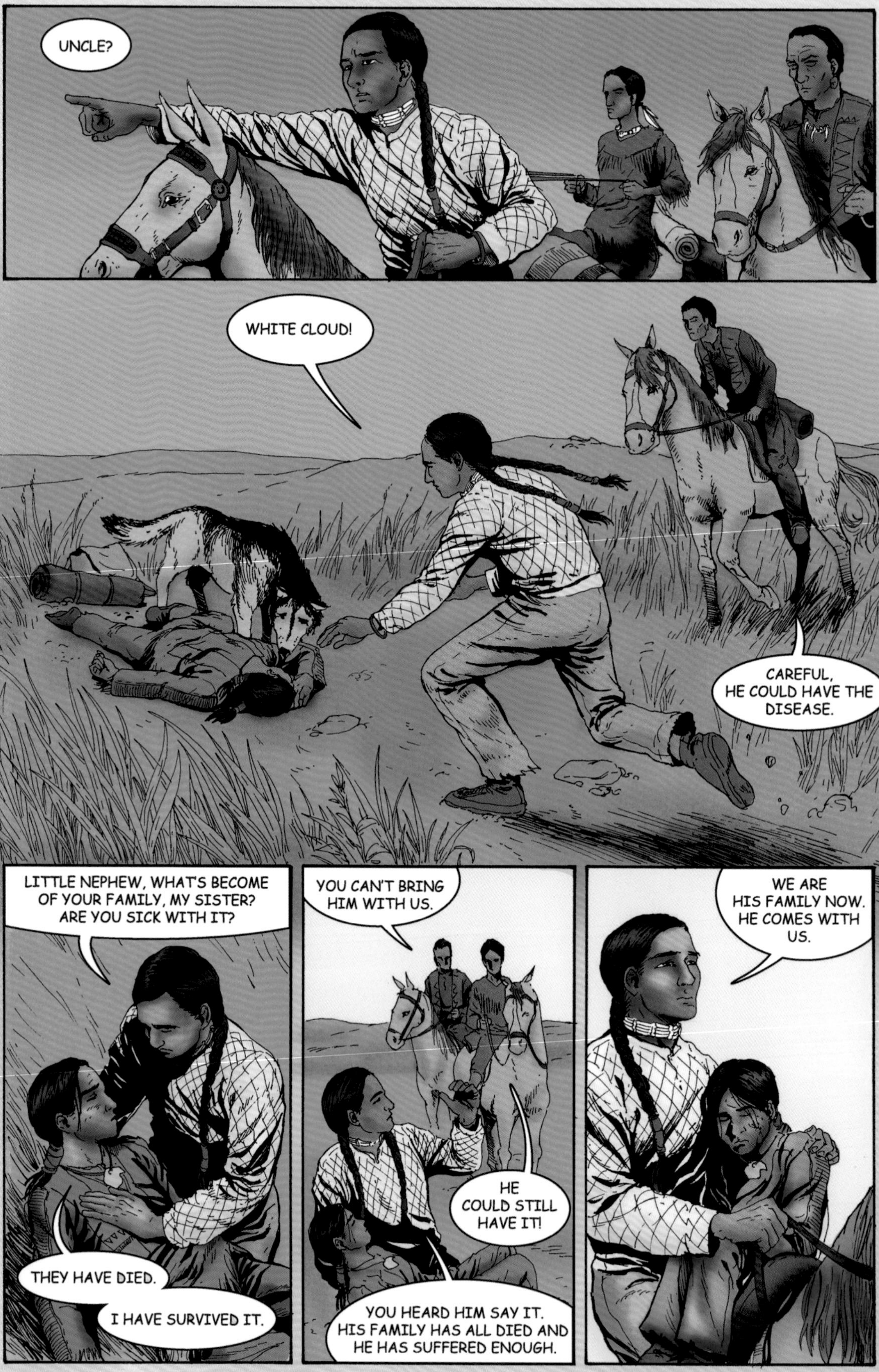
UNCLE?
WHITE CLOUD!
CAREFUL, HE COULD HAVE THE DISEASE.
LITTLE NEPHEW, WHAT'S BECOME OF YOUR FAMILY, MY SISTER? ARE YOU SICK WITH IT?
THEY HAVE DIED.
I HAVE SURVIVED IT.
YOU CAN'T BRING HIM WITH US.
HE COULD STILL HAVE IT!
YOU HEARD HIM SAY IT. HIS FAMILY HAS ALL DIED AND HE HAS SUFFERED ENOUGH.
WE ARE HIS FAMILY NOW. HE COMES WITH US.

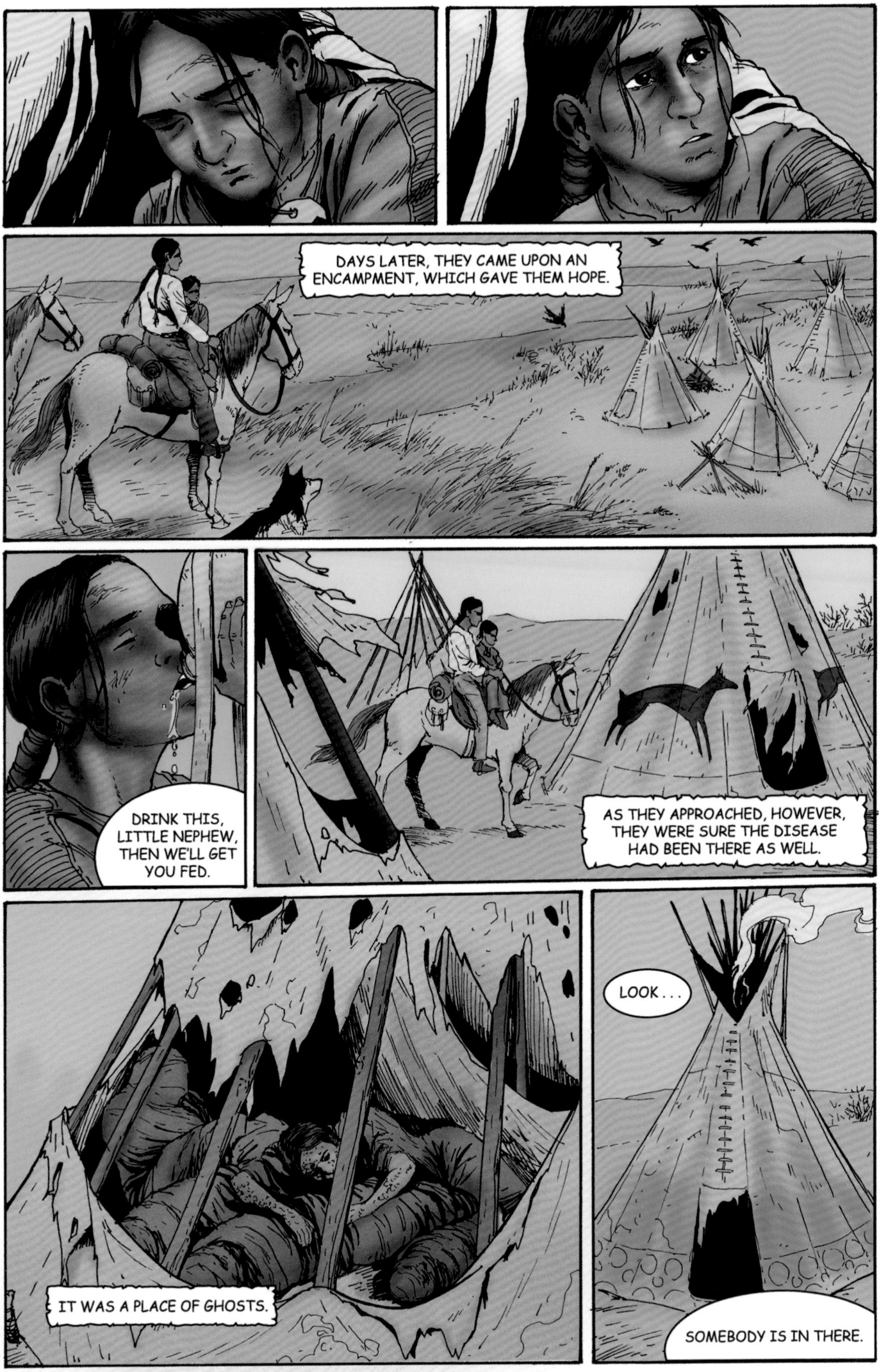
DAYS LATER, THEY CAME UPON AN ENCAMPMENT, WHICH GAVE THEM HOPE.
DRINK THIS, LITTLE NEPHEW, THEN WE'LL GET YOU FED.
AS THEY APPROACHED, HOWEVER, THEY WERE SURE THE DISEASE HAD BEEN THERE AS WELL.
IT WAS A PLACE OF GHOSTS.
LOOK . . .
SOMEBODY IS IN THERE.

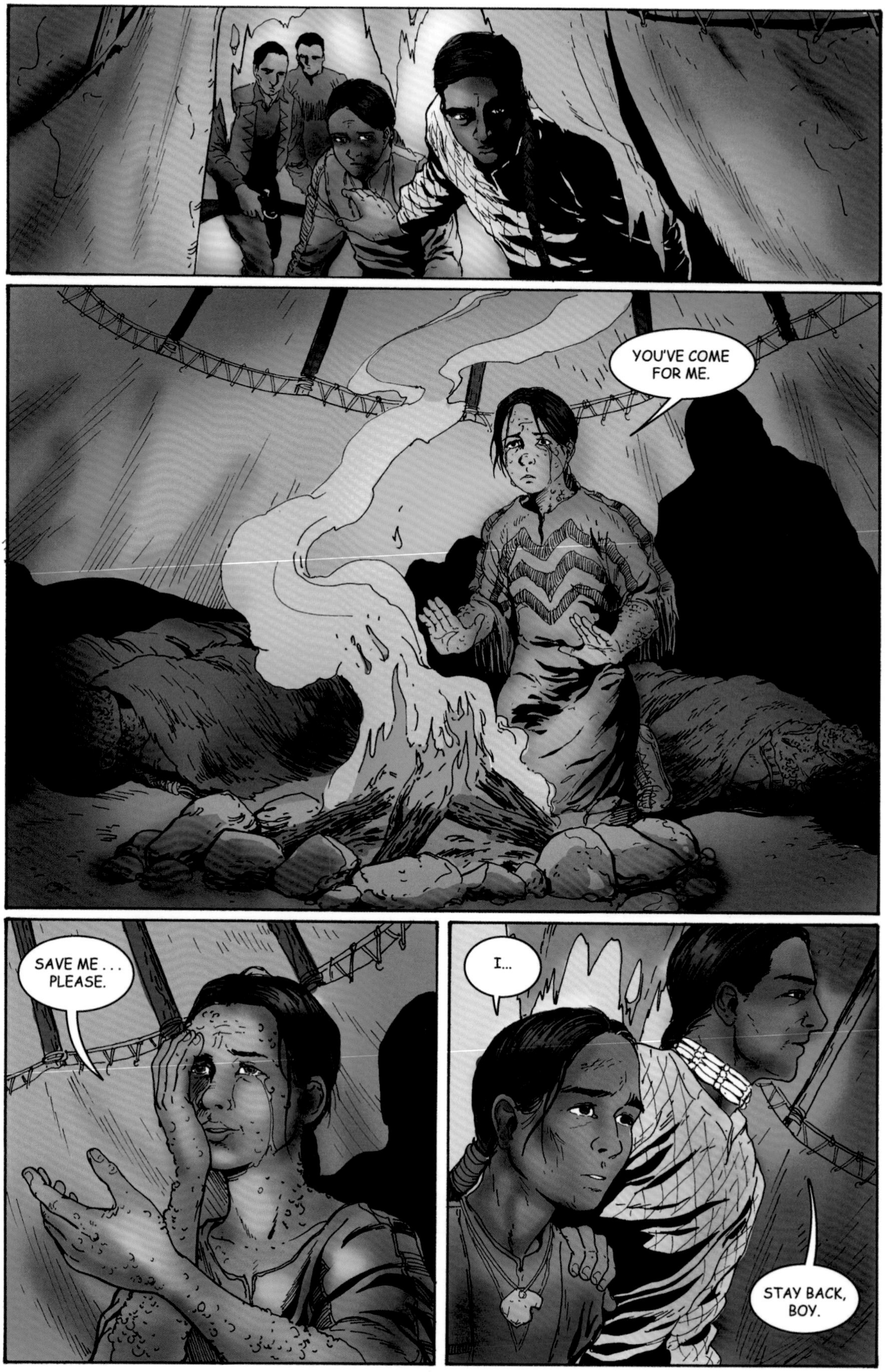
YOU'VE COME FOR ME.
SAVE ME . . . PLEASE.
I...
STAY BACK, BOY.

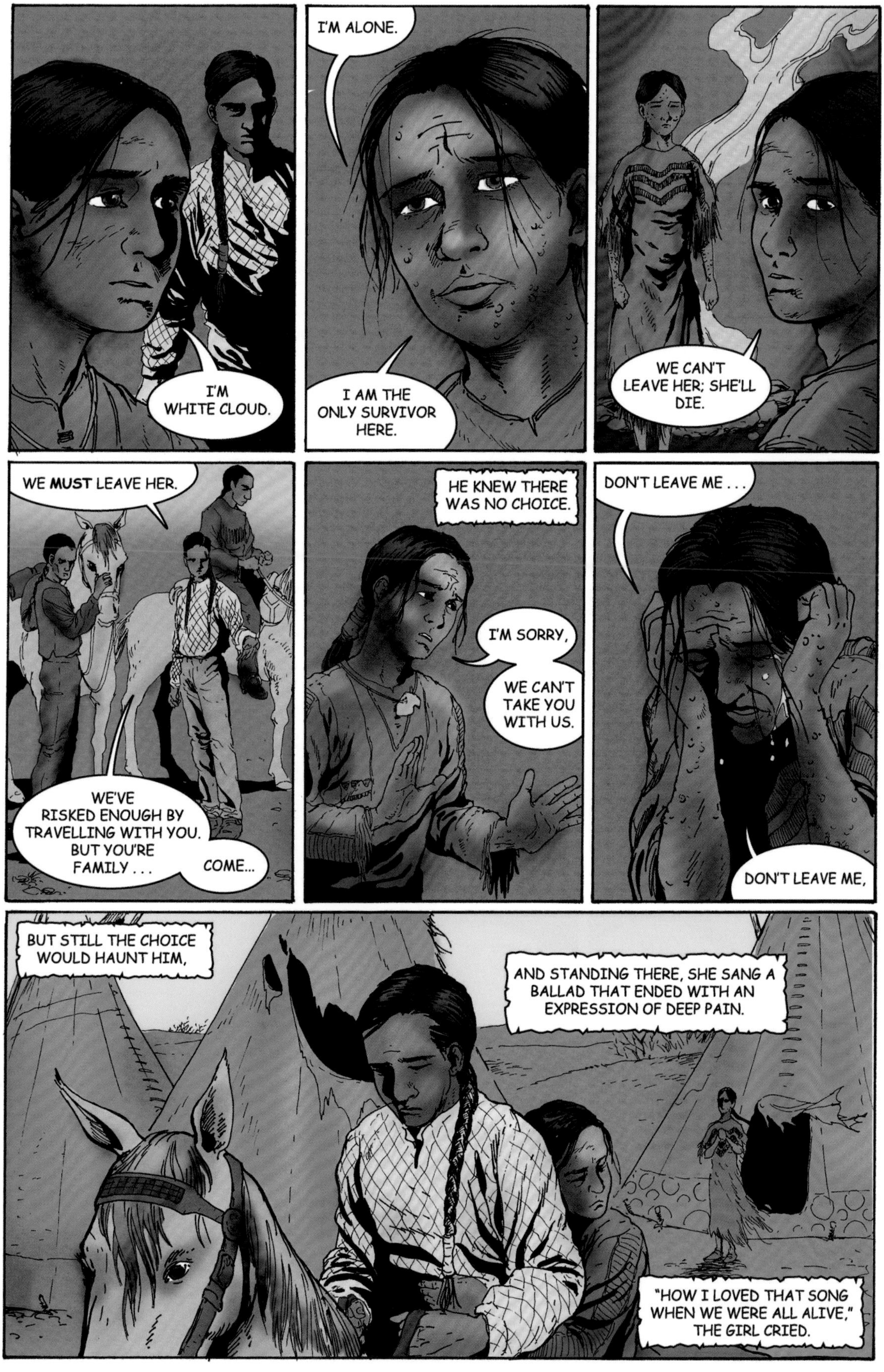
I'M WHITE CLOUD.
I'M ALONE.
I AM THE ONLY SURVIVOR HERE.
WE CAN'T LEAVE HER; SHE'LL DIE.
WE **MUST** LEAVE HER.
WE'VE RISKED ENOUGH BY TRAVELLING WITH YOU. BUT YOU'RE FAMILY . . .
COME...
HE KNEW THERE WAS NO CHOICE.
I'M SORRY,
WE CAN'T TAKE YOU WITH US.
DON'T LEAVE ME . . .
DON'T LEAVE ME,
BUT STILL THE CHOICE WOULD HAUNT HIM,
AND STANDING THERE, SHE SANG A BALLAD THAT ENDED WITH AN EXPRESSION OF DEEP PAIN.
"HOW I LOVED THAT SONG WHEN WE WERE ALL ALIVE," THE GIRL CRIED.

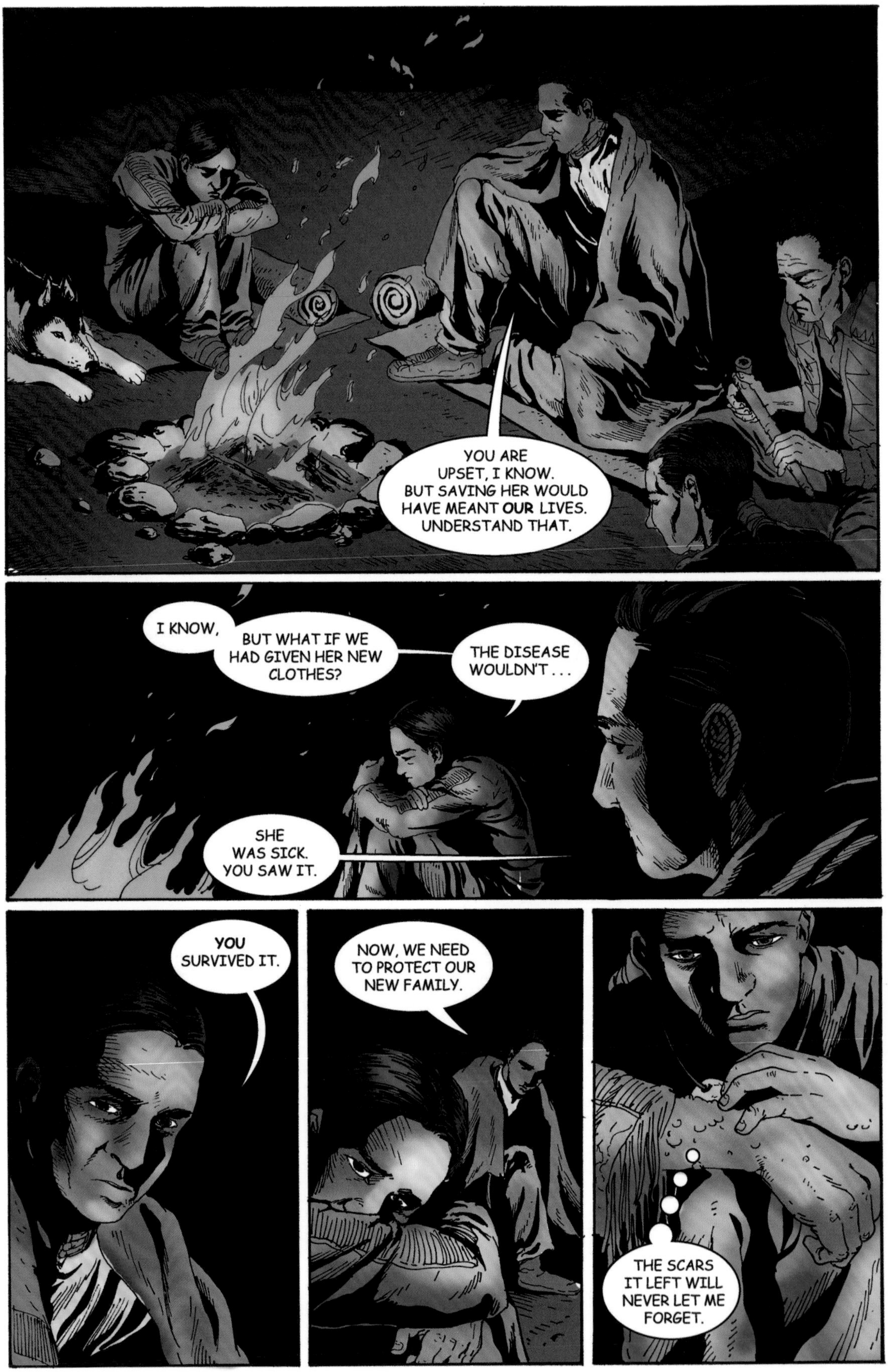
YOU ARE UPSET, I KNOW. BUT SAVING HER WOULD HAVE MEANT **OUR** LIVES. UNDERSTAND THAT.
I KNOW,
BUT WHAT IF WE HAD GIVEN HER NEW CLOTHES?
THE DISEASE WOULDN'T . . .
SHE WAS SICK. YOU SAW IT.
YOU SURVIVED IT.
NOW, WE NEED TO PROTECT OUR NEW FAMILY.
THE SCARS IT LEFT WILL NEVER LET ME FORGET.

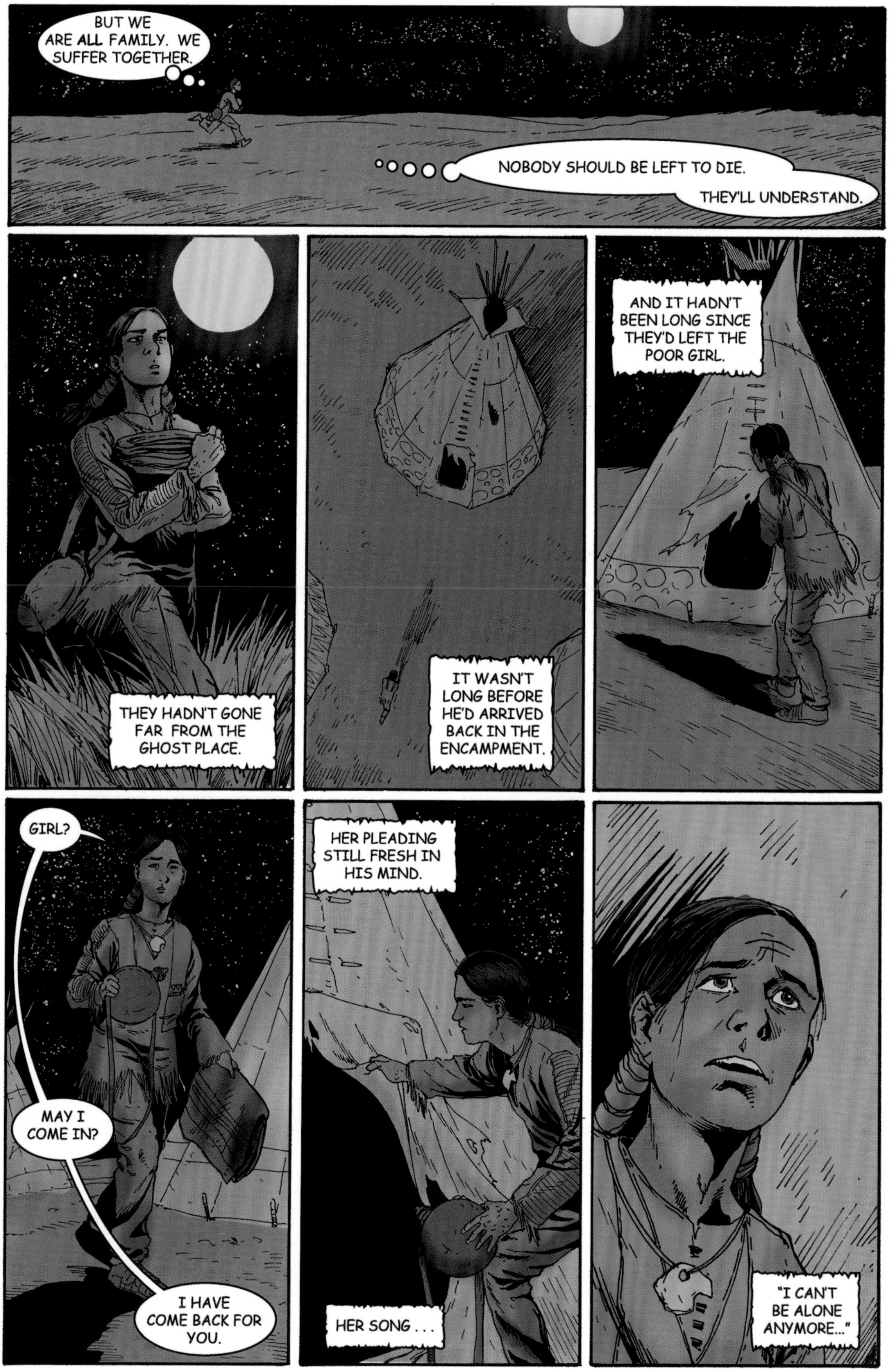
BUT WE ARE ALL FAMILY. WE SUFFER TOGETHER.
NOBODY SHOULD BE LEFT TO DIE.
THEY'LL UNDERSTAND.
THEY HADN'T GONE FAR FROM THE GHOST PLACE.
IT WASN'T LONG BEFORE HE'D ARRIVED BACK IN THE ENCAMPMENT.
AND IT HADN'T BEEN LONG SINCE THEY'D LEFT THE POOR GIRL.
GIRL?
MAY I COME IN?
I HAVE COME BACK FOR YOU.
HER PLEADING STILL FRESH IN HIS MIND.
HER SONG . . .
"I CAN'T BE ALONE ANYMORE..."

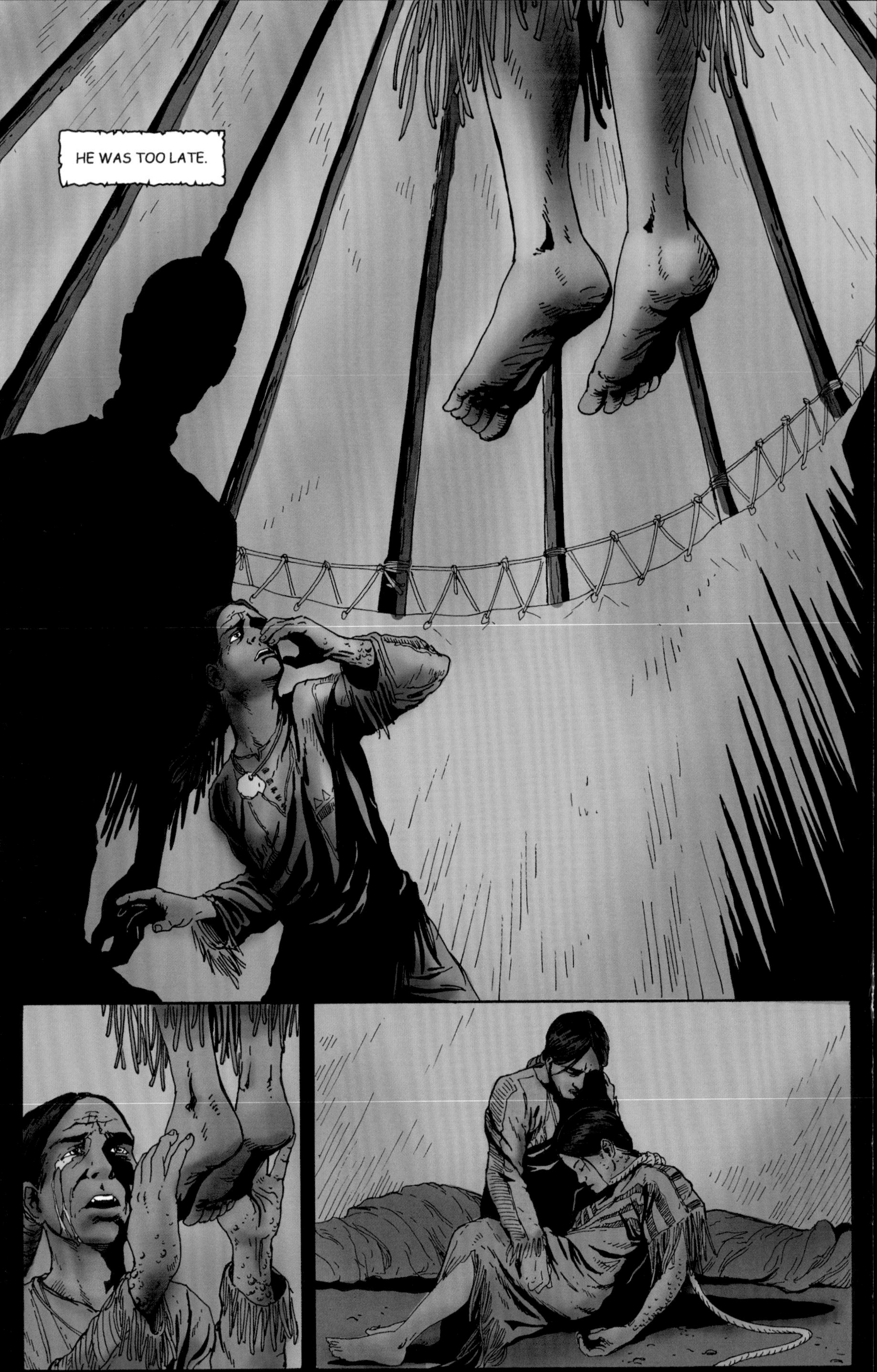
HE WAS TOO LATE.

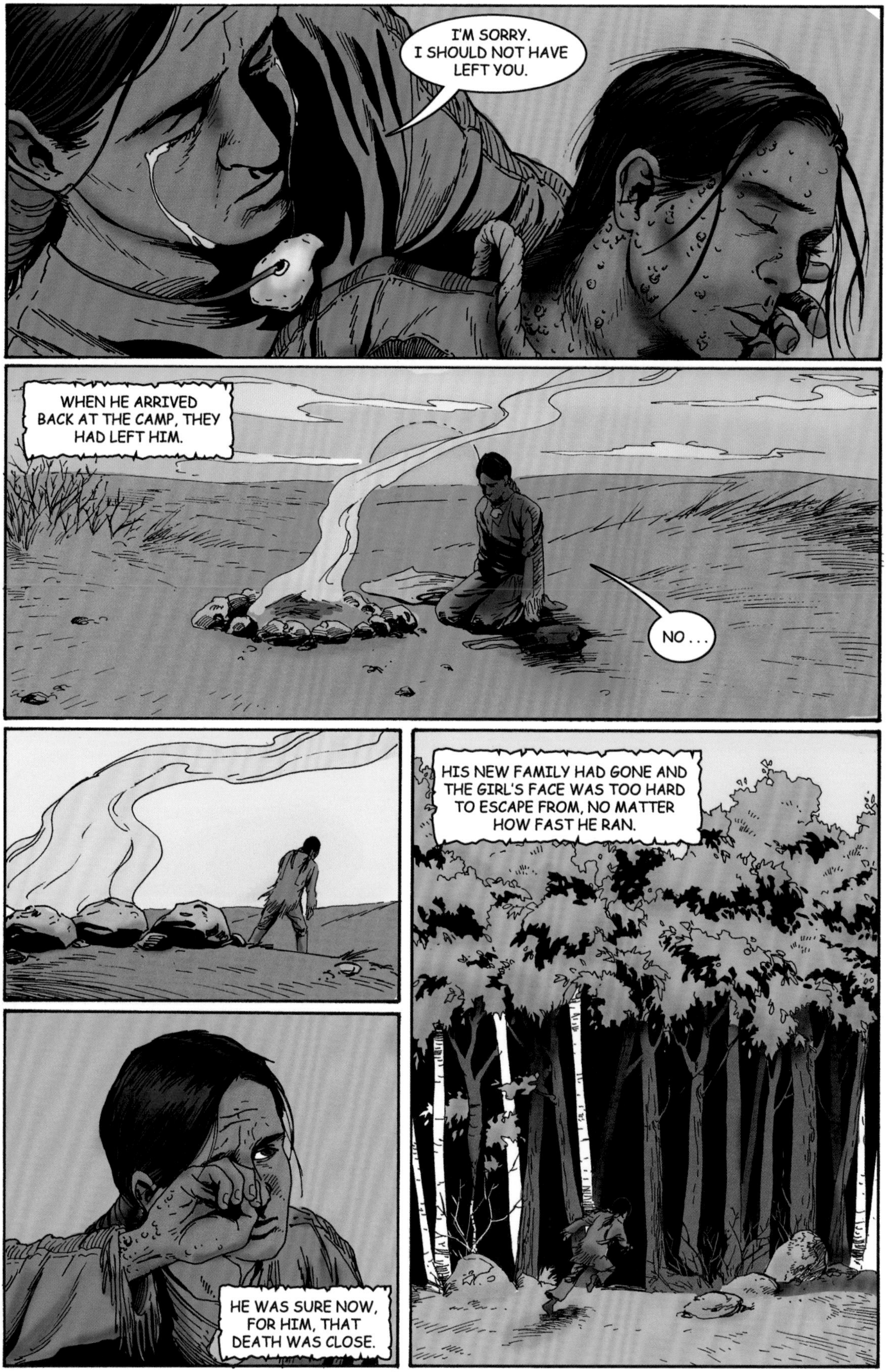
I'M SORRY. I SHOULD NOT HAVE LEFT YOU.
WHEN HE ARRIVED BACK AT THE CAMP, THEY HAD LEFT HIM.
NO . . .
HIS NEW FAMILY HAD GONE AND THE GIRL'S FACE WAS TOO HARD TO ESCAPE FROM, NO MATTER HOW FAST HE RAN.
HE WAS SURE NOW, FOR HIM, THAT DEATH WAS CLOSE.

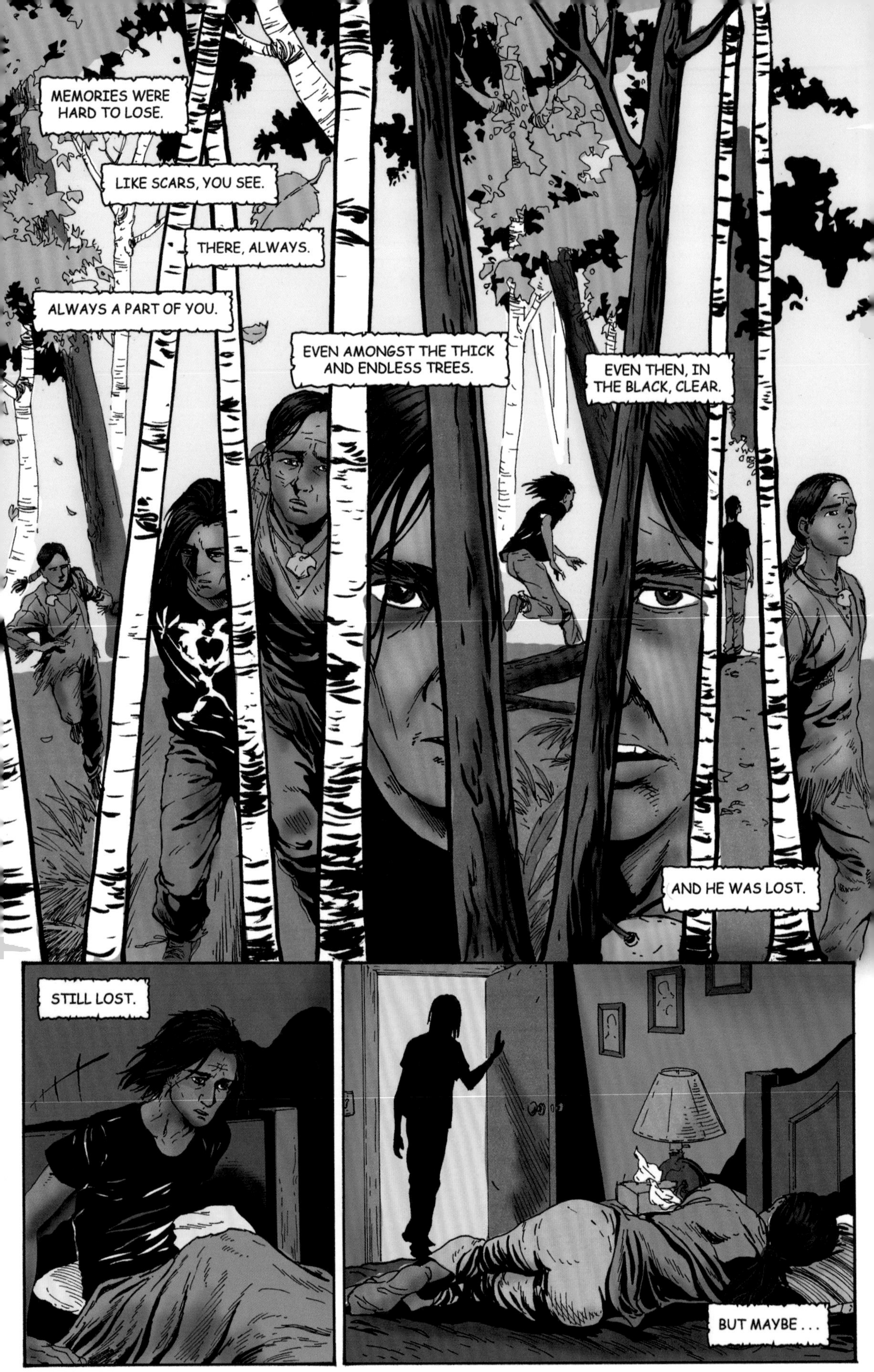
MEMORIES WERE HARD TO LOSE.
LIKE SCARS, YOU SEE.
THERE, ALWAYS.
ALWAYS A PART OF YOU.
EVEN AMONGST THE THICK AND ENDLESS TREES.
EVEN THEN, IN THE BLACK, CLEAR.
AND HE WAS LOST.
STILL LOST.
BUT MAYBE . . .

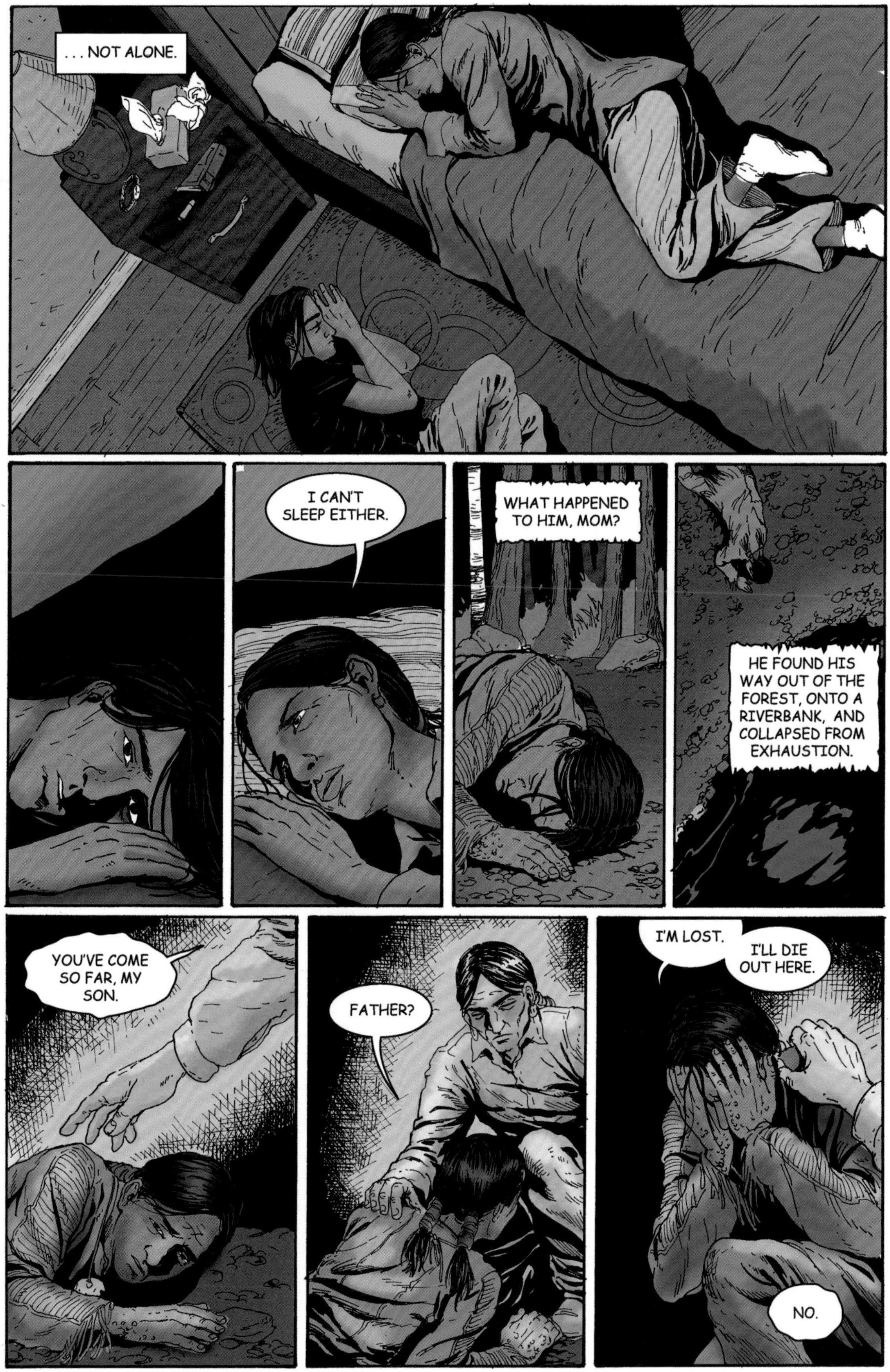
. . . NOT ALONE.
I CAN'T SLEEP EITHER.
WHAT HAPPENED TO HIM, MOM?
HE FOUND HIS WAY OUT OF THE FOREST, ONTO A RIVERBANK, AND COLLAPSED FROM EXHAUSTION.
YOU'VE COME SO FAR, MY SON.
FATHER?
I'M LOST.
I'LL DIE OUT HERE.
NO.

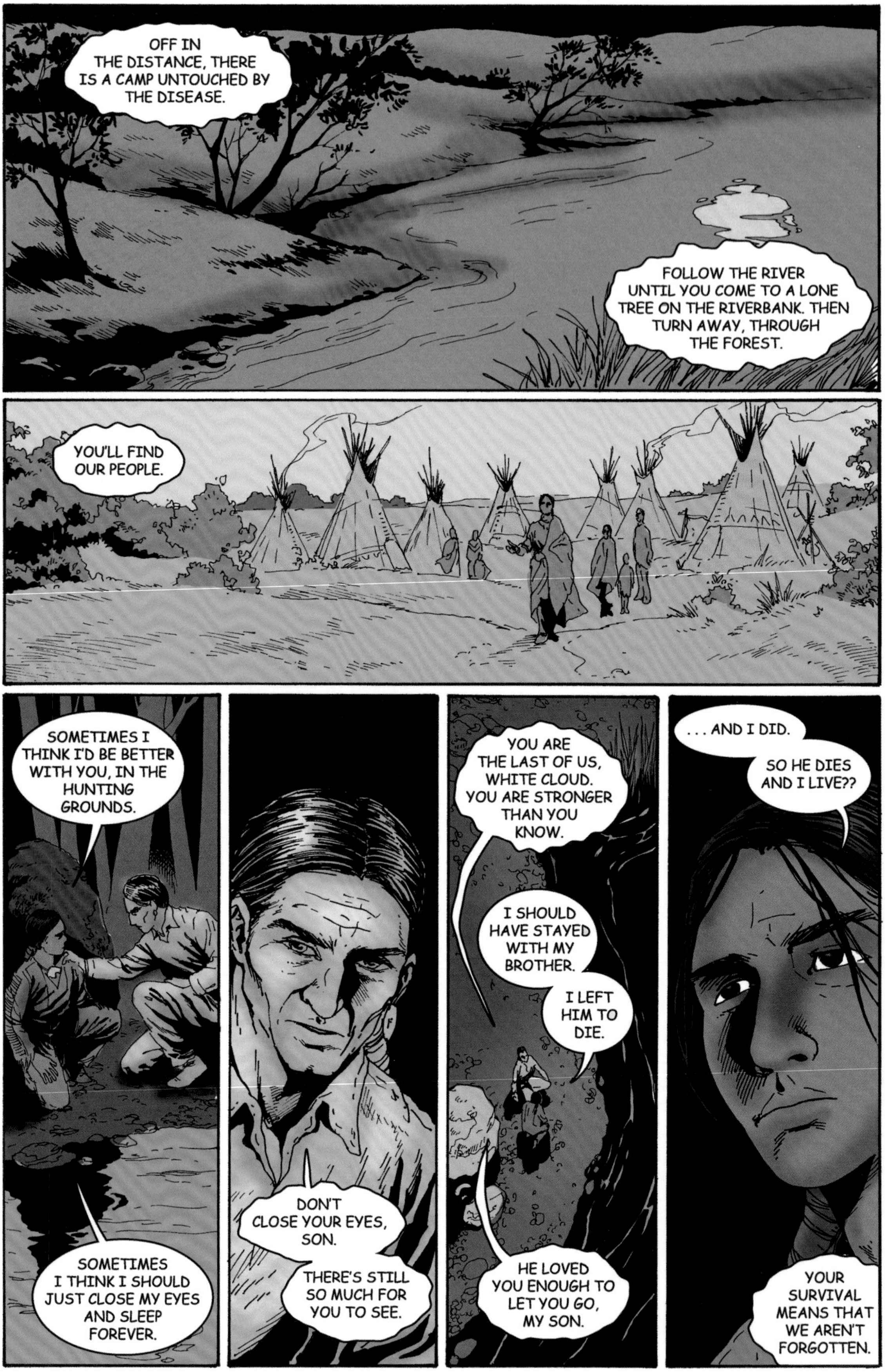
OFF IN THE DISTANCE, THERE IS A CAMP UNTOUCHED BY THE DISEASE.
FOLLOW THE RIVER UNTIL YOU COME TO A LONE TREE ON THE RIVERBANK. THEN TURN AWAY, THROUGH THE FOREST.
YOU'LL FIND OUR PEOPLE.
SOMETIMES I THINK I'D BE BETTER WITH YOU, IN THE HUNTING GROUNDS.
SOMETIMES I THINK I SHOULD JUST CLOSE MY EYES AND SLEEP FOREVER.
DON'T CLOSE YOUR EYES, SON.
THERE'S STILL SO MUCH FOR YOU TO SEE.
YOU ARE THE LAST OF US, WHITE CLOUD. YOU ARE STRONGER THAN YOU KNOW.
I SHOULD HAVE STAYED WITH MY BROTHER.
I LEFT HIM TO DIE.
HE LOVED YOU ENOUGH TO LET YOU GO, MY SON.
. . . AND I DID.
SO HE DIES AND I LIVE??
YOUR SURVIVAL MEANS THAT WE AREN'T FORGOTTEN.

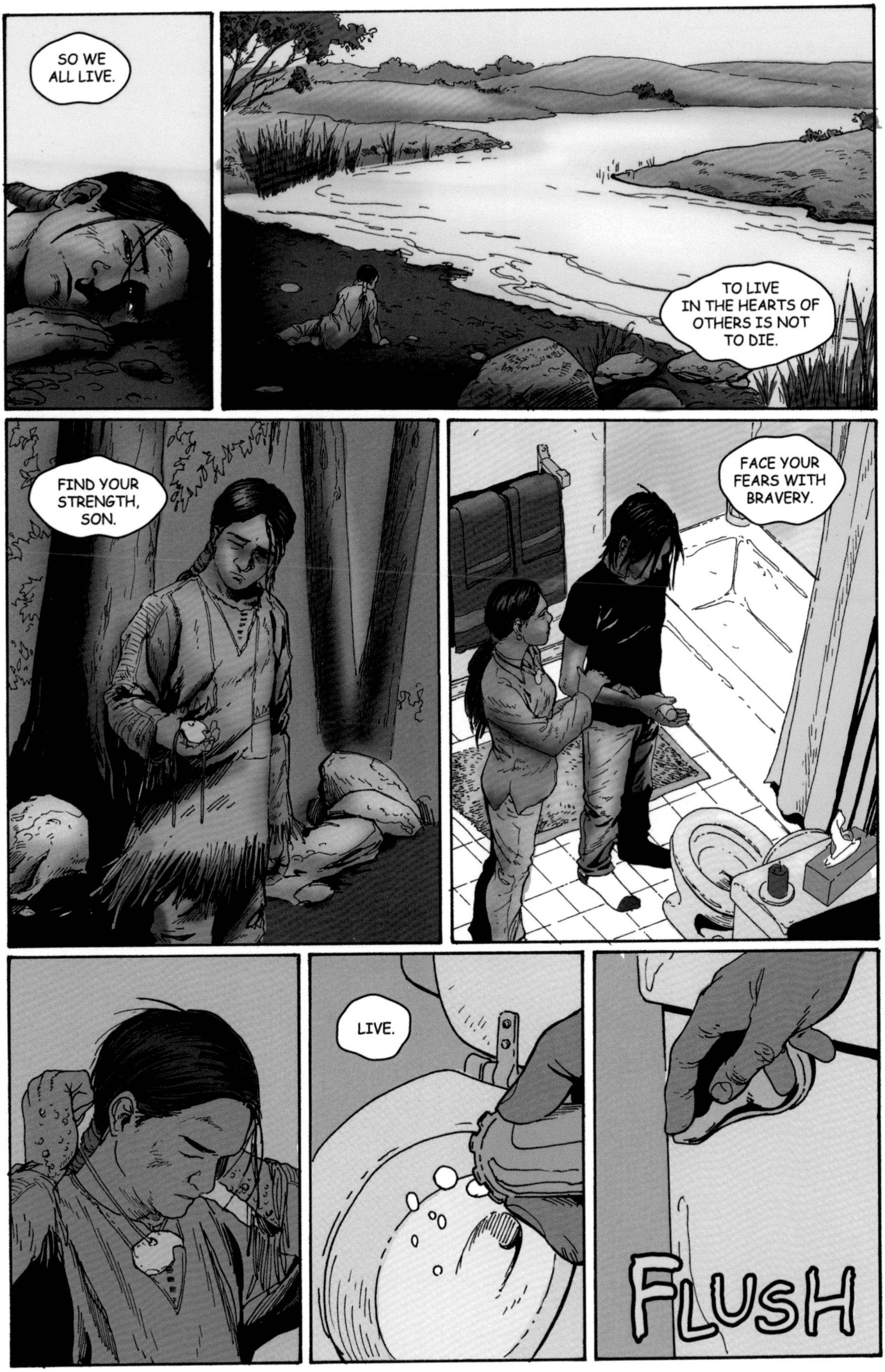
SO WE ALL LIVE.
TO LIVE IN THE HEARTS OF OTHERS IS NOT TO DIE.
FIND YOUR STRENGTH, SON.
FACE YOUR FEARS WITH BRAVERY.
LIVE.
FLUSH

HE SET OUT THAT MORNING, INTENT ON MAKING THE JOURNEY AND FINDING A NEW HOME.

THE AMULET THAT STONE AND WHITE CLOUD WORE HAS BEEN IN OUR FAMILY FOR SEVEN GENERATIONS.

IT HAS THE POWER OF OUR CULTURE WITHIN IT.

IT WILL HELP **YOU** ON YOUR JOURNEY OF HEALING.

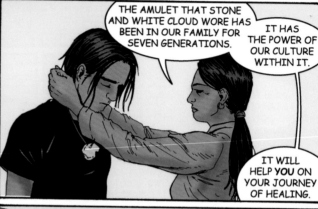

HE'D WALKED FOR A DAY AND A HALF ALONG THE RIVER UNTIL FINDING THE TREE.

AND STILL, THE CAMP WAS FAR AWAY.

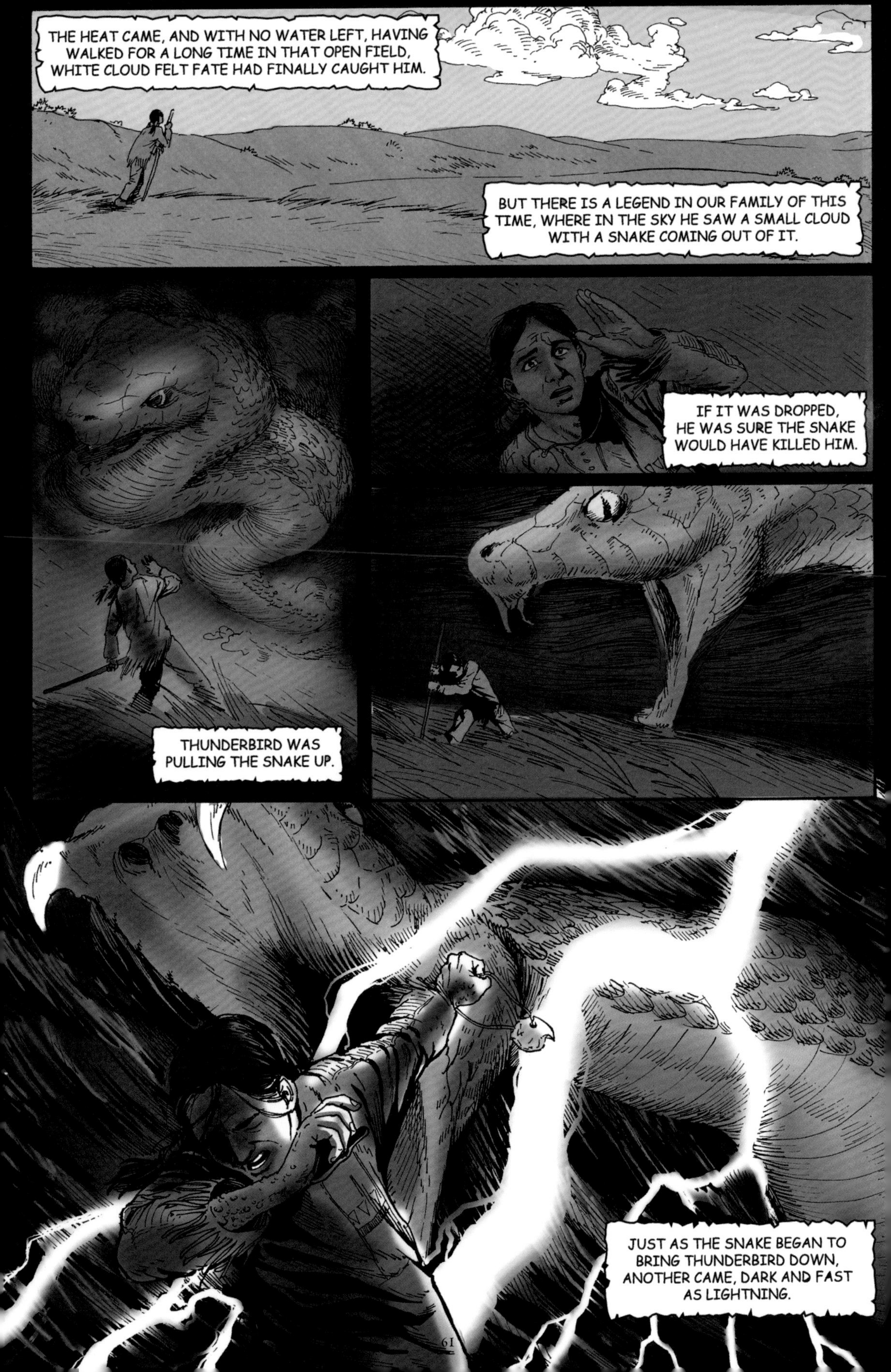
THE HEAT CAME, AND WITH NO WATER LEFT, HAVING WALKED FOR A LONG TIME IN THAT OPEN FIELD, WHITE CLOUD FELT FATE HAD FINALLY CAUGHT HIM.
BUT THERE IS A LEGEND IN OUR FAMILY OF THIS TIME, WHERE IN THE SKY HE SAW A SMALL CLOUD WITH A SNAKE COMING OUT OF IT.
THUNDERBIRD WAS PULLING THE SNAKE UP.
IF IT WAS DROPPED, HE WAS SURE THE SNAKE WOULD HAVE KILLED HIM.
JUST AS THE SNAKE BEGAN TO BRING THUNDERBIRD DOWN, ANOTHER CAME, DARK AND FAST AS LIGHTNING.

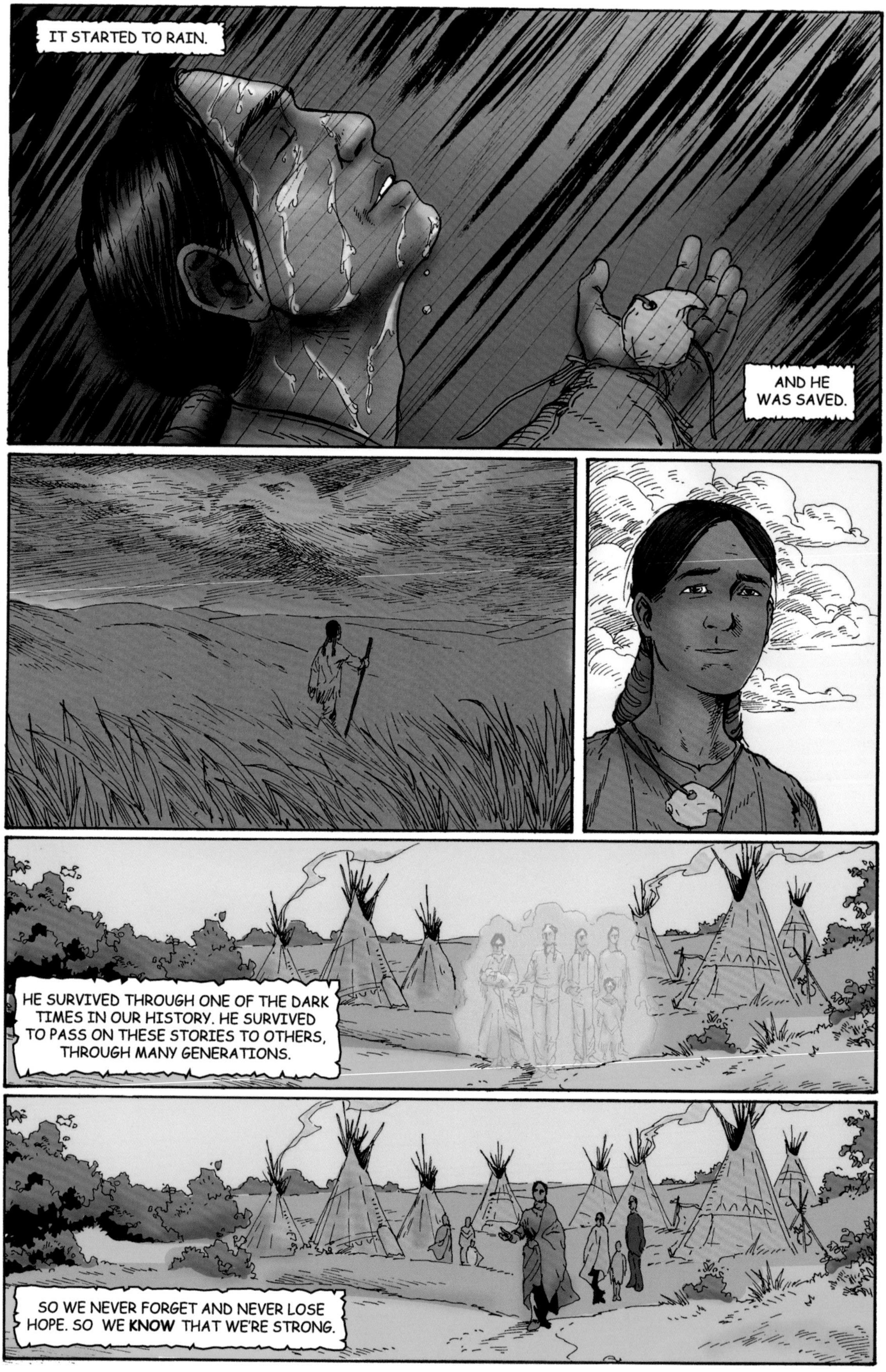
IT STARTED TO RAIN.
AND HE WAS SAVED.
HE SURVIVED THROUGH ONE OF THE DARK TIMES IN OUR HISTORY. HE SURVIVED TO PASS ON THESE STORIES TO OTHERS, THROUGH MANY GENERATIONS.
SO WE NEVER FORGET AND NEVER LOSE HOPE. SO WE **KNOW** THAT WE'RE STRONG.

WE CALLED SMALLPOX THE DISEASE OF SCABS.

OVER OUR HISTORY, IT KILLED HUNDREDS OF THOUSANDS OF US.

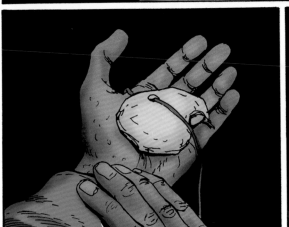

IT LEFT SCARS BEHIND ON THOSE WHO SURVIVED.

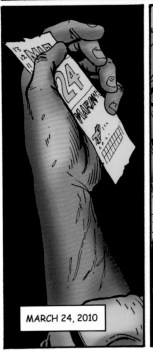

MARCH 24, 2010

SCARS FOREVER TO REMIND US OF THE PAST.

WE ALL HAVE SCARS, MEMORIES OF HARDER TIMES.

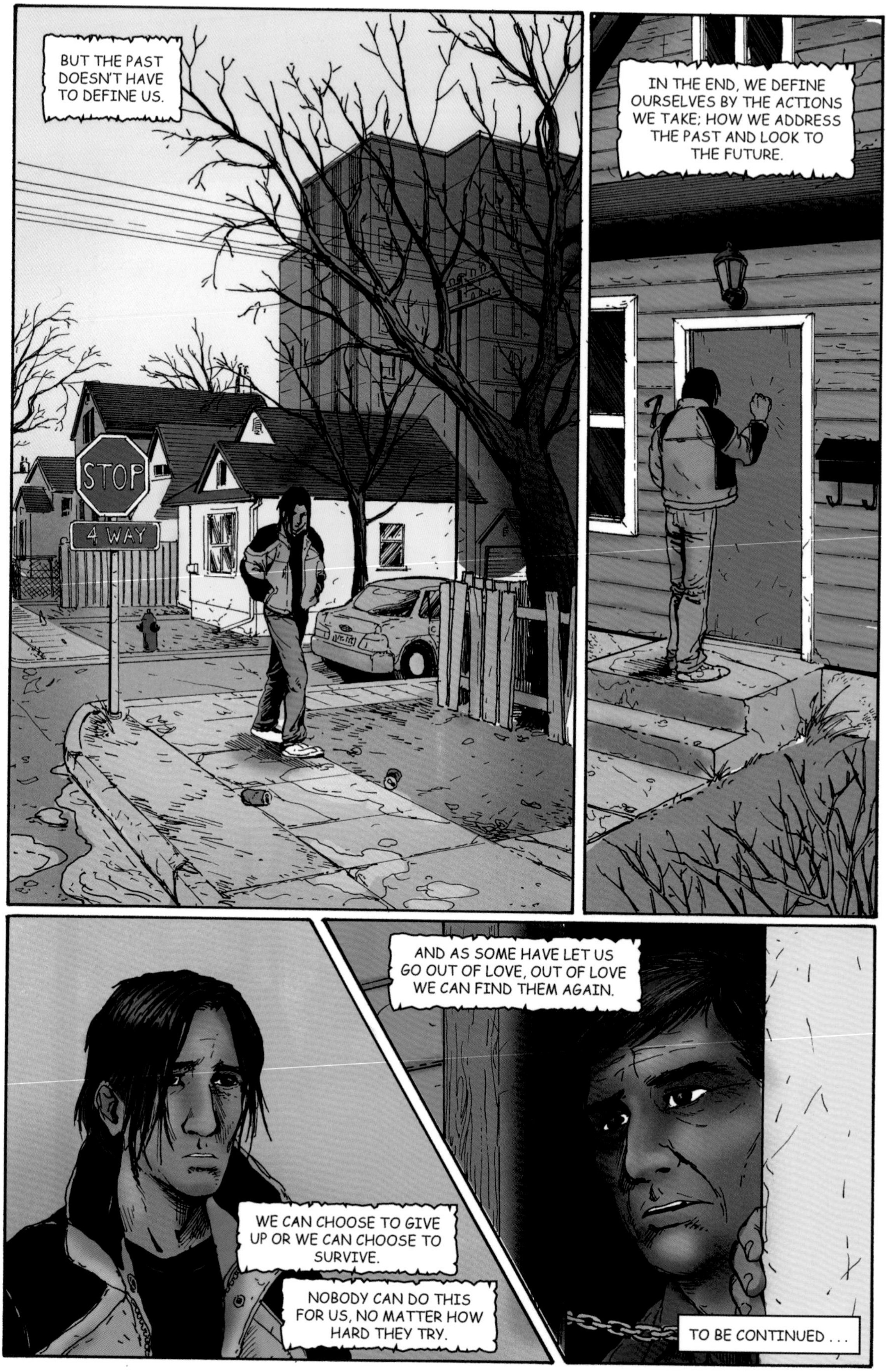
BUT THE PAST DOESN'T HAVE TO DEFINE US.
STOP
4 WAY
IN THE END, WE DEFINE OURSELVES BY THE ACTIONS WE TAKE; HOW WE ADDRESS THE PAST AND LOOK TO THE FUTURE.
AND AS SOME HAVE LET US GO OUT OF LOVE, OUT OF LOVE WE CAN FIND THEM AGAIN.
WE CAN CHOOSE TO GIVE UP OR WE CAN CHOOSE TO SURVIVE.
NOBODY CAN DO THIS FOR US, NO MATTER HOW HARD THEY TRY.
TO BE CONTINUED . . .

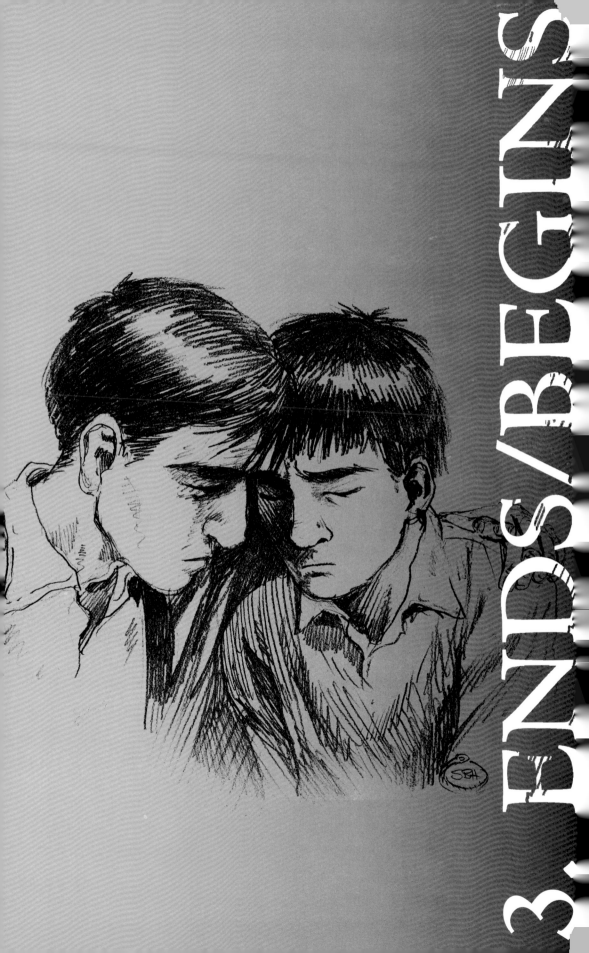

3. ENDS/BEGINS

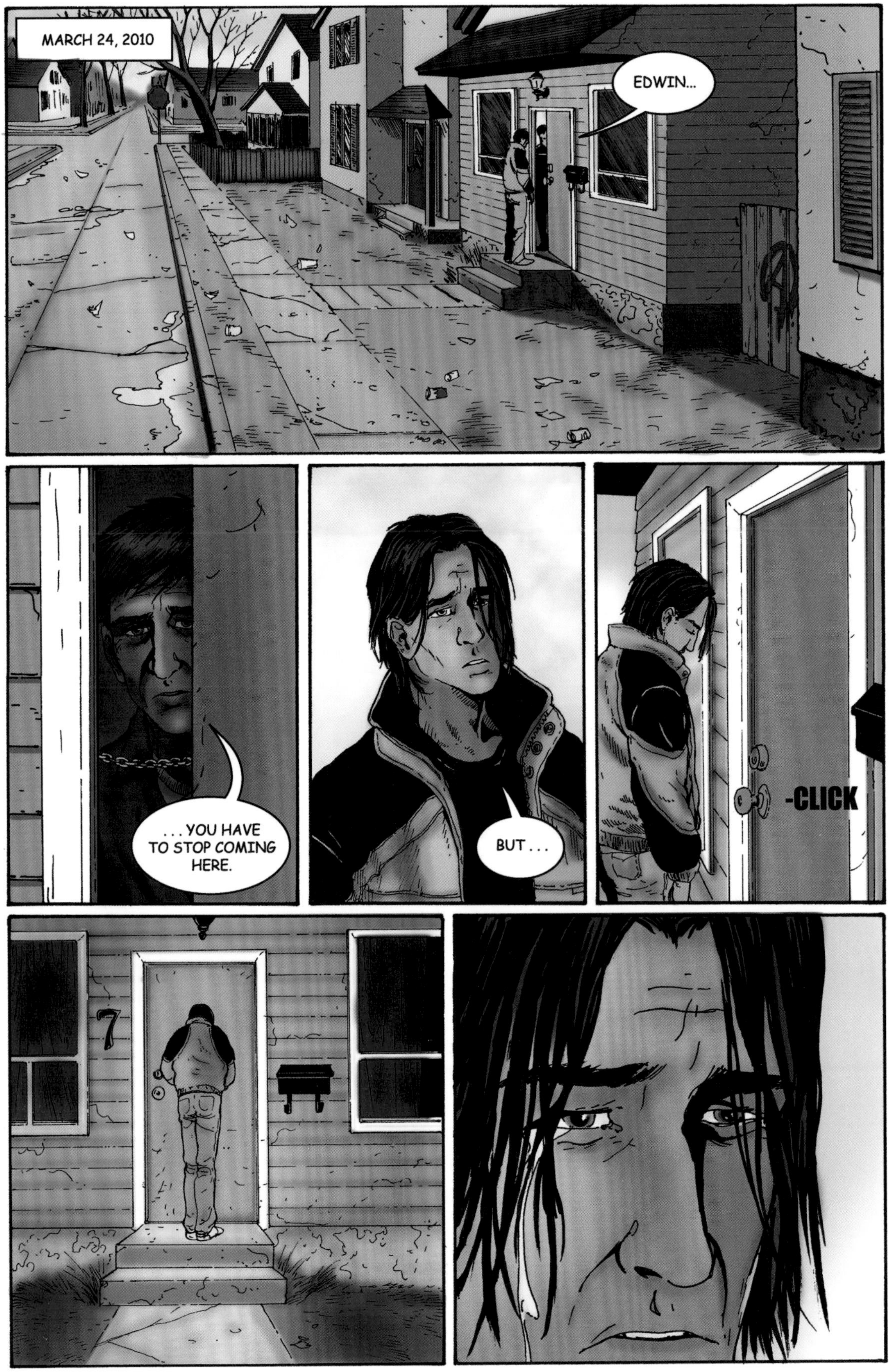
MARCH 24, 2010
EDWIN...
. . . YOU HAVE TO STOP COMING HERE.
BUT . . .
-CLICK

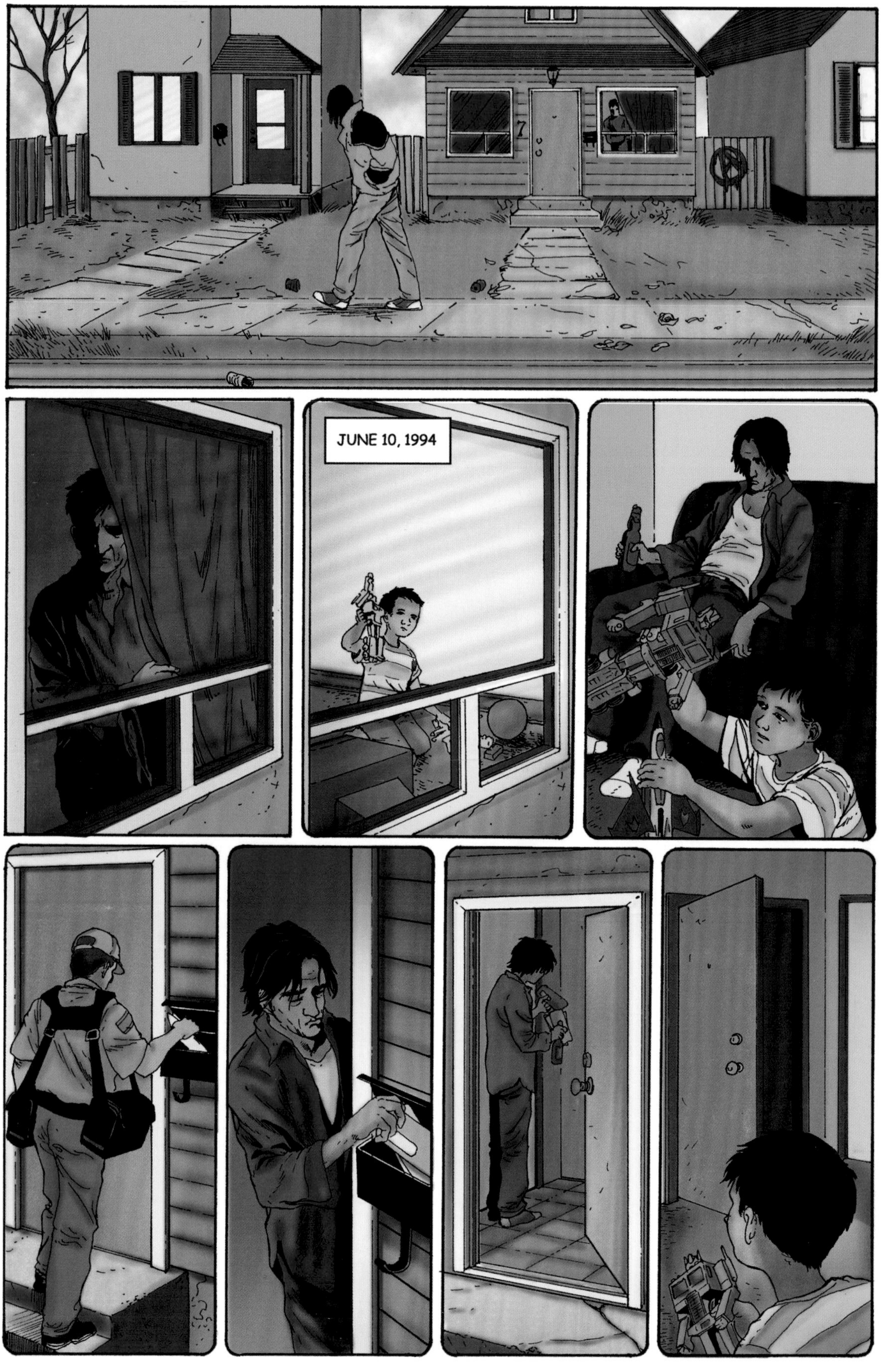
JUNE 10, 1994

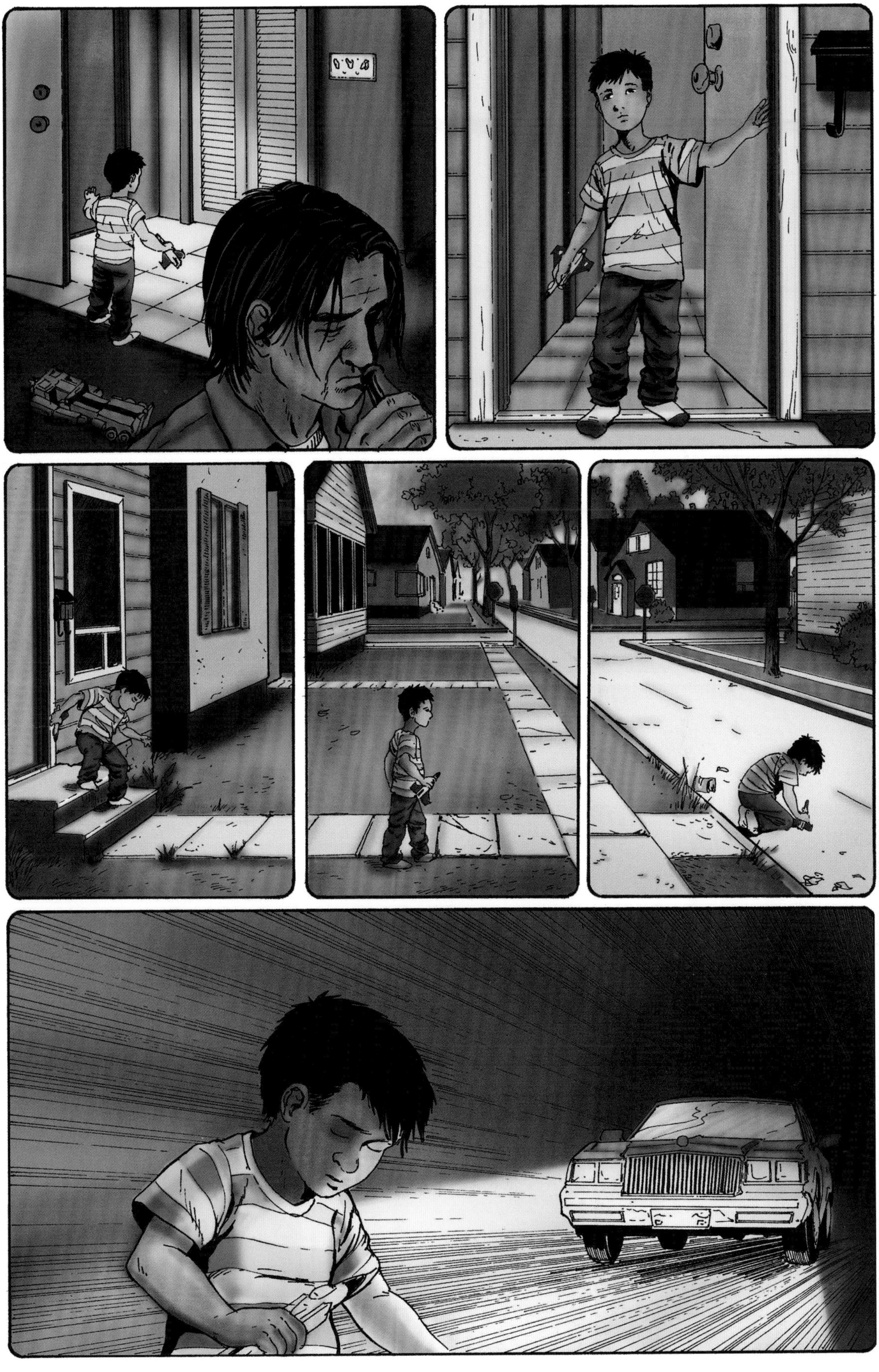

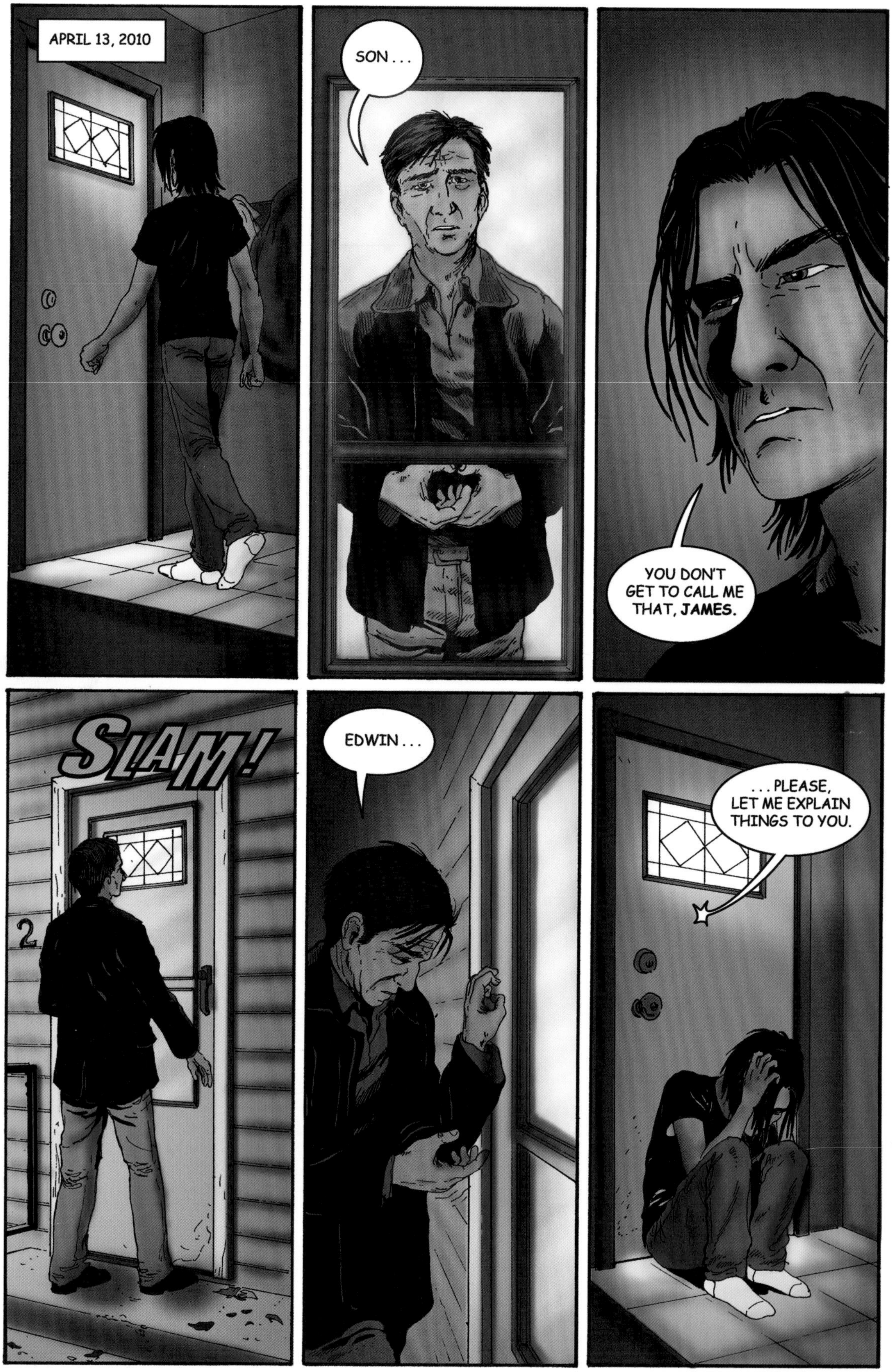
APRIL 13, 2010
SON . . .
YOU DON'T GET TO CALL ME THAT, JAMES.
SLAM!
EDWIN . . .
. . . PLEASE, LET ME EXPLAIN THINGS TO YOU.

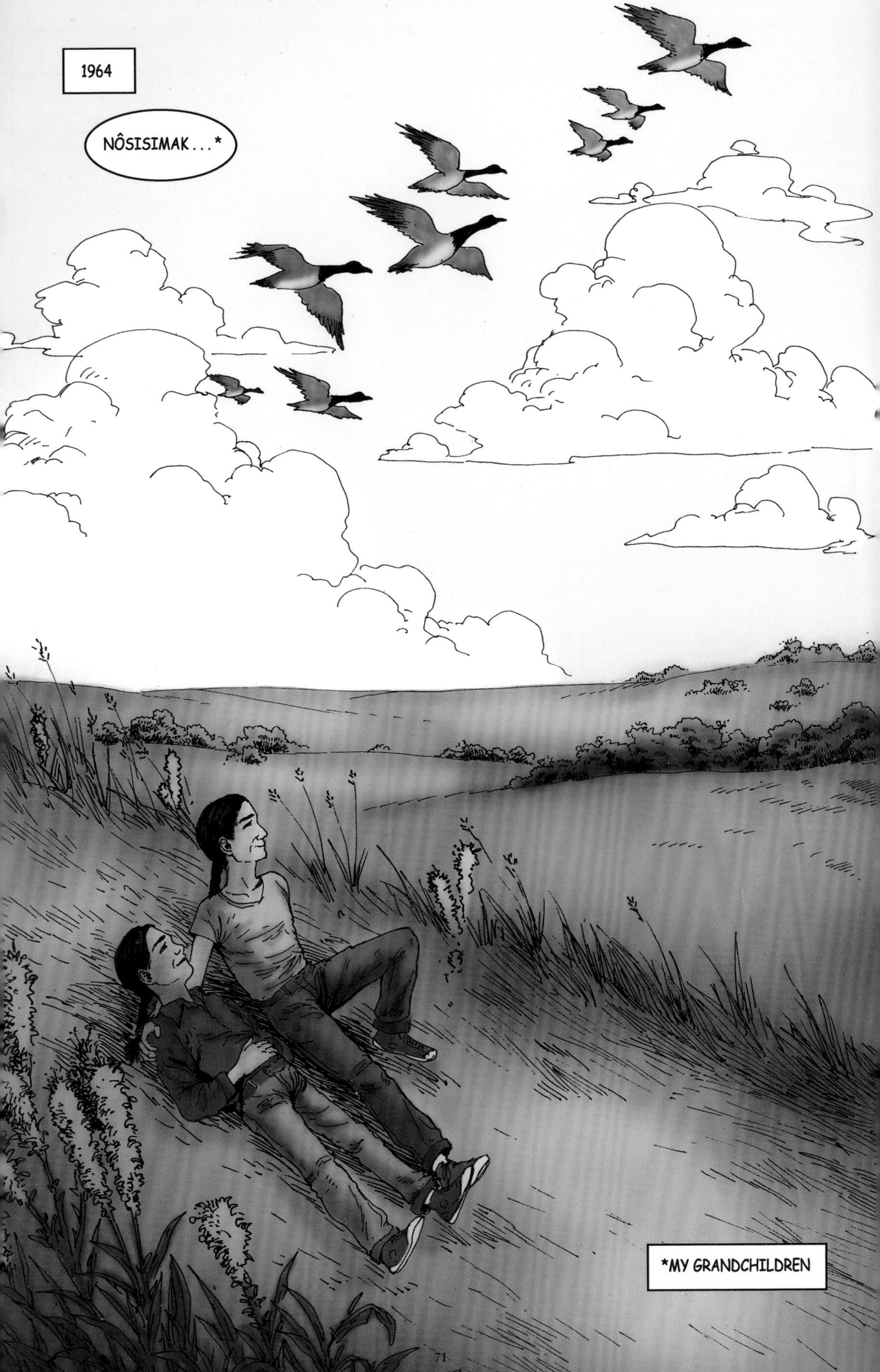
1964
NÔSISIMAK...*
*MY GRANDCHILDREN

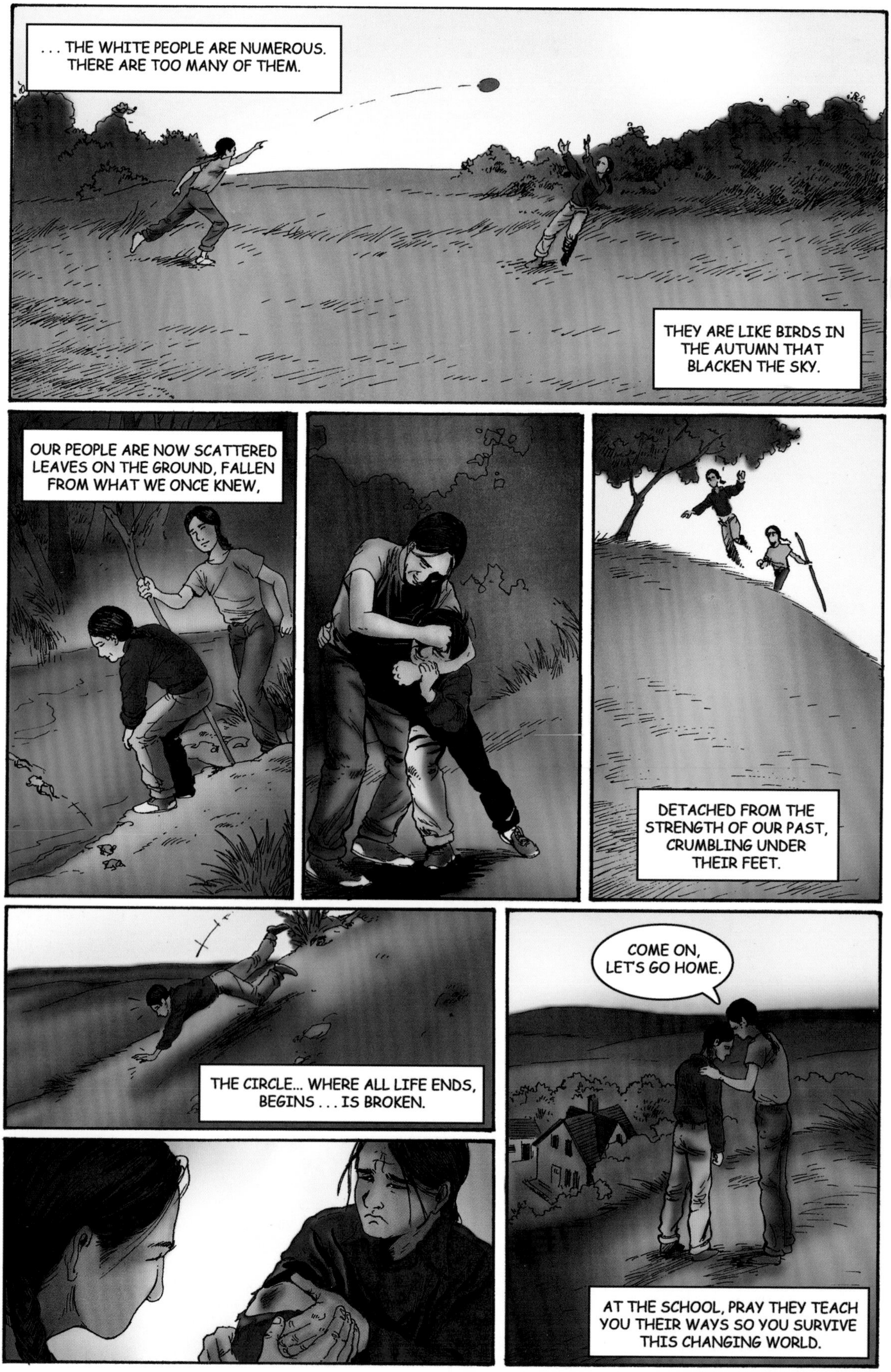

. . . THE WHITE PEOPLE ARE NUMEROUS. THERE ARE TOO MANY OF THEM.
THEY ARE LIKE BIRDS IN THE AUTUMN THAT BLACKEN THE SKY.
OUR PEOPLE ARE NOW SCATTERED LEAVES ON THE GROUND, FALLEN FROM WHAT WE ONCE KNEW,
DETACHED FROM THE STRENGTH OF OUR PAST, CRUMBLING UNDER THEIR FEET.
THE CIRCLE... WHERE ALL LIFE ENDS, BEGINS . . . IS BROKEN.
COME ON, LET'S GO HOME.
AT THE SCHOOL, PRAY THEY TEACH YOU THEIR WAYS SO YOU SURVIVE THIS CHANGING WORLD.

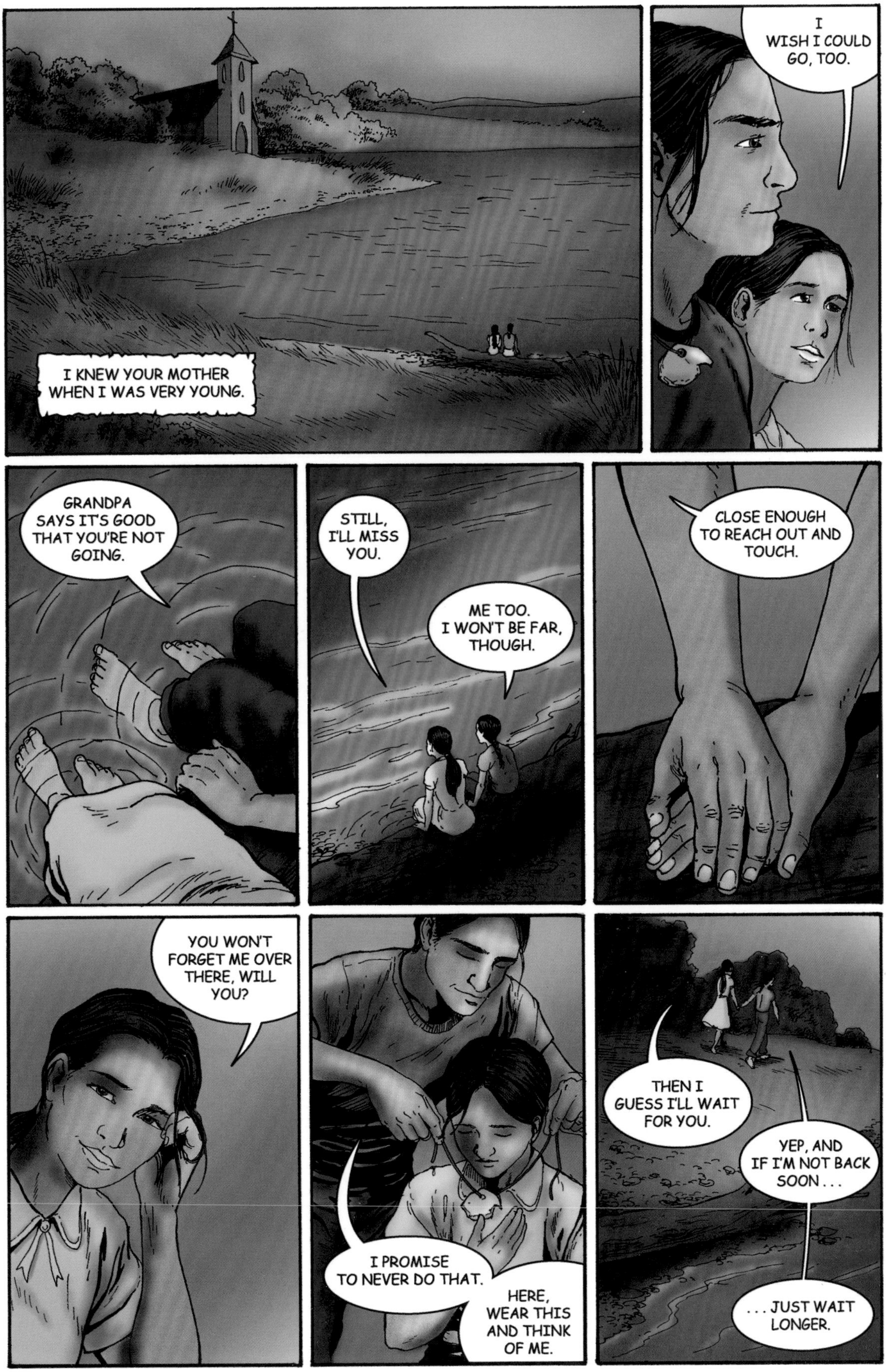
I KNEW YOUR MOTHER WHEN I WAS VERY YOUNG.
I WISH I COULD GO, TOO.
GRANDPA SAYS IT'S GOOD THAT YOU'RE NOT GOING.
STILL, I'LL MISS YOU.
ME TOO. I WON'T BE FAR, THOUGH.
CLOSE ENOUGH TO REACH OUT AND TOUCH.
YOU WON'T FORGET ME OVER THERE, WILL YOU?
I PROMISE TO NEVER DO THAT.
HERE, WEAR THIS AND THINK OF ME.
THEN I GUESS I'LL WAIT FOR YOU.
YEP, AND IF I'M NOT BACK SOON . . .
. . . JUST WAIT LONGER.

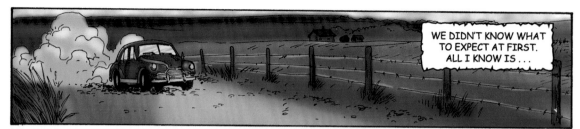

WE DIDN'T KNOW WHAT TO EXPECT AT FIRST. ALL I KNOW IS . . .

. . . WE WEREN'T GONE FOR A MOMENT, BUT HOME SEEMED LIKE A LONG WAY OFF.

THE SCHOOL WAS ONLY ABOUT 2 KILOMETRES AWAY, YOU KNOW. BUT I SWORE IT WAS ANOTHER PLANET. IT JUST FELT THAT WAY.

I'M SCARED, GRANDPA.

DON'T BE AFRAID, THOMAS.

YOU JUST LISTEN TO THEM.

JAMES WILL LOOK AFTER YOU.

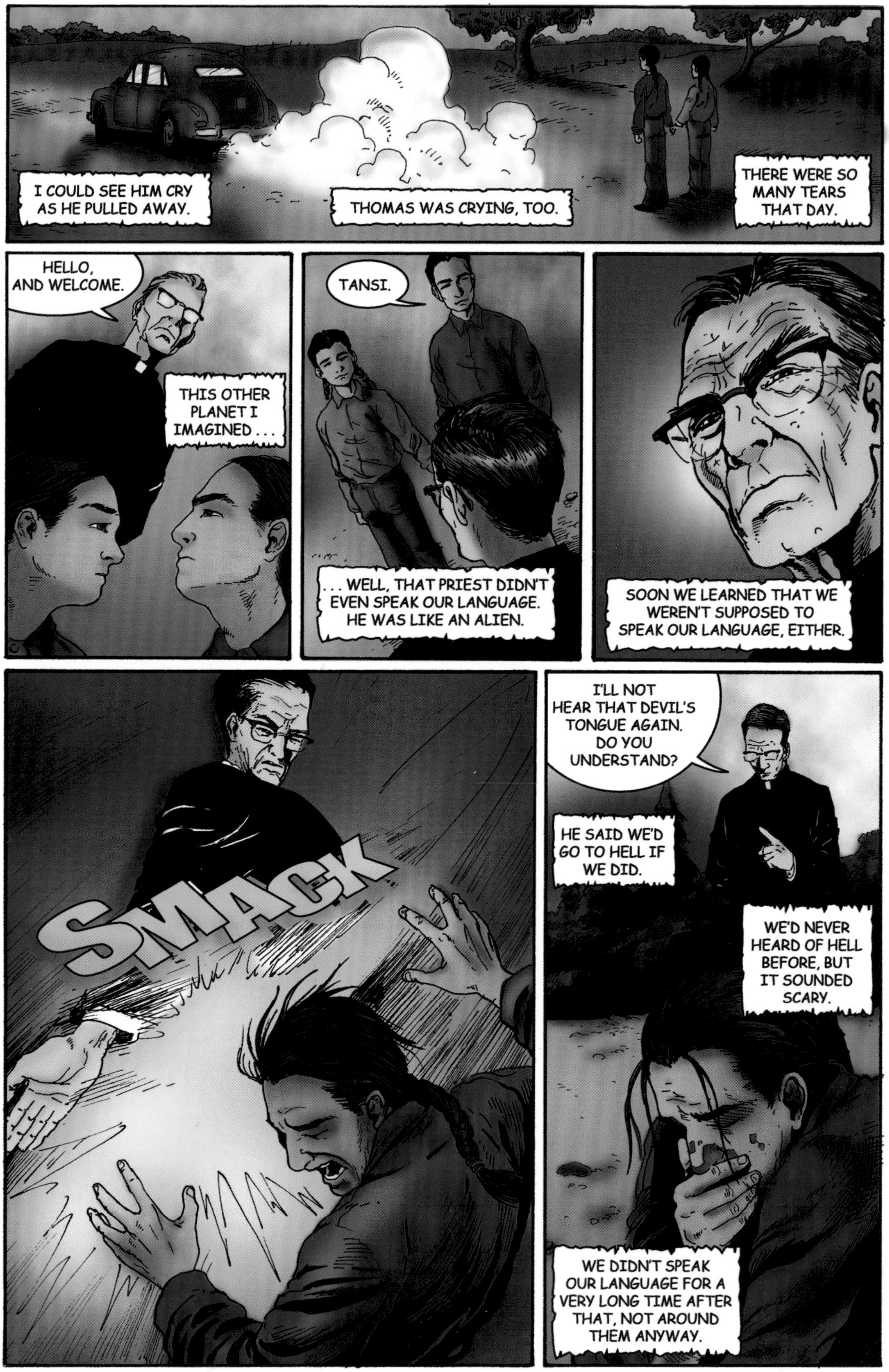
I COULD SEE HIM CRY AS HE PULLED AWAY.
THOMAS WAS CRYING, TOO.
THERE WERE SO MANY TEARS THAT DAY.
HELLO, AND WELCOME.
THIS OTHER PLANET I IMAGINED . . .
TANSI.
. . . WELL, THAT PRIEST DIDN'T EVEN SPEAK OUR LANGUAGE. HE WAS LIKE AN ALIEN.
SOON WE LEARNED THAT WE WEREN'T SUPPOSED TO SPEAK OUR LANGUAGE, EITHER.
SMACK
I'LL NOT HEAR THAT DEVIL'S TONGUE AGAIN. DO YOU UNDERSTAND?
HE SAID WE'D GO TO HELL IF WE DID.
WE'D NEVER HEARD OF HELL BEFORE, BUT IT SOUNDED SCARY.
WE DIDN'T SPEAK OUR LANGUAGE FOR A VERY LONG TIME AFTER THAT, NOT AROUND THEM ANYWAY.

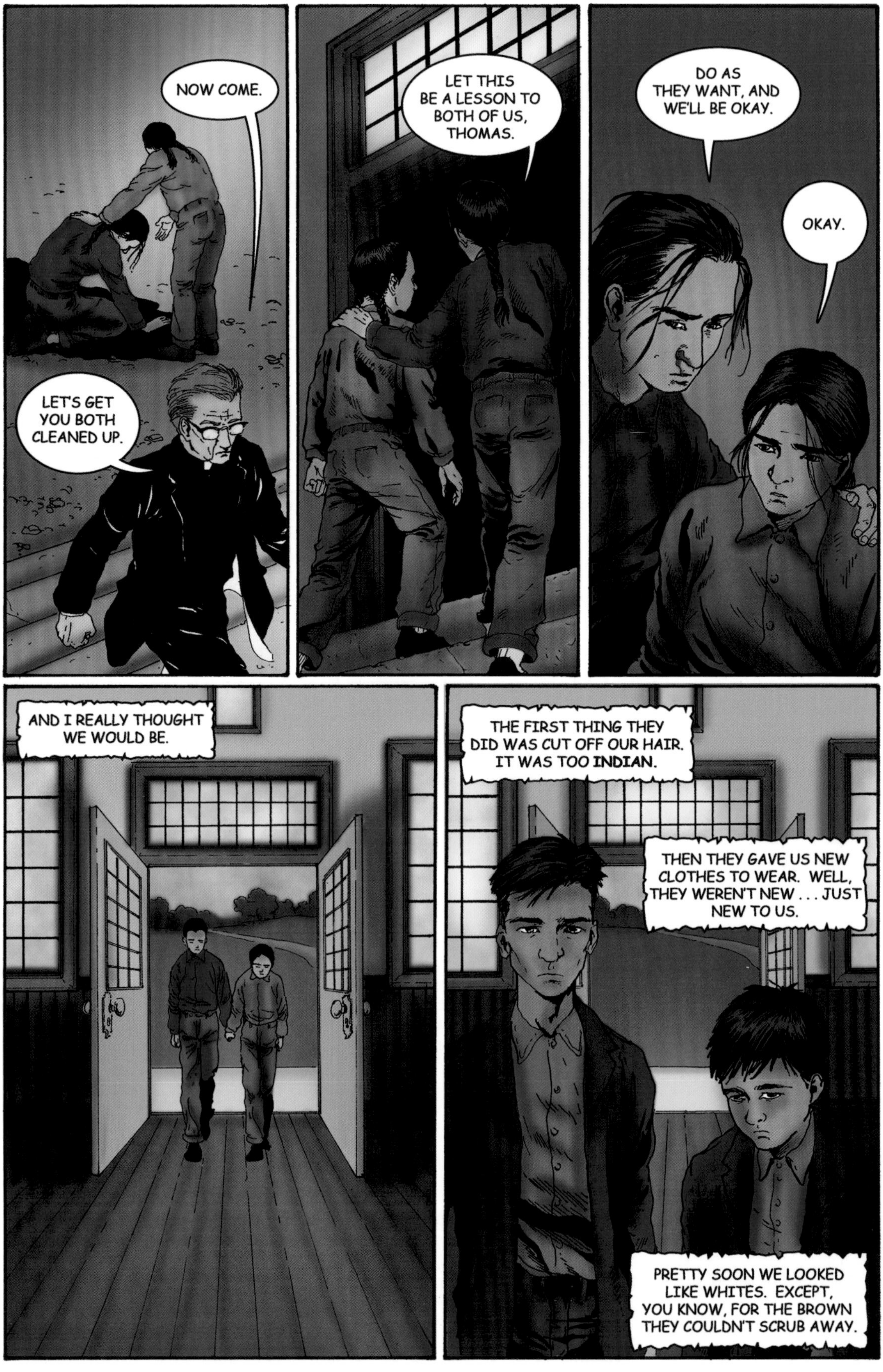
NOW COME.
LET'S GET YOU BOTH CLEANED UP.
LET THIS BE A LESSON TO BOTH OF US, THOMAS.
DO AS THEY WANT, AND WE'LL BE OKAY.
OKAY.
AND I REALLY THOUGHT WE WOULD BE.
THE FIRST THING THEY DID WAS CUT OFF OUR HAIR. IT WAS TOO INDIAN.
THEN THEY GAVE US NEW CLOTHES TO WEAR. WELL, THEY WEREN'T NEW . . . JUST NEW TO US.
PRETTY SOON WE LOOKED LIKE WHITES. EXCEPT, YOU KNOW, FOR THE BROWN THEY COULDN'T SCRUB AWAY.

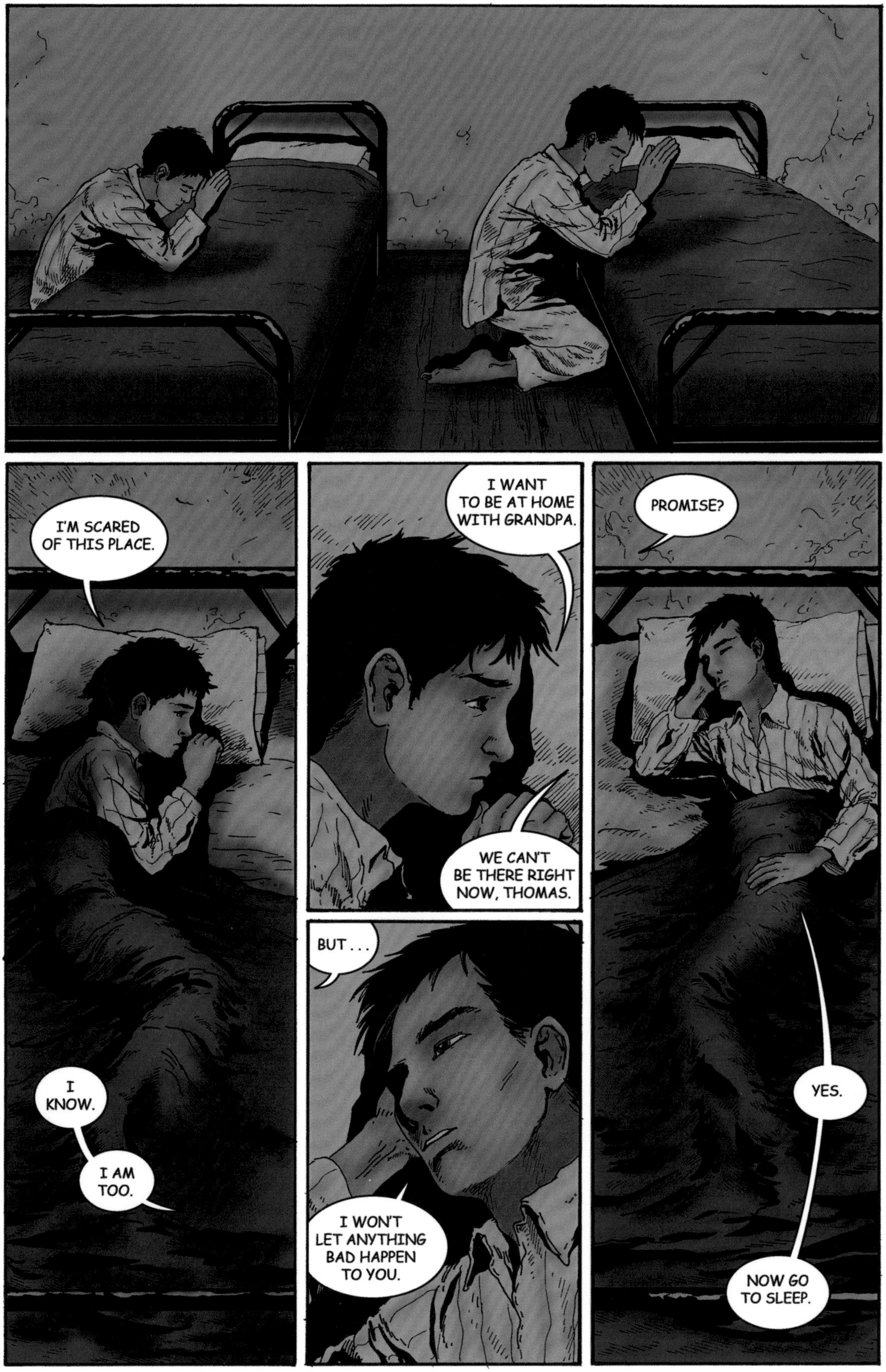
I'M SCARED OF THIS PLACE.
I KNOW.
I AM TOO.
I WANT TO BE AT HOME WITH GRANDPA.
WE CAN'T BE THERE RIGHT NOW, THOMAS.
BUT . . .
I WON'T LET ANYTHING BAD HAPPEN TO YOU.
PROMISE?
YES.
NOW GO TO SLEEP.

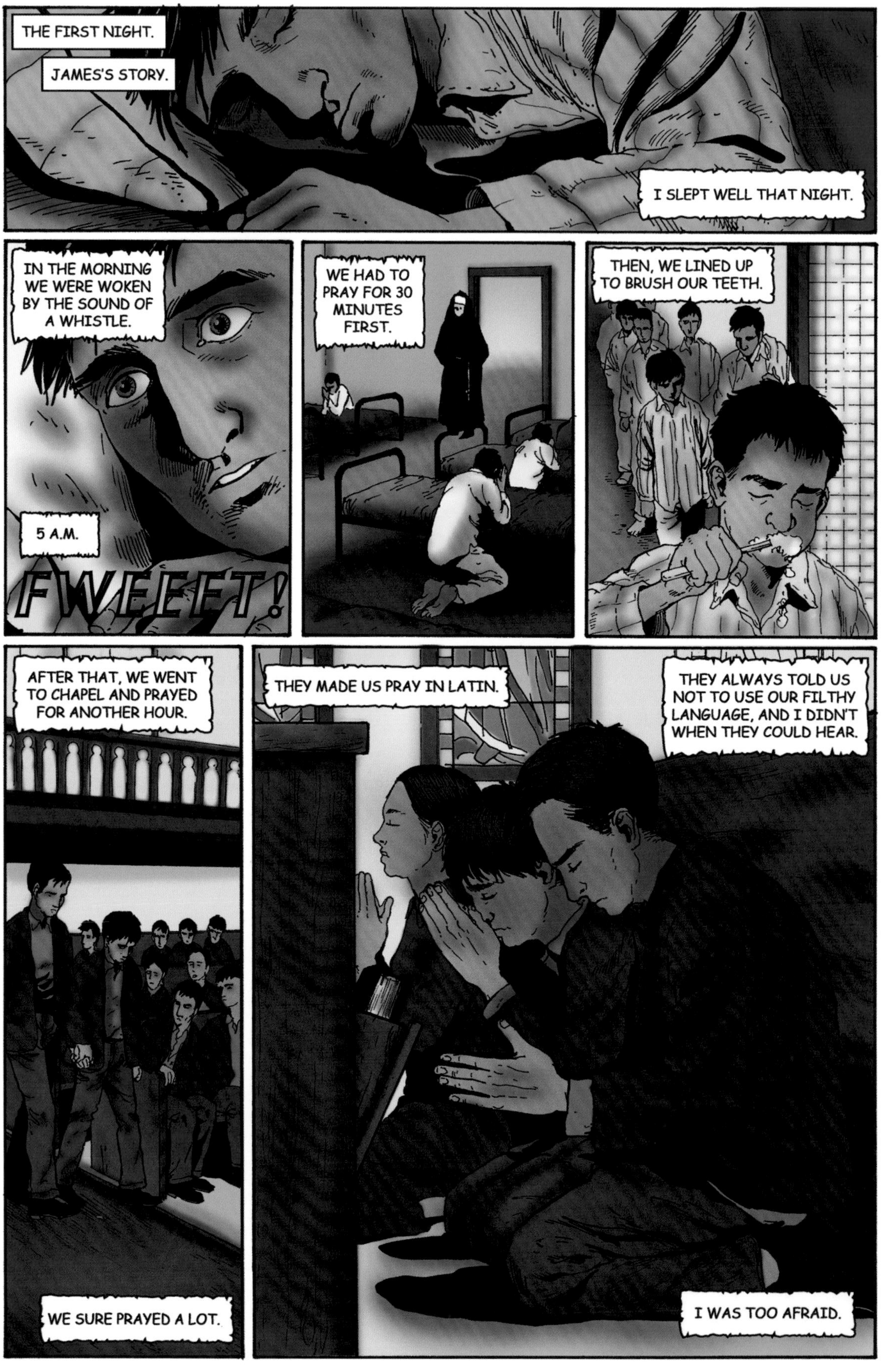
THE FIRST NIGHT.
JAMES'S STORY.
I SLEPT WELL THAT NIGHT.
IN THE MORNING WE WERE WOKEN BY THE SOUND OF A WHISTLE.
5 A.M.
FWEEET!
WE HAD TO PRAY FOR 30 MINUTES FIRST.
THEN, WE LINED UP TO BRUSH OUR TEETH.
AFTER THAT, WE WENT TO CHAPEL AND PRAYED FOR ANOTHER HOUR.
WE SURE PRAYED A LOT.
THEY MADE US PRAY IN LATIN.
THEY ALWAYS TOLD US NOT TO USE OUR FILTHY LANGUAGE, AND I DIDN'T WHEN THEY COULD HEAR.
I WAS TOO AFRAID.

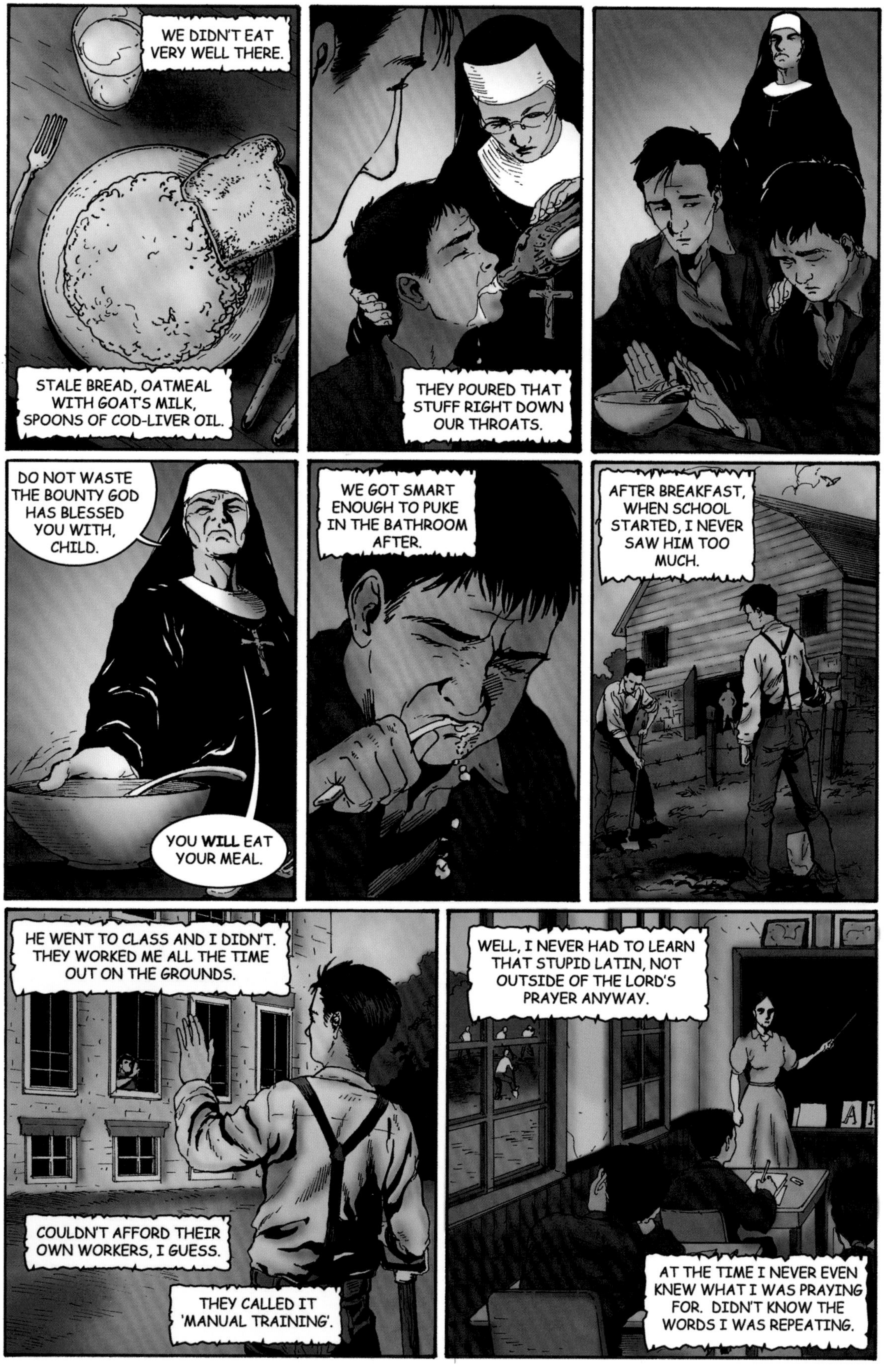
WE DIDN'T EAT VERY WELL THERE.
STALE BREAD, OATMEAL WITH GOAT'S MILK, SPOONS OF COD-LIVER OIL.
THEY POURED THAT STUFF RIGHT DOWN OUR THROATS.
DO NOT WASTE THE BOUNTY GOD HAS BLESSED YOU WITH, CHILD.
YOU **WILL** EAT YOUR MEAL.
WE GOT SMART ENOUGH TO PUKE IN THE BATHROOM AFTER.
AFTER BREAKFAST, WHEN SCHOOL STARTED, I NEVER SAW HIM TOO MUCH.
HE WENT TO CLASS AND I DIDN'T. THEY WORKED ME ALL THE TIME OUT ON THE GROUNDS.
COULDN'T AFFORD THEIR OWN WORKERS, I GUESS.
THEY CALLED IT 'MANUAL TRAINING'.
WELL, I NEVER HAD TO LEARN THAT STUPID LATIN, NOT OUTSIDE OF THE LORD'S PRAYER ANYWAY.
AT THE TIME I NEVER EVEN KNEW WHAT I WAS PRAYING FOR. DIDN'T KNOW THE WORDS I WAS REPEATING.

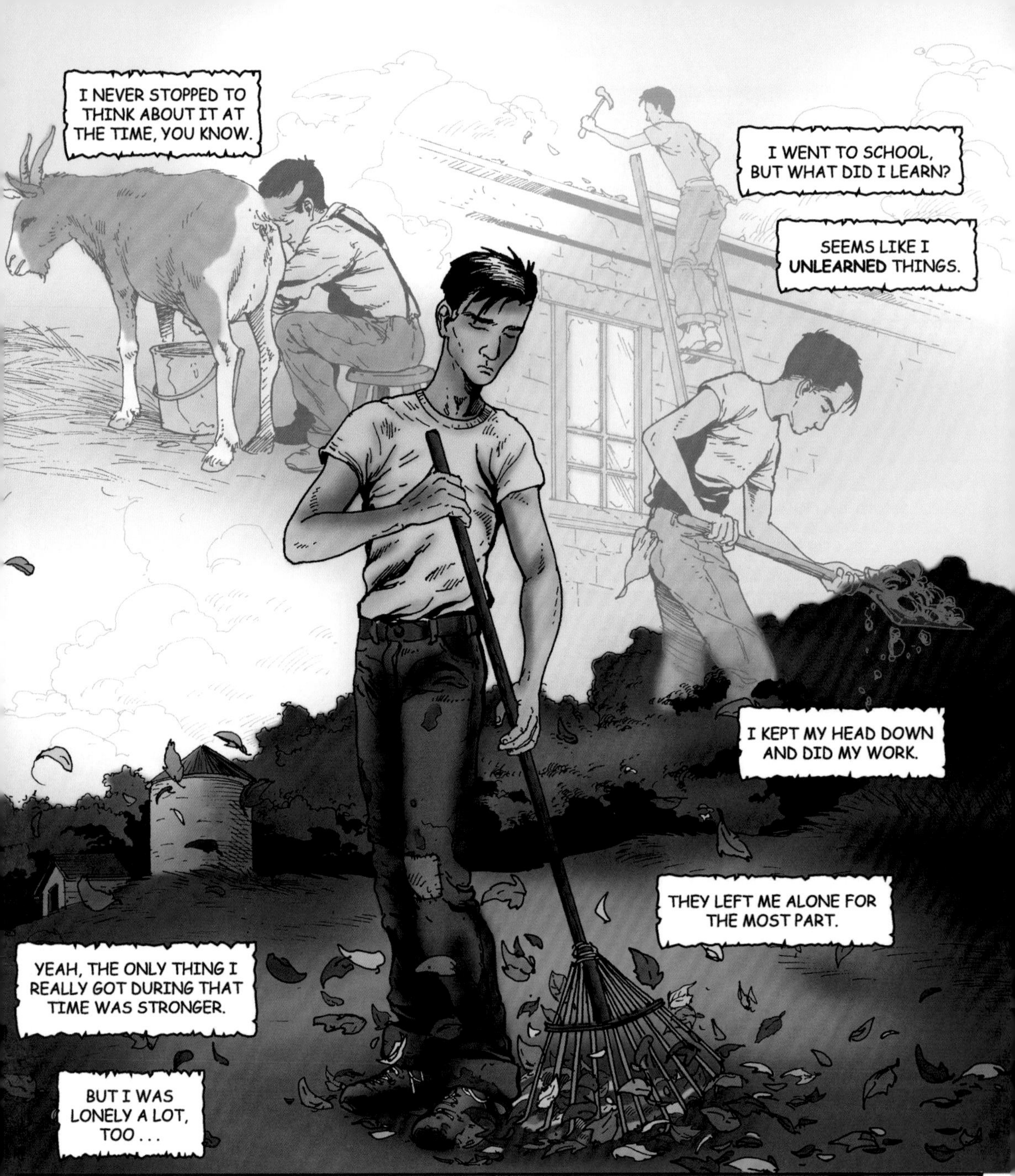
I NEVER STOPPED TO THINK ABOUT IT AT THE TIME, YOU KNOW.
I WENT TO SCHOOL, BUT WHAT DID I LEARN?
SEEMS LIKE I **UNLEARNED** THINGS.
I KEPT MY HEAD DOWN AND DID MY WORK.
THEY LEFT ME ALONE FOR THE MOST PART.
YEAH, THE ONLY THING I REALLY GOT DURING THAT TIME WAS STRONGER.
BUT I WAS LONELY A LOT, TOO . . .

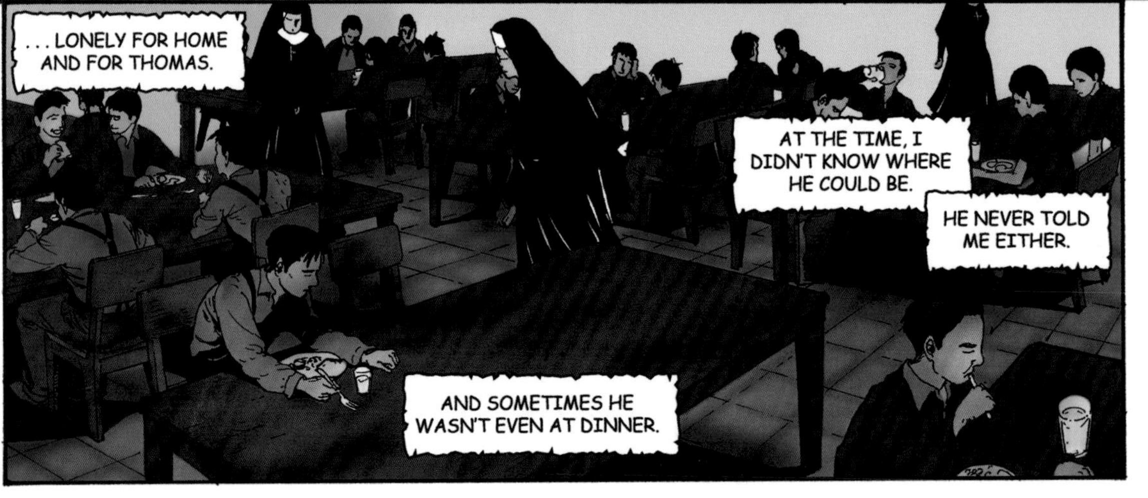
. . . LONELY FOR HOME AND FOR THOMAS.
AT THE TIME, I DIDN'T KNOW WHERE HE COULD BE.
HE NEVER TOLD ME EITHER.
AND SOMETIMES HE WASN'T EVEN AT DINNER.

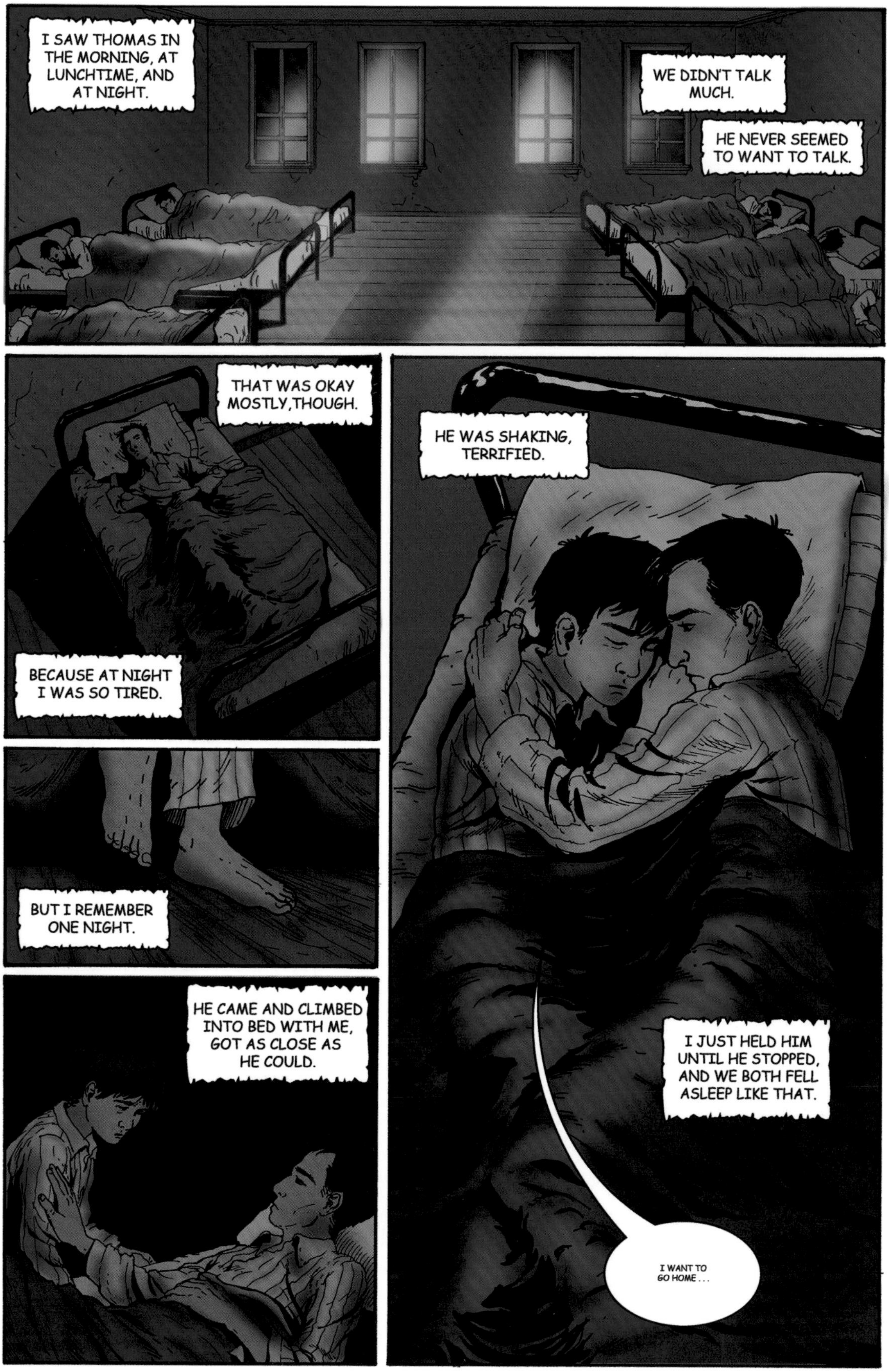
I SAW THOMAS IN THE MORNING, AT LUNCHTIME, AND AT NIGHT.
WE DIDN'T TALK MUCH.
HE NEVER SEEMED TO WANT TO TALK.
THAT WAS OKAY MOSTLY, THOUGH.
BECAUSE AT NIGHT I WAS SO TIRED.
BUT I REMEMBER ONE NIGHT.
HE CAME AND CLIMBED INTO BED WITH ME, GOT AS CLOSE AS HE COULD.
HE WAS SHAKING, TERRIFIED.
I JUST HELD HIM UNTIL HE STOPPED, AND WE BOTH FELL ASLEEP LIKE THAT.
I WANT TO GO HOME . . .

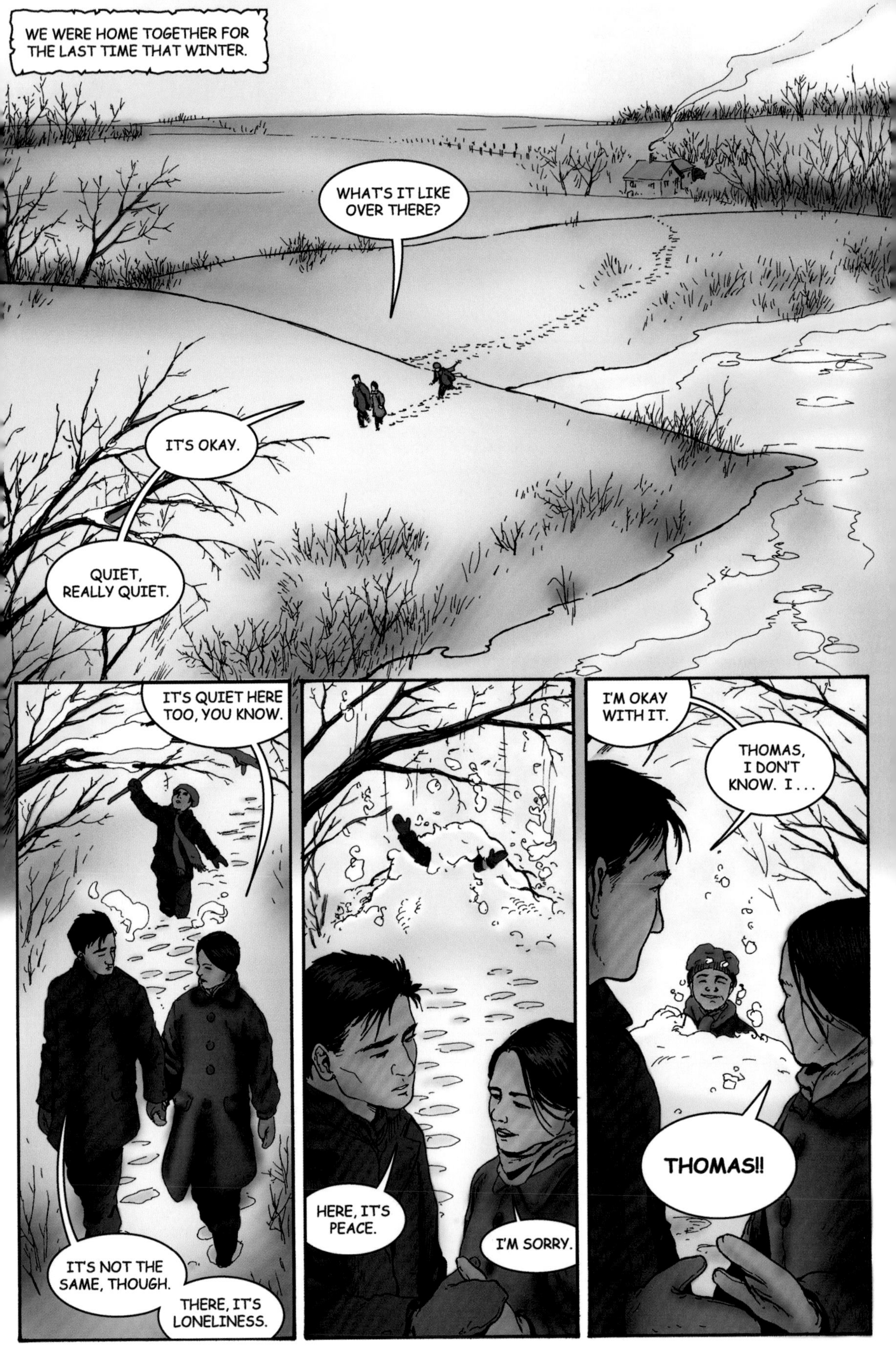
WE WERE HOME TOGETHER FOR THE LAST TIME THAT WINTER.
WHAT'S IT LIKE OVER THERE?
IT'S OKAY.
QUIET, REALLY QUIET.
IT'S QUIET HERE TOO, YOU KNOW.
IT'S NOT THE SAME, THOUGH.
THERE, IT'S LONELINESS.
HERE, IT'S PEACE.
I'M SORRY.
I'M OKAY WITH IT.
THOMAS, I DON'T KNOW. I . . .
THOMAS!!

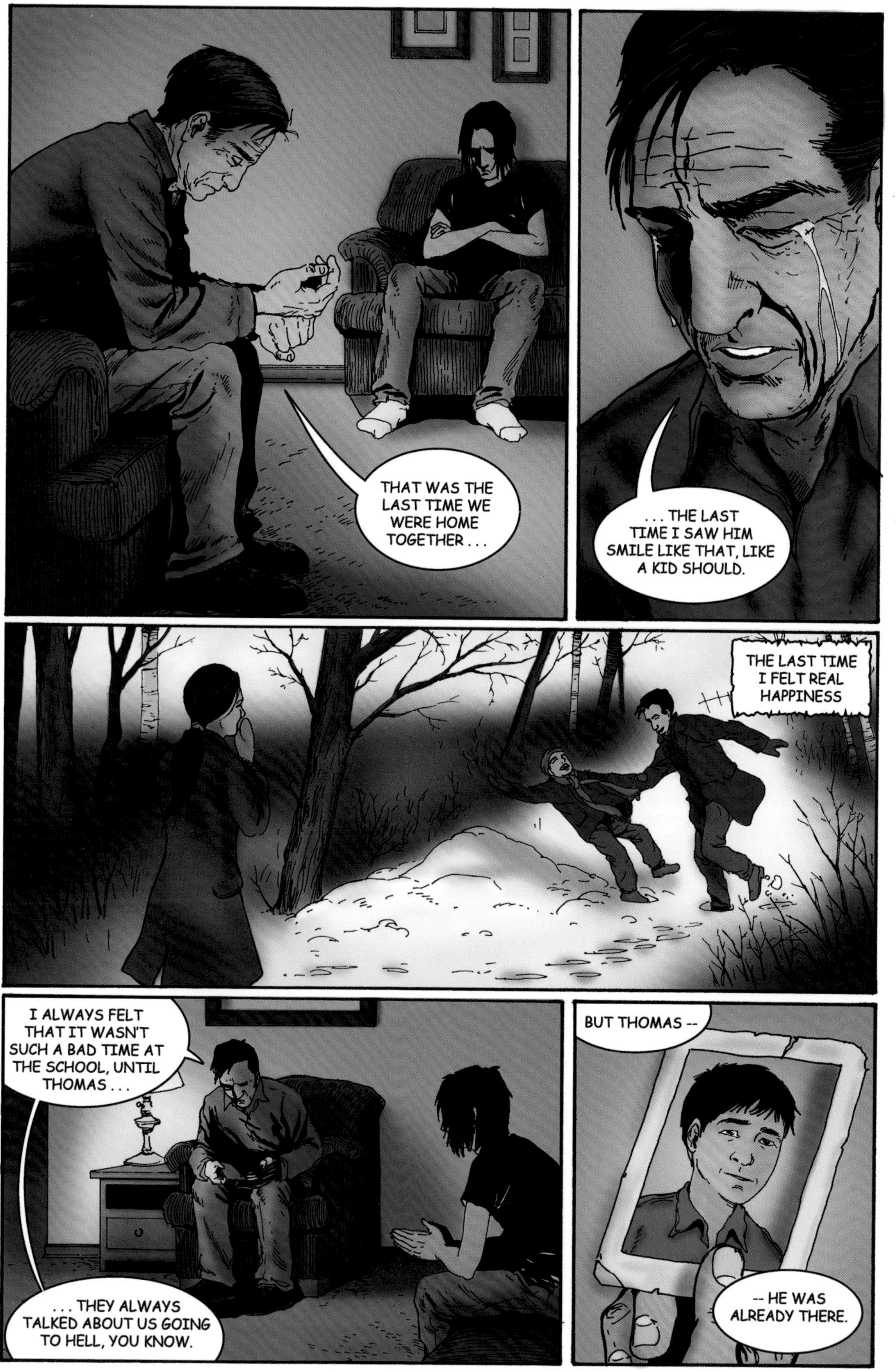
THAT WAS THE LAST TIME WE WERE HOME TOGETHER . . .
. . . THE LAST TIME I SAW HIM SMILE LIKE THAT, LIKE A KID SHOULD.
THE LAST TIME I FELT REAL HAPPINESS
I ALWAYS FELT THAT IT WASN'T SUCH A BAD TIME AT THE SCHOOL, UNTIL THOMAS . . .
. . . THEY ALWAYS TALKED ABOUT US GOING TO HELL, YOU KNOW.
BUT THOMAS --
-- HE WAS ALREADY THERE.

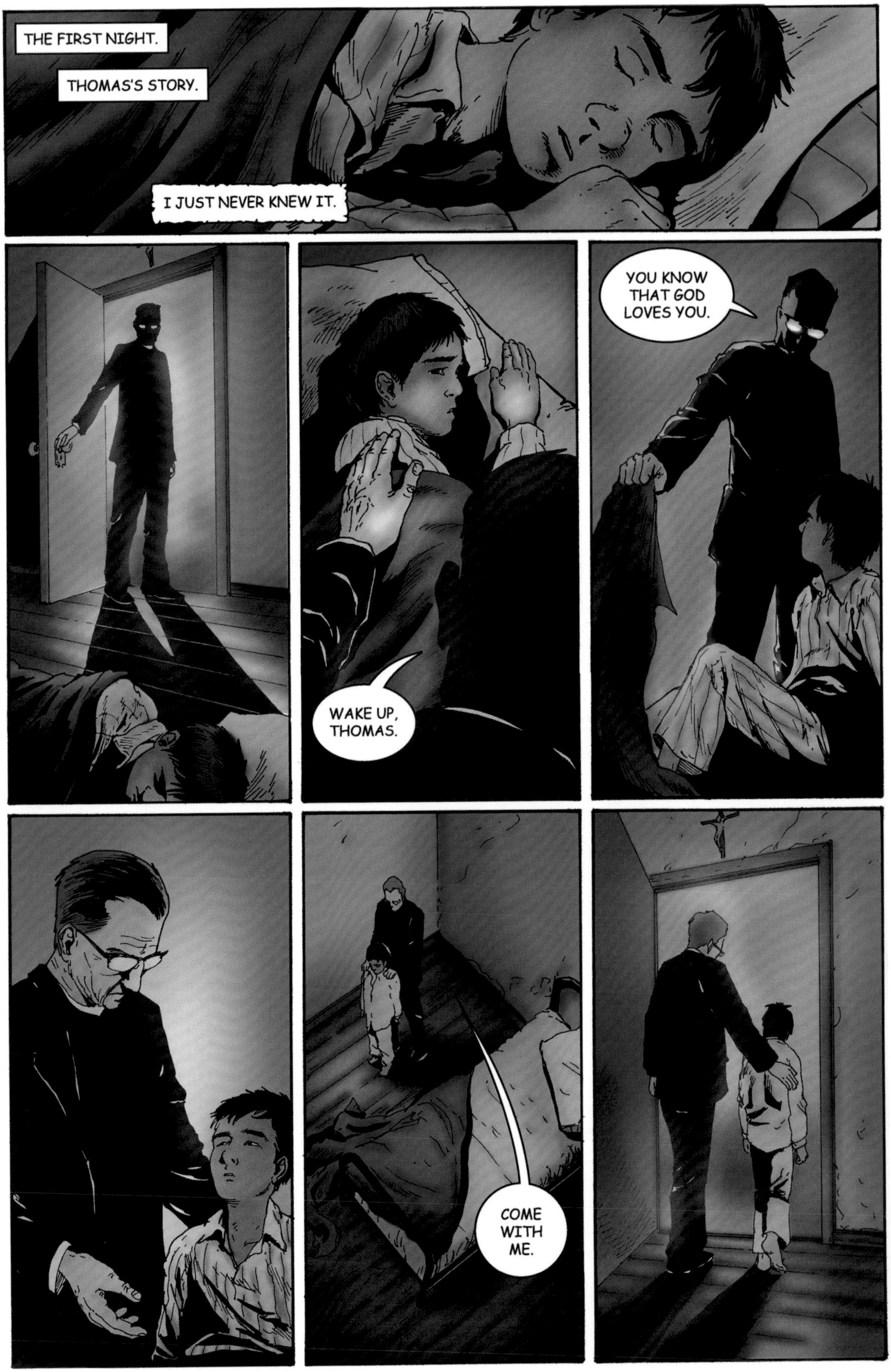
THE FIRST NIGHT.
THOMAS'S STORY.
I JUST NEVER KNEW IT.
WAKE UP, THOMAS.
YOU KNOW THAT GOD LOVES YOU.
COME WITH ME.

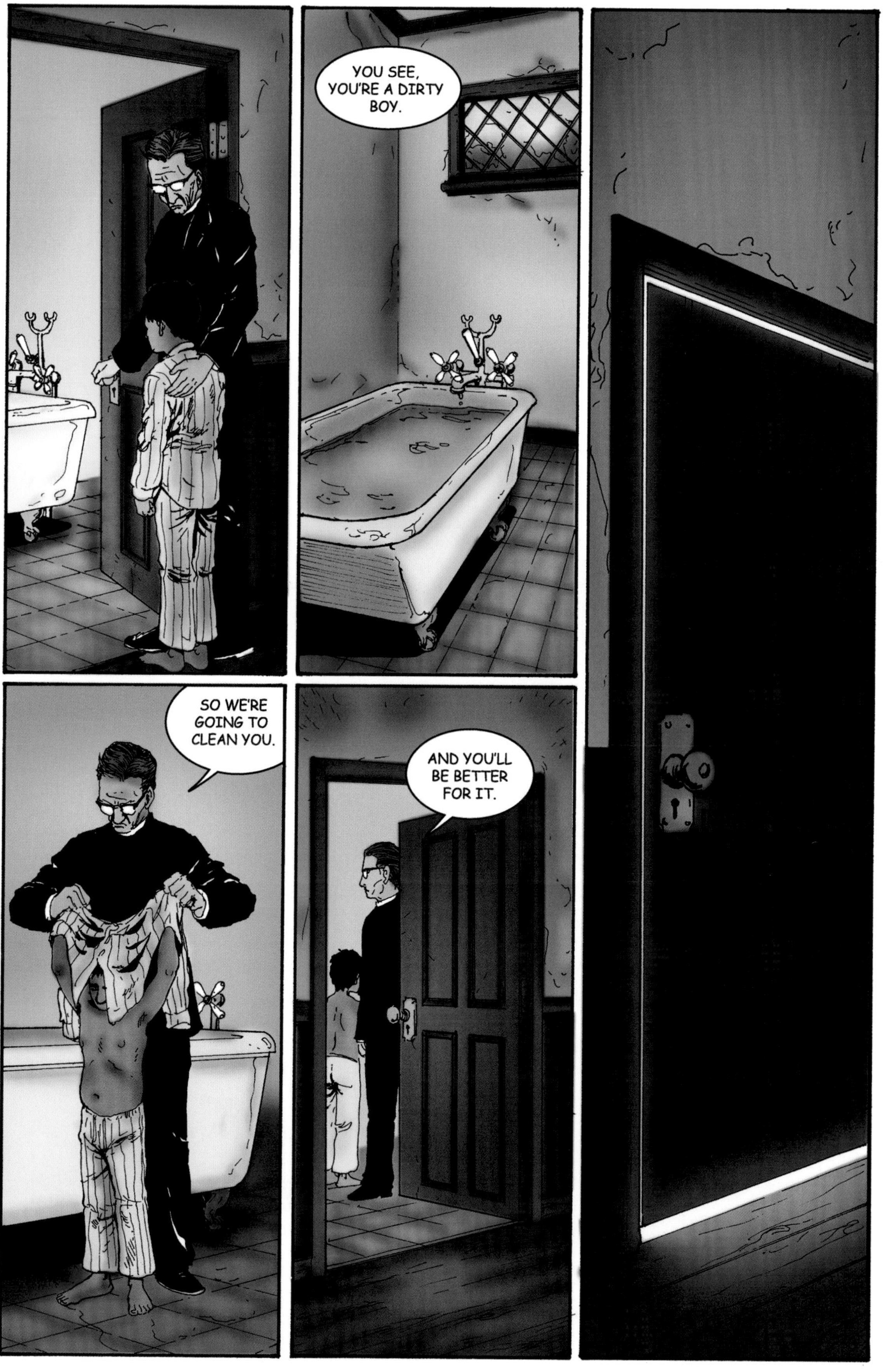
YOU SEE, YOU'RE A DIRTY BOY.
SO WE'RE GOING TO CLEAN YOU.
AND YOU'LL BE BETTER FOR IT.

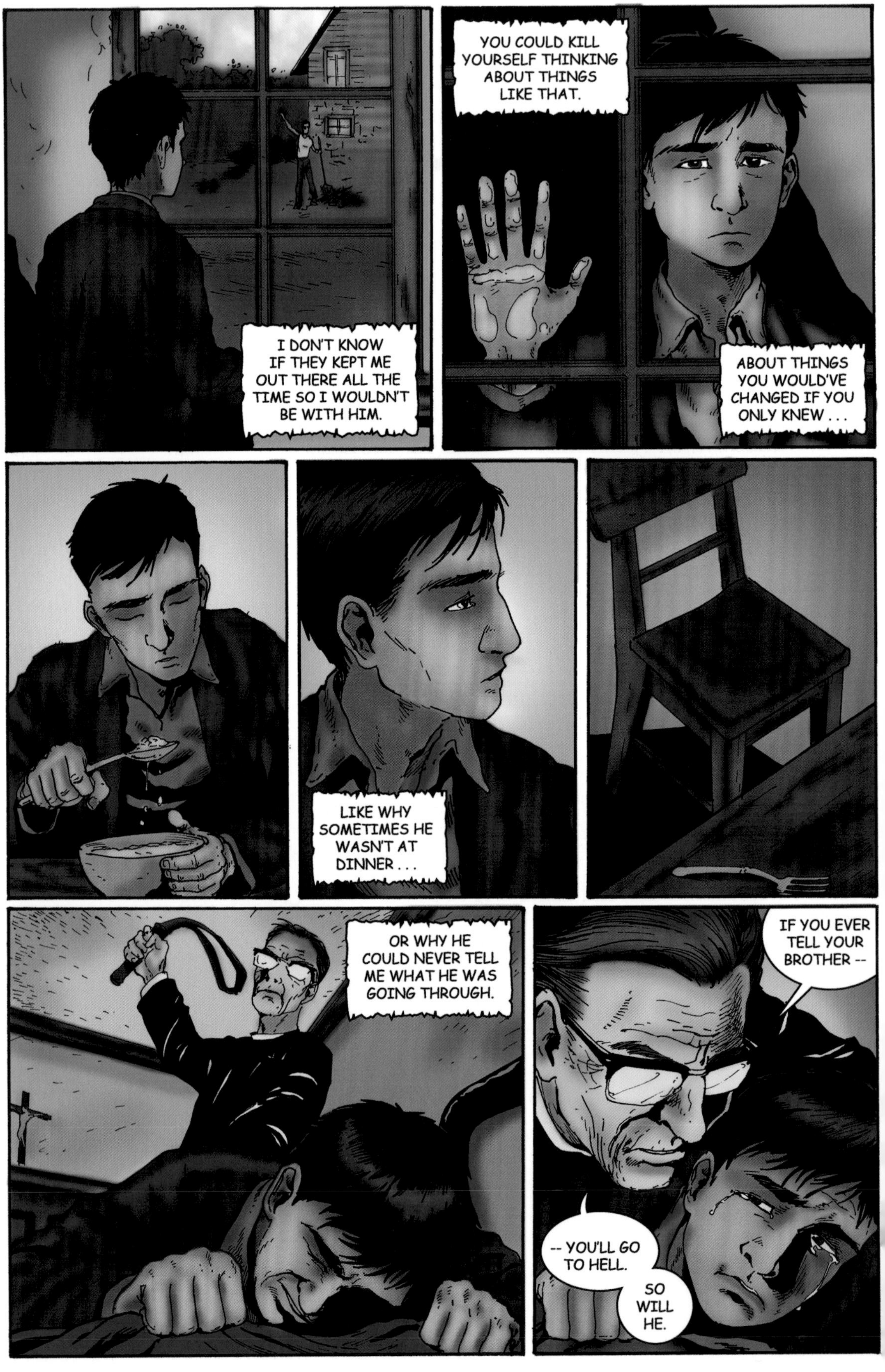
I DON'T KNOW IF THEY KEPT ME OUT THERE ALL THE TIME SO I WOULDN'T BE WITH HIM.
YOU COULD KILL YOURSELF THINKING ABOUT THINGS LIKE THAT.
ABOUT THINGS YOU WOULD'VE CHANGED IF YOU ONLY KNEW . . .
LIKE WHY SOMETIMES HE WASN'T AT DINNER . . .
OR WHY HE COULD NEVER TELL ME WHAT HE WAS GOING THROUGH.
IF YOU EVER TELL YOUR BROTHER --
-- YOU'LL GO TO HELL.
SO WILL HE.

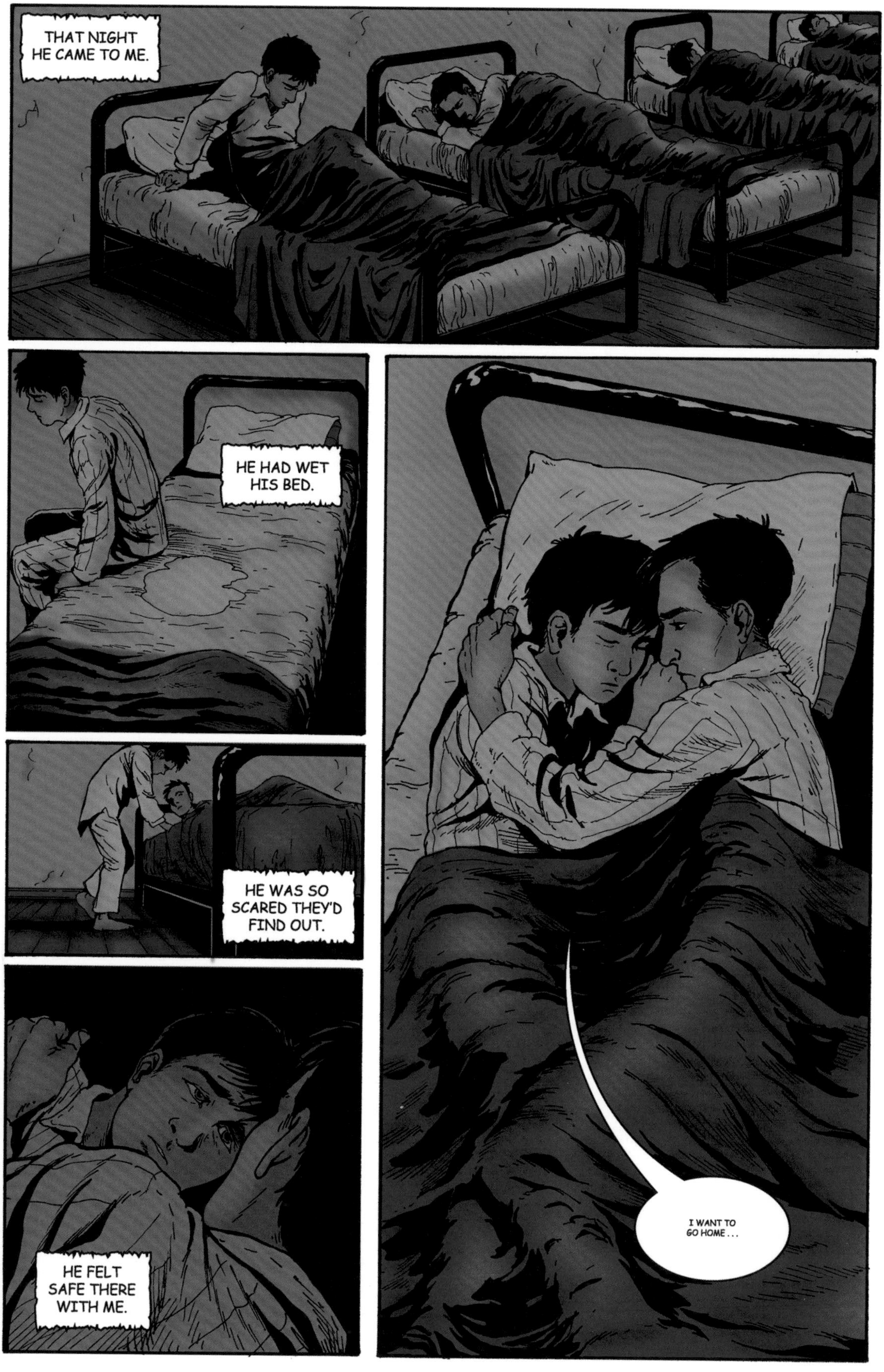
THAT NIGHT HE CAME TO ME.
HE HAD WET HIS BED.
HE WAS SO SCARED THEY'D FIND OUT.
HE FELT SAFE THERE WITH ME.
I WANT TO GO HOME . . .

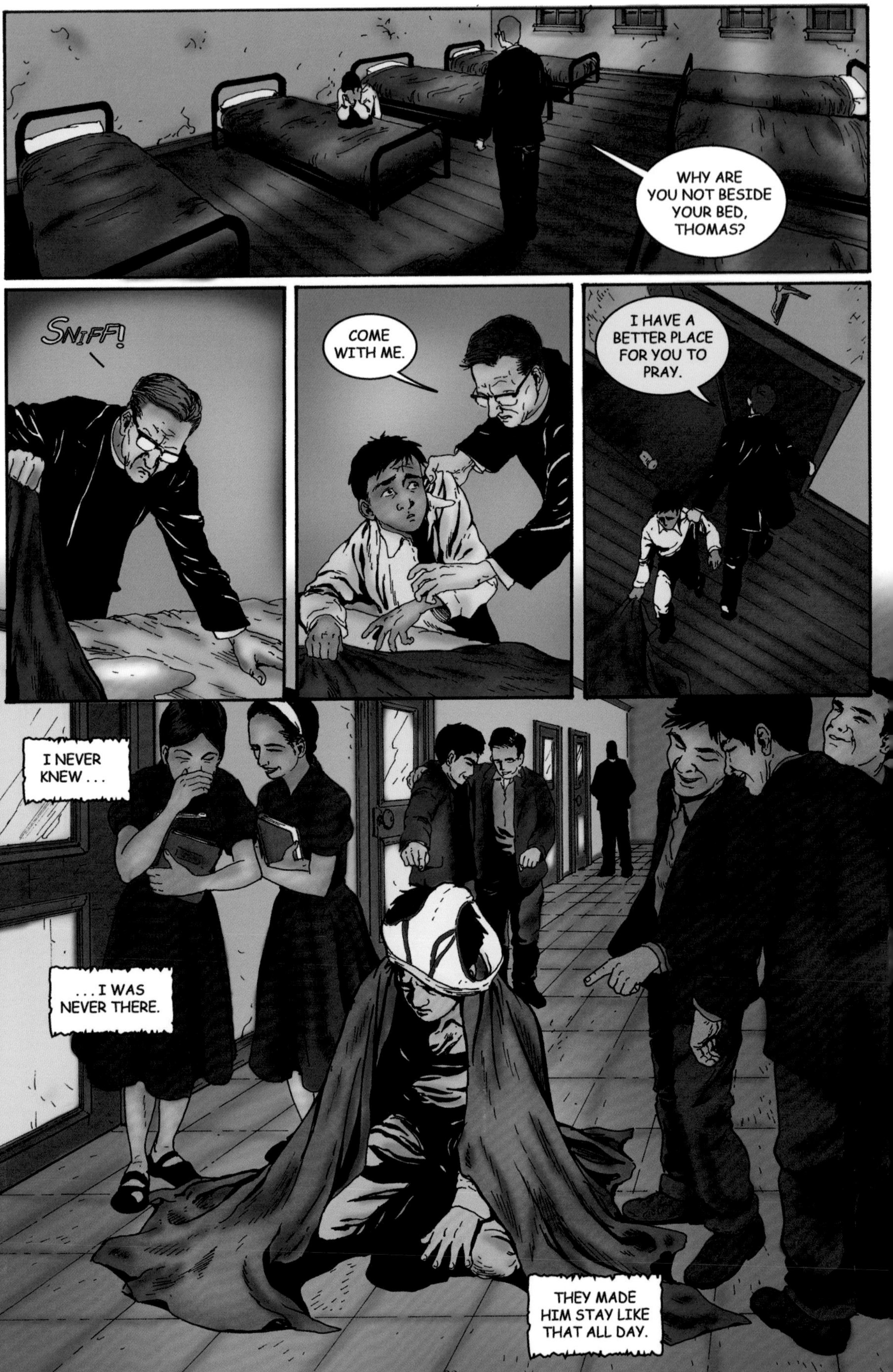
WHY ARE YOU NOT BESIDE YOUR BED, THOMAS?
SNIFF!
COME WITH ME.
I HAVE A BETTER PLACE FOR YOU TO PRAY.
I NEVER KNEW . . .
. . . I WAS NEVER THERE.
THEY MADE HIM STAY LIKE THAT ALL DAY.

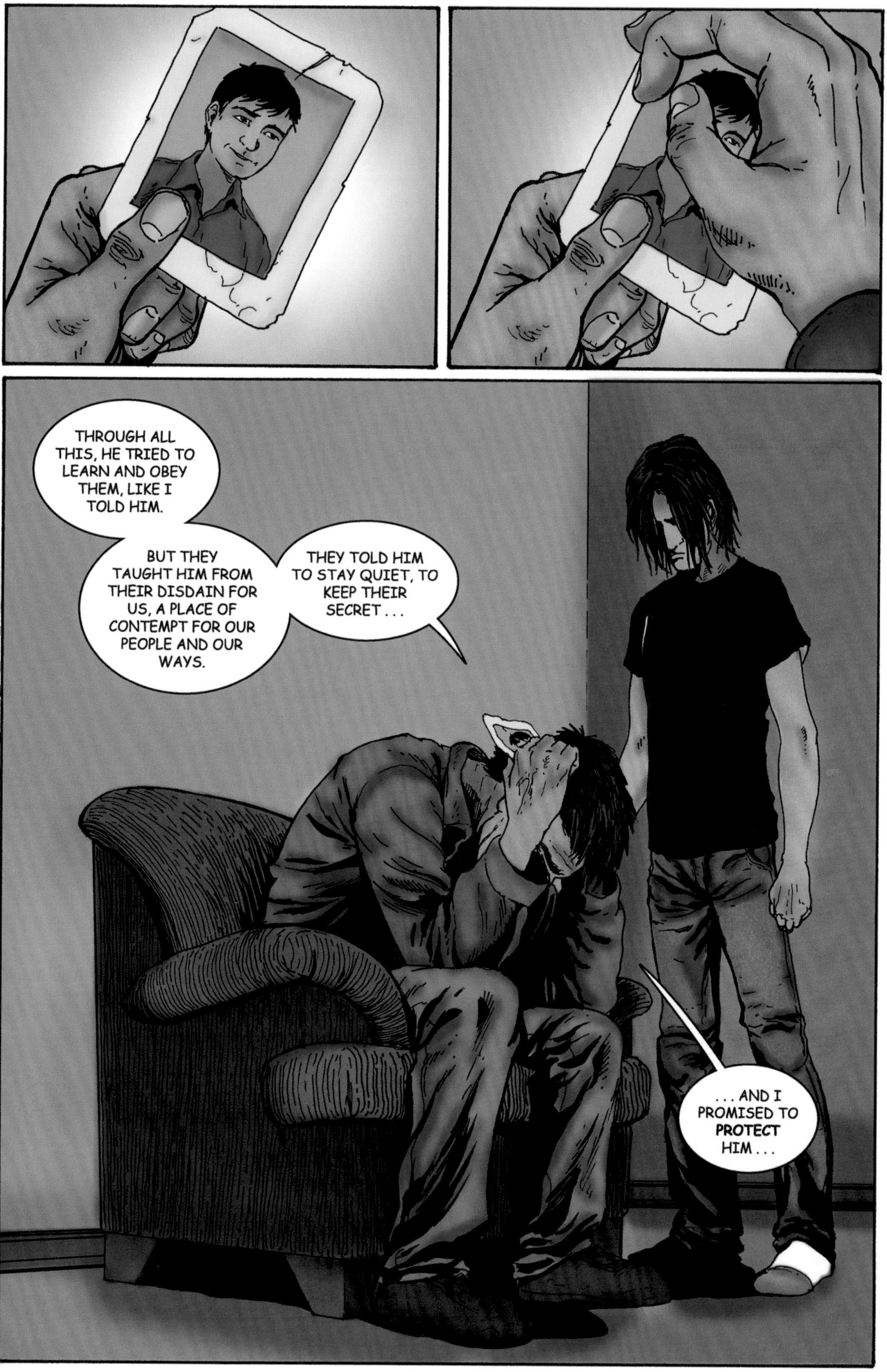
THROUGH ALL THIS, HE TRIED TO LEARN AND OBEY THEM, LIKE I TOLD HIM.
BUT THEY TAUGHT HIM FROM THEIR DISDAIN FOR US, A PLACE OF CONTEMPT FOR OUR PEOPLE AND OUR WAYS.
THEY TOLD HIM TO STAY QUIET, TO KEEP THEIR SECRET . . .
. . . AND I PROMISED TO **PROTECT** HIM . . .

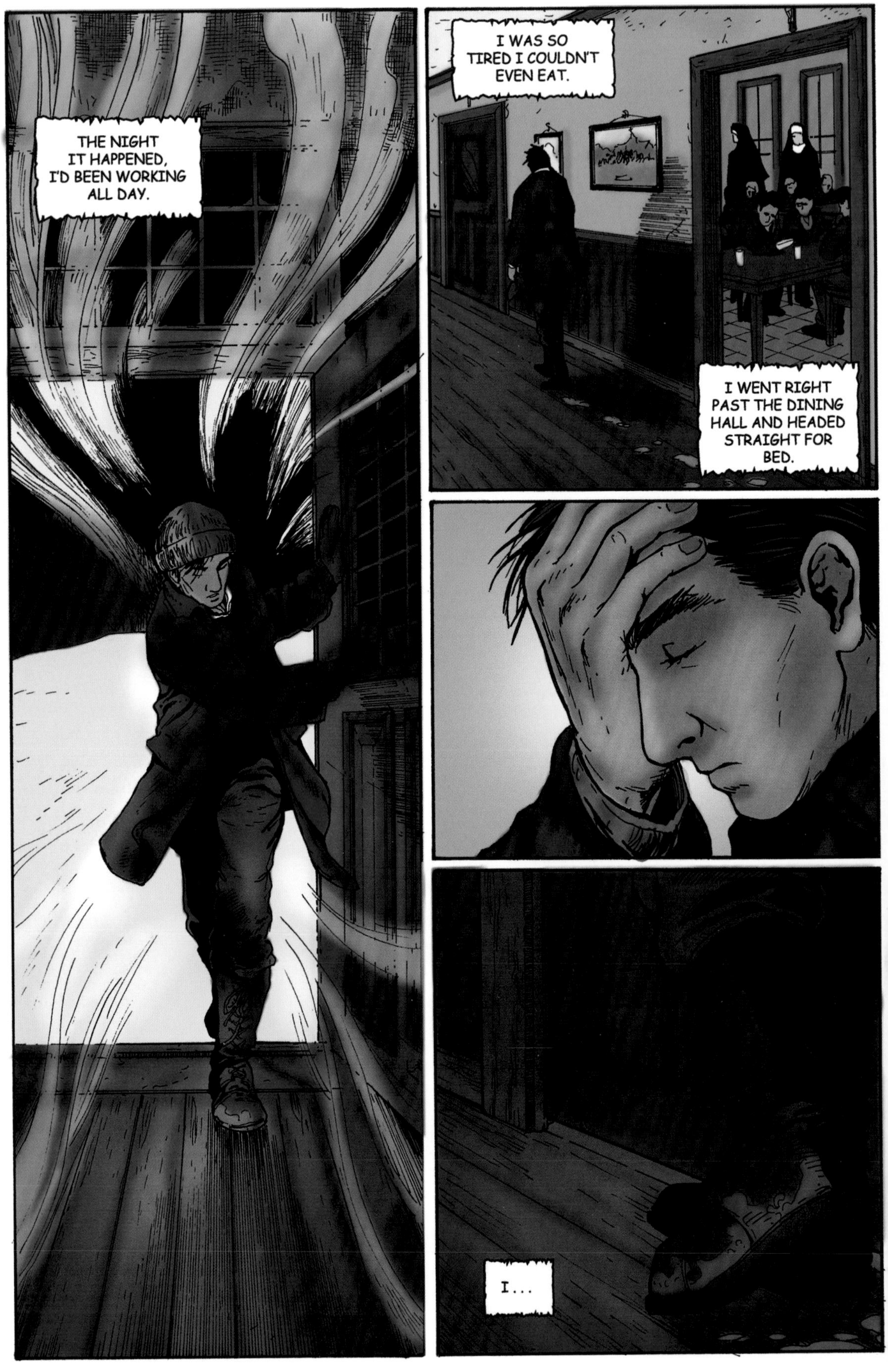
THE NIGHT IT HAPPENED, I'D BEEN WORKING ALL DAY.
I WAS SO TIRED I COULDN'T EVEN EAT.
I WENT RIGHT PAST THE DINING HALL AND HEADED STRAIGHT FOR BED.
I...

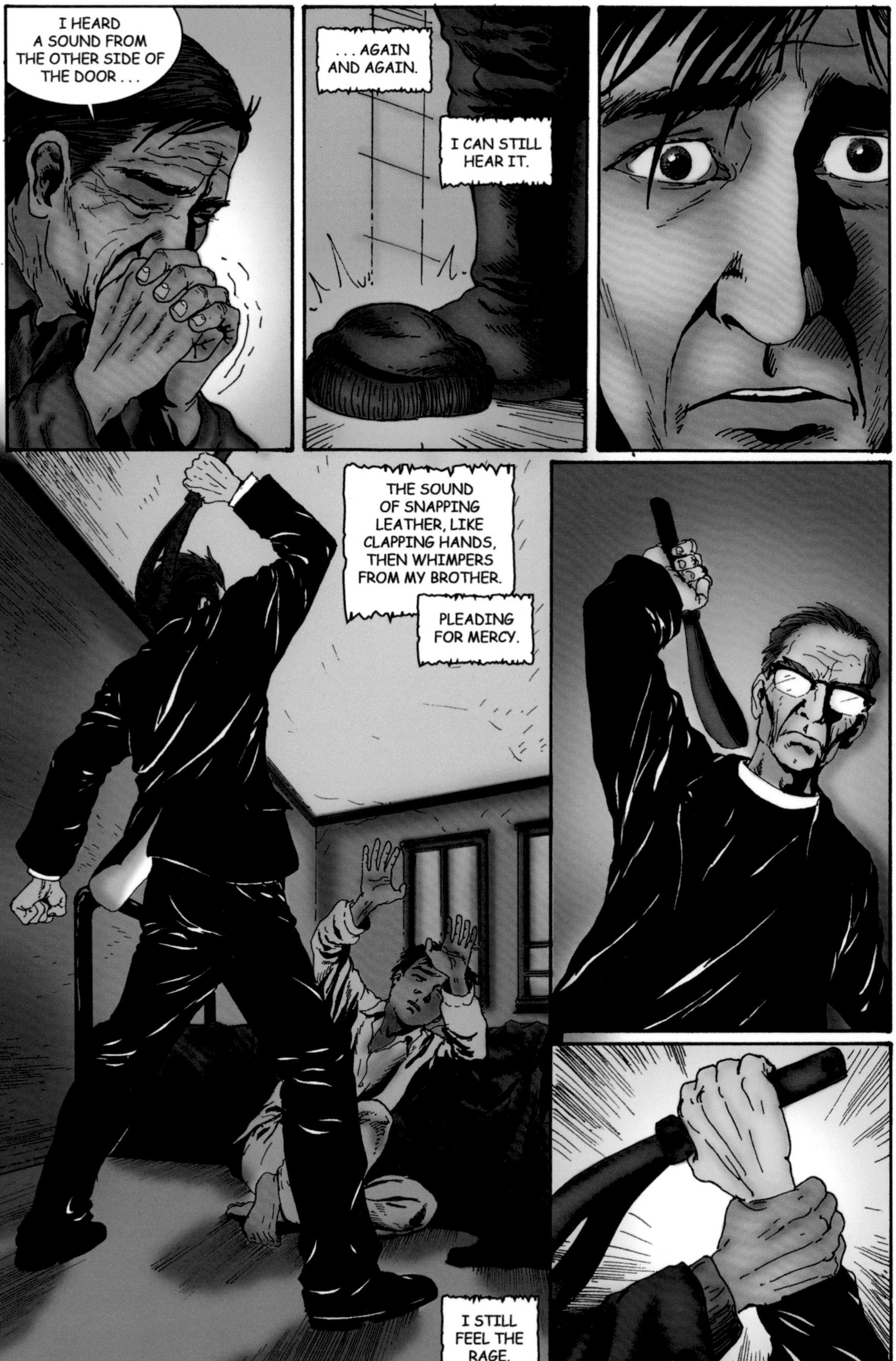
I HEARD A SOUND FROM THE OTHER SIDE OF THE DOOR . . .
. . . AGAIN AND AGAIN.
I CAN STILL HEAR IT.
THE SOUND OF SNAPPING LEATHER, LIKE CLAPPING HANDS, THEN WHIMPERS FROM MY BROTHER.
PLEADING FOR MERCY.
I STILL FEEL THE RAGE.

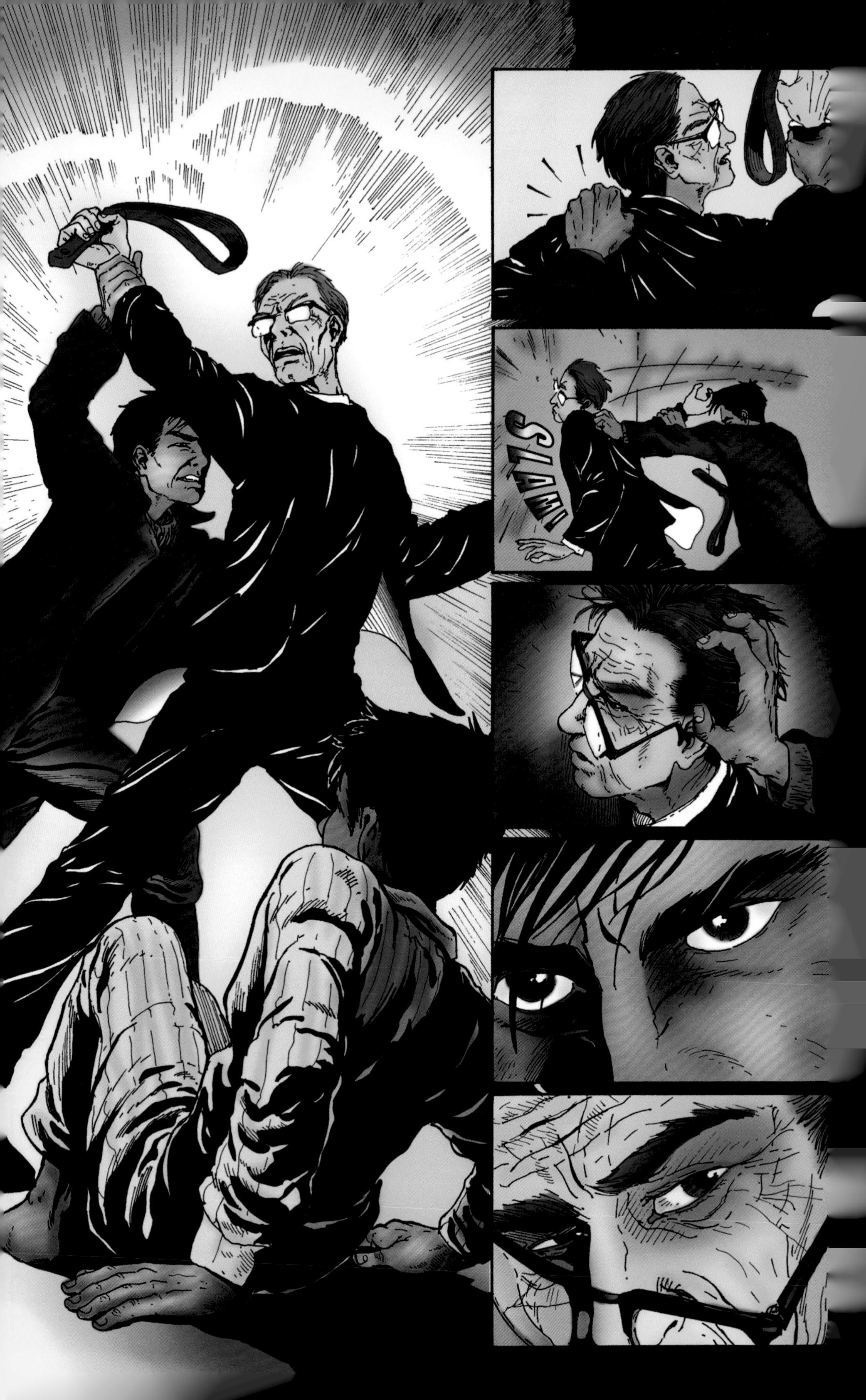
SLAM!

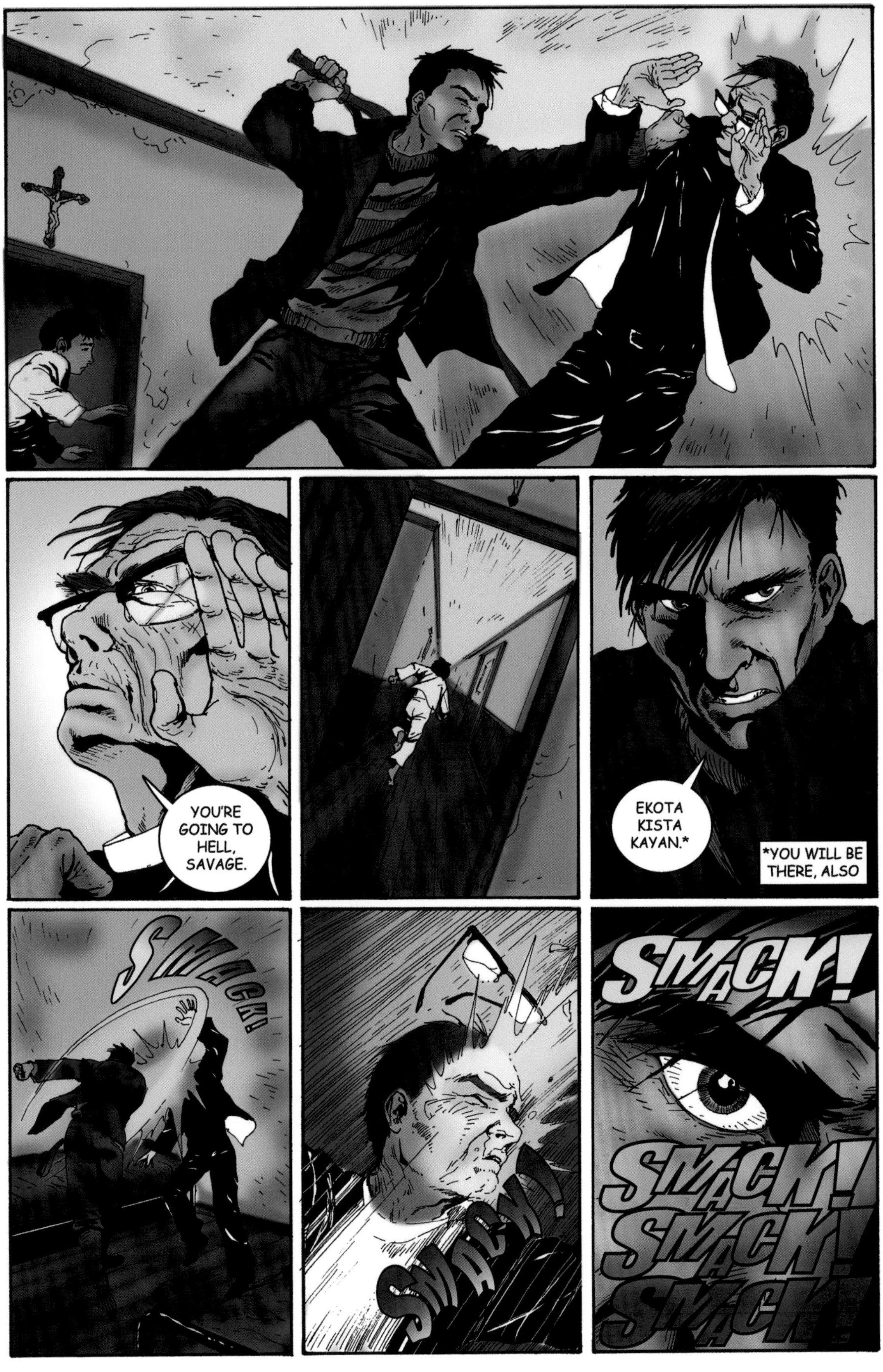
YOU'RE GOING TO HELL, SAVAGE.
EKOTA KISTA KAYAN.*
*YOU WILL BE THERE, ALSO
SMACK!
SMACK!
SMACK!
SMACK!
SMACK!
SMACK!

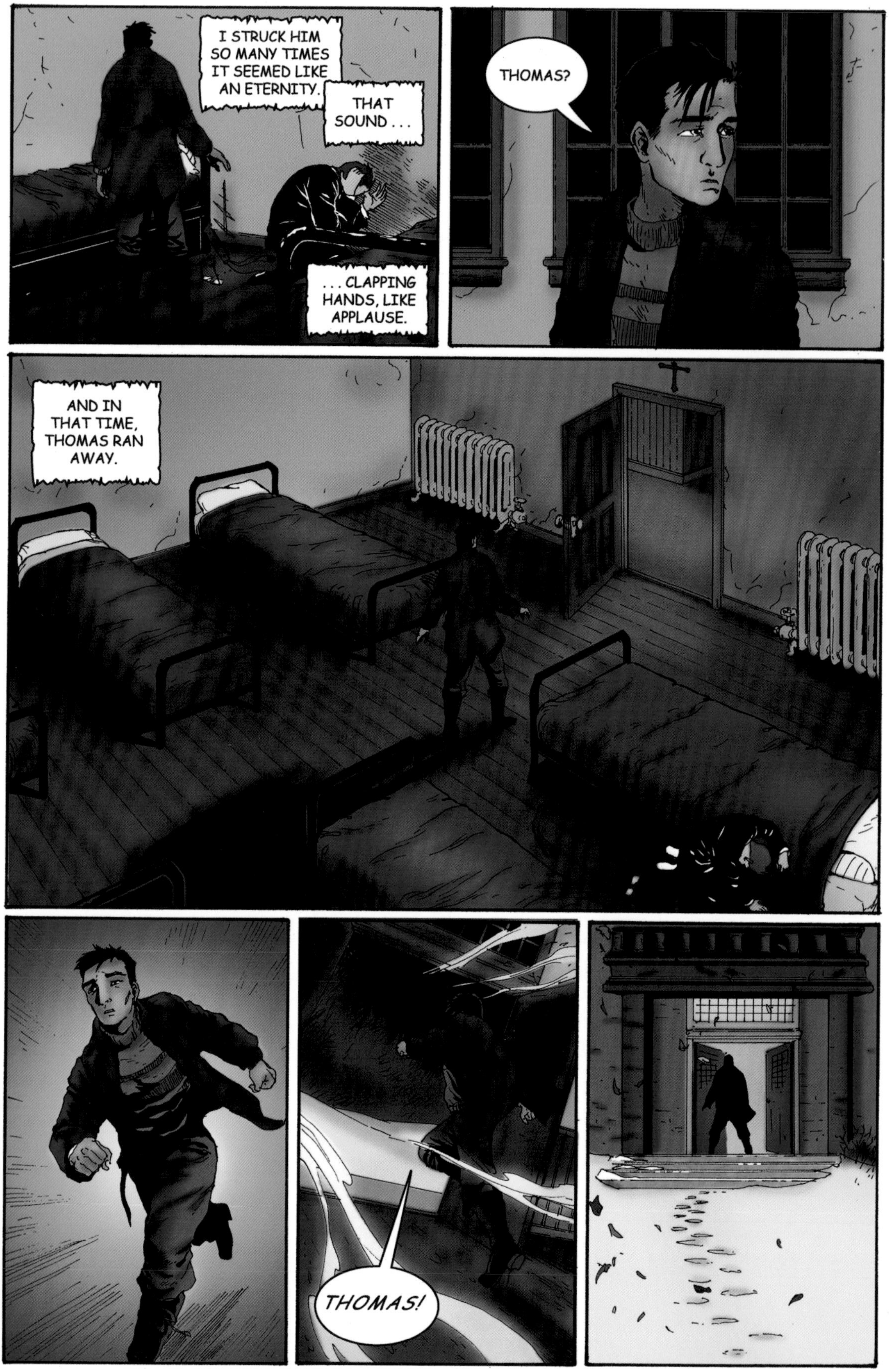
I STRUCK HIM SO MANY TIMES IT SEEMED LIKE AN ETERNITY.
THAT SOUND . . .
. . . CLAPPING HANDS, LIKE APPLAUSE.
THOMAS?
AND IN THAT TIME, THOMAS RAN AWAY.
THOMAS!

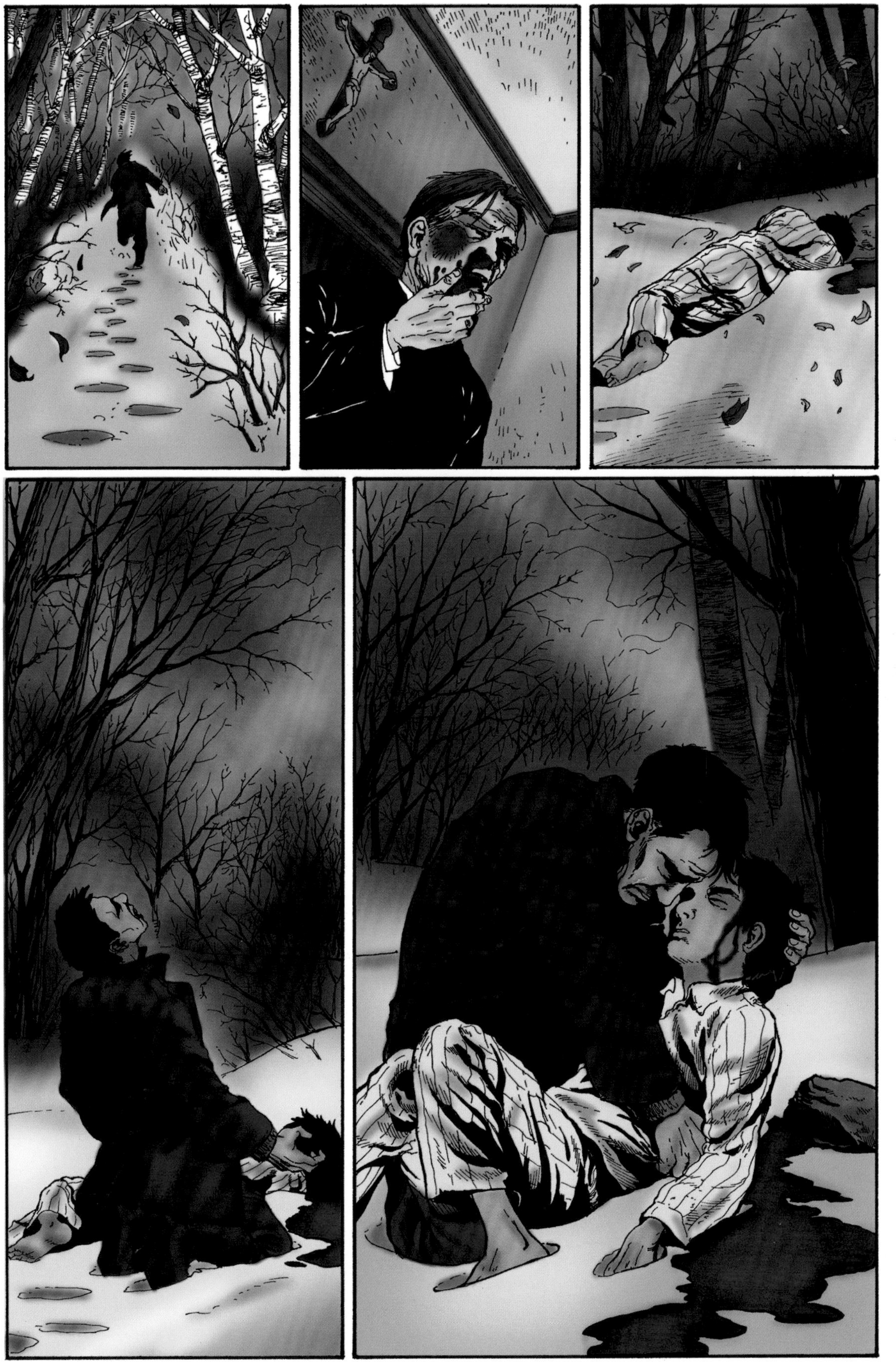

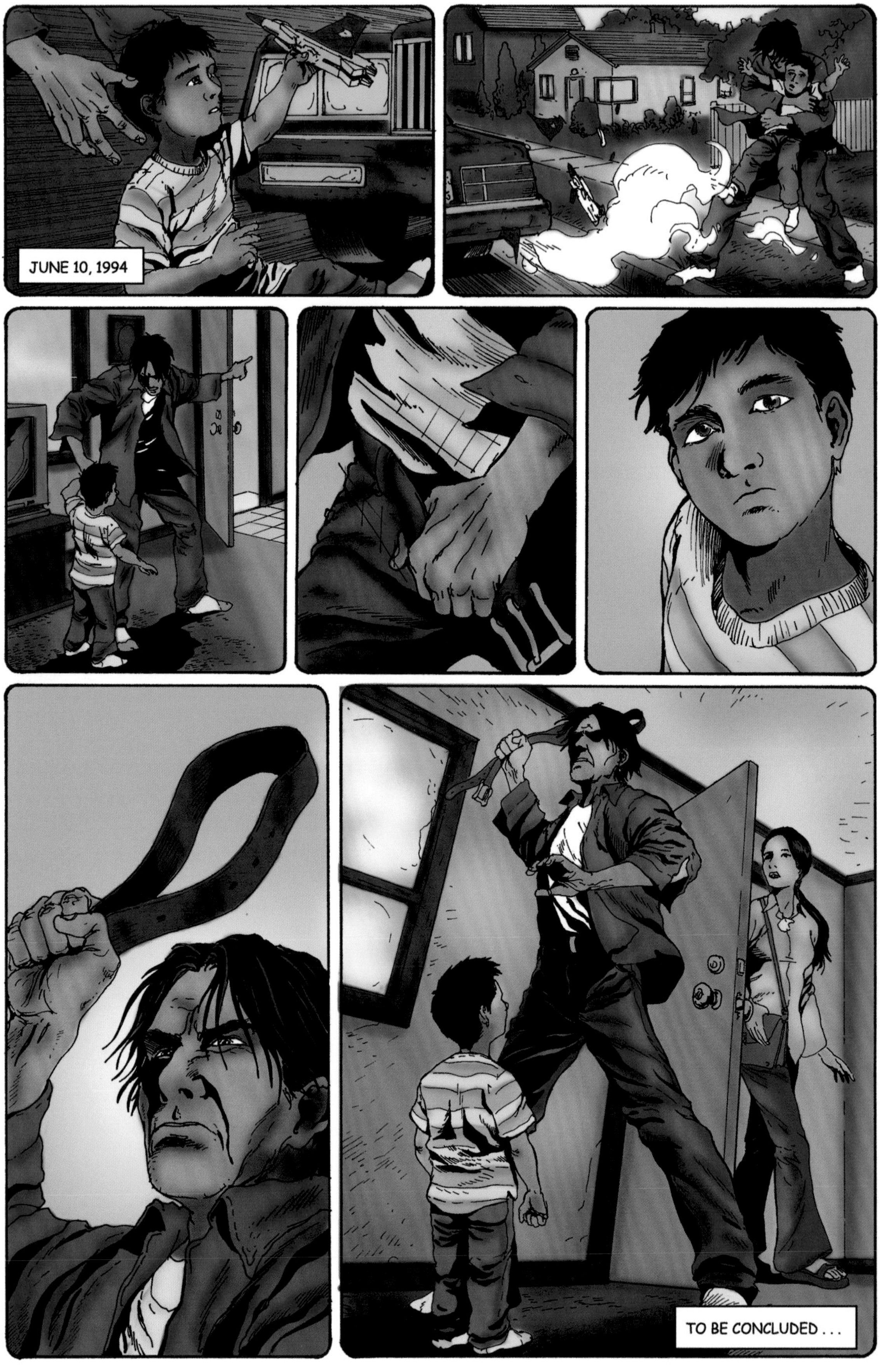
JUNE 10, 1994
TO BE CONCLUDED . . .

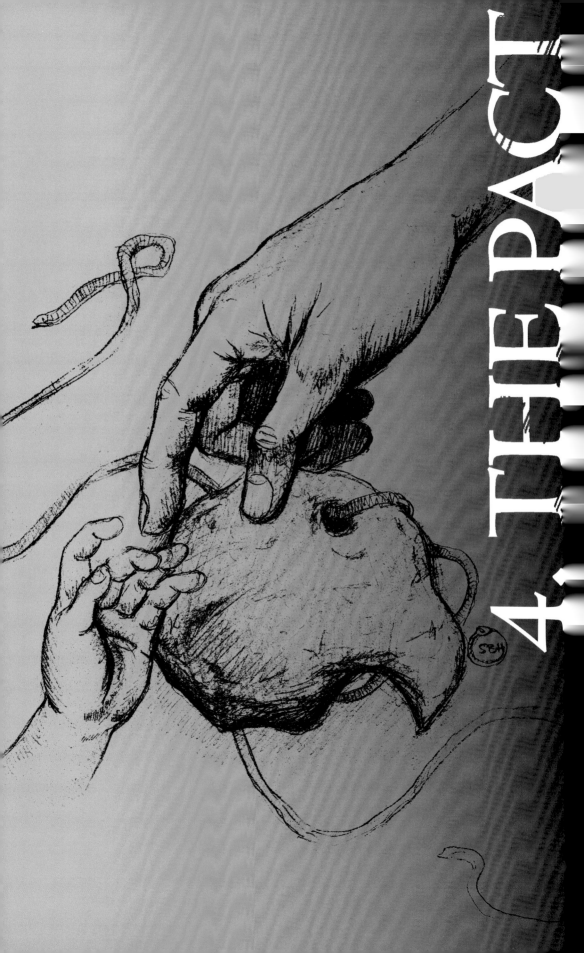

4 THE PACT

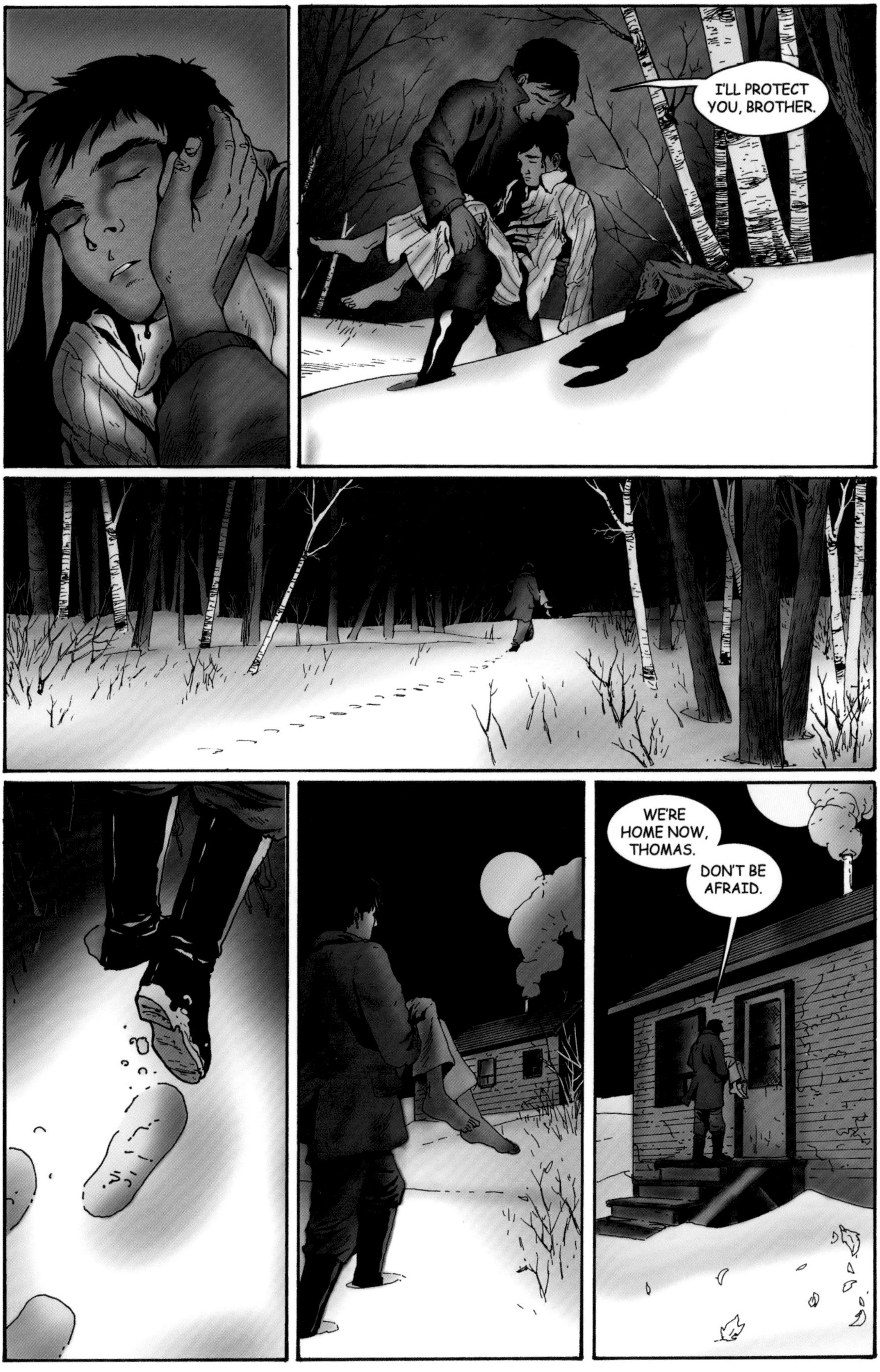
I'LL PROTECT YOU, BROTHER.
WE'RE HOME NOW, THOMAS.
DON'T BE AFRAID.

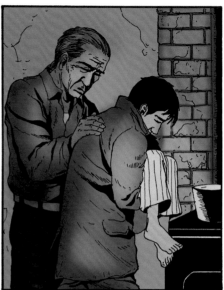

IT'S WARM HERE.

YOU'LL BE SAFE NOW.

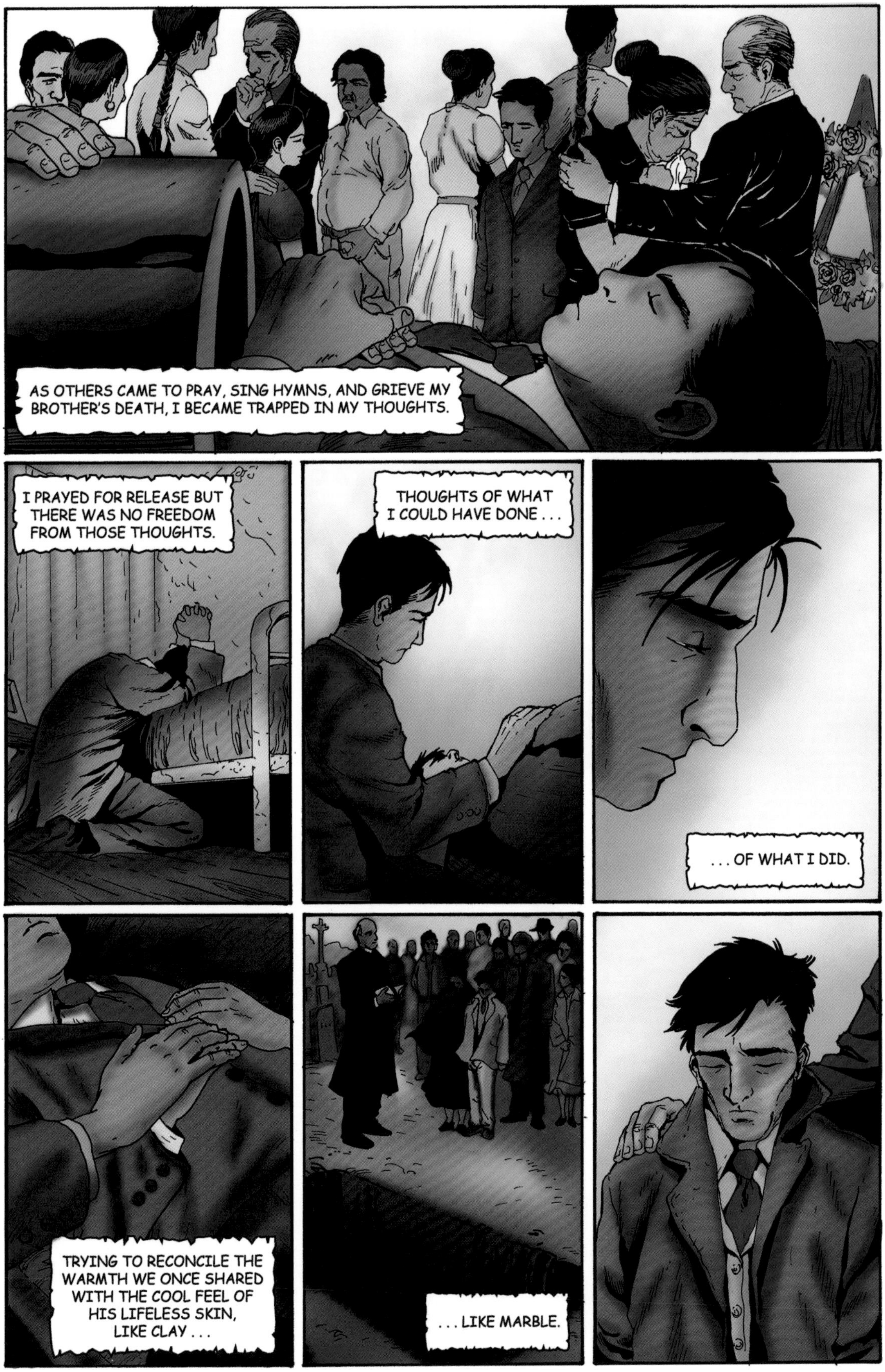
AS OTHERS CAME TO PRAY, SING HYMNS, AND GRIEVE MY BROTHER'S DEATH, I BECAME TRAPPED IN MY THOUGHTS.
I PRAYED FOR RELEASE BUT THERE WAS NO FREEDOM FROM THOSE THOUGHTS.
THOUGHTS OF WHAT I COULD HAVE DONE . . .
. . . OF WHAT I DID.
TRYING TO RECONCILE THE WARMTH WE ONCE SHARED WITH THE COOL FEEL OF HIS LIFELESS SKIN, LIKE CLAY . . .
. . . LIKE MARBLE.

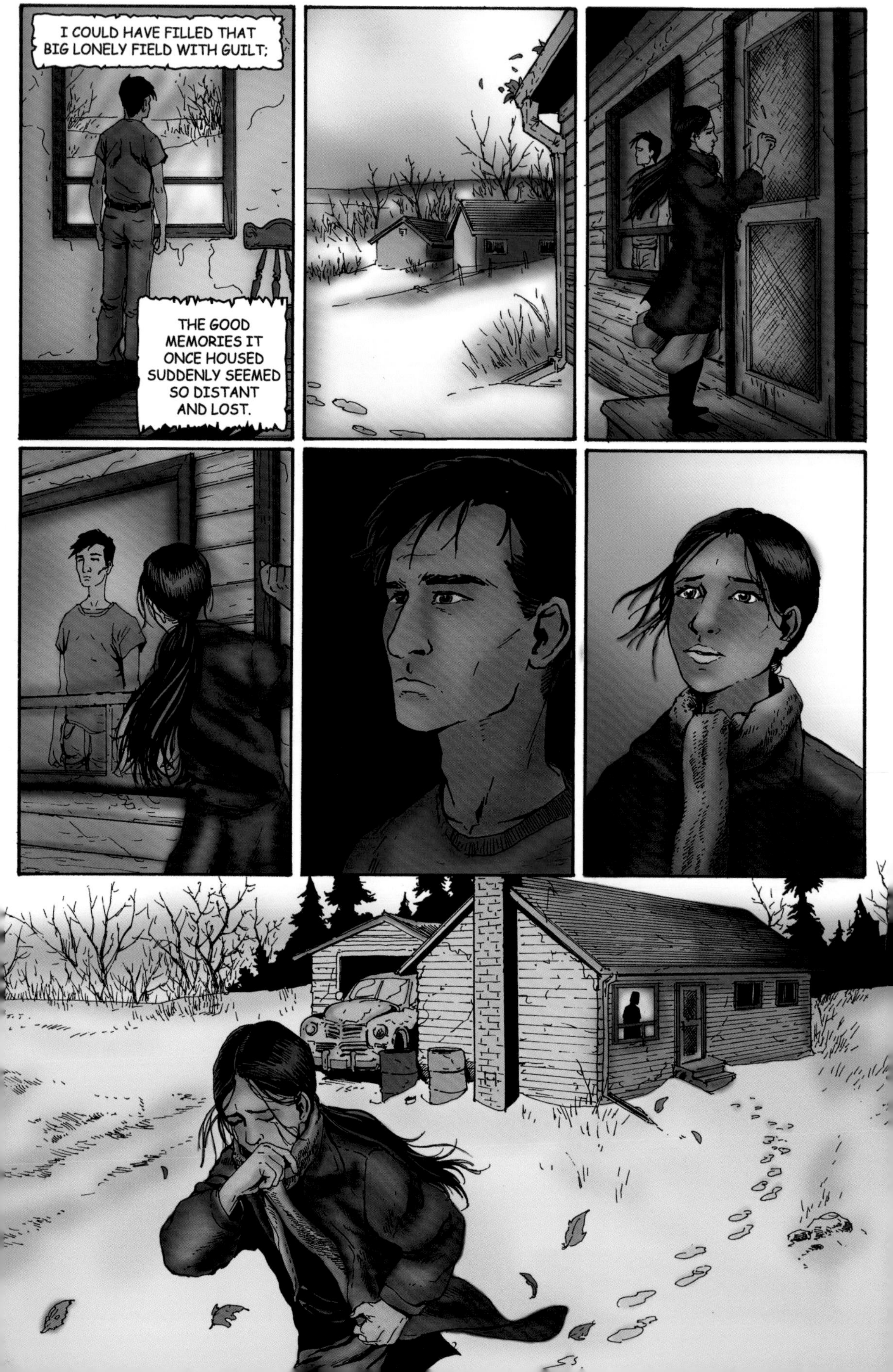
I COULD HAVE FILLED THAT BIG LONELY FIELD WITH GUILT;
THE GOOD MEMORIES IT ONCE HOUSED SUDDENLY SEEMED SO DISTANT AND LOST.

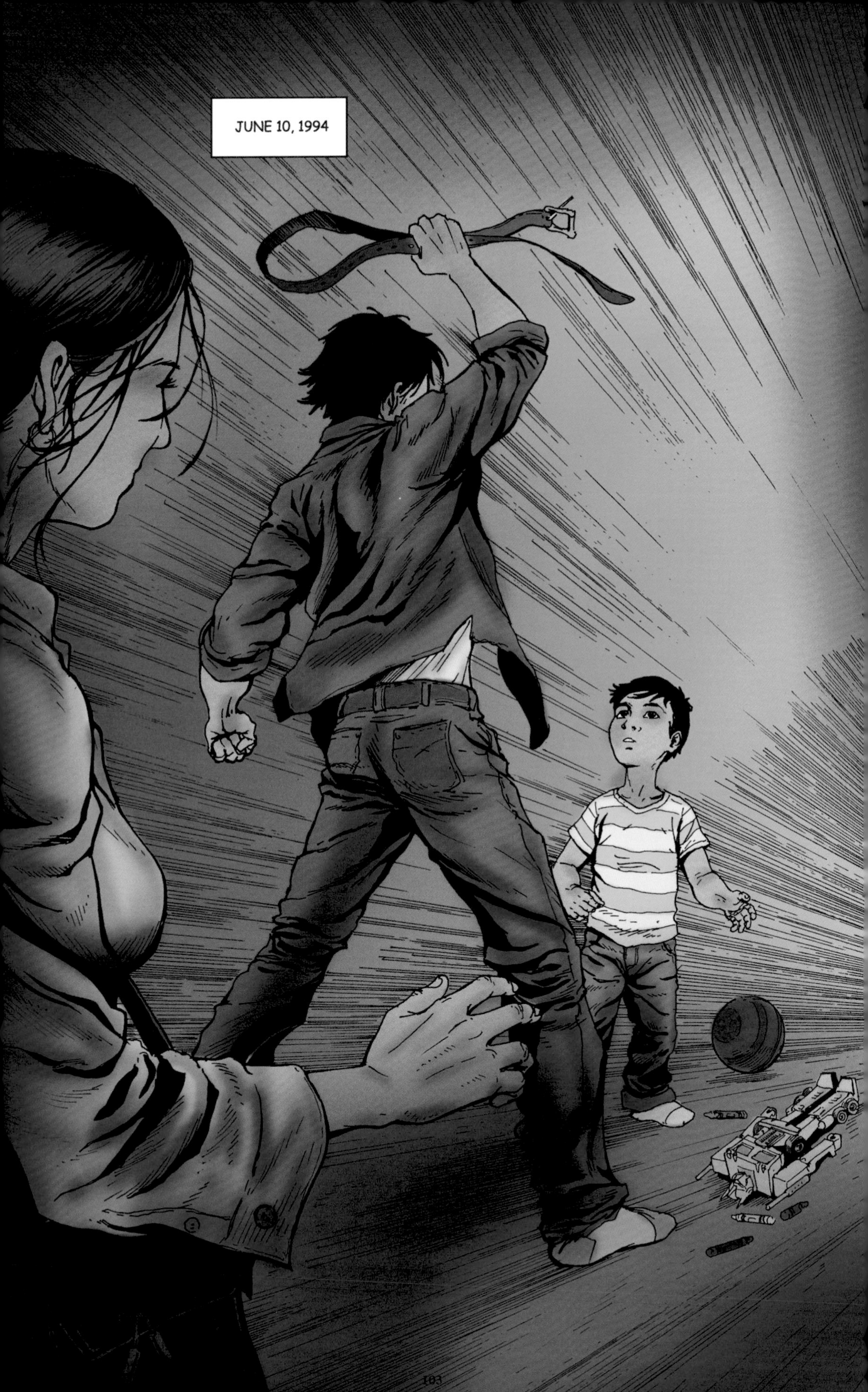
JUNE 10, 1994

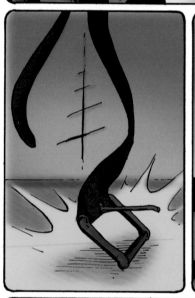

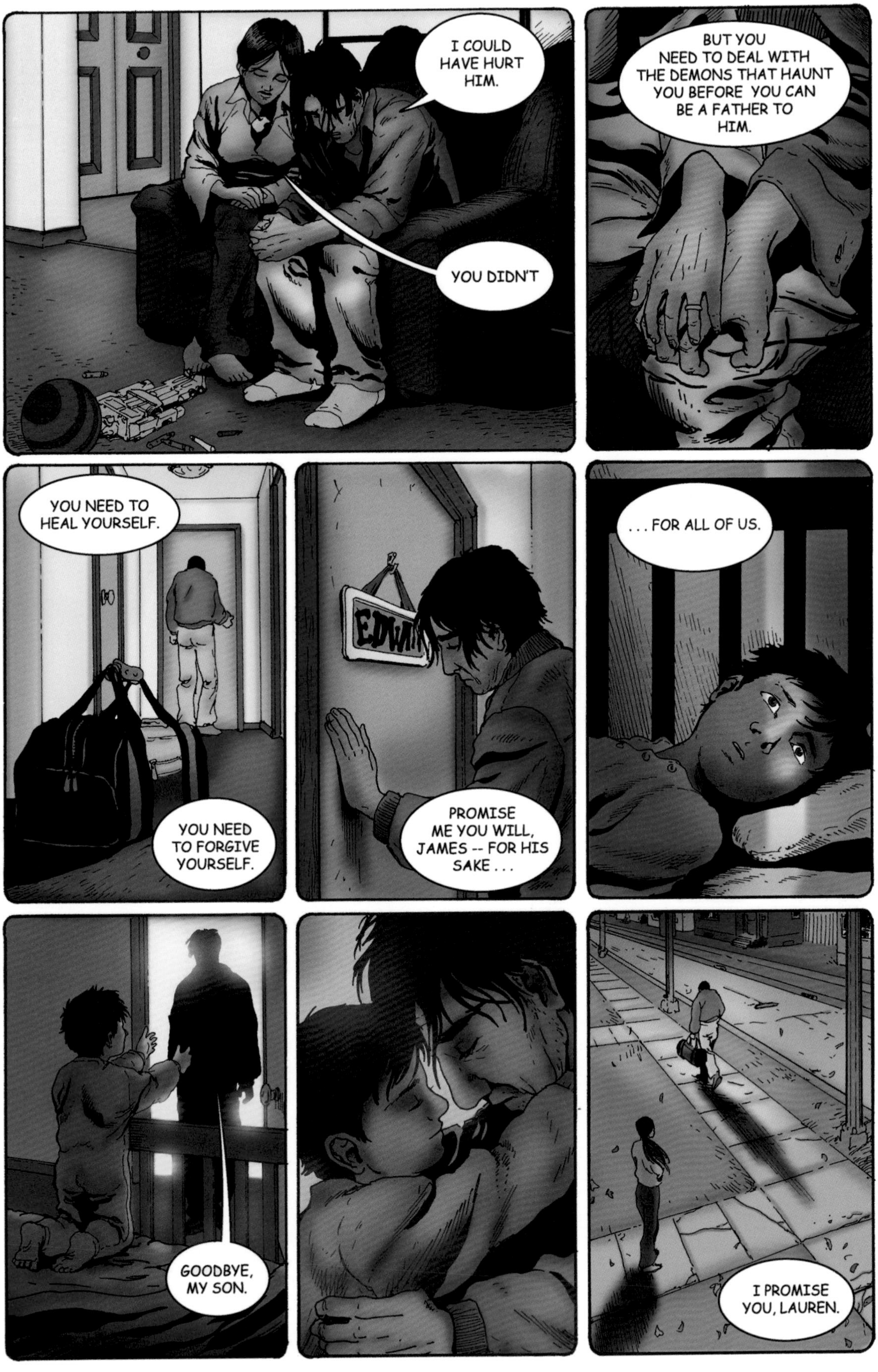
I COULD HAVE HURT HIM.
YOU DIDN'T
BUT YOU NEED TO DEAL WITH THE DEMONS THAT HAUNT YOU BEFORE YOU CAN BE A FATHER TO HIM.
YOU NEED TO HEAL YOURSELF.
YOU NEED TO FORGIVE YOURSELF.
PROMISE ME YOU WILL, JAMES -- FOR HIS SAKE . . .
. . . FOR ALL OF US.
GOODBYE, MY SON.
I PROMISE YOU, LAUREN.

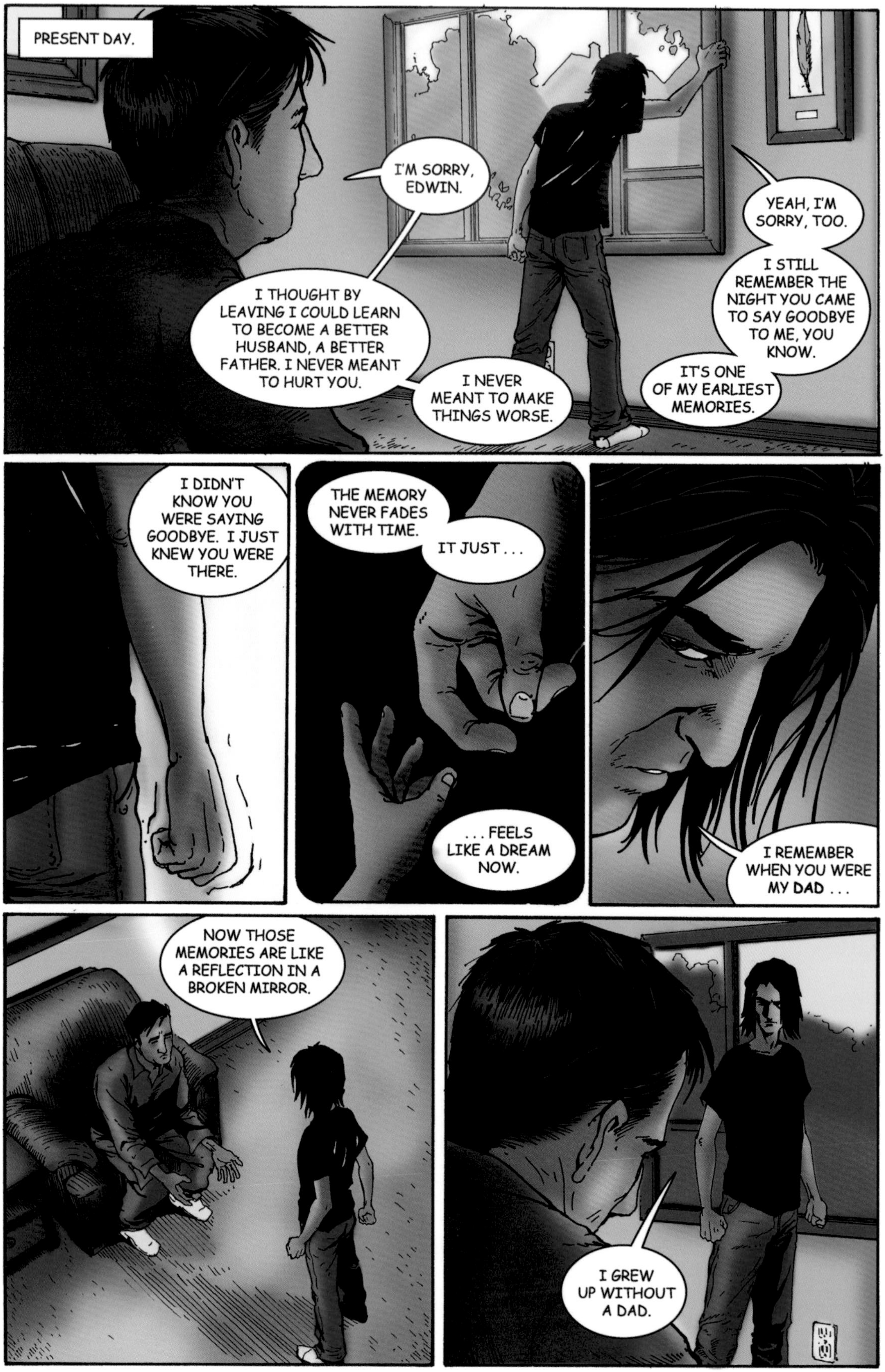
PRESENT DAY.
I'M SORRY, EDWIN.
I THOUGHT BY LEAVING I COULD LEARN TO BECOME A BETTER HUSBAND, A BETTER FATHER. I NEVER MEANT TO HURT YOU.
I NEVER MEANT TO MAKE THINGS WORSE.
YEAH, I'M SORRY, TOO.
I STILL REMEMBER THE NIGHT YOU CAME TO SAY GOODBYE TO ME, YOU KNOW.
IT'S ONE OF MY EARLIEST MEMORIES.
I DIDN'T KNOW YOU WERE SAYING GOODBYE. I JUST KNEW YOU WERE THERE.
THE MEMORY NEVER FADES WITH TIME.
IT JUST . . .
. . . FEELS LIKE A DREAM NOW.
I REMEMBER WHEN YOU WERE MY **DAD** . . .
NOW THOSE MEMORIES ARE LIKE A REFLECTION IN A BROKEN MIRROR.
I GREW UP WITHOUT A DAD.

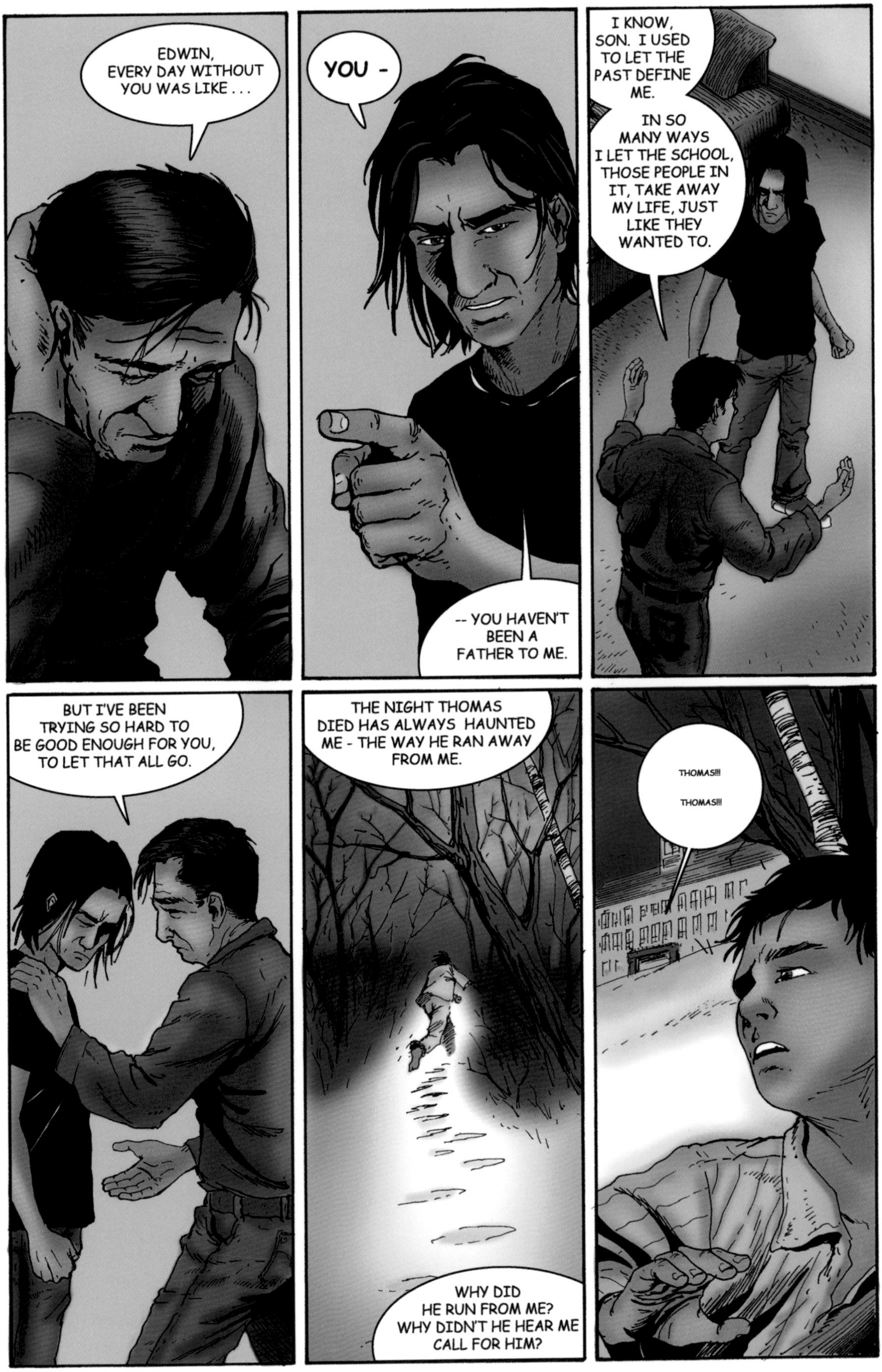
EDWIN, EVERY DAY WITHOUT YOU WAS LIKE . . .
YOU -
-- YOU HAVEN'T BEEN A FATHER TO ME.
I KNOW, SON. I USED TO LET THE PAST DEFINE ME.
IN SO MANY WAYS I LET THE SCHOOL, THOSE PEOPLE IN IT, TAKE AWAY MY LIFE, JUST LIKE THEY WANTED TO.
BUT I'VE BEEN TRYING SO HARD TO BE GOOD ENOUGH FOR YOU, TO LET THAT ALL GO.
THE NIGHT THOMAS DIED HAS ALWAYS HAUNTED ME - THE WAY HE RAN AWAY FROM ME.
WHY DID HE RUN FROM ME? WHY DIDN'T HE HEAR ME CALL FOR HIM?
THOMAS!!!
THOMAS!!!

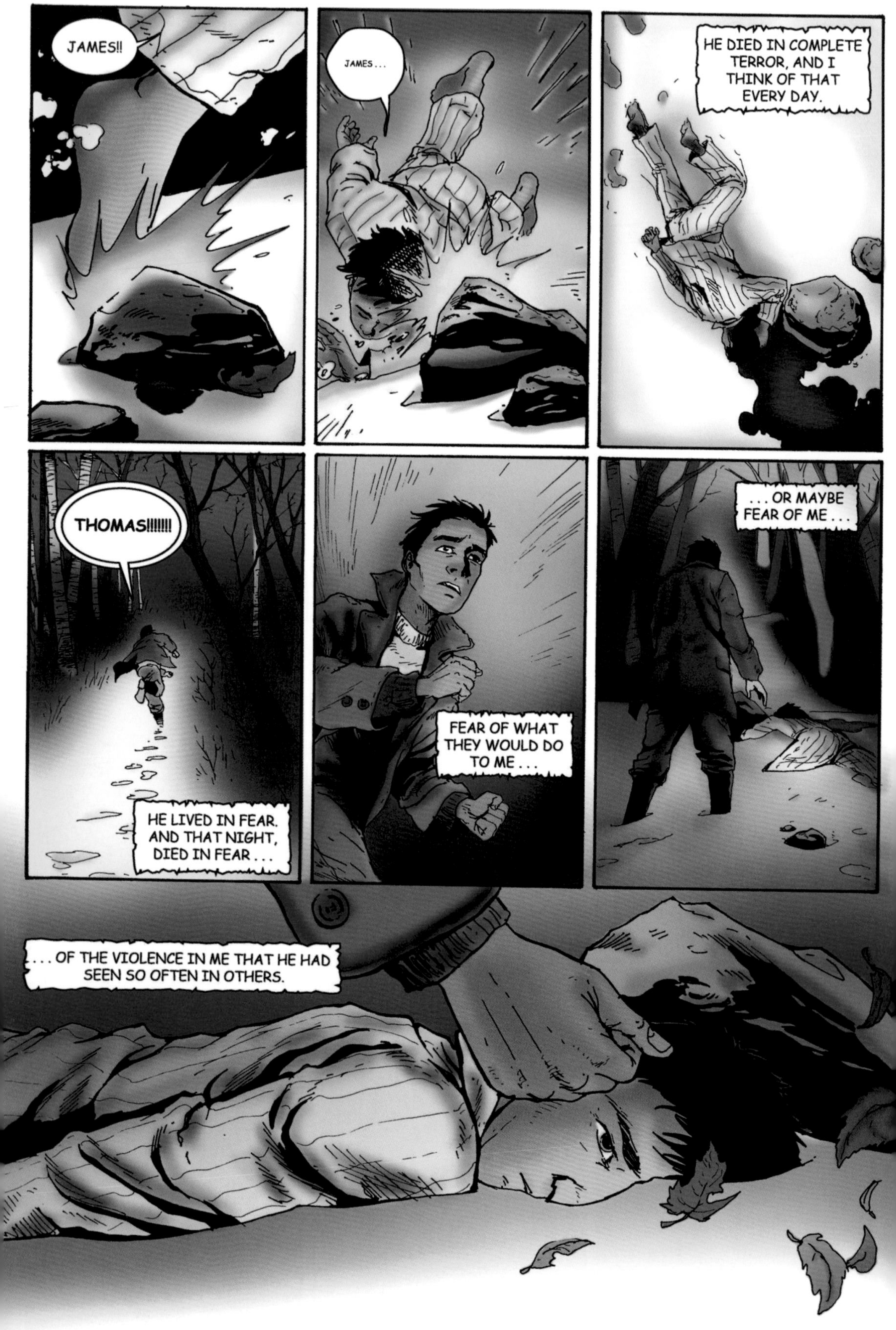
JAMES!!
JAMES . . .
HE DIED IN COMPLETE TERROR, AND I THINK OF THAT EVERY DAY.
THOMAS!!!!!!
HE LIVED IN FEAR. AND THAT NIGHT, DIED IN FEAR . . .
FEAR OF WHAT THEY WOULD DO TO ME . . .
. . . OR MAYBE FEAR OF ME . . .
. . . OF THE VIOLENCE IN ME THAT HE HAD SEEN SO OFTEN IN OTHERS.

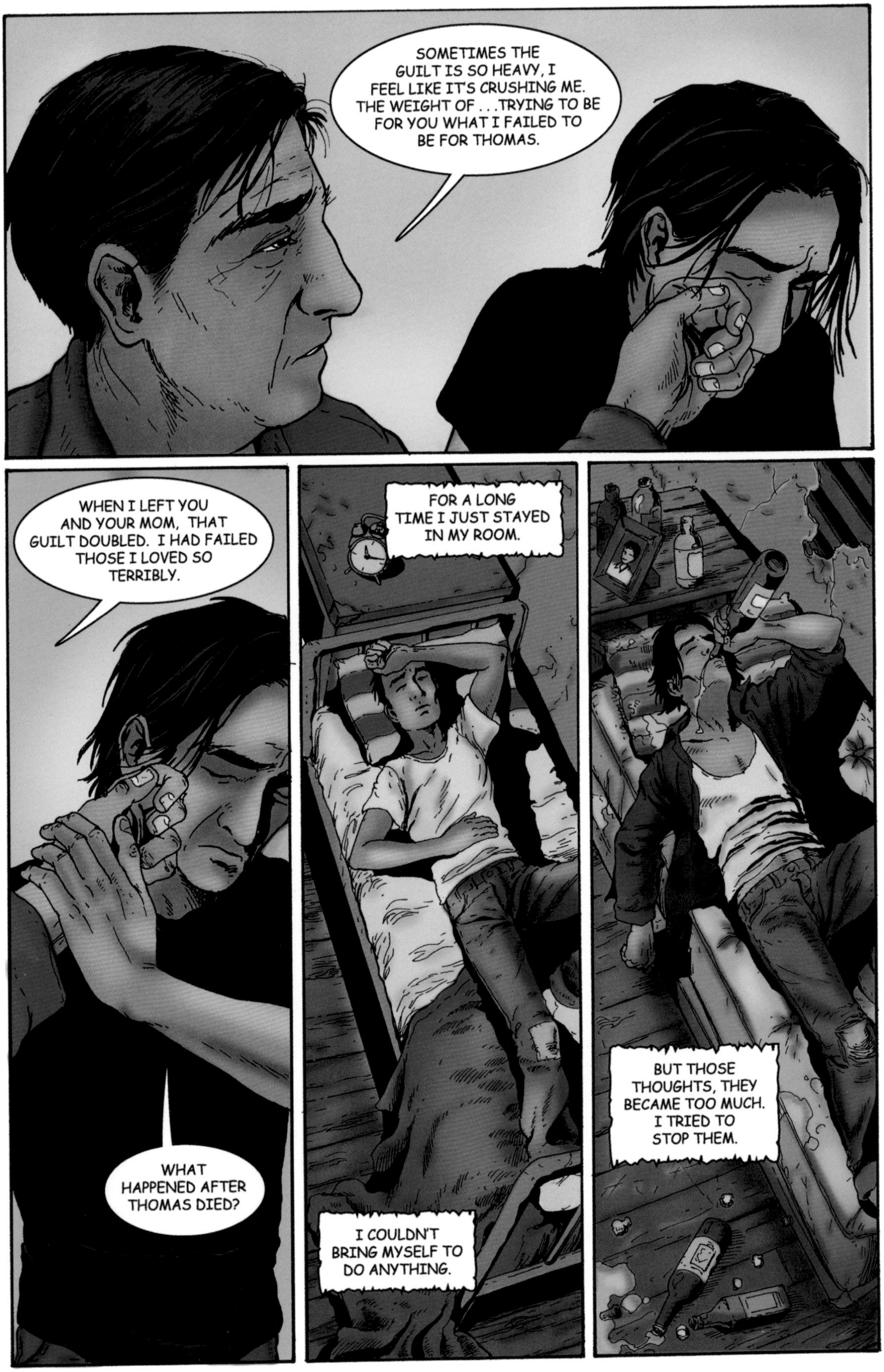
SOMETIMES THE GUILT IS SO HEAVY, I FEEL LIKE IT'S CRUSHING ME. THE WEIGHT OF . . . TRYING TO BE FOR YOU WHAT I FAILED TO BE FOR THOMAS.
WHEN I LEFT YOU AND YOUR MOM, THAT GUILT DOUBLED. I HAD FAILED THOSE I LOVED SO TERRIBLY.
WHAT HAPPENED AFTER THOMAS DIED?
FOR A LONG TIME I JUST STAYED IN MY ROOM.
I COULDN'T BRING MYSELF TO DO ANYTHING.
BUT THOSE THOUGHTS, THEY BECAME TOO MUCH. I TRIED TO STOP THEM.

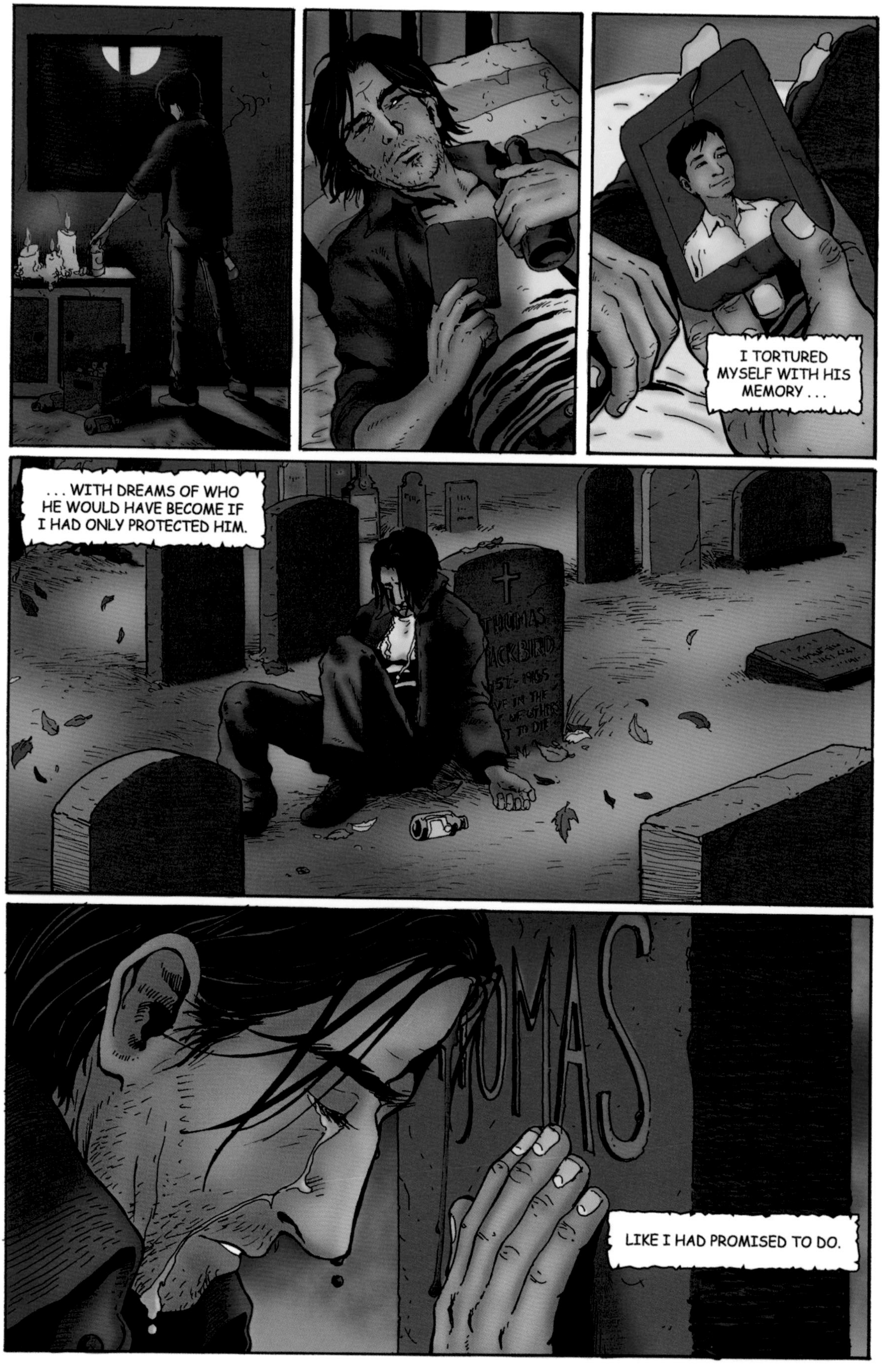
I TORTURED MYSELF WITH HIS MEMORY . . .
. . . WITH DREAMS OF WHO HE WOULD HAVE BECOME IF I HAD ONLY PROTECTED HIM.
LIKE I HAD PROMISED TO DO.

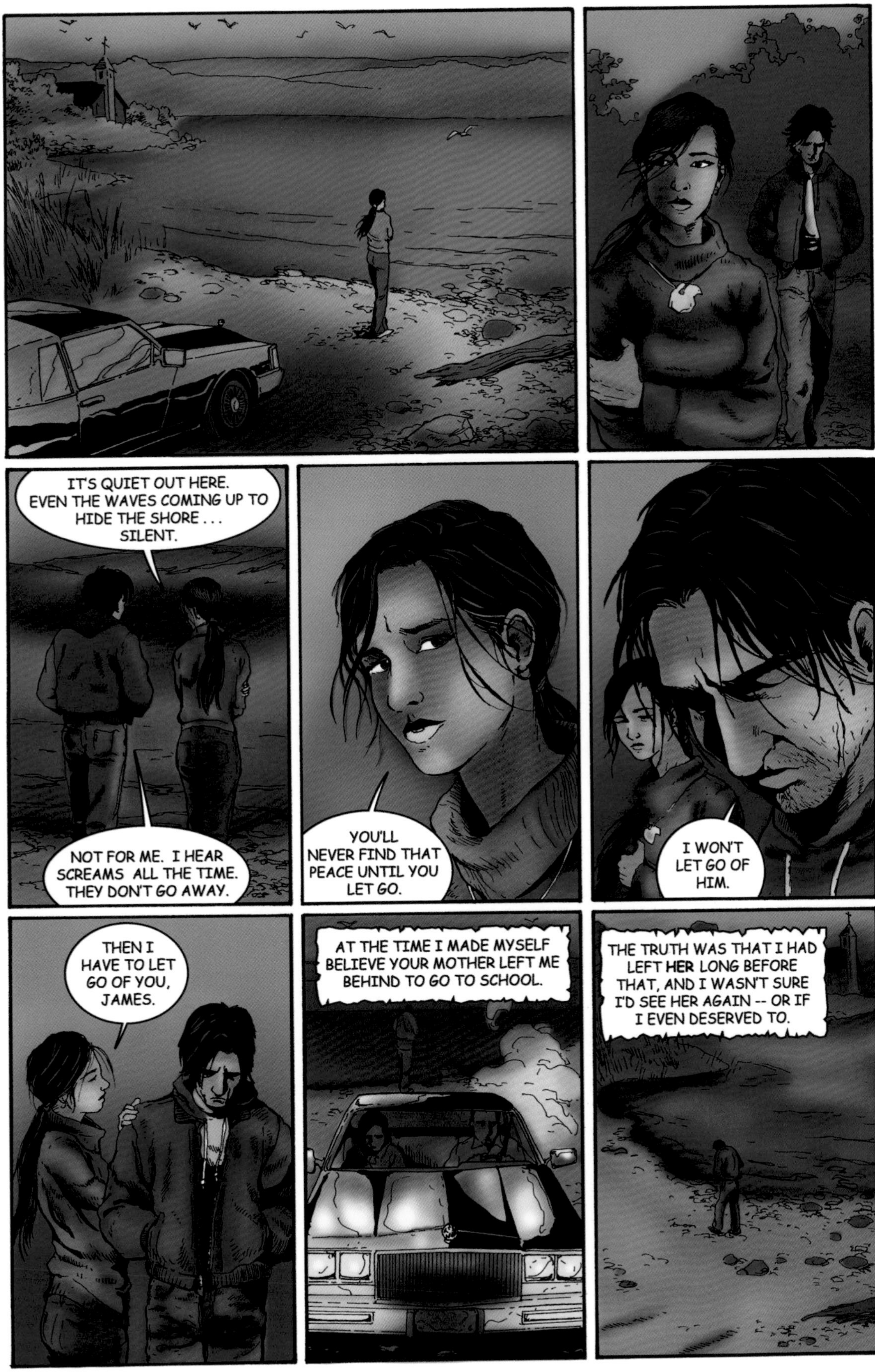
IT'S QUIET OUT HERE. EVEN THE WAVES COMING UP TO HIDE THE SHORE . . . SILENT.
NOT FOR ME. I HEAR SCREAMS ALL THE TIME. THEY DON'T GO AWAY.
YOU'LL NEVER FIND THAT PEACE UNTIL YOU LET GO.
I WON'T LET GO OF HIM.
THEN I HAVE TO LET GO OF YOU, JAMES.
AT THE TIME I MADE MYSELF BELIEVE YOUR MOTHER LEFT ME BEHIND TO GO TO SCHOOL.
THE TRUTH WAS THAT I HAD LEFT HER LONG BEFORE THAT, AND I WASN'T SURE I'D SEE HER AGAIN -- OR IF I EVEN DESERVED TO.

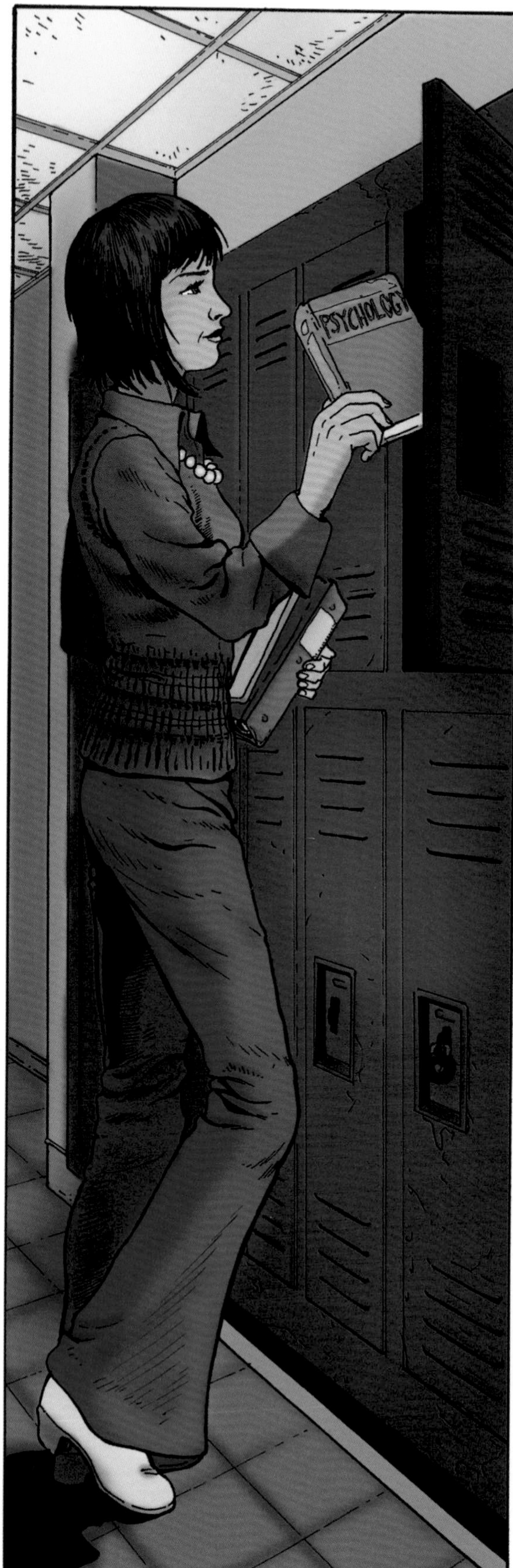
PSYCHOLOGY
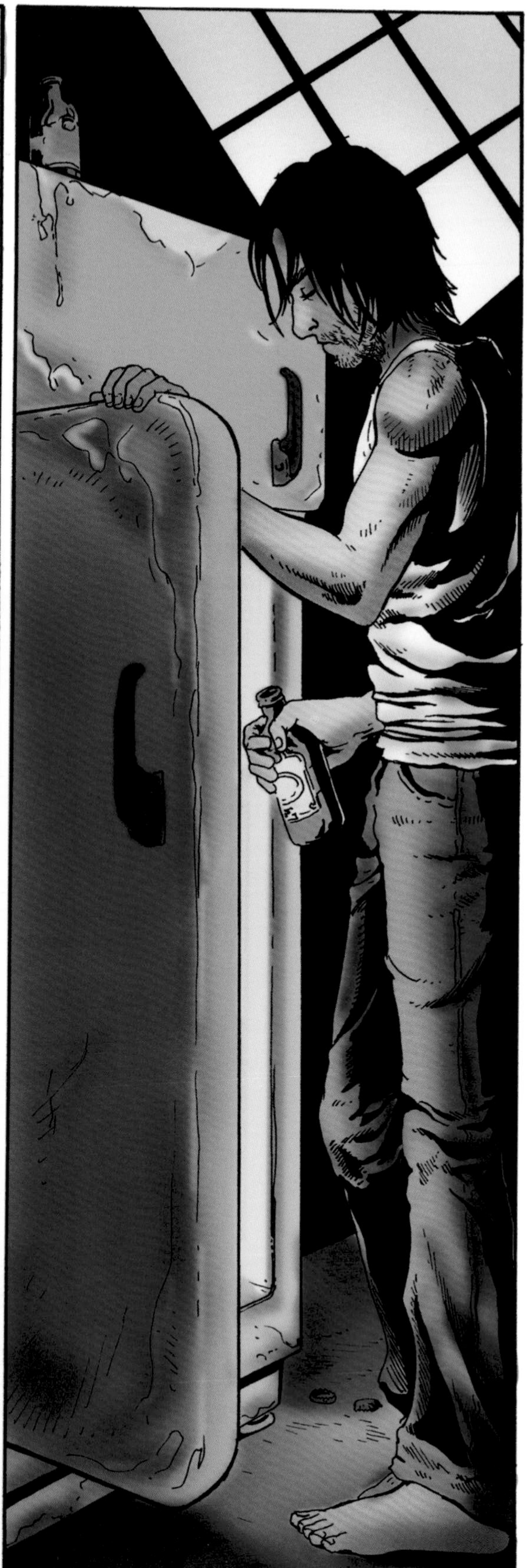

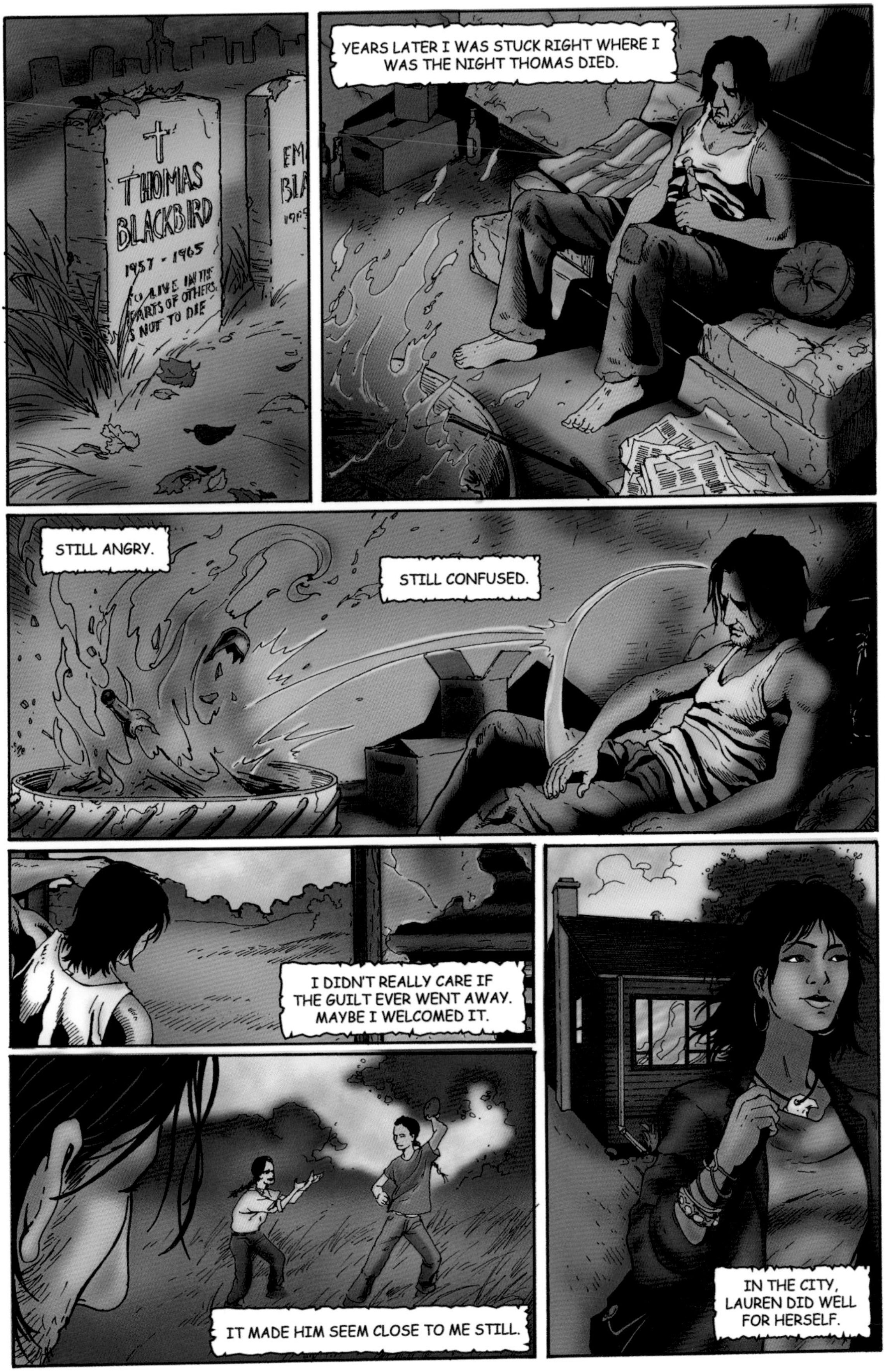
THOMAS
BLACKBIRD
1957 - 1965
TO LIVE IN THE
HEARTS OF OTHERS
IS NOT TO DIE
YEARS LATER I WAS STUCK RIGHT WHERE I WAS THE NIGHT THOMAS DIED.
STILL ANGRY.
STILL CONFUSED.
I DIDN'T REALLY CARE IF THE GUILT EVER WENT AWAY. MAYBE I WELCOMED IT.
IT MADE HIM SEEM CLOSE TO ME STILL.
IN THE CITY, LAUREN DID WELL FOR HERSELF.

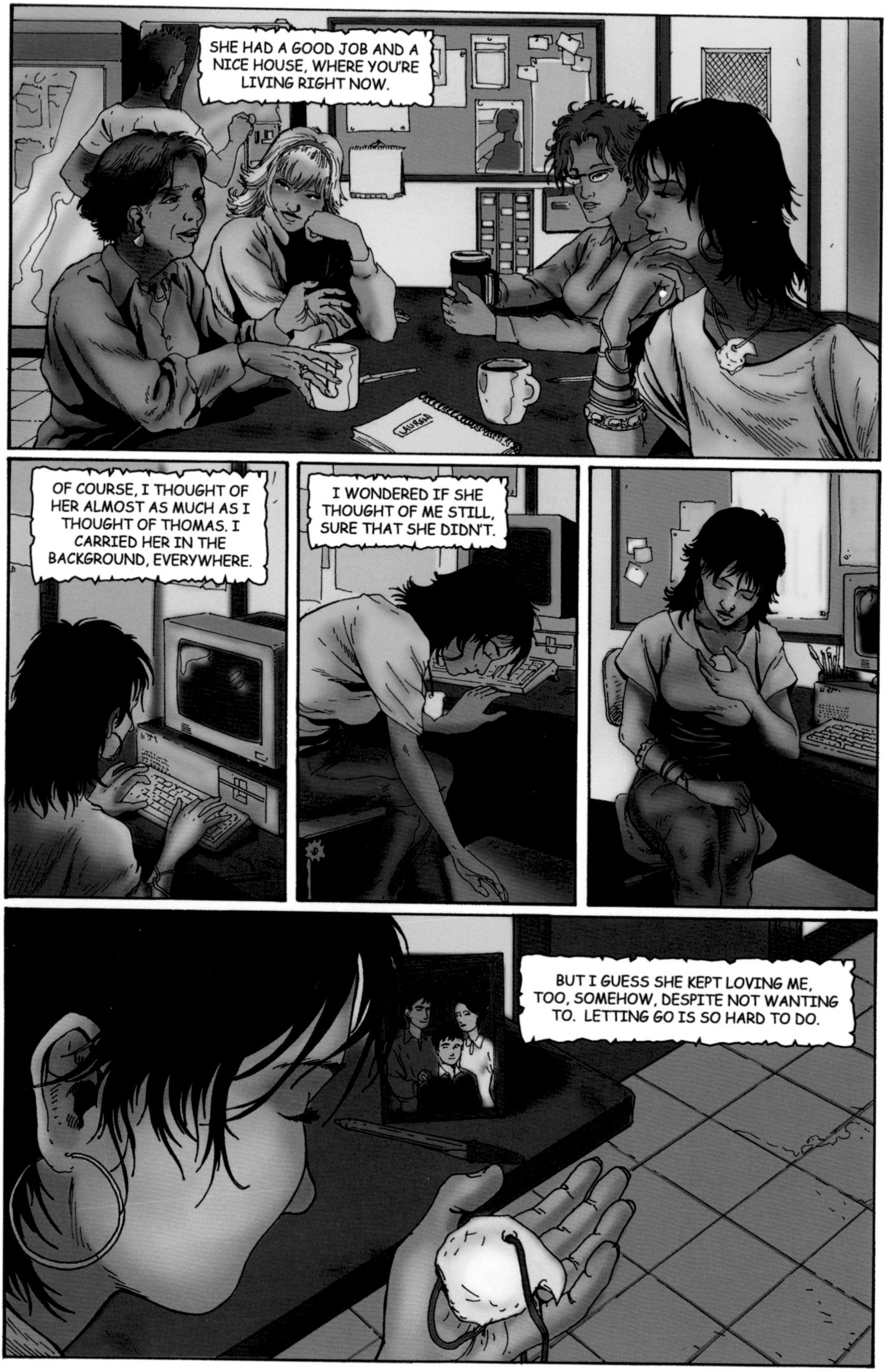
SHE HAD A GOOD JOB AND A NICE HOUSE, WHERE YOU'RE LIVING RIGHT NOW.
OF COURSE, I THOUGHT OF HER ALMOST AS MUCH AS I THOUGHT OF THOMAS. I CARRIED HER IN THE BACKGROUND, EVERYWHERE.
I WONDERED IF SHE THOUGHT OF ME STILL, SURE THAT SHE DIDN'T.
BUT I GUESS SHE KEPT LOVING ME, TOO, SOMEHOW, DESPITE NOT WANTING TO. LETTING GO IS SO HARD TO DO.

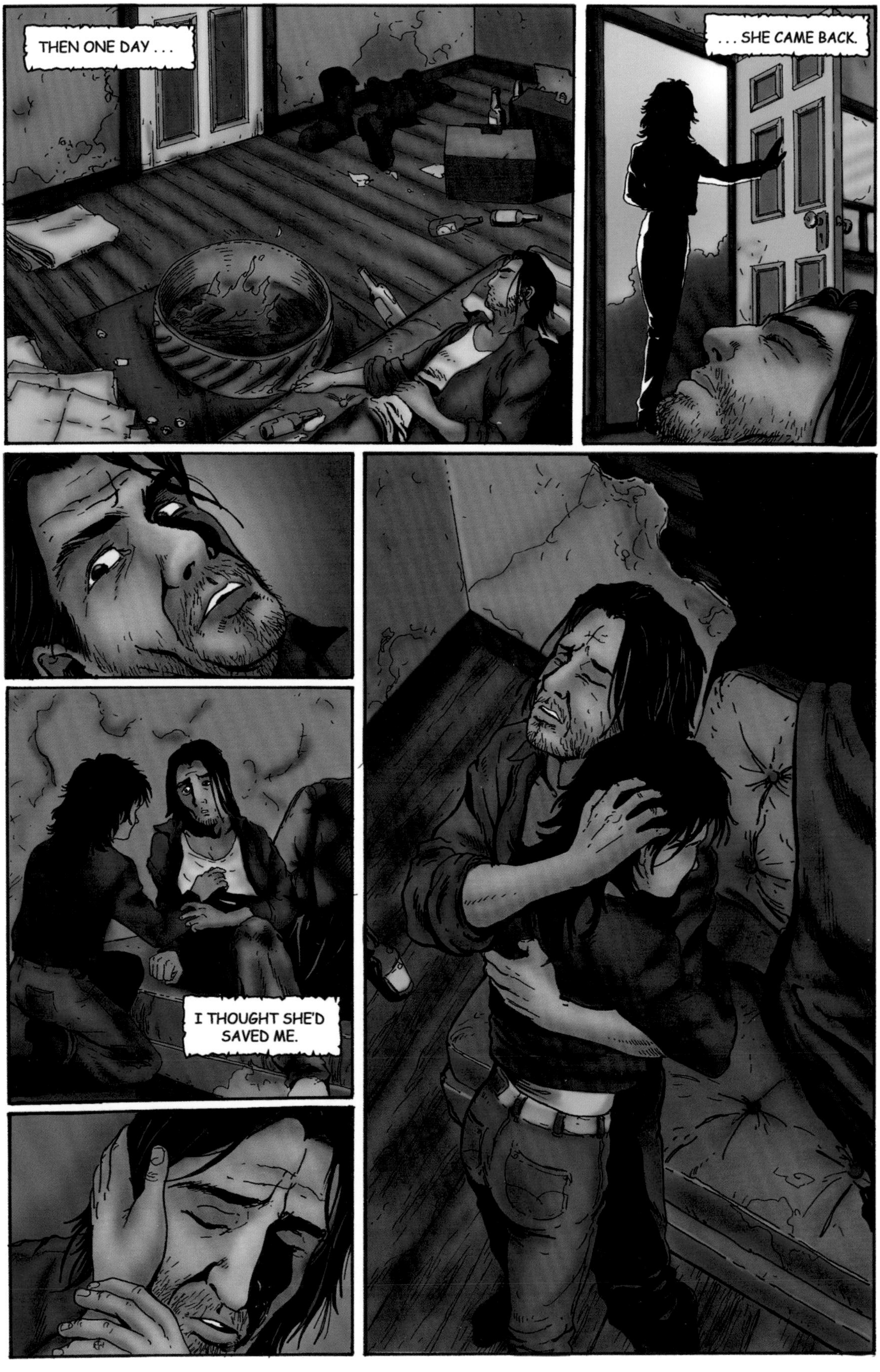
THEN ONE DAY . . .
. . . SHE CAME BACK.
I THOUGHT SHE'D SAVED ME.

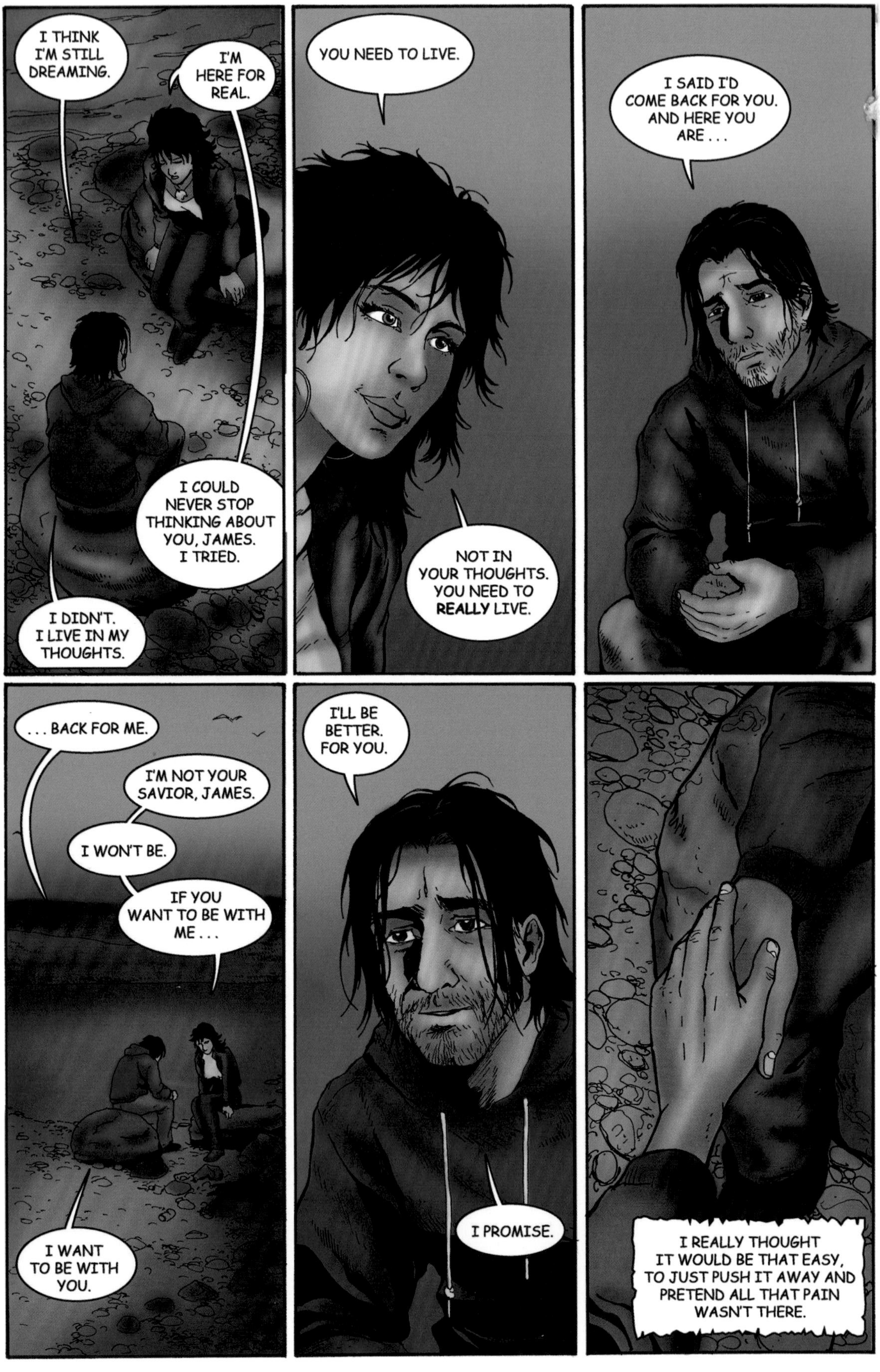
I THINK I'M STILL DREAMING.
I'M HERE FOR REAL.
I COULD NEVER STOP THINKING ABOUT YOU, JAMES. I TRIED.
I DIDN'T. I LIVE IN MY THOUGHTS.
YOU NEED TO LIVE.
NOT IN YOUR THOUGHTS. YOU NEED TO **REALLY** LIVE.
I SAID I'D COME BACK FOR YOU. AND HERE YOU ARE . . .
. . . BACK FOR ME.
I'M NOT YOUR SAVIOR, JAMES.
I WON'T BE.
IF YOU WANT TO BE WITH ME . . .
I WANT TO BE WITH YOU.
I'LL BE BETTER. FOR YOU.
I PROMISE.
I REALLY THOUGHT IT WOULD BE THAT EASY, TO JUST PUSH IT AWAY AND PRETEND ALL THAT PAIN WASN'T THERE.

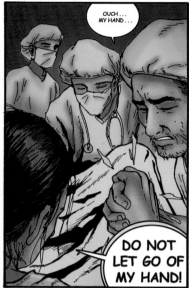

OUCH...
MY HAND...

DO NOT LET GO OF MY HAND!

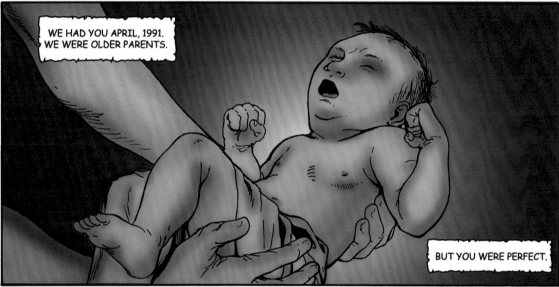

WE HAD YOU APRIL, 1991.
WE WERE OLDER PARENTS.

BUT YOU WERE PERFECT.

AND FOR THE FIRST TIME I REALIZED SOMETHING GOOD COULD COME FROM ME, EVEN AFTER SO MANY YEARS OF HOPELESSNESS.

YOU WERE MY HOPE.

MY LIGHT.

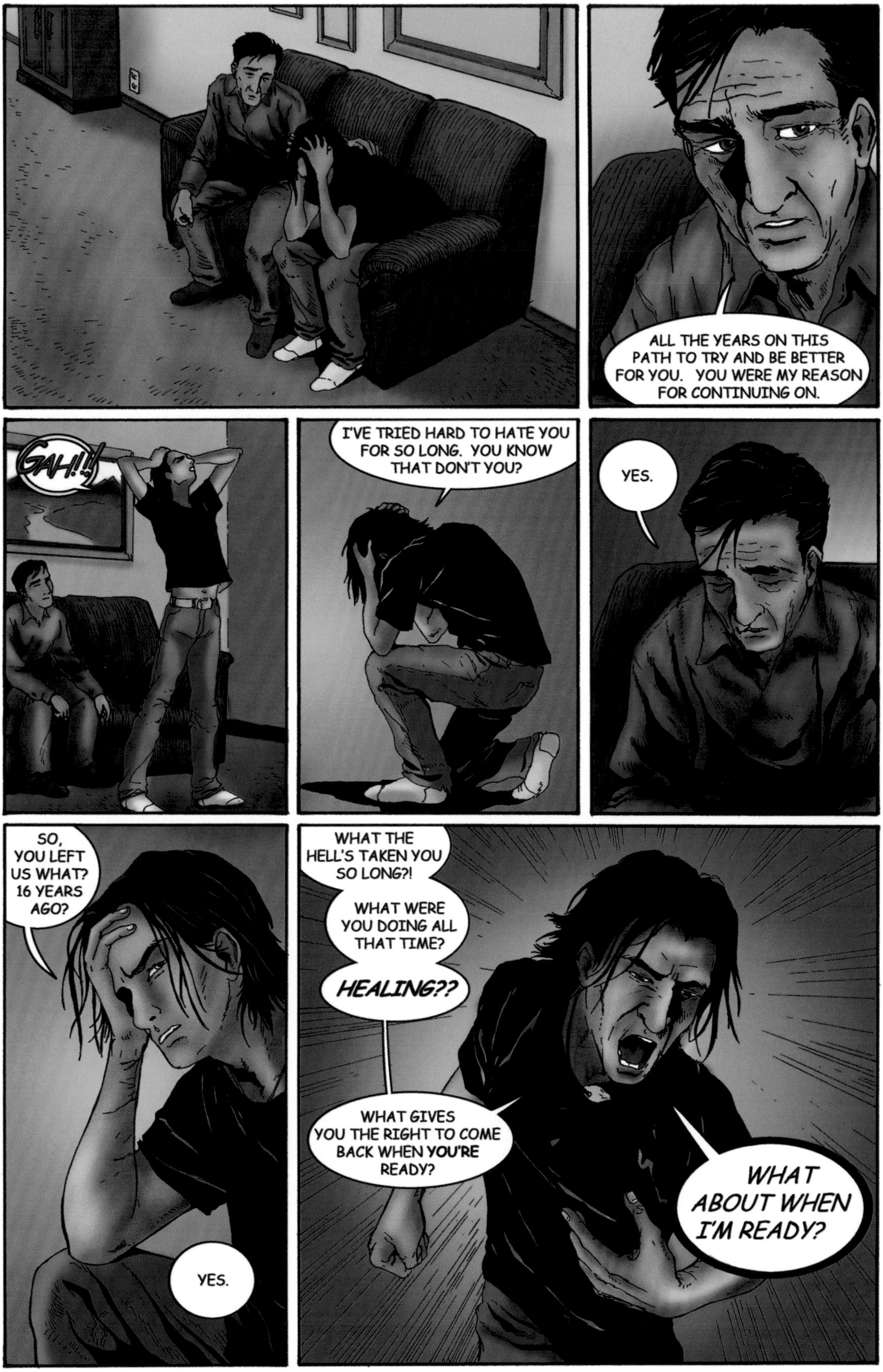
ALL THE YEARS ON THIS PATH TO TRY AND BE BETTER FOR YOU. YOU WERE MY REASON FOR CONTINUING ON.
GAH!!!
I'VE TRIED HARD TO HATE YOU FOR SO LONG. YOU KNOW THAT DON'T YOU?
YES.
SO, YOU LEFT US WHAT? 16 YEARS AGO?
YES.
WHAT THE HELL'S TAKEN YOU SO LONG?!
WHAT WERE YOU DOING ALL THAT TIME?
HEALING??
WHAT GIVES YOU THE RIGHT TO COME BACK WHEN YOU'RE READY?
WHAT ABOUT WHEN I'M READY?

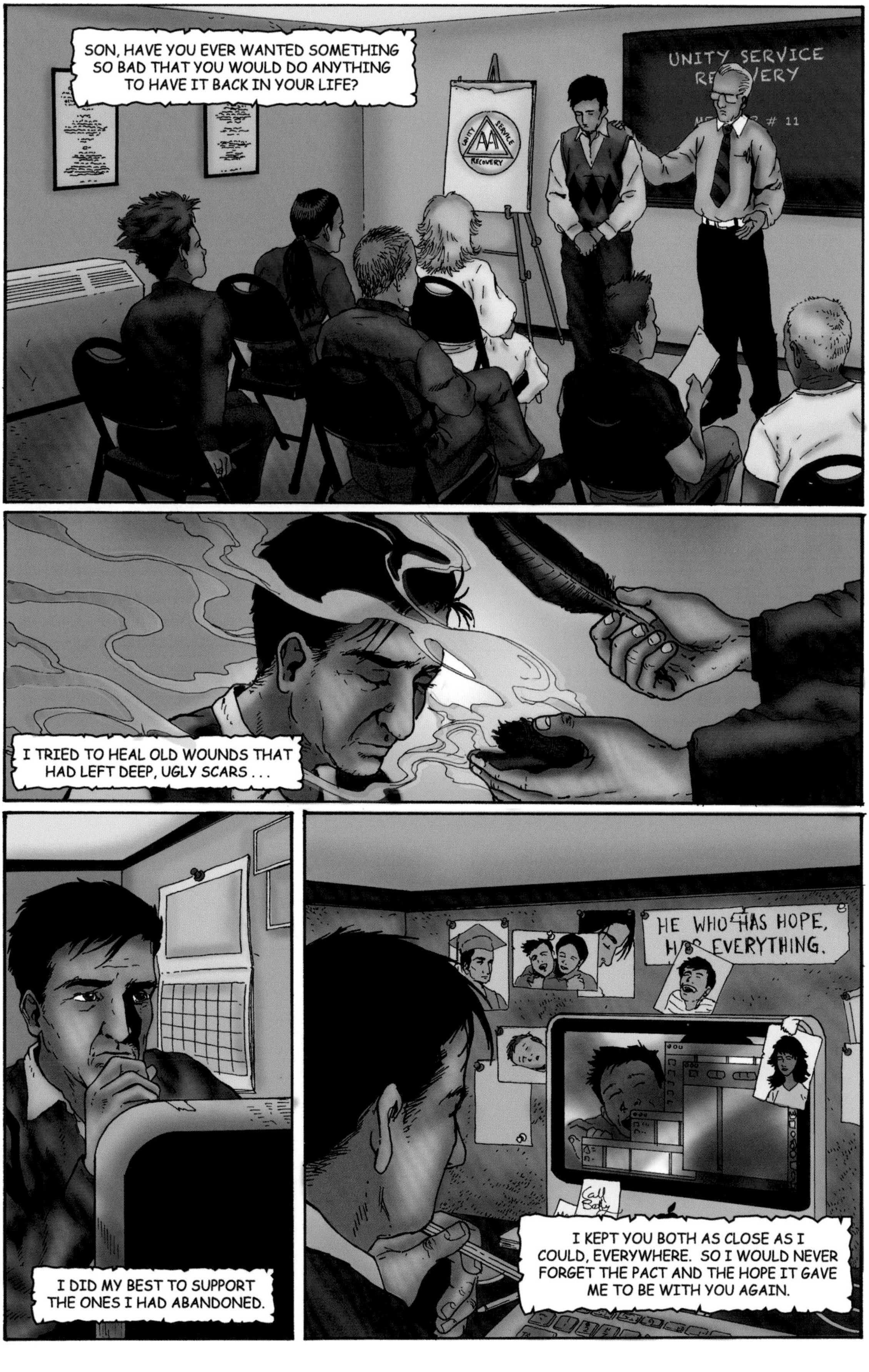
SON, HAVE YOU EVER WANTED SOMETHING SO BAD THAT YOU WOULD DO ANYTHING TO HAVE IT BACK IN YOUR LIFE?
UNITY SERVICE
I TRIED TO HEAL OLD WOUNDS THAT HAD LEFT DEEP, UGLY SCARS . . .
I DID MY BEST TO SUPPORT THE ONES I HAD ABANDONED.
HE WHO HAS HOPE,
I KEPT YOU BOTH AS CLOSE AS I COULD, EVERYWHERE. SO I WOULD NEVER FORGET THE PACT AND THE HOPE IT GAVE ME TO BE WITH YOU AGAIN.

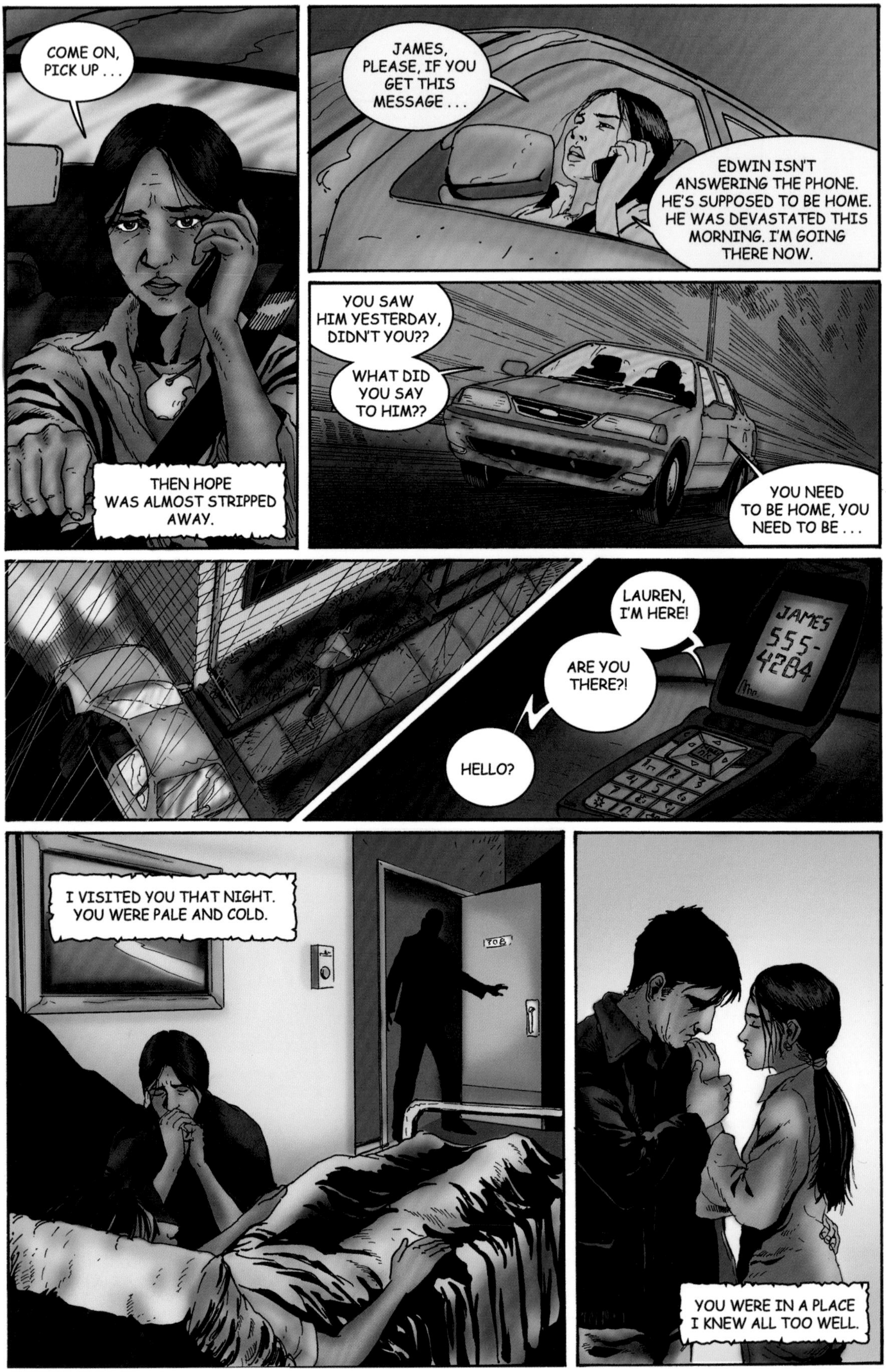
COME ON, PICK UP . . .
THEN HOPE WAS ALMOST STRIPPED AWAY.
JAMES, PLEASE, IF YOU GET THIS MESSAGE . . .
EDWIN ISN'T ANSWERING THE PHONE. HE'S SUPPOSED TO BE HOME. HE WAS DEVASTATED THIS MORNING. I'M GOING THERE NOW.
YOU SAW HIM YESTERDAY, DIDN'T YOU??
WHAT DID YOU SAY TO HIM??
YOU NEED TO BE HOME, YOU NEED TO BE . . .
LAUREN, I'M HERE!
ARE YOU THERE?!
HELLO?
JAMES 555-4284
I VISITED YOU THAT NIGHT. YOU WERE PALE AND COLD.
308
YOU WERE IN A PLACE I KNEW ALL TOO WELL.

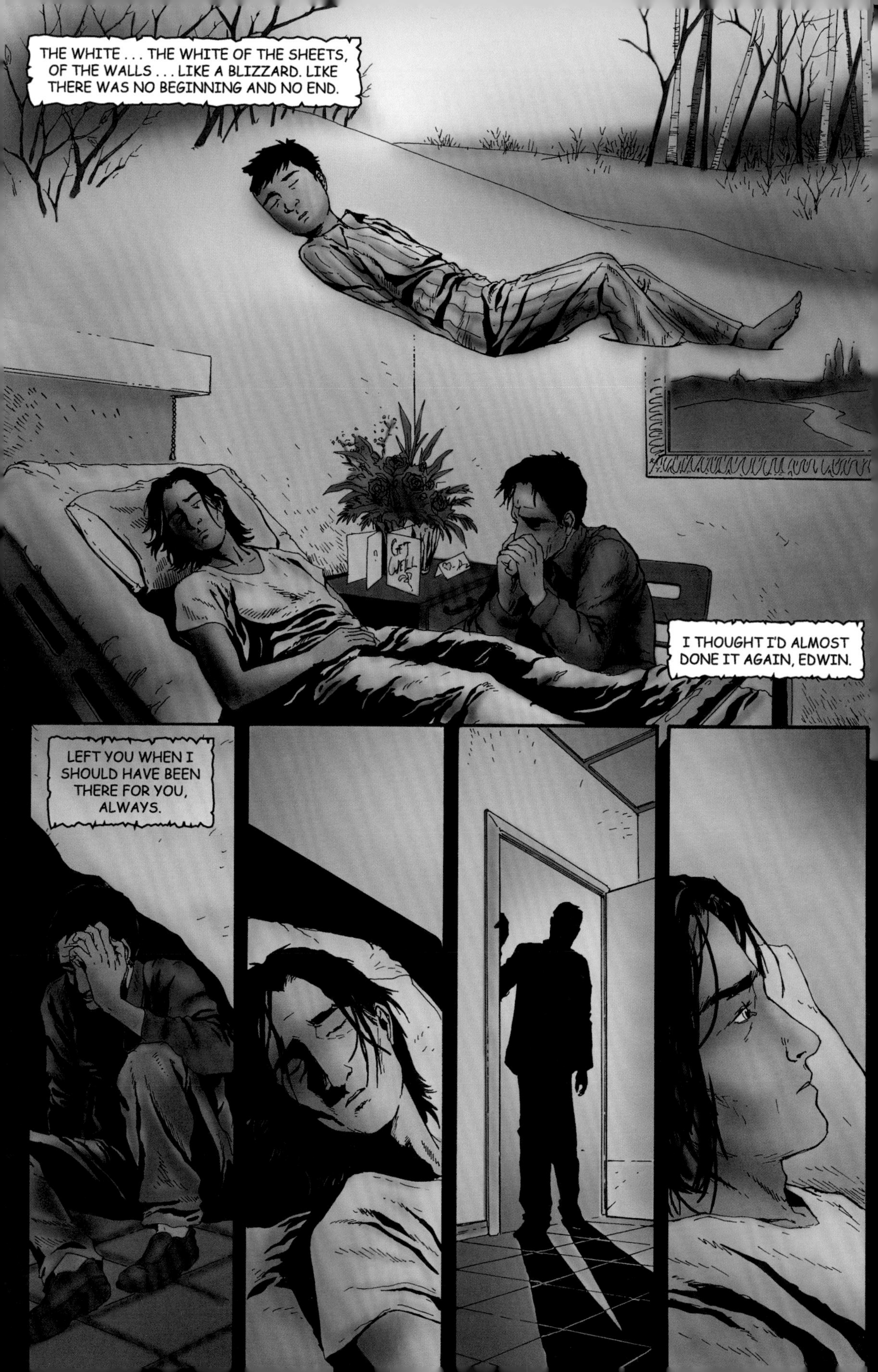
THE WHITE . . . THE WHITE OF THE SHEETS, OF THE WALLS . . . LIKE A BLIZZARD. LIKE THERE WAS NO BEGINNING AND NO END.
GET WELL
I THOUGHT I'D ALMOST DONE IT AGAIN, EDWIN.
LEFT YOU WHEN I SHOULD HAVE BEEN THERE FOR YOU, ALWAYS.

I DON'T WANT TO BE AWAY FROM YOU AGAIN.

I WANT TO BE HOME. I'M READY TO BE HOME

YOU KNOW WHAT? I HAVE WANTED SOMETHING SO BAD FOR SO MANY YEARS.

I WANTED A **FATHER**!!!!

YOU CAN'T MAGICALLY BECOME THAT AGAIN.

NOT SO QUICKLY.

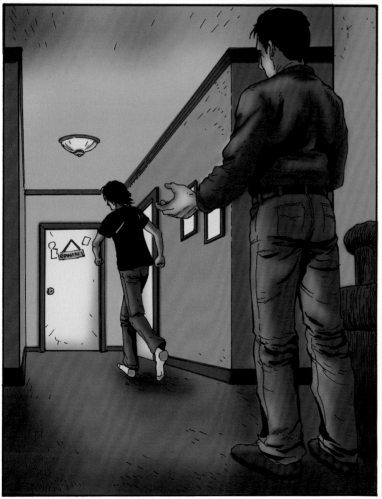

EDWIN, WAIT . . .

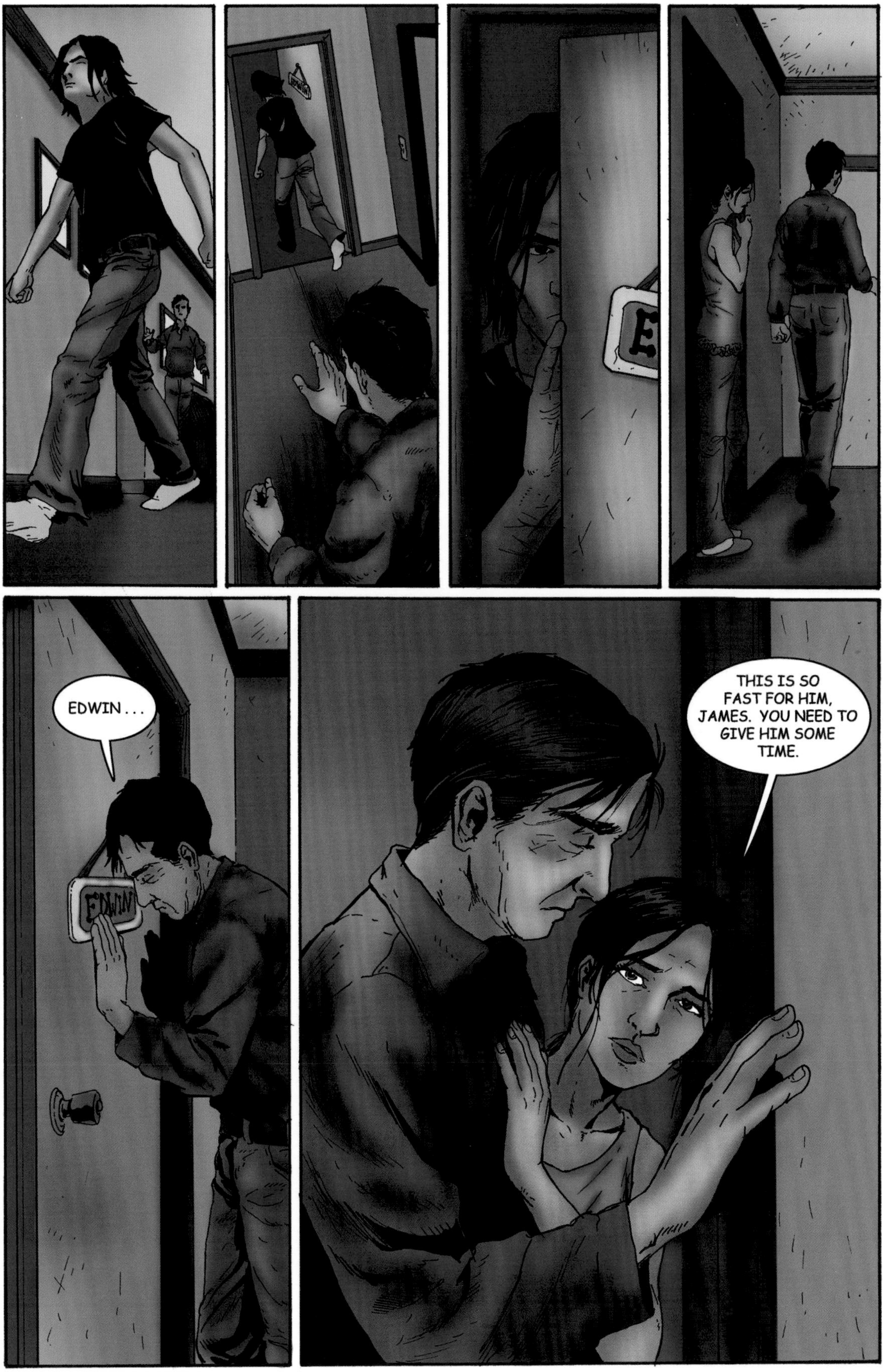
EDWIN
EDWIN
EDWIN . . .
EDWIN
THIS IS SO FAST FOR HIM, JAMES. YOU NEED TO GIVE HIM SOME TIME.

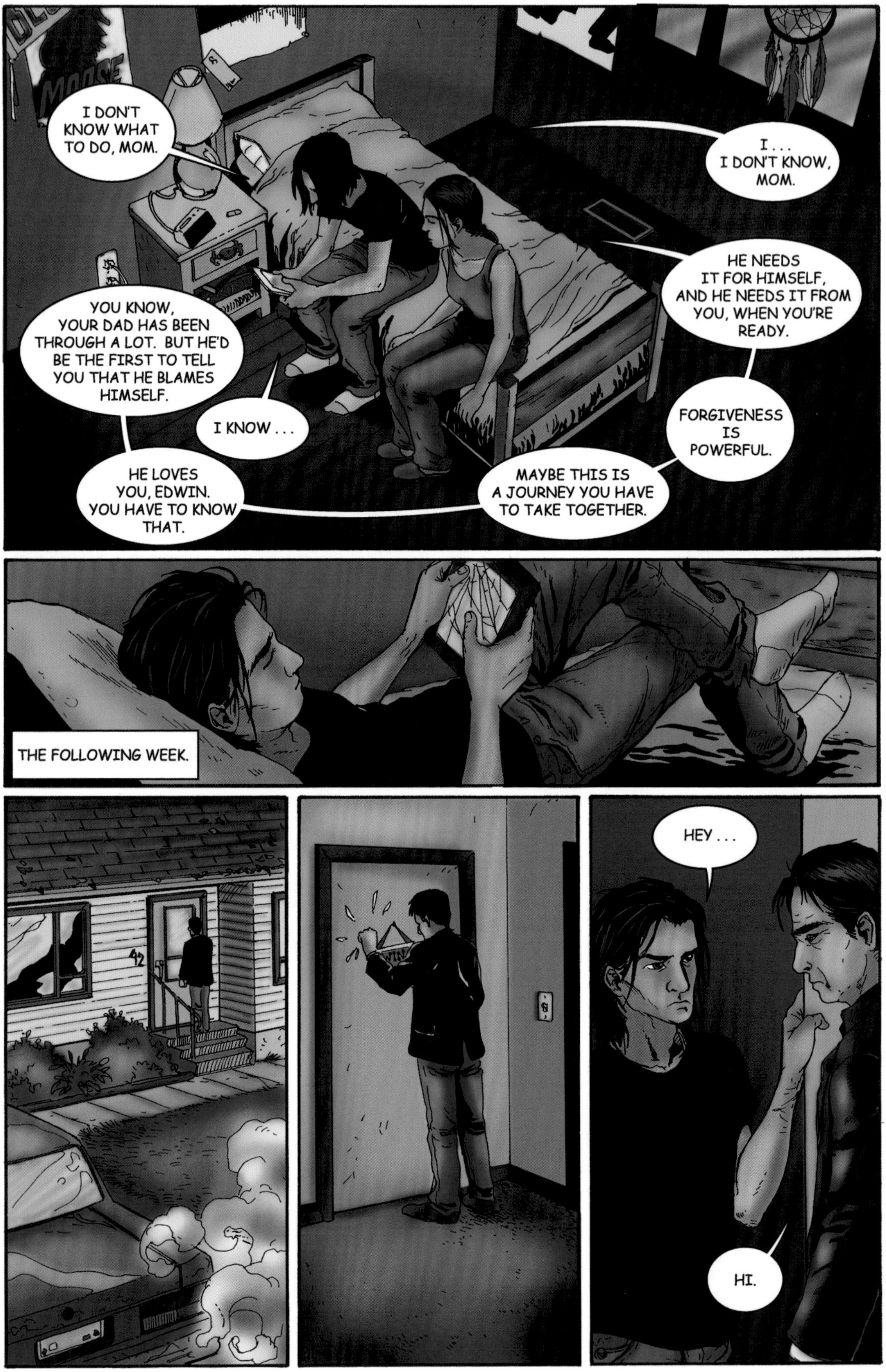
I DON'T KNOW WHAT TO DO, MOM.
YOU KNOW, YOUR DAD HAS BEEN THROUGH A LOT. BUT HE'D BE THE FIRST TO TELL YOU THAT HE BLAMES HIMSELF.
I KNOW . . .
HE LOVES YOU, EDWIN. YOU HAVE TO KNOW THAT.
MAYBE THIS IS A JOURNEY YOU HAVE TO TAKE TOGETHER.
FORGIVENESS IS POWERFUL.
HE NEEDS IT FOR HIMSELF, AND HE NEEDS IT FROM YOU, WHEN YOU'RE READY.
I . . . I DON'T KNOW, MOM.
THE FOLLOWING WEEK.
HEY . . .
HI.

DOES THIS HELP YOU?

I STILL HAVE NIGHTMARES.

HOW DO YOU KNOW THEY'RE NIGHTMARES?

BECAUSE I'M SCARED.

WE ALL GET SCARED, SON.

YEAH . . .

THERE IS ALWAYS A WAY OUT.

YOU JUST HAVE TO FIND THE PATH.

ONE OF THE THINGS THAT HELPED ME WAS COMING TO KNOW OUR WAYS AGAIN, FINDING THOSE THINGS I'D LOST WHEN I WAS YOUNG.

THOSE PARTS OF US HELP TO MAKE US WHOLE, SON.

THEY'RE PIECES OF WHO WE ARE.

I WANT TO TAKE YOU SOMEWHERE.

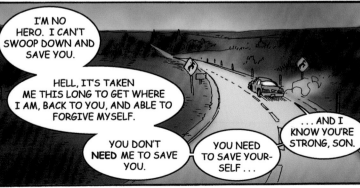

I'M NO HERO. I CAN'T SWOOP DOWN AND SAVE YOU.

HELL, IT'S TAKEN ME THIS LONG TO GET WHERE I AM, BACK TO YOU, AND ABLE TO FORGIVE MYSELF.

YOU DON'T **NEED** ME TO SAVE YOU.

YOU NEED TO SAVE YOURSELF . . .

. . . AND I KNOW YOU'RE STRONG, SON.

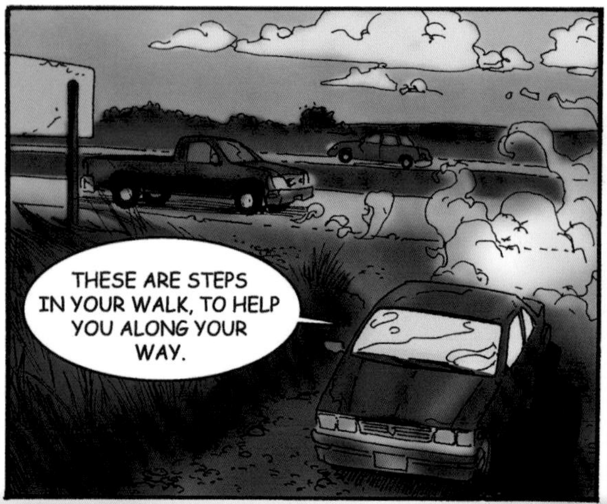
THESE ARE STEPS IN YOUR WALK, TO HELP YOU ALONG YOUR WAY.

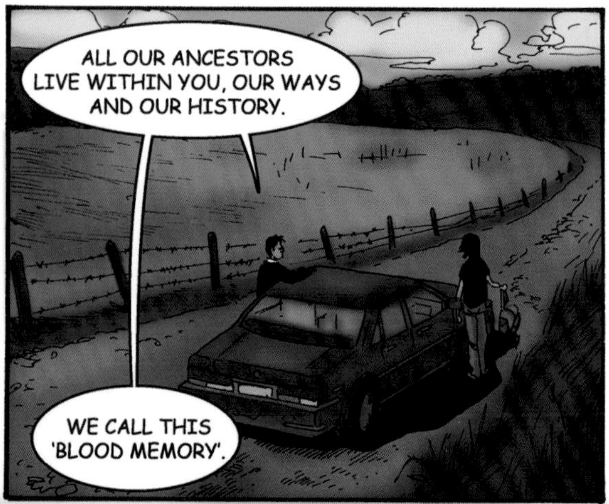
ALL OUR ANCESTORS LIVE WITHIN YOU, OUR WAYS AND OUR HISTORY.
WE CALL THIS 'BLOOD MEMORY'.

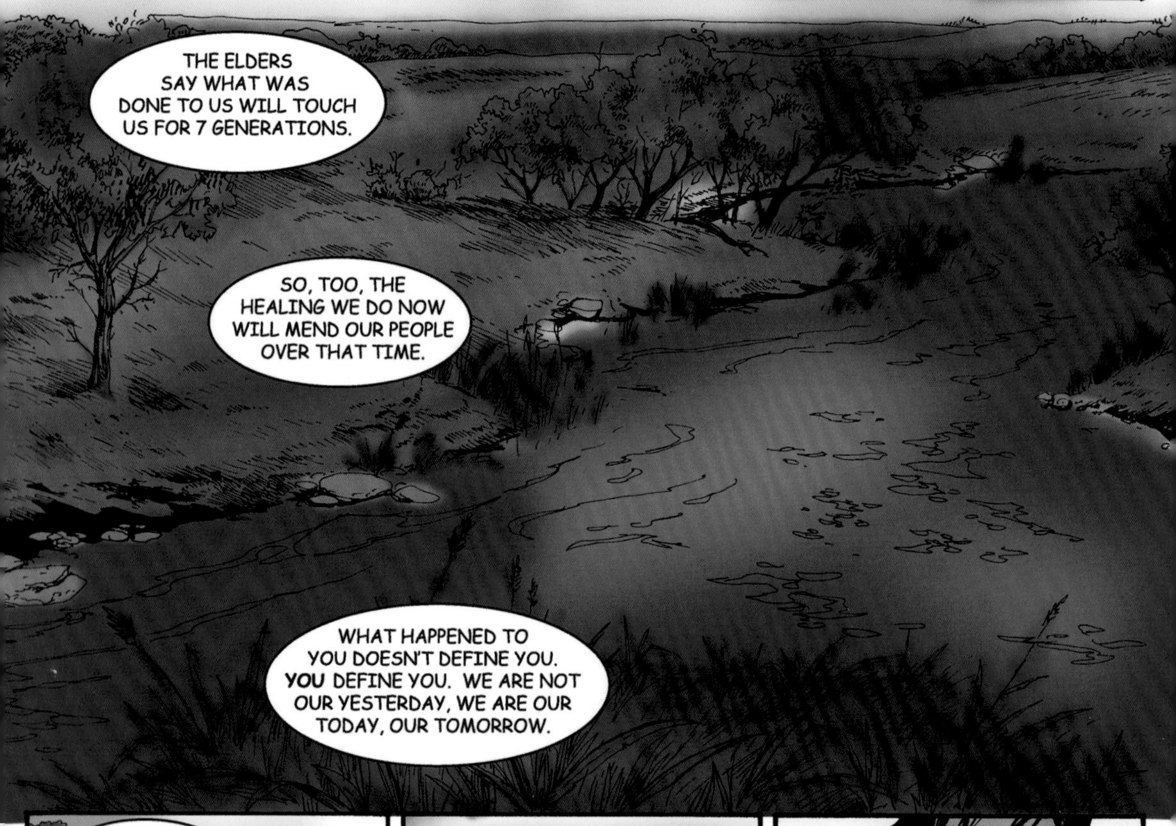
THE ELDERS SAY WHAT WAS DONE TO US WILL TOUCH US FOR 7 GENERATIONS.
SO, TOO, THE HEALING WE DO NOW WILL MEND OUR PEOPLE OVER THAT TIME.
WHAT HAPPENED TO YOU DOESN'T DEFINE YOU. **YOU** DEFINE YOU. WE ARE NOT OUR YESTERDAY, WE ARE OUR TODAY, OUR TOMORROW.

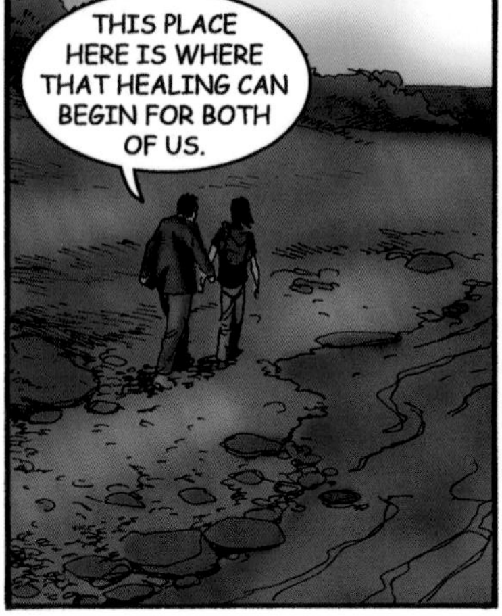
THIS PLACE HERE IS WHERE THAT HEALING CAN BEGIN FOR BOTH OF US.

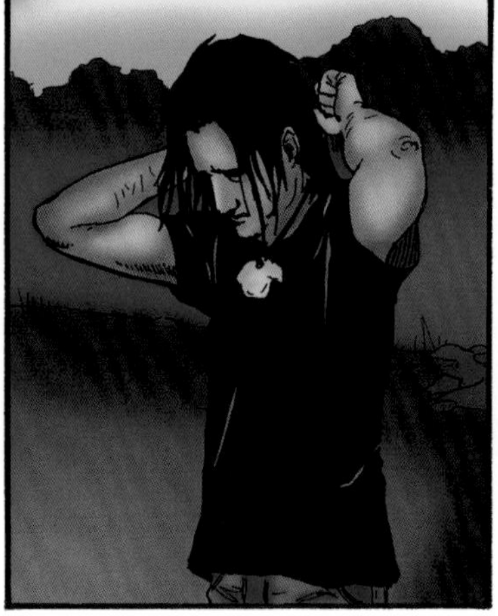

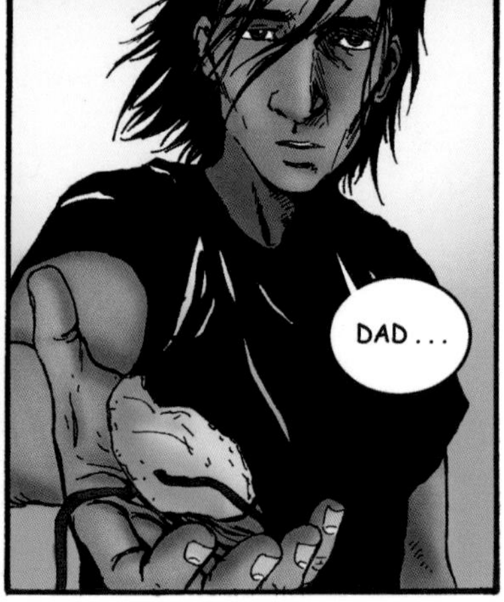
DAD . . .

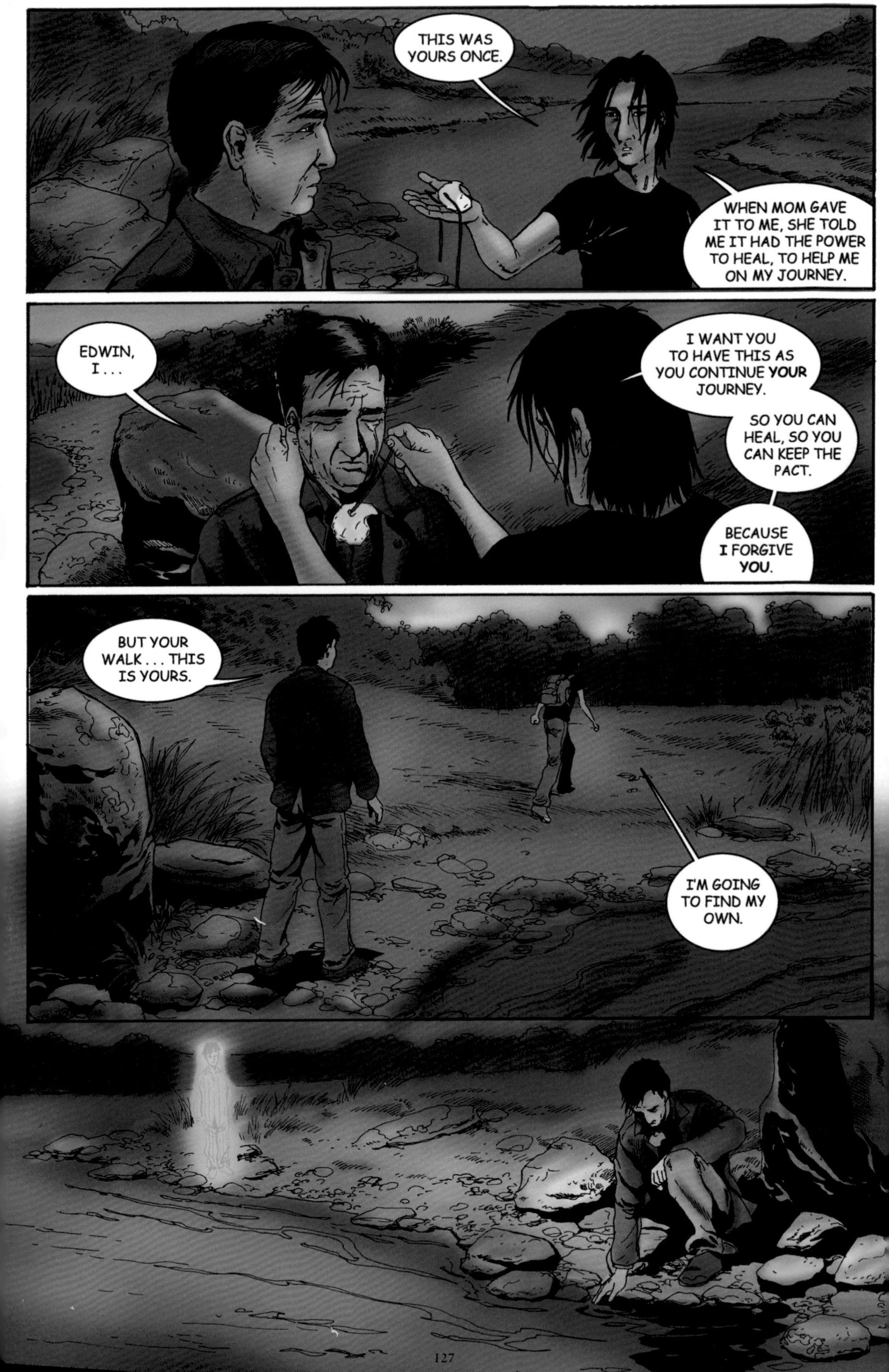
THIS WAS YOURS ONCE.
WHEN MOM GAVE IT TO ME, SHE TOLD ME IT HAD THE POWER TO HEAL, TO HELP ME ON MY JOURNEY.
EDWIN, I . . .
I WANT YOU TO HAVE THIS AS YOU CONTINUE YOUR JOURNEY.
SO YOU CAN HEAL, SO YOU CAN KEEP THE PACT.
BECAUSE I FORGIVE YOU.
BUT YOUR WALK . . . THIS IS YOURS.
I'M GOING TO FIND MY OWN.

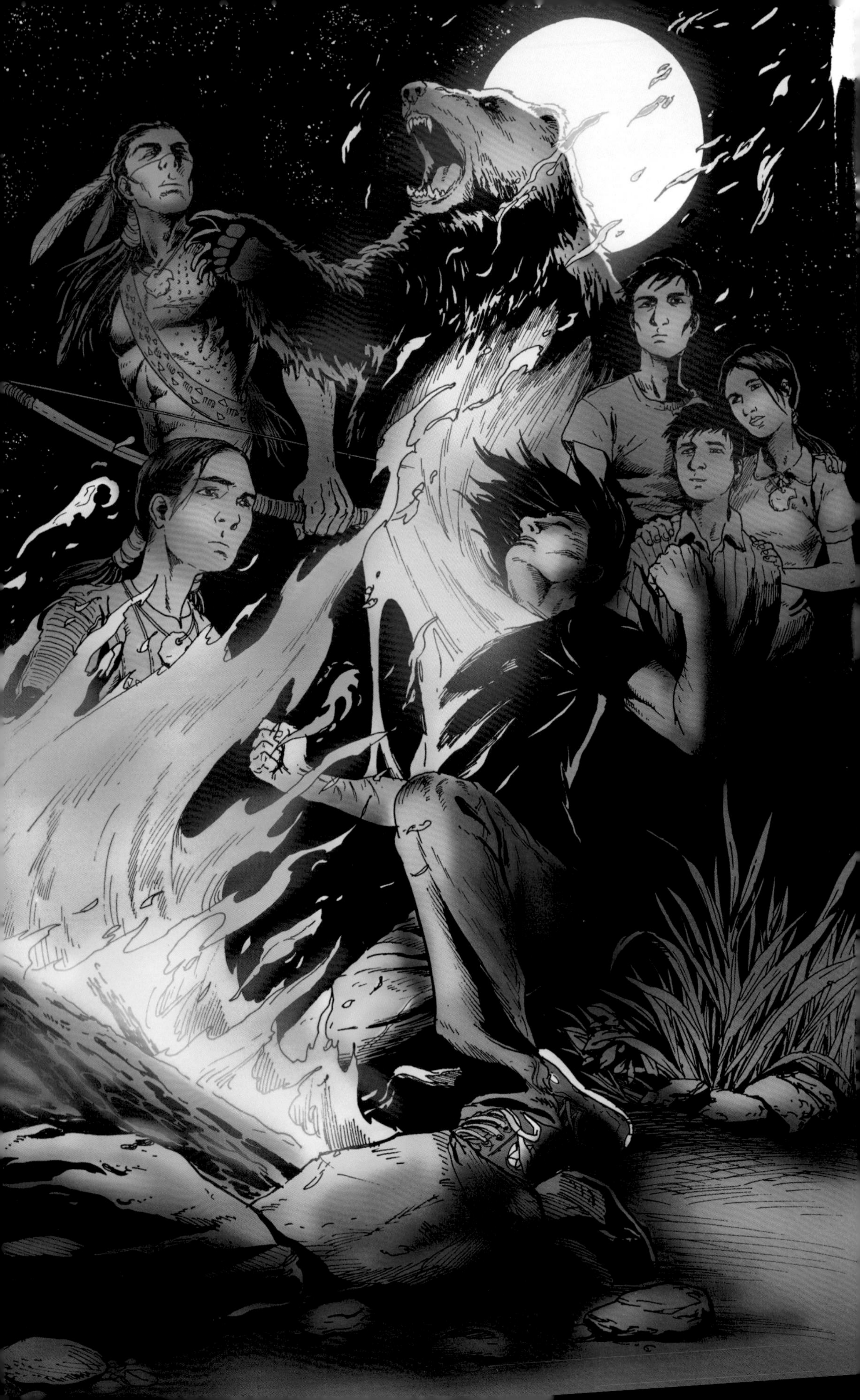

About the author

DAVID A. ROBERTSON (he/him/his) is an award-winning writer. His books include *When We Were Alone* (winner *Governor General's Literary Award*), *Will I See?* (winner *Manuela Dias Book Design and Illustration Award*), *Betty, The Helen Betty Osborne Story* (listed In *The Margins*), and the YA novel *Strangers* (winner of *The Michael Van Rooy Award for Genre Fiction*). David educates as well as entertains through his writings about Indigenous Peoples in Canada, reflecting their cultures, histories, communities, as well as illuminating many contemporary issues. David is a member of Norway House Cree Nation. He lives in Winnipeg.

About the illustrator

SCOTT B. HENDERSON (he/him/his) is author/illustrator of the sci-fi/fantasy comic, The Chronicles of Era and has illustrated select titles in the Canadian Air Force's For Valour series, Tales From Big Spirit series, the graphic novel series 7 Generations, *Betty: The Helen Betty Osborne Story*, select stories in *This Place: 150 Years Retold*, and Eisner-award nominee, *A Blanket of Butterflies*. In 2016, he was the recipient of the C4 Central Canada Comic Con Storyteller Award.